Gift Of The Shaper

Book One of the HIGHGLADE Series

by
D.L. Jennings

"The Breaker of Dawn, the Hammer of Darkness,

bound in His prison and resting in chains.

Binder of Worlds, the Keeper of Shadows,

in Her embrace, the world remains.

Shaper of Ages, the Anvil of Light,

Her power descended; Her Children, Her might."

From The Book of the Shaping War: A Written History of Athrani and Khyth

Copyright © 2017 by D.L. Jennings

This is a work of fiction. All names, places, and incidents are the product of the author's imagination. Any resemblance to actual persons, living or dead; events; or locales is entirely coincidental.

All rights reserved. No portion of this publication may be reproduced, stored in a retrieval system, or transmitted by any means—electronic, mechanical, photocopying, recording, or any other—except for brief quotations in printed reviews, without the prior written permission of the publisher.

Editors: Earl Tillinghast and Regina Cornell

Cover Artist: Chris Jeanguenat

Interior Design: 3SIXTY Marketing Studio

Cartographer: Michael Dains

Indigo River Publishing
3 West Garden Street Ste. 352
Pensacola, FL 32502
www.indigoriverpublishing.com

Ordering Information:

Quantity sales: Special discounts are available on quantity purchases by corporations, associations, and others. For details, contact the publisher at the address above.

Orders by U.S. trade bookstores and wholesalers: Please contact the publisher at the address above.

Printed in the United States of America

Library of Congress Control Number: 2017964194

ISBN: 978-0-948080-07-1

First Edition

With Indigo River Publishing, you can always expect great books, strong voices, and meaningful messages. Most importantly, you'll always find… words worth reading.

ACKNOWLEDGEMENTS

First and foremost, this book is dedicated to my amazing friend Nicole Holmes. Without her enthusiastic response to my early writing, it would never have happened.

To my Mom, who fostered my love of fantasy and storytelling by reading me C.S. Lewis and J.R.R. Tolkien when I was just a boy; to my brother, Matt, and my best friend, Joshua Galbincea, who used to stay up way too late with me playing D&D; to my beautiful sister, Sara, who always believed I could do this; to my Dad, who did everything in his power to make sure this book got published. To my test readers: Matt Jennings, Paul Truong, Lori Carlin, Pat Flaherty, Andrew Baldwin, John Burkle, Jack Van Houten, Matt McBrien, Pam Brodman, and John Leifels.

To Dan and Hamishe from Indigo River, who loved what they saw in a young author; and to my editor, Earl, with his great eye for detail and fantastic input to help guide me toward the best story I could possibly tell.

None of this would have been possible without everyone listed here along with the love and support of my friends and family, who amazed me and humbled me with their support. Thank you all.

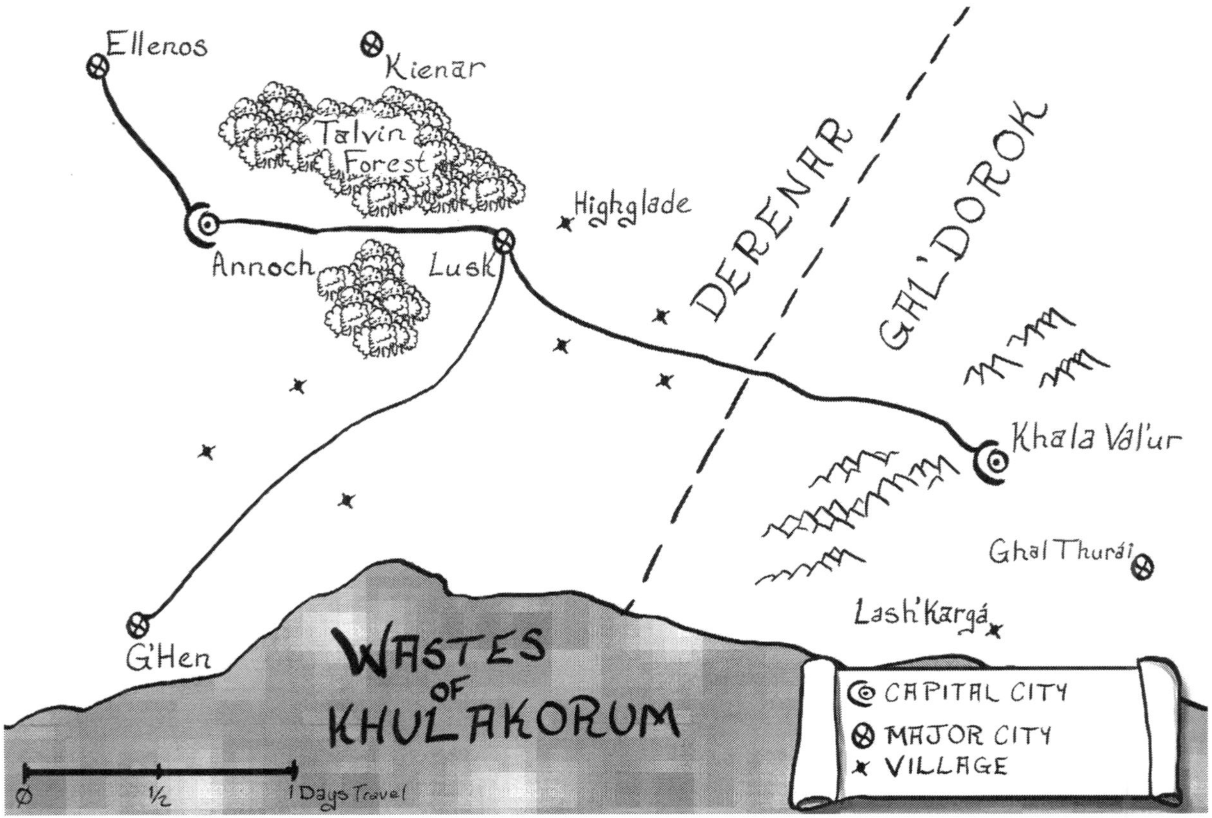
Ellenos
Kienar
Talvin Forest
Highglade
DERENAR
GAL'DOROK
Annoch
Lusk
Khala Val'ur
Ghal Thurái
Lash'Kargá
G'Hen
WASTES OF KHULAKORUM
CAPITAL CITY
MAJOR CITY
VILLAGE
Ø
½
1 Days Travel

TABLE OF CONTENTS

PROLOGUE 13

CHAPTER 1 15

CHAPTER 2 23

CHAPTER 3 31

CHAPTER 4 37

CHAPTER 5 53

CHAPTER 6 63

CHAPTER 7 69

CHAPTER 8 75

CHAPTER 9 83

CHAPTER 10 93

CHAPTER 11 99

CHAPTER 12 111

CHAPTER 13 117

CHAPTER 14 125

CHAPTER 15 135

CHAPTER 16 141

CHAPTER 17 149

CHAPTER 18 155

CHAPTER 19 163

CHAPTER 20 167

CHAPTER 21 175

CHAPTER 22	191
CHAPTER 23	199
CHAPTER 24	205
CHAPTER 25	213
CHAPTER 26	223
CHAPTER 27	229
CHAPTER 28	243
CHAPTER 29	255
CHAPTER 30	261
CHAPTER 31	265
CHAPTER 32	271
CHAPTER 33	277
CHAPTER 34	281
CHAPTER 35	287
CHAPTER 36	291
CHAPTER 37	305
CHAPTER 38	309
CHAPTER 39	315
CHAPTER 40	321
CHAPTER 41	327
CHAPTER 42	333
CHAPTER 43	343
CHAPTER 44	347
CHAPTER 45	353

CHAPTER 46	361
CHAPTER 47	369
CHAPTER 48	379
CHAPTER 49	383
CHAPTER 50	391
CHAPTER 51	401
CHAPTER 52	411
CHAPTER 53	425
CHAPTER 54	439
CHAPTER 55	441
CHAPTER 56	445
EPILOGUE	449
APPENDIX	451

PROLOGUE

Mordha's hand trembled as she loosened her grip on the blade and looked at the Kienari before her.

"I was so scared that day. Until then, death and cruelty had been strangers to me, yet suddenly they appeared before me in the flesh. Never before had I felt such relief and such terror at the same time." Her voice trembled with emotion. "I thought the creature wanted nothing more than to slit my throat and the throat of my sister, as it had just done to our captors," she said.

She closed her eyes in sorrow and turned her face to the ceiling.

"It was a death I welcomed. I'd had enough of begging for my life."

Chapter 1

Highglade

Gift of the Shaper

Thornton

Night breathed out as the dawn breathed in, and Thornton Woods awoke to his father's big hand shaking his shoulder.

"Time to wake up," grunted Olson as he towered over his son's bed. "We've got some chains to make today. Simple work, but tedious." The worn leather of the blacksmith's vest creaked softly as Olson tightened it over his shirt, protecting his chest while allowing his muscular arms to move free. He patted his son on the back once more to hasten his waking before walking downstairs to start breakfast.

"Nnnn," Thornton mumbled groggily in response as he rolled onto his back to rub the sleep from his dark brown eyes. He lay there staring at the ceiling, not wanting to get up, and wondering how much longer he could put it off. Eventually he managed to convince himself to sit up, knowing that his father would insist more strongly if he didn't get moving soon.

Despite working alongside his father for nearly a decade, Thornton was still slow to get going. He could feel that the night had made a mess of his thick brown hair as he pushed it out of his face with a yawn. His strong jawline capped off what was otherwise a youthful face, light and even, with the firmness that came from years of exposure to open flame and molten steel.

Swinging his feet off the low-lying bed, Thornton trudged over to the wash bucket beside it to splash a bit of water on his face to aid the waking process. He pushed his hair back behind his ears as he looked around for his own protective vest, which he had tossed on the floor before collapsing in a fit of exhaustion. Finding it, he pulled it over his tan short-sleeved tunic and gave his reflection a final look, taming his hair before heading downstairs.

Thornton was met at the bottom by the welcome smell of roasting meat. His father was a master with fire, and food was no exception. Some of the villagers liked to say that he spent just as much time over the fire of his cook stove as he did over the fire of his forge, and it was easy to see why: Olson's shoulders and chest looked like they were carved from solid oak, and his arms—hardened by a lifetime of swinging a hammer—were bigger around than most men's legs.

"Have a seat," Olson said, chewing and pointing a chicken leg over the plain wooden table. "But don't take too long. Those chains won't pour themselves." Thornton pulled a chair up and helped himself to some boiled eggs.

Moments later, the large frame of Olson Woods disappeared through a door into the kitchen of a modest house that, Thornton was constantly being reminded, had been built by his grandfather. "With his own two hands," Olson would say.

Taking a few sluggish bites out of a chicken leg, Thornton watched his father come back into the room with a plate of meat that could have easily fed four men. He sat down and gave his son a smile, still chewing, and proceeded to devour most of it.

Thornton had barely finished his first few bites by the time his father was wiping his hands off, stepping outside to begin stoking the flames and preparing the casts for the chains. *He's always a step ahead,* Thornton thought. He shook his head and kept eating, making sure to finish off what his father had left for him.

When his stomach was pleasantly full, Thornton walked out to see his father already pouring the first links into the mold.

"You're late," said the elder Woods. Nodding to the forge, he added, "Keep that fire going."

Thornton walked listlessly to the flames and grabbed a shovel to add more coal to the fire; it had to be especially hot to melt the iron that would eventually become the chains. After a few heaping shovelfuls, both he and the fire woke up.

For as long as Thornton could remember, he'd been helping his father with the smithing. When he was still too small to hold a hammer, Thornton had been put to work filling buckets with water to douse whatever needed tempering. When he had outgrown that, his father let him handle the shovel to get coals from the pile and dump them into the fire. He did that for a long time and became quite good at it, some days even looking forward to working in front of the roaring flames of the furnace.

When Thornton had turned thirteen, his father finally decided that he was big enough to swing a hammer. The one he gave him had belonged to his father before him—also a black-smith, as was his father before him. It was the first day Thornton ever felt important.

It was an unusually large hammer, used in forging the heaviest of materials. Its handle was carved from straight-grained white ash, giving it a lighter appearance, and the head of the hammer—a dark black steel that stood in stark contrast to the lightness of the handle—was as solid as it had been the day it was crafted. In this sense, it was perfectly suited to be a striker's hammer: huge, heavy, and well-balanced. Hammers like it could be found in the hands of any blacksmith's assistant worth his salt.

But it was clear that the hammer which had found its way into Thornton's hands—passed down through generations of Woods men longer than any of them could say—was no ordinary apprentice's hammer. One glance at the handle was enough to see that.

Carved up and down the entire length of the solid white ash were intricate figures enveloped in smooth, swirling lines that gave the illusion of smoke. The years had eroded the surface and turned the deep grooves into shallow nooks, but the design was still largely visible: on one side was a figure holding a hammer above a forge, and on the opposite side was a second figure standing beneath a pillar, looking at a shining star above him. Whenever Thornton looked at it, he felt a sense of power and a sense of pride, knowing that his father had used it when he was small. His father wasn't sure where it came from, but he knew it had been in the family for generations.

When he'd first started using the hammer, he could hardly lift it. The first time he tried, he barely got it off the ground. But as the years passed and he grew stronger, Thornton found himself swinging it more and more easily, until it felt like it was a part of him. He would take every opportunity to use it when he worked with his father, even practicing his strikes on the anvil when there was no work to be done. He always felt powerful when his hands touched the handle, and he brought it with him wherever he went.

The smell of molten iron brought him back to reality as Olson barked orders. Thornton wasn't sure how long they had been working; it felt like days.

Pour the cast, add to the fire, let the cast set, hammer the iron.

Pour the cast, add to the fire, let the cast set, hammer the iron.

Pour, add, set, hammer.

Pour.

Add.

Set.

Hammer.

His father was right—it was tedious. The order had called for ten five-foot chains, and they had already produced six by the time the sun peeked out from behind the trees. As they finished the last one, it was nearly midday.

"Nothing left to do now but to take these into town," Olson said. His shaggy brown hair was damp with sweat as he wiped his hands off on his vest, moving his thick beard aside in the process.

Thornton had just finished finished cleaning off the soot from his hammer when his eyes lit up. "I'll take them," he said, jumping to his feet. He knew that Miera would be headed there soon, and he couldn't pass up the chance to ride with her. "Tell me where and I'll load them up."

His father eyed him uncertainly. The halfday's ride into town would mean that Thornton would be on his own, away from home, for longer than normal. Even a quick delivery like this meant coming back at night or early tomorrow morning. The look on his father's face told Thornton that he thought of that as problematic.

"I'd rather we make the trip together," he countered. "Lusk isn't as safe as it once was."

Thornton frowned and patted the head of his hammer. "I know you won't admit it, but I'm not a boy anymore. I can take care of myself."

The big, bearded blacksmith sighed and grabbed half of the pile of chains, hoisting them over his broad shoulders and making for the wagon.

Gift of the Shaper

"I suppose you're right," he said. Nodding to the rest of the chains, he added, "You can start by bringing out the rest of those, then."

Thornton made a face his father couldn't see and picked up what he could carry. Even after years of wielding a heavy blacksmith's hammer, Thornton was still dwarfed by his father and could only manage to take three of the big chains at a time. With a quick second trip, the cart was full.

His father held out a small piece of parchment that had the order for the chains on it. On the reverse, handdrawn and scrawled in black, was a map showing a path leading away from Lusk.

"Here's where you'll drop off the chains," he said. He then reached into his pocket to produce a few pieces of silver, holding them up and looking at Thornton. "And this should buy you a place to sleep for the night. But I need you to be back before sunset tomorrow," he said. "There's more work to be done, and that striker's hammer won't lift itself."

Thornton took the map and the silver, stuffing them both in his pocket with a smile. "I'll be back before you light the forge."

His father put a big hand on Thornton's head and rustled it through his wild brown hair. "Just be careful. And say hello to Miera for me." He didn't even wait for a protest before he disappeared back inside to put another chicken on the fire.

Thornton shook his head in bewilderment and walked off down the path that connected his house to the rest of the village—a village that was wide awake and humming with life.

Looking around at the smoke billowing from chimneys as the other families prepared their food, Thornton heard the familiar sounds of children shrieking with laughter as they chased each other around the village. He waved to a few of the onlooking parents as he stopped to exchange some hellos. After a short chat, he excused himself and found his way to a small dirt road that lay just ahead. With any luck, he could catch Miera as she finished loading her cart.

Hidden in the shade of a small thicket of trees was an unassuming house with brown shutters and a door to match. There was a small vegetable garden in the front, presently guarded by an old but sturdy-looking brown mare that was happily munching on some grass. As Thornton walked up, out from the house stepped a blonde girl wearing a white cloth dress and clutching a bunch of flowers.

"Miera!" Thornton said as he waved.

The girl looked up and shielded her eyes from the sun. When she saw Thornton, a smile spread across her lips.

For years now, Miera Mi'An had been collecting, planting, growing, and selling flowers from all over. There was hardly a spot of bare ground visible behind her house, as most of it was taken up by the rivers of blossoms that flowed through her yard. She carried an armful of deepred roses, freshly pruned and bound for her cart, which she promptly tossed inside as she went over to meet Thornton.

"Master Woods," she said, giving him a mock curtsy. They had been friends for years now; and, despite her thinking of him as a brother, Thornton looked at her differently than he did other girls. She was lovely, with stunning blue eyes and a laugh that came easily. Shorter than him by almost a foot, she had a tenacious spirit that rivaled that of even the largest of men.

"So here's where you've been hiding," Thornton said with a smile. He looked over the dozens of flowers seated in the back of her cart but stopped counting around twenty.

"You know very well I wasn't hiding," Miera protested. "I was getting ready for a trip into town."

"Well, it just so happens I'm headed there too," Thornton said slyly, "and could use some company."

Miera smiled a half-smile with the left side of her mouth and looked away. "Is that so? What makes you think I'd want to go with you?"

Thornton scratched his chin. "A pretty girl like you? You need to keep an eye out for bandits. And you're less likely to be bothered if you've got a strong blacksmith riding beside you."

Miera put her hands on her hips and looked at Thornton skeptically. "Well, if you happen to see a strong blacksmith, tell him he's welcome to join us."

Gift of the Shaper

Thornton feigned laughter as Miera latched the cart onto her horse, Matilda. She walked up beside her and gently patted her nose. "Okay, Matty, time for another ride to town." Leaning in to whisper in her ear, she said, "Maybe if we're lucky, we'll run into that handsome stallion Jericho." Matilda clearly recognized the name of Thornton's workhorse, because she stomped her back foot in excitement.

"Well, if Matty says it's alright," Thornton began, "I'll meet you on the north side of the village."

Miera smiled and said, "Suit yourself."

Chapter 2

Lusk

Gift of the Shaper

Thornton

It was a half day's ride west from the village of Highglade into the town of Lusk, and most of it was spent quietly. The soft, steady thumping of the horses' hooves on the dirt road provided a backdrop for the silence. Jericho, the taller of the two horses, even-tempered and strong, was in front. He made a good leader since he was familiar enough with the route that Thornton barely had to tell him where to go. The horse's bold brown coat had started to fade with age, but his demeanor remained unchanged. He led the way comfortably, with Miera and Matilda bringing up the rear.

Thornton had made this trip many times before. When he was a boy, he used to ride in the back of the cart as his father walked beside them. He would watch in awe as Olson unloaded the cart himself and then watch as the customers struggled to lift what had been delivered.

After that came the ride back home, with most of it spent talking. Olson was a man of few words, yet as good as he was at carrying heavy things, Thornton was even better at carrying conversation. Some trips Thornton spent the whole time talking. He loved every minute of it. It was always just him and his father.

Then, a few years ago, Miera and her father had come to Highglade, choosing to settle in a home not far from Thornton's. He could still remember the first time he saw her; she was this energetic little thing with bright blue eyes and an ever-present smile. The other girls in the village seemed to be jealous of her, but Miera had never minded. She always carried herself with an air of confidence, even at such a young age. The women of the village were always grabbing her cheeks and telling her how precious she was. She was always pleasant and well-mannered, offering a polite *thank you* accompanied by a curtsy. The village women ate it up, and it wasn't long until they all knew her by name.

Before he passed away, Miera's father had been a peddler who sold his wares in town, leaving Miera by herself in the village to do as she pleased. Sometimes she would watch the boys as they rough-housed, rolling around in the dirt, climbing trees, and making up games. She was never asked to join, but more often than not, it looked like she could barely hold herself back. The girls, however, mostly jealous of the attention Miera got from their mothers, never asked her to play. They would all sit cross-legged in a circle, making sure to leave her out, laughing a little too loudly and smiling a little too broadly.

That all went on for a few weeks until, on a dare from the boys and more out of sympathy than adventurousness, a mud-covered Thornton raced over to her and rubbed his hands all over her face. The laughter from the girls' circle suddenly went quiet, and there were even a few gasps of surprise from the boys. Miera stood there looking at Thornton, who was standing so still it looked like he'd forgotten to breathe. Then, calmly and deliberately, Miera walked a few feet over to the nearest mud pile, scooped some up in her hands, and threw it right in Thornton's face. Laughter erupted from all around, boys and girls alike, as the biggest mud fight in Highglade history broke out right in front of them. Thornton wiped the mud from his eyes and looked at Miera, who was doubled over in laughter. He grinned, then threw a mud ball right back at her. It was a filthy start to a long friendship.

The town of Lusk had recently become a trade hub in Derenar and was always busy during the daytime: people going in and out with trinkets to peddle, shouts from shopkeepers advertising their wares, children running around giggling and chasing invisible monsters. His father told him of a much different Lusk from when he was a boy, when, perhaps thirty years ago, everyone knew each other. That was not the case anymore, as he said he recognized maybe five people out of a hundred. That was before the wall was built, too.

A little more than waisthigh and made of mortar and unpolished stone, a wall encircled Lusk and delineated the town from the countryside and villages around it. There were a good deal of fields and pastures between the wall and the town proper, but the fields outside the wall were largely ignored by the people living inside. In truth, the wall was used less for defense and more for the sense of belonging it provided. But it was still a wall, and it made Thornton feel like he was an outsider whenever he passed through it.

Walls give people a sense of stability, Olson used to say, *because they keep the outside out and the inside in.*

Gift of the Shaper

Looking at the town that still lay a fair distance away, Thornton could see that his father was right: he was an outsider looking in.

He glanced back at Miera, who was following about twenty feet behind him and had dismounted a ways back to walk alongside Matilda. She was talking to the old brown mare and stroking her mane, giving her a short break from pulling her weight on the cart. He hopped off his own cart and grabbed Jericho's reins to wait up for her. While he did so, he pulled out the makeshift map to study it again.

"I'm not sure where this is, so I might have to do some looking around. It looks like it's back outside the wall," he said, squinting at the map as she approached. "I guess I'll let you go on by yourself. Will you be in the usual place?"

Miera nodded and looked up at the sinking sun. "I've got some daylight left, so I'll set up when I get in. I'll sell what I can today and leave the rest for tomorrow."

"Then you'd better get moving," Thornton said with a smile.

Miera flashed him a smirk and a *thank you*, then led Matilda further in toward the town. Thornton's eyes followed the road and watched as the dirt and mud paths from the outlying villages turned into streets of worn cobbled stone.

Looking at the town, Thornton was surprised at how big it seemed now. Maybe it was the fact that his father wasn't there with him, but he felt like he was seeing it for the first time. He shook his head and turned, setting himself back on the path to the wall.

Outside the town was mostly just trees and grass, with the Talvin Forest to the west and the numerous, ambling roads around it that led to other villages in its vicinity.

After a bit of walking, with nothing but the chirping of birds to keep him company, Thornton glanced again at the crumpled map.

It should be around here, he thought. He wondered if he'd taken a wrong turn somewhere—he was no tracker, that much was certain. Looking to his right, though, in a clearing past some trees, he spotted a building. Glancing around and seeing no signs of life, he walked toward it and tied Jericho to a tree to wait while he looked around.

It was a large stone structure with double doors on the front, big enough to let two horses through, and looked like it had seen some very recent use. Thornton couldn't tell how far back the building went, as the trees behind it swallowed it up, but it looked big enough to at least be an inn or a warehouse.

Odd place for an inn, he thought to himself.

On one of the doors was a knocker made of iron, right in the middle, poised over a metal face plate. After another glance around to satisfy his curiosity, and still seeing no one, Thornton reached out and gave it a quick trio of knocks. Jericho snorted uneasily from behind him and stomped his hoof.

A quiet moment passed before Thornton knocked again. He was contemplating leaving when he heard faint footsteps approaching.

The *clank* of a metal bolt being released was followed by the heavy sound of wood sliding and dropping to the floor.

One of the doors creaked open.

Inside stood a man garbed in long black robes, whose face was obscured by the shadow of a hood pulled over his head. His sleeves hung down to his fingertips, and he made no eye contact with Thornton.

"Bring them inside." His voice was low and raspy, like its essence had been burnt away by fire.

Thornton nodded warily and walked over to the cart where he began unloading the chains, two by two. He carried them inside the entryway where he saw the man standing and pointing a long, sleeved hand toward the center of the room. Surrounding him were high, vaulted ceilings, with windows lining the tops of the walls.

"Place them there," the man said, pointing to a spot in the middle of the floor.

Thornton put the chains down in a pile and returned to the cart to repeat the process for the rest, making sure to keep a watchful eye on the hooded stranger. Back outside, Thornton could see that Jericho was equally distraught, shaking his head and stomping a hoof.

Gift of the Shaper

"It's okay, boy," Thornton said softly, placing a hand on Jericho's muzzle to reassure the big brown stallion. "Nothing to worry about. Just wait here until I'm done, and then we can go home. Maybe even get you some carrots." Jericho's eyes widened at the mention of the word, and he nudged Thornton's shoulder in approval.

Laughing, Thornton made his way to the cart again to load up more chains. He brought them in, one thick length draped across each shoulder, and placed them in the same spot as the others, needing no instruction from the man in the hood. Silently, he returned for the others, intending to repeat the process without incident.

After loading up the last of the chains he walked in again to see that he was alone in the room. He furrowed his brow in confusion and walked to the center of the room where the other chains had been piled. He dropped them with a loud *clank* and looked around for his cowled customer. From the back of the building, behind a locked door, came a low rumbling that sounded like a growl. Thinking he could not get out of there fast enough, Thornton made his way back out to the cart to await his payment.

When he stepped outside, though, he was surprised to see the man from inside had beaten him there and was looking at something inside the cart. He seemed startled by Thornton's footsteps, turning around to face the young man from Highglade like he'd been caught stealing.

"Ah! You've finished," the man said, stretching his arms out innocuously. His sleeves fell back to reveal hands that looked charred and blistered. His hood hung conspicuously low over his face, which Thornton imagined was similarly scarred, so that only his mouth was visible. *No wonder he kept himself concealed*, he thought to himself.

"That's the last of the chains," Thornton said, eyeing him suspiciously.

"Good," came the reply from below the hood. The stranger turned to the cart and seemed to be looking at the hammer. "Such craftsmanship is rare outside Gal'dorok," he said. "Your father is more talented than I thought."

"That?" Thornton said, looking at his hammer. "My father didn't make that."

The man seemed surprised at this. "Oh?" he asked, "Who did? I might have some work for him."

Thornton looked at him warily but did not answer right away. "I don't really know. It's just some old heirloom given to my father by his and his father before him. It's nothing special."

The man was now ignoring Thornton almost entirely, fixated instead on the hammer. "I've never seen one like it," he said. His hands began to move to the white ash handle, but as he did, Jericho reared up and caused the stranger to back away. Thornton was at his horse's side in an instant, putting a calming hand to his face and staring death at the man in the robe.

"Easy, boy," Thornton said gently, his eyes still locked on the stranger. "He won't hurt you."

Seeming to come out of a trance, the man turned to Thornton. "I suppose you would like your payment." He patted around his robe absentmindedly and finally produced a small bag of coins. He handed it to Thornton and turned to leave without another word.

Thornton thanked the man and watched as he retreated back inside the building. Turning to Jericho and giving him a quizzical look, he tossed the coin purse into the cart, climbed up, and began the trek back toward Lusk to find Miera.

Chapter 3

Lusk

Gift of the Shaper

Thornton

Thornton knew that it wasn't every day Miera traveled to Lusk. She shared a stand in the town with two other people, rotating in and out every few days: one day it was a clothing shop with items made of silk or cotton; another day it was a perfume and scented-oil stand; when she was there, it was a flower shop. She liked the arrangement, and the customers didn't seem to mind—she even had a stream of regulars, some of whom Thornton recognized.

So when he saw her admiring the clear evening sky, unusual for Lusk at this time of year, he smiled. Her cart was still mostly full of flowers, but it looked like she had managed to sell a few dozen. By tomorrow she might have enough to stock up on food for a few weeks.

As he trotted up with an empty cart, her eyes found his. He urged Jericho to a stop in front of her stand and smiled.

"It looks like you've had some luck," he said, looking down at her cart. He climbed off and looked back at Miera, whose face had suddenly gone white, flecked with worry.

"What is it?" he asked. "What's wrong?" No sooner had the words left his mouth than he saw something move on the edge of his vision. He turned to see a dark-clad man approaching from behind, brandishing a knife, and heading straight for Miera, a white skeletal hand embroidered into the cloth on his shoulder.

"You've got something we want," he said in a deep, nasally voice.

Miera opened her mouth to shout, but the man leveled his knife at her, wagging a finger to keep her quiet. Immediately, her eyes went to her coin purse, filled with a modest amount of silver from her long day's work, and her spirit sank visibly as the man closed in, raising his knife to her chest.

"And you," he said nodding at Thornton, "can stay over there." He was a tall, thin man with a patchy gray beard whose face looked as if it were caught in a permanent scowl. His nose was broad and flat, looking like it had been broken a few times and topping off what Thornton thought was the ugliest face he'd ever laid eyes on.

"Don't want no heroes," stuttered a second voice from right behind Thornton, high-pitched and shaky. Turning his head just enough to see where it came from, Thornton's gaze met the eye of a short, wiry young man with wild red hair and bandages covering his right eye, a red stain in the middle speaking of its recent loss. He was moving slowly toward Thornton, a knife in his hand pointed hesitantly at the young blacksmith.

"It's one of them," said the low voice of a third man, who seemed to come out of nowhere. He was holding something that looked like the white horn of an animal. "Grab 'em both," he said. His face was partially obscured by shadows, but Thornton could see that it was covered in scars. His skin was as thick and as rough as the leather of his boots, looking like it had been on the wrong end of a few sharp knives over the years. He was the biggest of the three by far, roughly Olson's size, and Thornton knew they stood no chance of taking him down in a fight.

Thornton saw Miera look at him with a mixture of uncertainty and fright. As she did, the man with the gray beard grabbed her, bringing up his knife within inches of her throat. "Any coins you have," he said, nodding to the pouch in Thornton's cart, "would be greatly appreciated as well." His face twisted into what Thornton assumed was a grin. *

Time seemed to freeze as fear and rage washed over Thornton, who was suddenly forced to watch as his friend's life and livelihood were being threatened by a bunch of thugs. In a surge of madness, he threw his elbow backward, catching the face of the one-eyed man behind him. Then he launched himself forward at the bearded man holding Miera. The man let out a panicked cry of confusion as he wildly thrust the knife in Thornton's direction, missing twice and only stopping when his jaw met the fist of the blacksmith from Highglade. Whirling around to find the biggest of the three, Thornton found him just in time to have the wind knocked out of him by a swift kick to the stomach. He stumbled backward as Miera began to scream for help.

He dodged a first punch, but the second one caught him on the cheek and sent a few drops of blood from his nose to the ground. There was a flash of steel as the man unsheathed a knife, giving Thornton no time to think. In quick succession, he charged, swung his right arm down in an arc that caught the knife-wielding hand coming up to meet him, and backhanded the stranger across the face with his closed fist, staggering him and dropping him to one knee. The knife clinked as it landed on the cobblestone, and Thornton covered the ground between them in a flash. He stepped on the knife, keeping his eyes on the big man with the scars, who rose to his feet slowly, glaring at Thornton.

Adrenaline was still surging through his body as he looked around for the other thugs. The gray-bearded man with the broad nose lay behind Miera's flower stand, groaning and clutching his jaw. The other man was holding his face with his hands over his remaining eye.

By now, the blood from Thornton's nose had gone from drops to a steady trickle. One eye was blurry from the blow to his face, and his ears were ringing. He shook his head as he met the eyes of the big man with the low voice who seemed to be their leader. He was rubbing his jaw where Thornton had hit him.

"I don't know what you want with us," Thornton said as he reached in his cart for his hammer. With his fingers wrapped around the handle, he felt something flow through him, mixing with his adrenaline and causing the hairs on his neck to stand up. "But I'll give you the coins if you'll leave us alone."

The man with the scars scowled and seemed to consider the offer. "Not gonna happen," came his gruff reply.

"Fine." Thornton took a step toward the man and clenched tightly the ash handle of his hammer. With no time to react, the man was upon him, and Thornton instinctively swung his hammer to meet him, but he was too slow. The bruising fist of the man slammed into Thornton's face, sending him flying backward like a limp doll, landing on his back, and rolling two or three times before coming to a stop by a wall. Beside him fell his hammer, joining him in crashing to the ground.

The stranger smiled as if he had just claimed his prize, and walked over to Thornton. Just as he closed in, though, an arrow flew by, narrowly missing his head and burying itself deep into the wall above.

"Your pride or your life," came the words from a man on horseback. He was wearing blue chainmail inlaid with gold—the famed colors of the

D.L. Jennings

Guardians of Lusk. He had a second arrow nocked and ready, aimed at the man standing over Thornton. "Keep one or lose them both."

The scarred stranger spit blood onto the ground and wiped off his mouth. "Fine," he growled, moving to drag away the small man missing an eye. He picked him up easily and swung him over his shoulder like a father picking up a child. "Bunch," he shouted to the man with the beard, "you heard the man."

A weakened groan of protest from the man called Bunch was soon followed by a kick to his ribs by the man with the scars, who pulled his cohort to his feet and sulked away in defeat, cursing at the guard in the gold and blue.

Thornton wasn't sure how long he'd been lying there, clutching his head, but Miera's frantic voice snapped him back to reality as he felt her raising a cloth to his nose to stop the bleeding. He was in a daze and his head ached.

After she cleaned him up a bit more, Miera picked up the coin purse that had been torn from her and glanced down the alley where the three men had retreated.

The guard, who had now dismounted, looked around at the small crowd that had gathered and shook his head in disappointment. "Not the first time I've seen the Hand this far north. I just don't know why they decided that Lusk was a good place to make trouble."

Miera was visibly shaken and her hands trembled as she held her coin purse. "Well, thank you for coming along when you did," she said as she touched the spot on her neck where the man had placed his knife. Her skin was slightly indented, but, luckily, there was no bleeding. "Any later and . . ." Her voice trailed off as she stood there in a daze.

The runin with the strange man from earlier had already made Thornton uneasy. Now there was no question what he had to do. "We need to get you home," he said firmly. He had already started loading the carts behind Jericho and Matilda, but Miera made no indication that she'd heard him.

He stopped what he was doing and looked at her again. "Miera," he said, "did you hear me?"

Gift of the Shaper

"Hmm?" she said, snapping back to the present.

"I said we need to leave. My father was right—it's not safe here in Lusk."

Miera made no protest; she simply nodded and made her way over to Matilda, who buried her nose into the girl's shoulder. Shaking her head as if trying to rid herself of the events of the day, Miera stepped silently into the saddle.

Thornton was already seated atop Jericho and clicking his tongue to urge him forward by the time she was ready.

***

As the two of them rode out of town, a man in a black robe watched them leave.

"The Gwarái led us here," he said. His hood was pulled back and draped around his neck to reveal a face that was scorched and torn. Flanking him were the three men who had traded their dignity for their lives, looking all the worse for wear. "The blood of the Shaper must flow through one of them."

"You want us to follow them, Master D'kane?" the man with the scars asked.

"I want them followed," he answered. "But not by you three." A broad scowl had worked its way across his blistered face as he turned to address them. "Your foolishness nearly cost us everything. No, Rimbal, I will have them followed by someone who can finish the task he is given. I will have Master Khyth Rennick follow him."

"Of course," Rimbal said as he shrunk in shame.

"But you will have a chance to redeem yourself; I have another task for you," he said, staring right at the big man. "The Breaker awaits. And he does not tolerate failure."

Chapter 4

Derenar, East of Lusk

Gift of the Shaper

Thornton

The two horses walked in a line; Jericho was in front pulling the cart, and Matilda followed closely behind with the rest of Miera's flowers. The tiny sliver of moon above them was doing its best to light their way, but Thornton knew it would not be enough. He climbed down from the cart and pulled out a torch, sparking his flint until the oil-soaked rag caught fire, lighting up the dusk and the road ahead. Forcing a tight smile, he settled back into his seat to watch the waves of flames make shadows of the trees that lined the path. The light of the torch was welcome, as was the comfort it provided, and he and Miera were back on their way in no time.

Lusk was a ways behind them, but Miera still seemed jumpy. Though the road was almost not wide enough for it, she prodded Matty to the side so she could walk side by side with Thornton and Jericho. "I just don't understand," she started. "Lusk has always been peaceful."

Thornton grunted in agreement.

"I've never heard of anything like that happening, especially in a crowded market area," she continued. "And did you see all those people just standing around and watching? It was like nothing was going on!"

Thornton grunted again, causing Miera to narrow her eyes at him. "Are you listening to me?" she asked.

In truth, his head was still back in Lusk. "When I looked at the man lying on the ground," he started, "I saw something. It was a white hand—like a skeleton." Shaking his head, he added, "I can't stop thinking about it."

"I saw it too," Miera answered. "And I don't like it."

"I don't either," Thornton said as his voice trailed off, allowing silence to settle in.

The only other sounds as they traveled were the steady steps of the horses and the wooden creaks of the turning wheels. Their rhythmic repetition had lulled Thornton into complacency as he watched the road ahead of them, lazily scanning the route for anything out of the ordinary. But when he thought he saw a light go out ahead, he instinctively tightened his grip on Jericho's harness. Home was still a ways off, and he was wary. A *crunch* from somewhere in the trees ahead brought him to a stop, with Miera and Matty following suit.

"Did you hear that?" he whispered.

Miera nodded. "It sounded like it came from up there," she replied quietly, pointing to the trees off the road ahead.

Thornton started to reach into the cart for his hammer, but the sound of a bowstring being drawn made him freeze.

"Human, extinguish your light," came a voice, low and gravelly.

"Don't do it," Miera whispered cautiously.

"Listen to me," said the voice.

"Why should I?" Thornton shot back.

There was silence followed by a low growl. "You can argue with my arrow, but it flies whether or not you put out the light."

Thornton had no choice. With his free hand, he doused the light and almost instantly the bowstring twanged. An arrow whistled right past him. It must have hit its mark, as a gurgling sound came from behind them, slightly off the road.

Two more arrows flew through the air, and twice more they struck home. This time a female voice said, "There are more ahead, five or six."

Thornton strained his eyes and turned to see where the voices were coming from. He studied the area for a moment and saw nothing. He was about to give up when he heard the low voice of the male again.

"Those three had been following you for some time. They were about to make their move."

Out from the darkness of the trees stepped two black figures barely discernible against the shadows as they approached Miera and Thornton. They were thin and tall—a good foot taller than Thornton—and almost completely invisible in the blackness. As they got closer, Thornton could see why: their entire bodies were covered in what looked to be fine black fur that caught just the tiniest glint of moonlight. Trailing behind each was a tail about as long as Thornton's arm, and pointed ears sat atop their heads, moving and twitching as they followed sounds. They each held a longbow, and the only clothing they had looked to be made from a single hide. Their dusty and well-worn packs suggested that they had been traveling for some time.

"Kienari," Miera whispered. "What are you doing outside of your forest?"

"The Mother told us of your need," said the male. "You are in trouble. We must move." He turned to his companion and said, "Ynara, scout ahead. Bring me a count."

Ynara gave a quick nod and melted back into the shadows. Thornton strained his eyes to try to follow her, but it was like she was never even there. He blinked a few times at the vacuous blackness.

The male turned to them and bowed slightly. "I am called Kethras." Despite his narrow frame, nothing about the Kienari suggested frailty. Miera curtsied deeply in return as Thornton looked on, searching in vain for some sign of Ynara. "I'm Miera and this is Thornton," she replied.

Kethras walked over to one of the bodies and knelt down to examine it, rolling it onto its back. It was clad all in black, and there was a single white handprint on its shoulder.

Miera watched the Kienari closely. "Kethras, what do you mean we're in trouble? How did you find us?"

Kethras did not look up from examining the body but took a dagger and sheath from it and tucked them away in his belt. "We did not find you. We found them. Their pull is strong, and we can feel it from a great distance." He patted down the body a few more times, rifling through pockets, then stood up and sniffed at the air. "Quickly," he said, "off the road."

"What about the horses?" Miera asked.

"Bring them," Kethras answered. "They are not safe here either." His attention was focused ahead; he seemed to be looking for something. He turned quickly and motioned for them to follow.

Thornton took his hammer from the cart as he and Miera unhooked the horses, leading them off the road to be tethered. The two animals

40

shook their heads excitedly, happy to be rid of the burden. If they noticed Kethras, they didn't show it.

The Kienari crouched down, motioning again for Miera and Thornton to follow.

The three of them waited in silence for what seemed like an eternity. Then, suddenly, Ynara's voice came from behind them. "There are seven and they are cold."

Miera gasped and Thornton almost jumped out of his skin. They both turned to look at her in amazement.

"Cold?" Miera asked the Kienari. "Are they dead?"

"No," Ynara answered. "They only want to appear as such. They have masked their body heat well—but not well enough."

Thornton looked at her quizzically, barely able to make out her face in the moonlight. "I don't understand. Why would they do something like that?"

The female Kienari spoke again, saying, "They are waiting for someone and are very well hidden. But for someone who knows what to look for, they are a beacon in the night."

Kethras made a noise from beside them that sounded like laughter. "Ynara knows what to look for," he said smiling, revealing a mouth full of sharp teeth that flashed in the moonlight.

Thornton did his best to examine the two Kienari in the dark. Against the blackness, not much stood out. He did note one thing, though: both of them were as long and thin as tree branches, moving just as they looked—lightly and with ease. Their bearing and gait reminded him of elm trees, long-limbed and lofty, yet sturdy enough to endure even the harshest of storms. Just looking at them was enough to make the hairs stand up on the back of his neck.

Ynara swept her gaze over Thornton and Miera, regarding both of them coolly. Thornton, closer to her now, studied her face and felt his heart jump when he realized what was so unnerving: it was her eyes. They were three times the size of Thornton's and did not reflect even the tiniest bit of light. It was like looking into black pools.

Gift of the Shaper

Before Thornton had time to say anything, Kethras stood and said, "Move."

Miera hesitated, saying, "The horses . . ."

But Ynara took her by the arm and said, "Leave them. We will return."

Thornton followed, gripping his hammer and bringing up the rear in silence.

The two Kienari were masters of their craft. Kethras had taken to the trees, leaping effortlessly to a branch, catching it, and swinging upwards in one fluid motion without making so much as a sound. Ynara kept to the ground, acting as a guide for Miera and Thornton. She quietly pointed out twigs and dead leaves on her way so they could avoid stepping on them.

Thornton had still not completely made up his mind about the two creatures from the shadows. Miera seemed surprised to see them, but not incredulous, as Thornton most certainly was. He'd heard stories but only ever thought of them as just that—stories. When his father spoke of them, it was in the same way as he spoke of one day growing rich and fat, nothing more than something to let the mind wander. But here were two of them, standing right in front of him, like shadows come to life from the forest. Two predators perfectly suited for hunting at night—something they had grown to master over the years, as it was their sole means of survival. They were creatures of stealth and silence, stalking prey, and they did it better than any other living thing.

The sounds of low chatter could be heard from up ahead as they approached. Thornton looked to the trees for some sign of Kethras but found none, not even a telltale movement of a branch or a rustle of leaves. Ynara put up her hand, motioning for them to stop. She turned to Thornton.

"These men are prepared to kill you," she whispered. "You must not let them. Have you ever taken a life?"

"No," Thornton whispered. He did not look at her face as she spoke—he was still not used to it.

Miera was silent.

Ynara pulled out a dagger from a sheath around her leg and handed it to Miera, saying to them both, "The first one is the hardest, but never forget: any one of them will take your life if you give them the chance."

Miera nodded but did not speak.

Thornton gripped his hammer uneasily, tapping his fingers quietly on the handle as he adjusted his grip. The worn ash felt familiar and comforting, and he found himself wishing he were back home working the forge instead.

Since there was no fire to give them away, Thornton heard the group of men long before he could see them as the Kienari continued to lead their silent advance. Thornton strained his eyes in the dark but could only make out the faintest trace of shapes. He had no idea how Ynara could be so confident in her count, but he imagined it had something to do with those eyes of hers. He shuddered when he pictured them again.

Ynara took a stick from nearby and started drawing in the dirt. She made seven circles in the ground and four Xs. One X—*Kethras*, Thornton guessed—lay behind the group of circles. Two Xs were front and center—Miera and he—and the fourth X was behind those by a good distance.

Ynara spoke, addressing both of them. "You must meet them head on. You have the element of surprise on your side, so you can almost even our numbers with two swift blows. They will not expect you to act so quickly, and their defenses will be down. If you are swift enough, perhaps you can put one or two more on the ground." She rubbed her hand over three of the circles, leaving four.

Thornton spoke up. "You make it sound like it's just the two of us. Where will you be?"

Ynara made a low gurgling sound like laughter. "The Kienari are hunters, not creatures of brute force; our strength lies in stealth and distance. We will strike from the trees so they can never be sure if there is one or one hundred." Standing, she added, "But I assure you, we will be with you."

Thornton was quiet but nodded his approval.

Gift of the Shaper

"When I give the signal, you two will charge, swiftly as you can. Kethras and I will do the rest." She paused and looked up. "Above all else, you must not hesitate. If you do, even my truest arrow cannot help you." She looked past the group of men to something unseen. "He is ready. Move."

They approached the small clearing where the seven lay in wait. They were sitting in a loose circle with two of them facing the road as lookouts. Thornton could feel his palms sweating as he tightened his grip on the hammer. All his years of swinging it could not prepare him for this, he knew, hoping that he would be able to swing it when it truly mattered. He looked over at Miera, who seemed not to notice, like her mind was somewhere else.

From behind them, Ynara whispered, "Now," and the two of them were off, running headlong into danger.

Thornton had the longest reach with his hammer. By the time he landed the first blow with a deep "thud" to the head of his target, the others were on their feet.

One down, six to go, he thought coldly.

Reason and guilt were shut out as he opened himself up to instinct and the knowledge that these men would do the same to him—if not worse—given the chance. His heart raced as he tried to ignore the sick feeling creeping up his throat.

Thornton ducked as a sword swung at him from the left, and heard the sound of Miera's dagger going into the chest of a man to his right.

Two down, five left.

He thrust forward with the head of his hammer, ramming it into the stomach of someone coming toward him. The whisper of arrows came from behind him as he heard them hit their mark.

Two thuds, two more down.

Three left.

Sidestepping a slice from his left, he was not quick enough to dodge a second time as the followup slice caught him on the arm, shooting pain throughout his body. Adrenaline surging, he shrugged it off, slamming the butt end of his hammer into the face of his attacker. He dodged another slash but caught a kick to the ribs that sent him reeling back and off balance. He regained his footing long enough to swing his hammer down and catch his assailant in the forearm, splintering bone and dropping the man to his knees, screaming. An arrow from Kethras finished the job, leaving just two men standing side by side, staring at Thornton through the dark. No one moved a muscle.

In the dim moonlight, the dark clothing the men wore did a good job of obscuring them against the blackness of the night. Thornton tried to make out their faces, but they were nothing but outlines to him, two dim shapes in the darkness. But their eyes! Their eyes gave off a blood-red glow, flaring up and dying down like coals in a fire. Thornton was mesmerized as he watched them.

Glowing and dimming,

up and down,

rhythmic like breathing.

An eternity of silence passed as he stared them down, waiting for them to make a move or a sound, all the while feeling drawn to the lights behind their eyes. He adjusted the grip on his hammer, tightening his fingers around the white ash handle.

Then, in an instant, the night was illuminated with red as the darkness around gave way to a sickening glow, revealing a third figure standing behind them, most of his face covered by a black hood. He flashed a smile that sent a shiver down Thornton's spine.

"Khyth!" came the frantic cry from Ynara. "They are Khyth! Get back!" She followed the words with an arrow, but the hooded figure was quicker. He raised his hand, and the earth itself seemed to fly up to meet it, shattering the arrow into a thousand pieces and splintering it harmlessly onto the ground. The two figures in front looked like fire as Thornton watched them pulse with burning power. Neither so much as flinched.

The Khyth in the back doffed his hood to reveal a scarred and burnt face that reminded Thornton of the man who had bought the chains.

Gift of the Shaper

Ynara growled as she revealed herself, stepping forward from the shadows. "So, it was you three we felt," she said. "You hid yourselves well, servants of the Breaker."

The Khyth made no sounds as the one in back moved the palms of his hands to the ground, which began to tremble in anticipation. He flicked one hand toward the sky, and the earth cracked and split around them in a circle. Then Thornton watched as the three Khyth were raised into the air by a simple gesture that seemed to have summoned a mountain out of nothing. Rumbling and shaking, the earth leapt upward, shedding boulders and dirt as it grew. When it finally stopped, the Khyth were as high as some of the surrounding trees, staring down at Thornton and Miera like hawks eyeing a group of field mice.

"Go," said the hooded one, as the other two seemed to disappear in a flicker of flame, moving swiftly off the earthen platform and suddenly reappearing in front of Thornton, their eyes burning wildly.

"Look out!" Miera shouted. She had drawn her dagger and was running toward them.

Thornton stumbled backward in a panic as the Khyth closest to him lunged with both hands, sending him tumbling onto his back with a thud. He rolled to his right to escape a boot that barely missed crushing his skull. Then, coming quickly to a knee, he swiveled his head to see Miera caught up with fending off the second one. It was using the earth to ward off Ynara's arrows and was moving like the feat was effortless.

Thornton looked back up to the figure before him and stared right into its fiery eyes, flames moving around it like water. It seemed to be made of flesh but was burnt and split, making it appear more like charred wood than skin. Cracks on the surface glowed orange like the embers of a log in a fire. Thornton took to his feet and regained his balance just in time to sidestep a fist from the ashen figure. He countered with a punch of his own from his off-hand, but when his fist connected, it felt like he had hit a block of pure granite. He pulled back his stinging knuckles and stared wide-eyed at the Khyth before him, who bared his teeth in what might have passed for a smile. A swift backhand sent Thornton flying.

To his dazed and blurry vision, it looked like three of them were bearing down on him, and he struggled to his feet to try and defend himself. In a heave of desperation, he swung his hammer blindly, cursing aloud as it felt like he'd hit nothing but air. He clenched his teeth and braced for the impact from the counterattack.

When it didn't come, he opened his eyes to find nothing before him but a pile of ash. A roar of pain erupted from the Khyth above, who still stood atop the rocky peak.

Looking suspiciously at his hammer, Thornton turned his head again to Miera. The Khyth pursuing her had a dagger sticking out of his side and was swatting down arrows like flies. Thornton could see that Miera was empty-handed and defenseless, with nothing but a look of defiance masking her fear. Her fists, hanging loosely at her sides, were bloody from taking swings at the fiery figure.

Kethras and Ynara ceased firing arrows, finally conceding their futility, so that the only sounds were those of agony coming from the black-hooded Khyth above. Unsure of exactly what to do next, Thornton did what came naturally: he yelled, trying to divert the creature's attention away from Miera. It didn't work so he did the next best thing. He ran toward it.

Miera was continuing to back away from the creature, and the blood from her knuckles was welling up enough to drip onto the ground. Thornton had his hammer in his right hand as he ran, grasping it about halfway down, its head to the ground and handle to the sky. He placed his left hand at the end of the handle as he covered the last remaining steps between himself and the Khyth. Leaping, he raised it above his head as the creature made a lunge toward Miera, oblivious to the threat behind it.

To Thornton, the scene seemed to unfold in slow motion. The head of his hammer was the first to make contact as it caught the creature on the crown of its skull. Thornton had the same feeling as before when he felt like he was swinging through air. He followed through as the heavy black metal cut through the creature in a downward arc, meeting no resistance and splitting the creature in half without so much as a sound.

He swung so hard that the head of his hammer buried itself in the ground, standing on its own as Thornton released his grip on the handle and backed away. He watched as the creature stood there, two halves of what moments ago was a whole, frozen in mid-stride and still reaching

Gift of the Shaper

for Miera. The black charred skin of the creature revealed a fiery orange where it was split in half, running in an almost straight line from the top of its head to just above the waist, where it tapered off to the left. It stood there motionless as if it was unaware of what had happened. Then, in just enough time for Thornton to blink, the creature crumbled into a pile of ash.

Dumbfounded, Thornton looked to his hands for an explanation. Finding none, he reached out for his hammer again, letting his palm settle on the worn wood of the handle. It felt warm to the touch, like leather on a hot day, and the warmth spread through him as he held it. When a second cry of pain came from the last remaining Khyth, he picked it up and readied himself to strike again.

As he did, Ynara stepped in front of Miera and him. She looked up at the Khyth, who towered above her, and spoke. "You are an abomination, Khyth—you and all your kind."

The creature coughed, sending a spatter of blood onto the earth in front of him. He glared down at Ynara. "The Breaker of the Dawn is coming to Break this world and restore us to greatness." He turned his eyes to Miera, who gasped audibly and took a step back. Extending a finger toward her, his eyes darkened and he said, "Blood of the Shaper! You will be the one to free him!"

Thornton stood firm even as the ground beneath him trembled. He knew this was his chance, while the Khyth was distracted. He looked at the base of the rocky platform and made a break for it, swinging his hammer as hard as he could. He connected and felt the earth shudder, sending huge chunks of rock spraying off. A surprised cry from the Khyth filled his ears as he swung again, this time cleaving the platform in half to collapse under its own weight.

His foundation destroyed, the black-hooded creature fell helplessly along with it, landing sharply on the pile of rocks and dirt. Lying on his back, his eyes focused on Thornton. He opened his mouth to speak, but death found him first. An arrow fired from the bow of Kethras, still hidden, buried itself solidly in his throat. The Khyth made a choking sound as he grasped at the arrow and tried to pull it out, but it did him no good. The last of his breath left him in a sputter as he stared wide-eyed at the handle of Thornton's hammer.

"He is dead," Kethras said, stepping out from the shadows.

Thornton stared at the black-robed figure lying on the ground in front of him. He approached him cautiously, stooping to examine the body. He did not need the moonlight to see the huge white hand woven into the back of his robe. "But what is he?" he asked.

"The Khyth," Kethras answered, "serve the Breaker of the Dawn. They are blood-enemies of the Athrani and are a threat to all who would see the Breaker remain imprisoned."

Thornton knew enough about the Athrani to realize that an enemy of theirs was someone to be feared. He'd heard about them from his father, but only that they were powerful—and dangerous.

"How was he able to do that?" Thornton asked. "Move the earth like that?"

"*Breaking*, they call it," the Kienari answered slowly, as if the word itself were dangerous. "They harness the energy that exists beyond this world and use it to their own ends. And although they are not as powerful as they once were, they are still formidable."

Thornton's attention was still focused on the Khyth's robe. "This white hand, I've seen it before. Miera and I were attacked earlier today, and I saw it on the cloak of one of the men."

Kethras nodded. "The Hand of the Black Dawn. It is a symbol for all of those who are sworn in service to the Breaker."

"I don't know what they want," Thornton said. "But it can't be a coincidence that we keep running into them."

Miera still looked shaken up. "What did he mean by 'Blood of the Shaper'?"

Kethras approached, examining her from a distance. "I was hoping you could tell us."

She looked at the ground, as if a painful memory had somehow made its way back into her mind. She shook her head and was silent.

Gift of the Shaper

Ynara spoke suddenly. "We should leave. There may be more, and I am not one for being hunted."

"What about the bodies?" Thornton asked.

"The forest will take them."

Thornton backed away, suddenly realizing that unnamed dangers could still be lurking in the darkness.

The four of them made their way back onto the road, and Kethras led them back to their horses, which had not moved from where they had left them. Thornton scratched Jericho behind the ears, and the big brown horse flicked his tail with satisfaction. He started to hook up the cart, when Kethras put his hand on his shoulder.

"It will only slow us down."

Thornton looked at him, puzzled. "But I need to bring it back to my father."

Kethras shook his head. "You cannot go back. Whoever sent these men has surely sent more. You said yourself that you recognized the symbol on their clothing. You are not safe anymore, and you would only be endangering those around you, including your father."

"I don't understand. What do they want with me?"

"Do you really want to find out?" Kethras said, turning to face the forest and listen.

Thornton put down the cart's hitch. "Not from them."

"Agreed," Kethras said.

"But who else would know?" Miera asked as she took out Matilda's saddle from her cart.

"Perhaps our Mother can help," Kethras answered. "There is a road ahead that will take us north to Kienar." He pointed to the blankets in Thornton's and Miera's carts. "There are no beds on the roads we will take. Bring those. We have long to travel."

Thornton looked at Jericho and the blanket in his cart and thought of home. "I have to see my father one last time."

Kethras looked at him, considering, thrumming his long black fingers on his chin in thought. Glancing down the road toward Lusk and the other way toward Thornton's village, he said, "You will place him in great danger. It is still possible that he will be left alone. I do not know what draws the men of the Hand to you, but if you go back there, you could lead them right to him."

Thornton looked at the ground in disappointment and back again to Jericho. The tall workhorse buried the end of his nose in Thornton's palm, bringing the slightest crack of a smile to Thornton's lips. He scratched behind Jericho's ear and worked his hand through his gray-flecked mane. "I just need to see him, at least to tell him that I'll be taking Jericho. He loves this old horse, maybe more than me."

Jericho snorted in apparent protest.

"We have no time for tearful goodbyes," Kethras said sharply.

The words made Miera laugh. "You don't know Olson Woods," she said. "The last time he cried, Lusk was just an inn."

Kethras eyed her and Thornton carefully. "Very well," he replied. "But quickly. We have no time."

Thornton looked at Miera, whose face reflected her uncertainty. He took the blanket and pouch of coins from his cart, taking a moment to prepare Jericho's saddle, and climbed on, urging him forward.

Miera, exasperated, did the same with Matilda.

Chapter 5

Highglade

Gift of the Shaper

Thornton

The horses' hooves beat against the dirt road as they rode toward the village. There was urgency in Kethras's voice when he told them they must hurry, and Thornton took him for the type that did not exaggerate.

The horses were running at a comfortable pace, but no less impressive to Thornton was that the Kienari were keeping up with them. Their big legs took long and graceful strides, rebounding off the ground with ease and making Thornton wonder if he was even seeing them at their fastest. Suddenly, he understood why neither of them had brought a horse of their own.

They slowed as they rounded a curve in the road, and Thornton could see his home through the trees. The dirt road meandered into offshoots of smaller roads, eventually making its way to one of the small number of houses in the village—houses that Thornton knew well, along with the names of everyone who lived in them. He'd spent his entire life here, among these trees: climbing, playing in the dirt, laughing, growing.

He breathed in, letting the familiar smells fill his nostrils: grass, dust, animals, trees. He didn't want to leave any of it behind.

They came to a stop with Kethras in front, breathing more heavily than normal, but not nearly hard enough to suggest he had been running stride-for-stride with a horse. Thornton swung his legs off the side of Jericho and hopped off.

"Say what you have to say," said Ynara. "We will stay here."

Thornton nodded and took off toward his house. He saw the telltale smoke rising from his father's forge. *Another late night, using just the moonlight as his lamp.*

As he got closer, though, something seemed wrong. He quickened his pace when he realized the smoke wasn't coming from the forge—it was coming from the house.

He raced to the door and flung it open, yelling for his father.

"Father!" he screamed.

No answer.

He yelled again.

"*FATHER!*"

Urgency and panic lined his voice.

When his shout was met with silence he turned back to his three companions, a look of wild desperation in his eyes, and shouted for Miera. She was on her feet and running before he finished her name. The Kienari both looked at each other and then back at Thornton, who was already making his way inside the house.

He burst inside, still shouting for his father. The smoke was not so thick yet that it was impenetrable, but looking upstairs he realized it was about to get much worse. A gray haze hung in the house as Thornton covered his mouth with his hand.

He scanned the floor for the source of the smoke but saw nothing. His eyes went back to the stairs that led to the single room he shared with his father. He was up them in a heartbeat, taking the stairs three at a time. As he reached the top, he headed toward the room, unsure if he wanted to find his father there and what it would mean if he did. He did not need to open the door; it was hanging off its hinges already, having been forced open from the outside.

He stared wide-eyed as the flames leapt from the bed, engulfing it almost entirely, and began to spread to the walls. Their bedside table had been overturned, and the lamp they used at night was smashed to pieces. There were two holes in the back wall, roughly human sized, and Thornton immediately knew that his father had put up a fight—Olson Woods never did anything easily.

The flames were now spreading to the ceiling, and Thornton knew he didn't have long. Seeing no signs of his father but plenty of a struggle, he backed out of the room and onto the stairs. Smoke stung his eyes as he coughed and made his way back onto the ground floor where Miera was waiting. Ynara and Kethras stood behind her.

"My father, he's—"

"Gone," Miera interrupted.

Thornton nodded and rubbed his smoke-stung eyes.

Gift of the Shaper

"We should not have come," Kethras said to Ynara, almost out of earshot, as she raised her nose to the air as if suddenly catching a scent, slipping quietly out the door.

"No!" Thornton shouted and turned to look at the Kienari. "Whoever did this got here before we did. There's no way they followed us." His voice quieted. "They knew what they were looking for." Thinking of the strange man who had asked about his father, who seemed so consumed with his hammer, he added, "This is my fault."

Miera slapped him across the face, hard, and pointed a finger right at him.

"Stop it right now, Thornton Woods. This is most certainly not your fault, and if Olson were here, he would tell you the same, but with a much firmer hand. This is no one's fault but the people who did it. And I most certainly want to find out who that is."

Thornton rubbed his face, shaking his head to rid it of the shock. "But how?" He looked past Miera at Kethras. "Is there some way of finding out who did this? Of tracking them?"

The tall Kienari looked up at the gathering smoke and said calmly, "Perhaps we should move outside," and stepped backward through the open doorway, standing just beyond the threshold.

Ynara was walking back toward them, a look of determination on her dark face. "The tracks lead north," she started. "But whoever did this took precautions, above the skills of even the greatest hunter." She paused before speaking again. "Whoever took your father used Breaking to try to cover their tracks."

Thornton's eyes darkened as he heard the word. He had only just found out what it meant, and he remembered the fear that coursed through him when he stood face to face with a Khyth. Now that fear had been replaced by hate.

"We can track them," Kethras said. "But we must be cautious. Meet us at the north side of the village. Ynara and I will find the trail."

By now, the flames had fully engulfed the upper part of Thornton's house. He stood numbly and watched as his boyhood home turned to ash and dust in front of him. The commotion had drawn the rest of the village out, with most of them dressed for sleep; but the calm manner in which Thornton stared at the flames, the oranges and reds dancing off his eyes, made them hesitate to approach him. He simply stood and stared while they worked around him to douse the fire.

The Kienari had slipped away unnoticed yet again, which came as no surprise. He looked around at the faces of his neighbors, then back to Miera. "I have to find him," he said, his voice calm against the flames.

"I'll come with you," Miera said. Her words were quiet yet firm.

Thornton looked up and studied her face. "Miera, no. You can't. Your home—"

She cut him off before he could finish. "Hasn't been a home since Father died. There's nothing left for me here. All I've had to look forward to are my trips to Lusk—and now even that's ruined." She looked despondently at Thornton's house, flames licking at the night sky. "Now there's nothing left."

Thornton's eyes followed hers. "Then I guess we've got no reason to stay." He turned his back on his house and walked over to Jericho, who stomped a foot and shook his head. Thornton took his reins and started toward the north of the village, Miera and Matilda following closely behind.

***

The journey north took them through the Talvin Forest, a densely wooded area that stretched on and on for miles. To the Kienari, it was comforting to be surrounded by forest; they were children of nature and were one with it. They seemed relaxed—almost cheerful.

To Thornton, it was not as relaxing. The only time he liked to be outside was when he was helping his father with his work, and it was starting to get to him. He was fighting off fatigue and exhaustion, swatting at the swarming mosquitoes—which Ynara found entertaining—and complaining of soreness from riding for so long.

Gift of the Shaper

"So walk," Kethras had said before catching a scent and disappearing into the forest, dagger already unsheathed. He'd been dipping into the forest at random intervals and had already caught enough for a small meal for each of them. By now, Thornton thought he was just showing off.

The road wound through the woods and occasionally split off in different directions, but the Kienari had no problem keeping them on the trail despite the darkness. Thornton wasn't sure how he did it, but whenever they came to a fork in the road, Kethras would survey the area for a moment or two before announcing which path they must follow.

As the night dragged on, the events of the day began to take their toll on Thornton. He was bruised, bloody, and drained, and the combined weight of those factors had finally started to catch up with him. He'd only meant to shut his eyes for a moment, but his body seemed to have other plans. His head lolled back and his torso wavered. Miera let out a cry as she watched him tumble from his saddle and crash to the ground.

His childhood friend was at his side in an instant. "Are you alright?" she asked as she helped him sit up. "What happened?"

"I don't know," he answered slowly while rubbing his head. "Just careless, I guess." He got up with Miera's help and started to walk back to Jericho.

"Thornton, no," Miera said, still holding onto his arm. "You're hurt. You need rest."

"I'll be fine. I'm just tired, that's all." He tried to pull his arm away but Miera wouldn't budge.

Kethras looked at Thornton, who was barely able to stand on his own. "She is right," he said. "You are in no condition to go much further."

Miera looked at the two Kienari. "What if we just stopped for a little while?" she asked. "Just for some rest. Could we pick up the trail again in a few hours?"

"I suppose we can," Ynara said. "We have covered a good amount of ground, and the tracks are still fresh. But we cannot stop for long if we have any hope of catching up." She looked at Thornton's arm that had been opened by the sword of the men they'd fought. She had done a good job of bandaging it with what she had. "We should look around for a place to rest, and I would like to look at your arm some more. Come."

Thornton was too tired to argue. He grabbed Jericho's reins and followed the Kienari as she led the way.

Up ahead they crossed over a small stream, and Kethras produced a pouch, which he proceeded to dip into the water. Thornton watched his long body, sleek and dark, as it worked so gracefully at even the simplest task. It reminded him of the foxes that would sometimes make their way into Highglade in hopes of finding a chicken coop left open at night. When the pouch was full the Kienari tied it to his belt, cupped his hands together, and drank straight from the stream. Between drinks he suggested the others do the same.

Miera led Matty to the water, from which the old mare happily drank. Jericho didn't need any help getting to the stream and almost took off Thornton's arm trying to get there. The two horses drank deeply beside the Kienari as Thornton looked on.

Standing up and wiping his mouth, Kethras went to look around for a place to stop for the night, fading into the trees as silently as ever.

Ynara took out a pouch of her own and dipped it in the stream, tying it off and turning to Thornton. Tapping her finger on the pouch, she said, "I will have to teach you how to make one of these." She hooked it to her belt and patted it. "Useful on travels such as these."

Thornton gave a sleepy smile and a nod, wishing he could be back indoors again.

"There is a small clearing up ahead," Kethras said, suddenly standing behind Thornton, who nearly leapt out of his skin in surprise. Miera pointed and laughed, while neither of the Kienari seemed to understand the joke.

Thornton regained his composure quickly, though. "Fine. Show us where so we can get some rest."

Kethras led them off the path into an open part of the woods, close enough to see or hear anyone coming by, but well-concealed enough so as not to give away their position. Seizing the opportunity, Ynara made

Gift of the Shaper

Thornton sit down while she unwrapped his bandage, washed off the blood, and rewrapped the arm.

"There," she said. "That looks better already."

Thornton groggily nodded his thanks.

Beside him, Kethras pulled six squirrels out of another pouch he was carrying and asked Miera if she knew how to skin an animal. When she stared wordlessly at him, he took the opportunity to demonstrate proper skinning technique to both her and Thornton.

The Kienari took two squirrels and hung them up with a small piece of twine, cutting them cleanly down the middle and spreading the skin to reveal the insides. Thornton did not fare well with the whole process, and Miera mostly stared in wide-eyed horror that ranged from disgust to fascination.

"All of this, we throw out," Kethras said as he held up the liver, emptying out the insides. "The rest, we keep." Thornton could not figure out why he was smiling and was unsure that he wanted to ask. Kethras used his knife to delicately cut away skin from muscle, then looked to Thornton. "Here," the tall Kienari said. "You try."

Begrudgingly, Thornton approached the animal and put his hands on the squirrel, surprised by how warm it was. Ynara pointed and began to talk him through the process. Trying to nod like he was listening, he had made no more than two errant cuts when he looked up to see Miera was already moving onto her second squirrel. He looked to the Kienari for help.

Kethras made an amused grunt and approached Thornton to finish the job himself. As he did so, Ynara pointed out how the skins could be used to carry things and that skinning techniques applied to larger animals as well.

After skinning the animal, Kethras had Ynara fetch some wood for a fire and offered another squirrel to Miera. She took it with enthusiasm and eyed the remaining ones. By the time Ynara had gathered enough for a small cookfire, Miera had finished the job and seemed pleased with herself, if not a little relieved to be done with it. The look in her eyes told Thornton that he would be hearing about it for a while.

Ynara then sharpened the ends of a couple of sticks to make skewers, while Kethras showed Thornton how to start a fire using just two pieces of wood and some twine. But as the flames took hold, Thornton was suddenly reminded of the eyes of the Khyth—those haunting, glowing orbs that seemed to float inside cracked and blackened skin. He turned to Miera with a worried look on his face.

As if reading his thoughts, Miera sat down beside him and put a hand on his shoulder.

"I know you're worried about him. But the fact that there are tracks at all means that they want your father alive."

Thornton rubbed a hand on his forehead as he grimaced. "But why did they take him in the first place? Why him? Why us?" His upturned palms hung in the air along with his questions.

"I don't know the answers," Miera said as she leaned in. "But I hope the Kienari might. If their Mother knew enough to send them to help us, then maybe she knows a lot more."

Thornton looked at her with pleading eyes. He had always had his father around—a fact that he knew better than to voice at the moment. Before he could speak, though, he caught a glimpse of a figure behind him. Turning, he saw Kethras flash his sharp teeth as he held up two roasted squirrels.

"You fought bravely today," said the Kienari. "It has been long since anyone has stood victorious in battle against one Khyth, let alone three." He passed the squirrel meat to Miera and Thornton. "And the way that you fought tells me you will do whatever it takes to find your father."

Thornton acknowledged this with a nod.

"And we will do everything we can to help," said Ynara. "But for now, you must take care of your hunger and your minds."

Thornton and Miera both nodded at this as they watched Kethras skewer two more squirrels and hold them over the fire.

Before long, they had full stomachs and heavy eyelids.

"Get what sleep you can," Kethras said after they all had finished eating. "We cannot stay for long."

Gift of the Shaper

Taking the blankets off the horses, Thornton knelt to place them on the ground, leaning over them and smoothing them out with his hands. When he had finished, he looked up at Miera. "Thank you for doing this," he said.

The look on her face told him that he was a fool for thanking her but that she cared for him more than anyone living. "Olson has been more of a father to me than mine ever was. You know I wouldn't have let you run off by yourself."

"I know. But I thought I should say something."

She walked over to him and took his head in her hands, kissed him lightly on the forehead, and smiled. "Then say it to Olson when we find him again."

Thornton watched her as she walked away to wrap herself up in one of the thick wool blankets they'd brought, a few feet away from where Matilda was tied.

Looking to find his own blanket, he watched Kethras grab a branch from a nearby tree to hoist himself up, lying down on his stomach with his hands folded under his chin. He pulled up the cloth hanging around his neck and covered his eyes with it. Ynara did the same thing on another tree nearby. Thornton shook his head in wonder and walked over near Jericho to lie down. It was warm enough to sleep on top of the blanket, which provided just enough padding to make him comfortable.

Exhaustion wrestled with his fear and his uncertainty—uncertainty over finding his father again and what more they would have to do to get him back safely. But soon his exhaustion emerged as the victor, giving way to slumber and the darkness of dreams.

Chapter 6

Derenar

Gift of the Shaper

Dailus

In a faraway cell made of mortar and stone, Dailus, son of Jecko, awoke to the smell of rotting wood and a headache that made him question his sanity. Blinking his way back to consciousness, he tried with little success to identify his surroundings. He was in some sort of prison—that much he could see—with a great wooden door standing between him and freedom. He gave a few more glances around the room and rubbed his eyes.

Like all Athrani, he was born with distinct multicolored eyes that served as a means of setting him apart from regular humans and identifying him as one born with the gift of Shaping. A treasure to their people, Athrani eyes had two colors: a first that made up the inner portion; and a second that replaced the white that existed in human eyes, making the eyes of the Athrani appear huge and unmistakable.

It was no surprise, then, that eyes were such an important part of Athrani culture. The color of the outer portion—the *ring*, which always passed from father to son—had become a symbol of strength and nobility over the ages. Since a darker ring meant a stronger affinity for Shaping, those who had them usually found themselves in positions of power, based solely on their perceived link to the Otherworld. "Dark eyes, fine lives" was a common phrase in Ellenos.

But to those who were born to an Athrani father and a human mother, their eyes were an inescapable curse that marked them for life; no matter how strong their affinity for the Other-world and how dark their ring, it only appeared in one eye. The other eye was indistinguishable from a human eye, with no ring at all.

These "half-eyes" were looked down on with pity and derision and were sometimes ostracized completely. Whether by force or by choice, most of them sought new lives among humans; some had even done so for generations. They were bastards, though, children of two worlds that would never be fully accepted in either. Rejected by humans and resented by Athrani, they carried the weight of their heritage on their backs and in their eyes.

None knew this better than Dailus, whose skyblue left eye floated on a pool of gold that brought him more than his fair share of poor treatment because of what he was—unquestionably different. And knowing that if the roles have been reversed—if his mother had been Athrani and his father, human—he would show no sign of his heritage whatsoever, there was not a day that went by that he did not curse his Athrani father for falling in love with a human.

As his wits slowly returned to him, he realized he had no knowledge of where he was or how he came to be there. His wrists were cold, and he discovered why once he glanced at them; two thick irons, one on each wrist, were held together by three loops of a chain that allowed him almost no freedom of movement.

About three-quarters of the way up the door was a horizontal window framed with iron. Three vertical bars, each about the length of a hand, were spaced evenly in the portal, denying even the smallest hope of an exit, even though the gaps between the bars were barely large enough to put his head through.

Heedlessly, he raised his hands and ran his fingers through his long white hair. He stopped when he felt something on his fingertips and pulled his hand away in confusion. *Blood?* He touched his scalp lightly and inhaled sharply at the pain.

"Is someone there?" a voice whispered.

He put his ear to the wall. "Who said that?" he asked.

The voice that answered him was smooth and light. "My name is Aidren. Did they bring you in today?"

"I . . . I think so. I can't be sure. I don't remember much . . . and I seem to have suffered a blow to the head."

"That's how they work," Aidren whispered. "They sneak up on you, mostly at night, when no one else is around to see. Smack you over the head, then drag you here and chain you up." He added with a sigh, "I know because that's how I ended up in here."

Dailus leaned his head against the wall in defeat. "How long has it been?"

Gift of the Shaper

There was a pause for calculation. "Three days ago, maybe four. It's just been me up 'til now."

Both of them froze at the sound of footsteps, heavy and slow. *Just like the owner, I'd wager,* Dailus thought with a chuckle. He considered standing up to take a look outside but thought better of it and stayed seated on the floor. If the guard was looking to drag out a body, he would rather pretend to be one than have it forced upon him. When they came to a stop, Dailus could make out the outline of a face through the opening in his door.

There was barely enough light to see; but, whoever it was, he saw what he was looking for; and the footsteps picked up again, moving away as heavily and slowly as they had come.

When they stopped, there was a shout in the distance, coupled with the sounds of a struggle. Then there was a yell from a different, rougher voice, followed by the crack of wood on bone and the sound of a body hitting the ground.

Dailus shrunk in his cell as he found himself frozen by the sounds. His eyes darted around as if willing his body to move, to hide, but his limbs stubbornly refused. His heart made it worse by thumping violently against his rib cage and sending blood screaming through his body. An audible gulp preceded the thought that whatever was making that noise would come for him next. His sweat glands seemed to be convinced that was the case.

After some scuffling and harsh whispers, footsteps once again approached his cell door. He heard the heavy clank of iron as the lock to his door was unbolted.

"In here," came a high-pitched voice.

This was followed up by the sound of something heavy being dragged and the door to his cell being flung open. Then the body of the biggest man he'd ever seen was dumped unceremoniously onto the floor beside him. After the door was slammed shut again, the only sounds were two pairs of footsteps and shallow breathing from the body beside him.

Dailus waited for the footsteps to fade as he watched the man, his eyes wide in amazement.

"What was that?" Aidren whispered from the next cell over, his voice punctuated with urgency.

"My new cellmate, apparently," Dailus quipped. By now his pulse had slowed, but the sweat on his palms and forehead remained.

Looking over the stranger, Dailus was amazed that their captors had not seen it necessary to chain him up as well. For one, he was an absolute mountain of a man—even bigger than the guard who had dragged him in. His clothes were torn and covered in blood—most likely a mix of his and a few others—and the callouses on his hands told the story of a man who relied on his strength alone to survive. His dark brown hair flowed into a thick beard.

"It sounded like they hit him pretty good," came Aidren's voice again. "Is he alive?"

Seeing that he was breathing and not wanting to startle the man if he happened to wake up, Dailus voiced a curt yes and retreated to the far corner of the room. The large heap of a man was certainly alive—but not by much.

After a pregnant silence, he turned again to the wall. "Do you know where we are?"

"The best I can figure is somewhere outside the Talvin forest. I was headed from Ellenos on my way back to Annoch when they grabbed me."

"Ellenos?" Dailus latched onto the word. "Are you Athrani?"

There was hesitation before an answer. "I am," Aidren said. "Through my father."

"A half-eye?" asked Dailus.

"All my life."

"That makes two of us."

Aidren's voice from the other cell sounded worried. "I don't like the sound of that—two Athrani held captive in the same place. I wonder if this new one is Athrani as well."

Gift of the Shaper

Just then he heard footsteps approaching, this time quickly. Both men fell silent. From the cell to his right, Dailus heard the clank of a lock and the door opening.

"Time to go," said a deep voice accompanied by the sound of chains moving around.

"Go? Go where?" said Aidren.

"You Athrani and your questions," the man said with a touch of amusement.

Dailus moved quietly to the window of his door and tried to peer through it to see what was happening. He placed his cheek against the wall and turned ever so slightly to get a better vantage point. He had to move all the way to the left of the hole to even see anything, but all he could manage was a glimpse of the outside of the open door to the cell on his right. Nevertheless, he watched and waited.

"Up with you," the voice barked. "D'kane won't like it if we're late." Chains scraped heavily against the stone floor.

The door swung shut with a heavy clank, and Dailus saw their captor, a man in a black tunic, holding a chain leading to the neck, wrist, and legs of Aidren. The Athrani's long, light hair hung down past his shoulders, and his youthful face was streaked with fear and sadness. His right eye was lined with only the lightest of a gray ring.

The man holding the chain—a brute of a man, with scars covering his face—looked through the small window into Dailus's cell, causing the Athrani to recoil in fright and nearly stumble over the slumbering stranger beneath him. The man's teeth revealed themselves to be as crooked as his grin. "Don't worry," he said through the rectangular opening in the heavy wooden door, his voice deep and mocking. "You're next."

As he walked away with Aidren, his laughter echoed down the halls and mixed with the horrific scraping of metal on stone.

Chapter 7

The Talvin Forest, North of Highglade

Gift of the Shaper

Thornton

Thornton awoke to the sound of the Kienari talking in low, rough tones. The first rays of light had already broken across the horizon, and Thornton could see them facing the road with their backs to him. He turned his head to see Miera asleep just a few feet from him. Rubbing the sleep from his eyes with his knuckles, he stood up and began folding his blanket, trying not to wake her. He finished, putting it on the ground next to the packs of the Kienari.

He walked over to Jericho and Matilda, who were nibbling on a nearby patch of grass. Giving them each a small pat on the head, he strained his ears to see if he could make out what Kethras and Ynara were saying but only caught fragments of words. He was sure he heard them say *Khyth* at least a half dozen times. Kethras raised his voice to say, "She must be protected," and both of them fell silent.

Miera stirred from her sleep, and the Kienari noticed. They came back to their makeshift camp and sat down.

"I am sorry if we woke you," Kethras started. "But we need to get moving. We have rested long enough, and the sun has already begun its climb."

Thornton looked puzzled. "What's that got to do with anything?"

Kethras stared at him uncomfortably, like he had let slip a secret he would rather not reveal. After a pause, he said, "When we met, do you remember the first thing I said to you?"

Thornton thought about it for a moment. "You told me to put out my light."

"Do you remember why?"

"You said you couldn't see."

Kethras nodded.

"But I don't understand," Thornton said. "It wasn't that bright."

"Not bright," Kethras said, "hot."

The same light seemed to come on in Thornton's mind as he slowly realized why the Kienari were such excellent night hunters. *They didn't use light to see at night—they used heat!*

"You're saying you can't see during the day?"

Kethras looked annoyed and answered, "Of course we can see. I'm looking at you now, aren't I?" He crossed his arms in protest. "We merely prefer our night vision to that of the daytime. Light can play tricks on the eyes, but heat does not lie."

Ynara spoke up. "But time is running short, and trails do not last forever."

Gathering himself up, Kethras said gruffly, "Enough talk. We must go."

Kethras walked over to his packs and picked them up, slinging his bow across his back and slipping dagger after dagger into sheathes tied neatly across his body. Thornton watched him, the tall creature covered completely in fine black fur, and understood why they would prefer the dark of night.

Ynara came up behind Thornton and whispered, "He doesn't like to be reminded that he has a weakness." She smiled at him gently and stooped to pick up her things. She pulled out a few pieces of bread from her pack and passed them around. By now, Miera was up and awake as well and had folded both blankets neatly and placed them on the backs of the horses. She happily accepted the piece of bread as she finished packing the rest of her things.

Dawn came streaming forth as the dark of night had turned into morning twilight. Kethras led them all back onto the road and oriented them north.

***

Thornton couldn't decide which would make him sorer: if he kept riding or if he got off to walk. For the moment, he opted to go on foot since the pace they were keeping was moderate. The Kienari, as always, were walking. He wondered if either of them knew how to ride a horse at all, then laughed to himself when he tried to picture it.

The day was warm, even for summer, so he was continually wiping sweat from his forehead and pushing his damp brown hair back behind his ears. Miera had tied hers back, which had absolutely fascinated Ynara, since her own hair was the same length all over. Ever since they started traveling together, Ynara had become obsessed with Miera's hair, constantly finding an excuse to touch it and run her fingers through it. Other times she would just watch as Miera put it up, only to ask her to put it down again so she could watch as she shook her head, sending her beautiful golden locks tumbling down to her shoulders. Ynara was entranced by it, and Miera was nice enough to indulge her.

Kethras had no time for any of that and chose instead to keep his eyes on the road and his ears alert. When they stopped to let the horses eat and rest, he was constantly on the lookout. He wanted to make sure that if they were being followed, they would be ready to defend themselves. At one point he stopped to examine a group of tracks on the road that appeared to be leading west. When he noticed Thornton casually glancing at him as he investigated, he called him over.

"Tell me what you can about these tracks," the Kienari said.

"There was one on horseback," Thornton said, pointing to the hoof prints, "and maybe two or three people walking."

"Good, but look here," Kethras said, pointing at a set of hoof prints. "These go deeper into the dirt than the other set, yet they are the same size." He looked at Thornton, waiting for him to connect the pieces.

"Someone was riding on it, on a second horse," Thornton answered slowly.

"Very good," Kethras said. "The tracks look to have been made in the mud. See how they go deeper in than our tracks do? More of the road was pushed away because it was soft and wet. They were traveling just after a rain."

Thornton was impressed.

"Always keep the track between you and the sun," Kethras went on, still looking at the ground. "You can catch tiny imperfections in the shadow of the track, and if you're good, you can tell the difference between one track and another. There were four people walking," he said as he stood. He looked over to see that the horses had finished grazing. Ynara and Miera were talking idly, with Ynara occasionally reaching out and flipping the ends of Miera's hair, smiling like a child with a new toy.

Thornton, still studying the tracks, asked, "What if these tracks were made by the people who took my father?"

Kethras stood with his back to Thornton. "That's one possibility."

"If there's a chance we could find him, we have to take it."

Kethras turned and looked at him, then back to Ynara and Miera, who were still talking and smiling. "I cannot guarantee these tracks will lead us to your father."

Thornton stood up. "Then let's see where they lead."

Kethras nodded, then walked over to Ynara and Miera to tell them the plan. Thornton walked back over to Jericho and climbed onto his back, hoping that they could make good time. If it was not his father's trail they were following, they could at least find out quickly.

Chapter 8

Derenar

Gift of the Shaper

Aidren

The chains on Aidren's neck were as cold as they were heavy, and the scraping sound made him cringe as they dragged against the stone floor. He found himself struggling to walk as they pulled him down, but he knew if he slowed even for a moment, he would be taking a sharp jab in the back from the big man behind him.

"Let's go, half-eye," the man said, jabbing him again. "You should know better than anyone how demanding the Khyth are."

Khyth, Aidren thought with a shiver. *That explains the decor*. He gathered up what strength he could find and kept walking.

He hadn't been paying close attention to the details of the halls they'd walked down, but they all looked the same to him anyway: stone wall after stone wall over a stone floor under a stone ceiling. The only sounds as they walked were the ones he made as he dragged his chains. It told him that they were most likely the only people being held captive.

"In here," the big man grunted. He shoved Aidren hard enough to make him lose his balance and fall flat on his face, chains clanking loudly. Inches in front of him was a heavy wooden hatch on the floor, which his captor opened easily. Towering over Aidren, he gave him a swift kick that sent him tumbling down a set of old wooden stairs. "After you," he said, laughing loudly at his own joke.

When Aidren hit the bottom, he had the wind knocked out of him as his chest landed right on a bunch of chains. He groaned weakly and sucked in a lungful of air to curse his luck. His oath was cut off, however, by a voice that gave him chills from down the hall.

"Rimbal," it said, "if you kill the Athrani before I've had a chance to work on him, you'll be joining him soon after." Raspy and low, the voice echoing through the cold stone enclosure sounded less like a man's and more like a phantom that had somehow clawed its way back to life. "Now bring him in."

Aidren squinted in the darkness, trying to see down the hallway and possibly catch a glimpse of the owner of the voice that scraped at his ears.

But the path ahead, illuminated only by dim candles, further convinced him that the voice had no corporeal form.

"He's fine, Master D'kane," came the gruff reply from Rimbal. "Just a little roughed up. Seemed content to take his time on the way here, so I had to help him along."

"As long as he's alive, he'll do."

Rimbal leaned down and whispered, "Hear that, Athrani? All I gotta do is not kill you."

Aidren felt the chains around him tighten as he found himself being lifted up. Rimbal gave him a boot to the middle of his back that made him nearly lose his footing. He dragged the heavy chains behind him as they walked, prodded ever forward by the big man behind him. And as they walked past the expansive gray walls, he found himself wanting less and less to see what was waiting beyond them.

After what seemed like an eternity, the hallway opened to a large, round room. In the middle was a stone table with a black-robed figure standing beside it with his back to them. He turned around, revealing a scorched and ravaged face streaked with scars.

"Alive," the man said with a dark smile. "Let's see for just how long." His voice crackled and groaned like a burning log.

Aidren's heart sank as he recognized the Master Khyth for what he was. His face felt heavy as he drooped in dread.

"Place him on the table," the Khyth said. Approaching Aidren and looking straight at him, he said, "I hope he has something we can use." Eagerness and power burned behind his eyes; it was the eagerness that was most unnerving.

Aidren looked down to a thin chain that hung from the Khyth's neck and what looked like an enormous tooth or a horn, huge, curved, and white.

Rimbal moved him over to the great stone slab and threw him on it roughly, jostling the chains and leaving him staring at the ceiling above. Aidren heard the clink as Rimbal fastened each chain to a ring on the

Gift of the Shaper

floor, securing him in place and taking away the final hope of escape. Without the use of his hands, Aidren's Shaping power was all but useless.

"The other two are still in their cages," Rimbal said. "One of them tried to escape earlier, but I bashed him on the head before he could try anything."

D'kane looked at Rimbal disapprovingly. "I thought I told you to keep them chained up."

"He was chained up," Rimbal countered. "I think he must've figured a way out of them or something. But . . . But if he finds a way out again—"

D'kane cut him off. "See that he doesn't."

"Of . . . Of course. But if by some unbelievable turn of events—"

"Stop," D'kane said sharply. "Very well." He lifted the chain that hung from his neck and handed the horn to Rimbal. "You will return this to me when you've finished."

"Thank you, Master Khyth," Rimbal said as he pocketed the horn.

"Now bring out the Gwarái," D'kane said. The word made Aidren's blood run cold as he started to feel faint. "I'll be needing a second horn."

Gwarái. The Night Stalkers. The Shape Eaters. Wretched spawns of the Breaker that fed on blood and power in their time before the Shaping War. Yet no one had seen one in . . .

A sharp slap on his cheek forced Aidren back to the present as his eyes met the Khyth's.

"I'll have none of that, Servant of the Anvil," D'kane growled. "This has killed quite a few of you before, but it doesn't have to. Although," he said as his lips curled into a sneer, "you will no doubt wish it had."

Begging would be fruitless, Aidren knew. He was a Khyth prisoner, and Khyth hated the Athrani more than anyone hated anything. No, begging would only bring him pain and humiliation. With a breath, he resigned himself to his fate.

He heard Rimbal's footsteps approaching again, trailed by a rhythmic click-clack, click-clack that sounded like heavy talons striking stone. Then nausea dug its claws in him as his fear was made real.

A Gwarái. Here. In this room! His head reeled at the impossibility of it all.

He craned his neck to try and see for himself, hoping beyond hope that it was a terrible lie, that everything he knew and felt was a deception. But when his eyes rested upon the creature, black and repulsive, he knew that he was seeing his end.

The Gwarái was young, standing about five feet taller than Rimbal, and had none of the scars and wounds that were described as typical of the ancient reptilian beasts. It was covered head to abominable toe in midnight-black scales that made its penchant for night hunting all the more effective. And, though it walked on all fours, its powerful forelimbs were long, built for grabbing and tearing; so its head was several feet higher than its waist, giving it a hunched appearance. And atop its long, thick neck was a head with two great horns, each one white and curved, with points as sharp as daggers.

Even when the Gwarái had stepped in the room, Aidren felt his power abandon him. The creatures had the terrifying and poorly understood ability to nullify Athrani Shaping. Their mere presence snuffed it out like water on a fire, leaving nothing but a void. Aidren felt his strength drain from him as the creature drew near, paralyzing him with fear and dread. The creature's cold yellow eyes looked over him hungrily, and Aidren could feel the warmth of its breath as it closed in.

It was as if the Gwarái could sense it—the power of the Otherworld—and were drawn to it. This one was already salivating at the presence of an Athrani, running its long tongue over rows of thin, sharp teeth, hungry for a taste of his blood. Its small, circular nostrils drank in the air as it drew closer, intoxicated with the aroma. Rimbal, big as he was, struggled to keep it restrained, despite the masses of chains holding it back.

"The strength of the Gwarái lies in their thirst for the blood of Shapers," D'kane began. "Whatever lets them do it—block the ability to tap into the power of the Otherworld—also lets them drain it. However, I've discovered," he said, looking rather pleased, "that if they drain enough power, it can be collected. I'm particularly fond of taking their horns," he said, fingering the one around his neck, "as they make for an impressive, if not functional, trophy."

Gift of the Shaper

By now Rimbal was struggling mightily to contain the creature that commanded the room. He grabbed the chains that held the Gwarái by the throat as it hovered only inches away from Aidren's face.

"Now, what I need from you," D'kane went on, "is just a bit of your power. Are you familiar with the Pieces of the Worldforge?"

At first, Aidren was unsure whether the Khyth was addressing him or simply speaking rhetorically. After a long silence, he croaked an answer. "Of course. All Athrani know the story. The Shaper used the Hammer and the Anvil to forge the chains that hold—"

D'kane slammed his hand down on the table. "The chains that hold the Breaker," he seethed. He turned the palms of his hands to the ceiling and recited:

"The Breaker of Dawn, the Hammer of Darkness,

Bound in His prison and resting in chains.

Binder of Worlds, the Keeper of Shadows,

In Her embrace, the world remains.

Shaper of Ages, the Anvil of Light,

Her power descended; Her Children, Her might."

Rimbal, still struggling with the Gwarái, said loudly, "Who cares?"

D'kane lowered his hands slowly and turned to Rimbal, the Khyth's dark face displaying the grave seriousness that was thick in his voice. "The Hammer of the Worldforge, one of the very tools of creation, is within our grasp. When the Shaper of Ages gave Herself to the Athrani and scattered the pieces throughout the world, She made it so that no Khyth could ever wield the Hammer and no Athrani could ever break the chains. But the Breaker had other plans," he sneered. "And He made the Gwarái with His last bit of strength, making them ravenous for the power of the Otherworld." He stopped and looked at the creature before him, almost marveling at it.

Rimbal spoke up again, "So that's why this one's so feisty."

D'kane nodded absently. "That which is broken always seeks to be remade whole. The Pieces of the Worldforge and the Shaping ability of the Athrani were once one and the same." He looked at the Gwarái and again at Aidren. "Even now, the Shaping power inside you is clawing at the surface, begging to be set free. Do you know why it is so important that we let it?" He turned to Rimbal, his face expressionless.

Rimbal looked drained as his purely physical struggle had now turned mental. "So you can use the Hammer of the Worldforge?"

D'kane clapped his hands together several times in mock applause. "And free the Breaker from His chains." He clasped his hands in front of his face in exasperation. "Now . . . loose the Gwarái," he whispered.

The Athrani's terror was as sharp as the scream that left his lungs.

At the words of his master, Rimbal dropped the only thing holding the monstrous beast back, and it lunged forward with unholy quickness and veracity, snapping its jaws open to reveal a set of needle-like fangs that sprung forth from their concealment in its mouth. Aidren felt the Gwarái's dagger-like teeth sink in as the creature clamped its jaws around his shoulder and upper chest and began to drink deeply.

The pain that coursed through Aidren's body was unlike any he'd ever felt. The fangs of the beast, sharp and terrible, were just the beginning. Perhaps it was the emptiness that he felt, the sudden absence of something so formative to his entire identity, that made him ache. Whatever it was, the feeling of powerlessness he felt had now overtaken him completely. He was sluggish and cold. When the Gwarái had entered the room, he'd felt himself weaken, as if he'd lost the power to stand. Now, with the creature feeding on him, he felt as if his connection with the Otherworld had been severed. It was like his legs had been cut off, and he would never walk again.

The distinct odor of perspiration, dirt, and red meat hit Aidren all at once as Rimbal appeared behind the Gwarái. He reached out to grab the chain around the creature's neck, and at his touch, the feeding stopped.

"You have done well, Rimbal," D'kane said as he tossed him a pouch of coins. "Cage our beast and bring the other Athrani to me. Use the horn only as a last resort. I must attend to my work," he said as he turned to leave, flicking his hands to part the stone wall that contained his study. "Our search for the blood of the Shaper continues." With those words,

Gift of the Shaper

the wall closed behind him, leaving Rimbal standing and staring at nothing.

The big man grunted and yanked on the chain, commanding the head of the huge black beast away from Aidren.

Aidren watched them leave as he struggled to move atop the cold stone table. He tried several times to move his hand to his chains but found the effort exhausting and let it simply drop to his side. Lying there, staring at the dead stone ceiling, he realized now what D'kane had meant: though he was alive, as the Khyth had said, he wanted nothing more than to have died along with his hope.

Burdened with the curse of a life without Shaping, Aidren closed his eyes and wept.

Chapter 9

Derenar

Gift of the Shaper

Olson

Olson Woods woke up and rubbed his head, which throbbed intensely. It hurt to open his eyes, and he let out a barely audible groan. A voice came from nearby. It was quiet but steady, with a hint of an Ellenos accent.

"You were out for hours. I was beginning to think you wouldn't wake up."

Olson blinked a few times and looked over to where the voice was coming from.

Smiling before him and sitting cross-legged on the ground was a man, thin and pale, with white hair that hung lightly above the shoulders of his blood-red tunic. His eyebrows were black, in stark contrast to the rest of him, but everything else about him spoke of softness and fragility.

Olson rubbed his eyes and looked up to the walls that surrounded him. "Where am I?"

"A prison cell, outside the Talvin forest." He sighed, adding, "That's all I know."

A sudden throbbing awoke in Olson's head, and he smashed the heels of his palms to his temples in agony. He uttered what sounded like *hnnngh*.

"I know. They did the same thing to me," the man replied. "There was another man in here, Aidren, in the cell beside us, who said that was how they operate," he went on. "They took him away before I could learn anything else." His voice dropped off. "I'm not quite sure if we will see him again."

Olson paused to internalize this information. "Who took him away?" he asked after a while. "The other prisoner, I mean. How many were there?"

The red-robed man gave it a bit of thought. "Two, I suppose. One, I saw; the other, I heard."

"Just two? No more?"

He paused to think. "Not that I recall. But sometimes I can hear voices coming from down the hall."

Olson rubbed his eyes again and muttered from behind his hands, "How long have you been in here?"

"About a day now, I think," the other man answered. He raised his hands up to touch his hair again, and that's when Olson noticed the chains. "My head still hurts from when they knocked me out, and it's still a bit . . . cloudy." He extended his hand out in greeting, as best as possible in chains. "But as long as we're sharing a cell, we might as well make it official. Dailus."

Olson cringed at the very thought of shaking hands in his current condition but managed to extend a huge hand in a somewhat acceptable fashion. "Olson," he whispered.

"Pleasure to meet you, Olson," Dailus said, rocking back. "Though unfortunate it has to be under these circumstances." When his eyes went to Olson's wrists, free of chains as they were, he frowned and turned his eyes to his own fetters. "I don't suppose you have anything to help with these?" he said as he displayed his bound hands.

Olson patted around his shirt for a few moments before producing a small, thin piece of metal. "Here," he said. "Try this." He flipped it to Dailus and started looking around the cell, examining it for strengths and weaknesses. He had no intention of staying put, especially with Thornton still in Lusk.

He's probably worried sick, Olson thought, *with no way of knowing I'm alive.*

It was a simple stone prison with no windows in the walls. There was no way to tell if escape lay just on the other side of the wall or if it merely led to more cells. *Too risky to try to tunnel through*, he thought, *and too time consuming*. The wooden door looked sturdy but old and was reinforced on the top and bottom with iron. There was a bucket in the corner of the cell, the purpose of which Olson quickly surmised, and a simple straw bed for sleeping, but not much else. He stood up and put his head to the window to try and get a look at the door next to him. He looked at the hinges, two of them, at the top and bottom of the door. *Terrible craftsmanship*, he thought. They were made of what looked to be iron, as was the hinge pin that held them in place. The outside of the door was a simple sliding lock.

Gift of the Shaper

"No offense, Dailus, but I don't plan on sticking around much longer," he said as he continued his examination of the cell.

"You have a plan, then," he laughed, still picking at the locks on his wrist. "Well, I certainly hope it involves me." He was biting his bottom lip in concentration, fully engaged in managing his own escape. A few seconds later, his shackles dropped to the floor.

Olson didn't bother with an answer. He reached out his hand and touched the door lightly, probing it for weakness. A smile spread across his face when he felt one. He lowered his shoulder and surged forward.

Dailus leapt off the floor in surprise as the sound of splintering wood filled his ears, followed shortly thereafter by the loud crash of wood hitting stone. He scrambled to his feet to see an open doorway before him, with his new cellmate kneeling on the one thing that had kept them from freedom.

The shoddy, old door never stood a chance.

Olson stood up and rubbed his shoulder. "I'd like to shake hands with the poor sap who built these things," he said, "and make sure I never, ever work with him." He looked back at Dailus, who was still too shocked to speak. "We should get going," he said, indicating the fallen door. "They probably heard that."

Dailus could do nothing but nod, moving quickly out of his cell and one step closer to escape.

Olson charged down the hallway of the prison, with Dailus close behind him. It was lined with cells just like the one he had been held in, but they were all empty. The end of the hallway came to a T and stopped.

He glanced left, then right; he saw nothing but the same endless stone walls and found no indications that they were headed in the right direction. Frustrated, he looked to Dailus.

"I don't suppose you know where we are, do you?" he asked.

Dailus peered down the hall. "To the right, I believe, is where they took the other prisoner."

Olson chewed on the words. *Then to the left could be the way out*, he thought. He glanced back to the right, considering.

After a silence, he spoke again. "I don't know how many of them are in there," he said, "but I can't leave someone in good conscience."

Dailus sighed deeply. "I was afraid you were going to say something like that."

Just as he finished his sentence, three men in black tunics walked through the door leading to the room next to them, whom Olson recognized immediately as the men who had taken him from his home in Highglade. The one in front was the biggest—nearly as big as him—and had a face covered in scars. The other two that stood behind him were smaller but armed with thick wooden cudgels. The smallest of the three had wild red hair and a bandage covering one eye, and the other one had a face as ugly as an axe wound, with a gray beard that did little to conceal the rest of it, capped off with a permanent scowl.

"Just where do you think you're going?" came the deep voice of the one in front, flashing a nasty grin full of yellow and brown teeth.

"Looks like they're trying to make a break for it, Rimbal," said the one with the red hair.

"I can see that, Twig," Rimbal said with annoyance.

Twig looked at Rimbal with confusion on his face. "Th-then why did you ask?"

The big, brutish man took one hand and made a fist, covering it with his other palm and cracking his knuckles with four sickening pops. "Because they're not going anywhere."

Olson squared off with the big man and readied himself for a fight.

"Hold them off," Dailus said as his eyes flashed with focus.

Olson had no time to think before the men were charging at him. He stepped back to avoid being hit, then surged forward, catching them each in the chest and sending them falling backward. The big man with the scars, Rimbal, took a swing at him with his fist, but Olson was just quick enough to move his head to the side and caught only a glancing blow. He answered with a wild punch at his head that landed right on the forehead, hurting both of them in the process.

Gift of the Shaper

Taking a couple of jabs to the face, Olson staggered back. He put his head down and made a desperate attempt to grab the big man. They both tumbled to the ground, with Olson managing to maneuver his way on top, getting a few punches in before a surge of pain shot through him as he caught a blow to the back of the head from one of the cudgels. Turning his head to where the shot came from, he saw one of the men winding up to take another swing, when suddenly a burst of bright light came from Dailus's direction, and the man stopped completely like his body had frozen over. Olson turned his head to Dailus in amazement.

"I said hold them back!" Dailus shouted as the second man shifted his attention and charged at him. Olson dove into the man from behind, stopping just short of Dailus, whose gaze fell on the largest of their assailants.

"There's three of them!" Olson protested in between punches to the face of the man below him.

Dailus crackled with energy. His face looked strained as he closed his eyes in concentration. The two men before him watched as his hands moved through the air, which somehow felt heavier all of a sudden.

Olson watched as what looked like a fog formed around the two men. It thickened with an unimaginable quickness, obscuring the men behind it, and then solidifying. With an audible *snap!* everything stopped. Olson blinked his eyes to be sure he was not seeing things. Where the two men had been standing only moments ago was now encased in some sort of cage made out of solid air. He could almost make them out as they stared back at him with fright-widened eyes. They pounded on the insides of it, their cries muffled by the opaque prison.

As Olson's fist met the jaw of the man on the floor one last time, he looked up in disbelief at Dailus. "What did you do?"

"Stopped them," he answered matter-of-factly.

Olson gaped. A gurgle came from Rimbal, so Olson took his head and banged it against the floor, causing the man's eyes to roll back in his head as he lost consciousness.

"But how?" he asked as he stood, scratching his beard in confusion.

"With Shaping," he answered. "While I might be a half-eye, I am still Athrani. I told the air what I needed it to do, and it listened."

Olson looked at Dailus's blue eyes and for the first time saw that behind one of them lay a golden sheen where any other man's eye would have been white. He'd never seen a socalled half-eye before and might not have noticed at all if Dailus hadn't called attention to it.

Olson continued to stare incredulously. "Well, why couldn't you have used that Shaping to escape earlier?"

"I did," Dailus answered. He lifted up the hair on the left side of his head and revealed a large gash that looked like it had been healing for a few days. "But I didn't get far. I barely made it out of my cell before they were on top of me. So you can imagine my relief when you showed up—I'm no good when I'm outnumbered." He wiped the fresh sweat away from his forehead and backed up against the wall for support. Dropping weakly to his knees, he closed his eyes and said, "Forgive me. I need a few moments."

The big blacksmith crossed his arms and frowned. "How many moments, exactly?"

Dailus looked up at Olson and smiled weakly. "It won't be long," he answered. "I tapped into a bit of power for that."

Olson looked around, making sure they were alone. His heart was still beating fast, and he was ready to fight again if he had to. He paced the length of the hall as Dailus rested, stopping to dig through Rimbal's pockets as he did so. He pulled out a few loose coins, a simple key, and a crudely drawn map.

Could come in handy, he thought.

Right as he pocketed them, there came a faint wailing down the hall, and Olson had a feeling that he knew where they had taken the other prisoner. He looked at Dailus, who sighed in exasperation and reached out his hand to be helped up, which Olson did easily.

Together they started down the hall, sidestepping the two men's fresh prison that had been made out of thin air.

Gift of the Shaper

They made their way down a series of corridors as the wailing continued. The walls around them were stone, and Olson could tell that it had not always been a prison. Windows lined the hallway, plain and unadorned, with not so much as bars on them to keep the prisoners in. Dim rays of light crept in, the first direct sunlight Olson had seen in days. They came to the end of a hallway where the sound was the loudest, and an open hatch on the floor was the only exit they could see. Dailus hesitated long enough for Olson to push him aside and venture down.

The stairs were wooden and smelled of rot, creaking under Olson's weight. He put up his hand, signaling Dailus to wait for him to get down them. When he took his foot off the last step, it seemed to groan with relief.

"If I can make it down, I think you'll be fine," he said quietly, motioning him to come down.

The hallway before them was small and dark, consisting of a single door no more than a few feet in front of them. Olson pushed on it, revealing a large room with a high ceiling. There were no windows, but the darkness was staved off by the hundreds of candles circling the room.

In the middle was a man chained to a table, looking frail and drained. His eyes were red from crying, and his clothes were torn at the shoulder, revealing a wound that looked like a snake bite—only Olson couldn't think of any snake large enough to have made the marks.

Dailus walked cautiously toward him and reached his hand out. "Aidren . . . what have they done to you?" he asked quietly. He looked at the wound on his shoulder that was soaked through with blood.

"The Master Khyth," Aidren whispered. "He . . . He took it."

Dailus's hands pulled back in astonishment when he looked Aidren in the eyes.

"What?" Olson asked. "What's wrong?"

Surely it was a trick of the light, but it looked for a moment like Aidren's ring, the center-piece of Athrani eyes, was gone. Dailus stood in muted shock as he seemed to search for an answer.

Realizing they could be there all night, Olson pushed him aside and produced a key he had taken earlier. "If this key works, we can talk about it on our way out," he said as he slid it into the lock of the chains binding Aidren to the table. The locking mechanism clicked as his shackles came unfastened.

Free of the chains, Aidren sat up slowly and rubbed his wrists.

"Can you walk?" Dailus asked.

Aidren looked at both of them and considered. His eyes were filled with pain and emptiness. "I can try," he said with a nod. He faltered as he tried to stand, but Dailus was there to catch him.

"I don't want to spend another moment here," Olson said, moving to Aidren and hoisting him over his shoulder. "I can carry him out, and then we can let him rest."

Dailus nodded in agreement and headed for the door and back up the stairs to the ground floor of the prison.

Chapter 10

The Talvin Forest, Northeast of Lusk

Gift of the Shaper

Thornton

The sun had just passed overhead and was beginning its slow descent to the west. They had been following the tracks for a few hours, every now and then stopping for Kethras to survey the area and point things out to Thornton. Kethras made him listen for the sound of birds, saying that it meant there was probably water nearby. Running water was better than standing water, and standing water was better than no water, he said.

Each time they came to a clearing, they would stop and let the horses graze while Kethras pointed out features of the tracks that they were following and asked Thornton to tell him what he saw.

"This horse has a chipped front left hoof. You can see it here," Thornton said, pointing to a print.

"Good," Kethras answered. "And?"

He scanned the area. "They slowed down here," he said, pointing ahead.

"How can you tell?"

"The tracks are closer together."

Kethras nodded. "There is one more thing that you should notice."

Thornton looked around the area, carefully inspecting the tracks. He frowned and scratched his head. Glancing back and forth, he put his hands up in defeat.

"Look over here, where the tracks are all clumped together. This horse came to a stop. Then the tracks from the same horse are shallower." Kethras said.

Thornton nodded. He looked over the tracks in silence. Coming up with nothing, he looked at Kethras for help.

"What would make tracks shallower?" Kethras asked, not wanting to give the answer directly.

Thornton grimaced and looked at the tracks again, hoping that inspiration would suddenly strike. It did not, and he looked again at

Kethras. The Kienari eyed him up and down, settling finally upon his hammer, which was strapped to his back. "Take a step and look at your tracks," he said. Thornton did as he was told. "Now put your hammer on the ground and take another step."

He did so, standing it on its head so that the handle was facing the sky. When he looked at his shallower tracks, his face flushed red. "They rid themselves of whatever they were carrying," he said to the ground.

"And this is the most important part—" Kethras said, ignoring his embarrassment and pointing nearby, "a new set of footprints."

Ynara turned to Miera and whispered, "He'll take any opportunity to show off."

The stifled laughter from both of them drew a stern look from Kethras.

"The tracks split here," he continued. "Three going this way, to the southwest, and the rest going off to the east." Standing up, he said, "If you can tell me which direction we should follow, I won't make you catch your own dinner tonight."

Thornton looked carefully at the tracks. His eyes went back and forth over the hoof prints and the footprints. He stood up and looked at Kethras, his eyebrows arched in a look of uncertainty. "East?"

"Ynara?" Kethras said over his shoulder.

"The poor boy will starve," she said as she approached them. "The new tracks lead southwest, toward Lusk."

Thornton put his hands in his face. He was not looking forward to hunting tonight.

They kept the sun in front of them as they traveled, always keeping an eye on the tracks. Kethras walked beside Thornton, who rode atop Jericho, and Ynara walked beside Miera. Neither of the Kienari had asked to ride, and Thornton was fairly certain they wouldn't have wanted to. And, despite how subtle he thought he was in staring at the Kienari, Thornton was surprised when Kethras asked, "Is something the matter?" without even taking his eyes off the trail.

Gift of the Shaper

Thornton jerked his eyes away quickly when he knew that he was caught. "Sorry. It's just, I thought Kienari were only stories. I still can't believe you're real."

This caused a hint of a smile to appear on Kethras's lips. "We do not venture much outside the forests of Kienar, it is true. Has it really been that long?"

Thornton looked puzzled. "That long?"

"Humans and Kienari have not always been strangers." His voice sounded distant as he spoke. "No doubt the stories you've heard are evidence of this. Once, we walked among you."

"What happened?" Thornton asked.

"The Khyth happened," he spat, like he had taken in a mouthful of poison.

Thornton was quiet, but the curiosity that showed on his face urged Kethras to continue. He drew in a deep breath and exhaled it loudly, hesitating.

"Our Mother is very old," he started. "She was old even when humans were young. She watched them as they grew, as they multiplied, and as they became enlightened. She watched them when they first felt the energy that is abundant in the Otherworld. Unlike Kienari, who are children of this world, humans are children of both. Their bodies are merely vessels for the energy inside them, which comes from the Otherworld. When humans were young, it was only their dreams that connected them to the Otherworld. They were never supposed . . . They were never meant to control that power. The energies that exist in the Otherworld are the powers of creation and destruction themselves."

He paused to look at the sky, which was starting to become red and purple as the sun sank lower and lower in front of them. "But the draw of power is not easily ignored. From the Otherworld came whispers—whispers with promises of power, promises of mastery over the energies that shaped the world. Its pull was too strong and humans were too weak. What they wanted was mastery over life and death. The true danger, though, was getting what they wanted."

He sighed as if the retelling was hard. "To have the power over death, they embraced the Breaker—they became death. And there was no room left for their humanity. Our Mother saw the darkness in them, and it made her sad and afraid—afraid for her children. She knew that humans had tasted the Breaker's power and would only spread his destruction to all that they touched. She could not stop them, so she withdrew. She took her children and left."

"But you humans—you saw it too. Those of you that embraced the darkness were forced out and set apart. They were the first Khyth."

"Was that what caused the Shaping War?" Thornton asked quietly.

"Yes. Because no matter how great the power of death, it will always be but a part of life. And a small pocket of humanity cried out for life, turning their backs on the Khyth, who once had the audacity to call themselves human. They cried out against the power that their own blood had embraced. Though they could not know it, their cries reached the ears of the Shaper of Ages Herself—and She listened. Knowing She could never erase the mark that the Breaker had laid upon humanity, She gave up Her own power in response, abandoning the Otherworld for this one and empowering the Athrani—those touched by the Shaper Herself. Using the gift She gave them through Her very being, they struck down the Khyth and pushed them out, pushed them away, into the depths of Khala Val'ur."

"That was a long, long time ago," said Miera, "so long that most of us have forgotten it ever happened."

"Humans do not have long memories," Ynara said flatly.

"But the Athrani are still young," Kethras continued, "and think highly of themselves. They think themselves greater than humans but conveniently forget that they were once human too. They only have to look to the Khyth to see what they are capable of."

Thornton pondered this quietly as the sun sank below the horizon and left just a sliver of the moon to light their path.

Chapter 11

Athrani Prison,
Outside of Lusk

Gift of the Shaper

Olson

Getting Aidren up the stairs was treacherous in its own right, and every step that Olson took was met with groans from the decrepit wood. When they reached the top, they kept on, straight down the hallway that led to the site of their earlier encounter.

As they approached the corridor where they had fought only moments before, they stepped past the translucent cage where Dailus had trapped their two assailants, who still pounded at its walls pleadingly. Olson eyed the body of Rimbal, who still lay on the ground in the same position he'd left him after he finished smashing his fist into his well-scarred face. He wasn't moving, and that suited Olson just fine.

"Let's get out of here," he said. Dailus and Aidren had no objections.

Just as they were about to leave the room, though, Olson heard a noise come from Rimbal's direction. He couldn't quite make it out—it sounded like a grunt of desperation more than anything—but it was followed by what sounded like a bone bouncing off the stone floor. He turned just in time to see the room flood with light.

Shielding his eyes from the emerald glow filling the room, Olson squinted in confusion as the walls began to tremble. He looked to Rimbal, who was still lying on the floor, to make sure he wasn't seeing things.

"What did you do?" Olson shouted.

"Like I'd tell you," Rimbal grunted. He followed it up with a sound like strained laughter.

Something on the edge of Olson's vision caught his eyes as he looked back to the trembling walls, from which progressively bigger and bigger chunks of gray stone had begun dropping onto the floor. Enough of them had come loose that he was sure the walls were about to collapse around them.

He watched as the stones on the floor came together in the same way that iron filings would attack a magnet. Then, when the pile of stone had grown large enough, it stood up.

"Dailus," Olson said as he backed up, "are you seeing this?"

The Athrani half-eye was staring at the pile of stone that had taken a human-like form. It was huge and sturdy-looking, despite being cobbled together from dregs of the prison walls.

"I am," was all Dailus said.

The hulking figure lumbered toward Olson, its feet sinking into the ground with each thunderous step that it took. Keeping his eyes on it, Olson knelt to place Aidren on the ground as he shouted gruffly to Dailus, "I hope you got some really great rest back there."

Dailus's eyes were white-hot. "We shall see," he said flatly. The stone creature continued toward Olson, who was gathering himself for either impact or counterattack. Dailus raised his hands into the air, and the fog that had come before began to swirl and thicken around the creature. The whole room seemed steeped in clouds that thickened and turned to a solid gray.

Olson watched, impressed, as the creature stopped in its tracks, trapped inside the impenetrable prison that Dailus had conjured from thin air.

"Nicely done," Olson said, dropping his guard.

But as the creature's arm burst through the cage, Dailus could do nothing but watch as its other arm broke free followed by a rocky torso and head. Both men stared with growing concern as the rest of the creature emerged and charged once more, straight at Olson.

"I take it back," Olson said, ducking a wildly swung fist from the creature. He lowered his shoulder and charged into the midsection of the great stone golem, driving it back toward the wall. It took every ounce of his strength to move the thing.

"Where did this come from?" he shouted to Dailus as they slammed against the wall.

"I hardly see how that is relevant right now," Dailus said.

Taking a blow to the stomach that knocked him halfway across the room, Olson inhaled sharply and looked up with narrowed eyes at his Athrani compatriot. "Because I'd like to figure out how to stop it."

Gift of the Shaper

Aidren had sat up and was looking at Rimbal. "Him," he said with all the strength he could muster. "It came from him."

Watching Rimbal wheeze with laughter between strained breaths, Olson asked, "Is he Athrani?" As the words left his mouth, the creature charged at him again.

"No, but he somehow has the power of Shaping," Aidren answered, confusion in his voice. "The Otherworld does not flow through him, but . . . it surrounds him."

The creature clasped its hands together and brought them down on Olson, who caught the brunt of the blow on his shoulders and dropped to his knees. Defiantly, he stood back up and smashed his fist into the creature's face with just as much pain as futility. He shook his hand in agony as the creature head-butted his chest and sent him staggering backward.

"I've used hammers softer than this thing," he yelled at Dailus, who looked to be wandering around the room in search of something. "Any help you can offer would be nice." Sidestepping a head-on charge from the creature, Olson watched as it crashed straight through the stone wall and into another room.

"Just give me a moment," Dailus said as he deftly checked the pockets of the barely conscious big man.

"Breaker's Hammer, Dailus! You and your moments!" Olson bellowed, trying to get a glimpse of the creature through the dust it had kicked up. He saw it early enough to take a dangling piece of the wall and throw it at the creature's head. The stone smashed to bits and appeared to not even faze the creature, but certainly served to enrage it.

"Ah, here it is," Dailus said. He held aloft the white horn that he'd found near Rimbal. "Catch."

Dailus tossed the bony growth to Olson, who caught it and looked more confused than when the creature had first showed up. "And?" he asked as he raised his forearm to shield himself from the moving statue that bore down on him.

"That horn somehow controls the creature," he answered simply.

Faster than he could think, Olson took the pointed end of the horn and brought it down in a merciless blow to the top of the creature's head. He buried it halfway in and kept going, following through with every bit of strength left in him.

It was enough.

In mid-stride the creature dropped to the ground and broke apart, leaving nothing but clouds of dust and a pile of stones that matched the walls of the prison.

After the air had finally cleared, Olson lowered the arm that shielded his face and looked at Dailus. "I think now is as good a time as any to make our way outside."

Dailus nodded in agreement. "This way," he said to Olson, who gave Rimbal a kick in the ribs before helping up Aidren.

"Just let me catch my breath," Olson mumbled. His fists were throbbing, and he was hoping that the pain in his shoulder wasn't serious. "Otherwise, you're going to have to drag both of us out of here."

A thin smile spread across Dailus's lips. "Of course."

"What do we do with him?" Olson asked as he sat down, nodding to Rimbal. The big man was drifting in and out of consciousness but still represented a threat. *Especially if he has any more of those horns*, Olson thought.

Dailus paled at the question. "Are you asking . . .," he leaned in to Olson and whispered, "are you asking if we should kill him?"

Olson laughed. "Relax, Dailus. I meant we should probably move him somewhere."

The half-eye visibly relaxed. "Oh, thank goodness," he said. "That's much better than the alternative." He looked back at Olson. "But I don't think any of us are in any shape to do so."

Olson looked at the big man on the floor and felt the pain surging through his shoulders and arms.

Dailus is right, he thought. After the beating he had just taken, he could barely help Aidren, who weighed maybe half as much. He watched

Gift of the Shaper

Rimbal's chest moving up and down, as it looked like the big man had slipped into unconsciousness.

"He's not going anywhere," Olson finally said. He knew that the longer they rested there, the less chance they had of escape. With a grimace, he stood up and said, "Leave him. Let's go."

Dailus helped Aidren to his feet, and the three of them made their way out of the room and toward some promising rays of light that seemed to point to an exit. After a fair amount of walking, the three of them found themselves in an entryway of sorts with a large set of double doors.

Olson eyed them warily and turned to Dailus. "I don't know too much about the men who captured us," he started. "Could this be rigged with a trap of some sort? With . . . Shaping?"

Dailus stepped forward and looked them over. The doors were huge and as ornate as they were massive. They had carvings from top to bottom depicting scenes from history and myth. A carving near the bottom showed a group of people raising their hands skyward and one figure surrounded by a light with a hammer in one hand and a glowing chain in the other, poised to strike an anvil. Another picture portrayed a dark figure reaching out his hand and a cluster of smaller figures reaching out for it. On the very top of both was a giant white skeletal hand about the size of a man.

"I don't think they're trapped," Dailus said. He reached out and traced one of the carvings on the door with his finger. "But what is this place?"

"I don't know," Olson answered. Besides the carving on the doors, he didn't see anything else remarkable about where they were being held. From what he could tell, it was nothing more than a prison. "And I'd really rather not find out. Help me get these doors open. Aidren is starting to get heavy."

Dailus shot an annoyed look back at Olson but did as he was asked. Pushing on one of the heavy doors, it opened with a groan.

The last of the light had retreated from the sky, leaving only darkness outside, with a tiny fingernail of a moon above.

Before them stretched trees in all directions, and the walls of the prison were overgrown with ivy. It looked like it had been abandoned for quite some time but had clearly been repurposed and revitalized for . . . whatever these men were using it for. Olson looked back at the huge stone structure and scratched his head, wondering just how many Athrani had seen the insides of it—and how many had managed to make it back out.

"This way," Dailus said, emerging from a trail that led into the woods. Olson turned and followed, with Aidren leaning on him heavily for support. When they were well clear of the prison, Olson stooped and helped Aidren to the ground, then stood up and stretched.

"We need to get him home," Dailus said to him, "to Ellenos."

The younger Athrani's face was pale, and his now-human eyes were focused on something in the distance.

"Oh no," Olson said sternly. "He's your problem. I have to get back to my son."

"Olson," Aidren said weakly; the words were soft, but enough to make both men stop and listen. "Whatever the Khyth have done to me, it's clear that there is more at stake here than your own life or even the life of your son. Know this: they will not stop with just one Athrani." He paused. "If the Khyth have their way, a missing father will be the least of your son's concerns."

"He's right," Dailus said. "Ellenos must be warned. If the Khyth have figured out a way to take our power, there may be no stopping them."

Aidren coughed and took a breath, "The one who did this . . ." He coughed again. ". . . D'kane—he is after the Hammer of the Worldforge."

Dailus stood up and stared into the emptiness of the night. "Then we have no choice."

Olson turned from both of them and looked at the sky, taking in the faint light of the moon, and put one hand on his chin, stroking the length of his beard in thought. "How far is Ellenos?"

"We would never make it in time by traveling on foot," Aidren admitted.

"Whatever the Khyth are planning," said Dailus, "must be dealt with swiftly and soon. We need horses—fast ones. Once we find some that suit our needs, we can make it in a few days' travel."

Gift of the Shaper

Olson scratched his head and frowned. He looked at Dailus, then at Aidren. *One is almost too weak to walk, and the other can barely handle himself in a fight.* He took a deep breath and resigned himself to help. "Fine, but we stop when I say, and you pay for my horse." He tossed Dailus a few coins. "This might help. I took it off one of the guards."

The half-eye smiled at the sight of coins. "Agreed. Now let's get him on his feet so we can put as much ground as possible between this place and us."

Olson and Dailus each took one of Aidren's hands and helped him up.

"Thank you," Aidren said weakly.

"We should head west to Annoch," said Dailus. "We have our best chance of finding some good horses for sale there."

Olson grunted as he looked up at the stars. "There are two things I'm good at: eating and hitting things. Navigation isn't on the list."

"Follow me," Dailus said. "I can at least get us pointed in the right direction."

The three men traveled westbound, deciding to keep to the roads by night and stay clear of them during the day. Dailus made a case for staying hidden in the fact that not one but two of them were Athrani, and obviously so. Both he and Aidren had the look. They were tall—though next to Olson they may have appeared normal—and Dailus's eye spilled the secrets of his birth to anyone who looked. "When the Athrani became enlightened," he had told Olson, "the power of the Otherworld came flooding into them and filled them up like a reservoir, full to the point of bursting."

Aidren was still struggling to walk, so they moved a little bit off the road and sat down. Dailus was examining him as best he could, using his Shaping abilities to prod and probe where his eyes could not, with Olson watching in wonder. When Dailus Shaped, there was a glow that emanated from his eyes, and when his hands would move close to Aidren, sparks of light would emanate from his fingertips like there was a current running through the two of them. He continued on like this for a few more minutes, then stood up to take Olson aside.

"I don't know how they did it, but they have completely taken away his Shaping ability," Dailus said quietly. "He's lost his link with the Otherworld."

"What's going to happen to him?"

"I can't say. Just a day ago I would have said this was impossible. A male Athrani with no Shaping ability is simply unheard of," he turned his head to look again at Aidren, "even for half-eyes like us. It's like taking the light out of the stars."

Just then Aidren made a loud groan of pain, and Dailus hurried back over to him. He called to Olson over his shoulder, "See if you can find some water for him. There's a skin over there."

Olson nodded and walked over to where Dailus indicated, finding an empty skin for water, then headed back toward the road. It was quiet on the path, and he listened for running water. When he heard none, in order to keep from getting lost, he rubbed his boots in the dirt to mark the location of their stop and headed down the road. For a while, all he heard was the sound of leaves rustling as the breeze danced through them and the occasional bird calling out.

Finally, the faint sound of running water came from up ahead, and he quickened his pace. He came to a small stream, narrow enough for him to step easily across. He took out Dailus's water skin and knelt down to fill it. Just as he finished, he heard a faint but terrible scream.

Aidren, he thought.

He tied the skin at the mouth and took off in a run, keeping his eyes open for the spot he had marked. He wouldn't need it though, as Aidren's agonized cries were enough of a beacon to guide him even if it were pitch black outside.

"What's the matter?" Olson asked as he handed the water skin to Dailus, who was seated on the ground cross-legged, Aidren's head in his lap. Aidren was staring blankly at the trees above.

"I don't know, but it isn't good. His body is hot all over, and he doesn't respond to my voice anymore. It's like he isn't here."

Gift of the Shaper

Suddenly, a thin red light shot out from Aidren's chest, and he made a choking sound as a hole tore itself open in his throat. Blood bubbled up to the surface and flowed out with every beat of his heart. Dailus's eyes opened wide, and he put his hands on the wound in a desperate attempt to stop the bleeding, but it was too deep, like an arrow had been shot clear through his neck.

"Can't you do something?" Olson asked as panic engulfed him.

Dailus looked up at him from the Athrani bleeding to death in front of him. His eyes were already glowing with the power of the Otherworld. "I am," he said flatly. A second wound opened itself and began to bleed from Aidren's chest. "His body is falling apart. I'm doing everything I can to hold it together."

Olson stood in silence, feeling powerless for one of the few times in his life. *If an Athrani can't help,* he thought, *it's all but hopeless.*

The Athrani ability to heal using the power that existed in the Otherworld was unique in all the world and was the source of much of their pride. Ever since the first Athrani had harnessed that power, their focus had been on preserving and improving life. But even that was slipping away from Dailus as he watched a life quickly being extinguished before him.

Aidren continued to gasp and choke as blood pooled beneath him, darkening the grass and creeping slowly outward as it gathered. Olson felt the air around them getting warmer as Dailus was suddenly enveloped in a glow that flickered like a white flame.

"I don't understand," Dailus said in a panic. "Everything I pour into him just seeps right back out, like his body is . . . rejecting it." He looked up at Olson, draped in power, but looking as helpless as a child.

Aidren's gasping finally stopped as the last of his breath left him, and Dailus let his head slip from his hands. The glow around him subsided, and he slumped forward in defeat. Olson stood quietly, unsure of what to say.

Dailus was the one to break the silence.

"What do you say now about our journey to Ellenos?"

Without even taking time to consider, Olson said, "I say we find the fastest horses we can buy."

Dailus nodded. "We will rest tonight and make for Annoch at first light. But for now," he said as he turned away, "I have a brother to bury."

Olson frowned as the Athrani walked away. Turning back to the forest that would be their room for the night, he looked for a comfortable spot on the ground to lay his head.

When he found one, sleep came quickly.

Chapter 12

The Talvin Forest,
Outside of Lusk

Gift of the Shaper

Miera

Despite Kethras's protests, Thornton lit the torch he had brought, insisting he use it to follow the tracks. Kethras was worried about giving themselves away—"an open invitation to predators and thieves," he'd called it—and the two had argued back and forth until Ynara finally spoke up in favor of Thornton, citing a chance to sharpen his "awful tracking skills," as she put it. Thornton had grumbled a thank you to her. Kethras glanced at her skeptically and then turned to the woods.

"Very well. I will find food," he said as he walked off. Without turning around, he added, "Don't worry—I will find you again."

Miera watched him go but quickly lost sight of him. She turned back to Ynara, who was a few steps behind Thornton. "How long have you known Kethras?" she asked.

Ynara looked at her with a smile. "Long enough to know that he is still the same Kethras," she said. "You can ask our Mother when you meet her. She delights in stories and memories."

"What is she like—your Mother?" Miera asked. The two of them were walking a good distance behind Thornton, who was slowly but surely keeping up with the tracks.

Ynara thought for a moment in silence. "She bears a great burden, one that has worn on her for some time. But despite this, she is full of love. You cannot find a more compassionate being in this world, perhaps even in the Otherworld. And she is beautiful."

"She sounds very much like someone I would like to meet," Miera answered.

"She is looking forward to seeing you again, as well," Ynara smiled.

Miera smiled, then blinked in confusion. Before she had a chance to respond, Ynara whispered sharply to Thornton, "Douse the light!"

Thornton did as he was told, looking around warily in the dark. Ynara put her fingers to her lips to signal for silence and took the reins of the horses. She moved into the cover of the trees, urging Miera and Thornton to follow.

"What is it?" Miera whispered.

"There, up ahead some distance. I see three figures," she answered, pointing in the direction they had been traveling.

Thornton and Miera were crouched low among the trees, mostly obscured by the foliage, but there was not much they could do about the horses. Ynara looked up at them in concern, then climbed deftly up into the branches of the tree over their heads.

". . . can't believe he just sent us out for more Athrani, like they should just f-f-f-fall into our laps. What are we supposed to do n-n-now?" The voice was high-pitched but belonging to a man.

A second voice that followed sounded nasal. "My head still hurts. That big one got me good."

"Stop your whining, you two," came a third voice, low and rough. "I should have just left you in that cage. D'kane probably thinks we're good at this. And besides," he said, taking out an object from a pocket in his shirt, "the Gwarái horn should lead us to the next one."

Audible gasps and mutterings of wonder followed as the two other men admired the white curved bone he held aloft.

"Well, when I see him again, I'm asking he double our pay," said the one with the nasal voice. "They made off with all my coins."

"You do that, Bunch. Just make sure I'm nowhere near you when you ask," the man with the low voice said, laughing. The three of them were coming down the trail that Thornton had been following and were headed right for them. Miera held her breath as the distance between them closed. Thornton put his hand on Jericho's nose and touched it reassuringly.

"If I never see that Kh-Kh-Khyth again, it will be too soon," said the one with the high-pitched voice.

"What's the matter, Twig?" came the low voice. Its owner was close enough to Miera that she could have touched him. "Afraid of a little coin?" He slapped the first man on the back and belted out a laugh that quickly tapered off as he came to a halt.

"What's wrong, Rimbal?" Twig asked.

Gift of the Shaper

"The horn . . ." There was a glow from the bone, and he looked around as if searching for something. His eyes came to rest on the bushes where Miera and Thornton were concealed. He lowered the horn and said calmly, "Boys, I think we've got company."

Miera gasped as she was lifted roughly by the throat. Her feet dangled as she left the ground, kicking desperately for something solid beneath her.

"Let me go!" she choked, doing her best to break free.

"Maybe we're good at this after all," Rimbal said over her sounds of choking. The glow from the horn continued to grow in intensity, and as he held it up with his free hand, it engulfed him.

Thornton jumped to his feet, drawing the attention of the two smaller men. Each of them produced a wooden club, twirling them around in their hands and beginning to circle him in the moonlight. One man with bandages over one eye took his right side; the other, his left. A flash of familiarity came over Miera—*I know these men! They were the ones who attacked us in Lusk!*

Thornton had his hammer out and gripped it in a wide defensive posture, ready to turn away the blows that were inevitably coming. He backed up, but the two men were on him in an instant. One came low and the other came high, and he chose to block high, taking a crippling blow to his thigh and crying out in pain. He dropped to his knees. Taking another blow to the back that knocked the wind out of him, he swung his hammer out in front of him in a desperate attempt to sweep the legs of the man coming at him. It worked, and Miera heard a snap followed by a scream as it broke bone. Thornton didn't have time to revel in the victory, as he caught a club on the back of the head and dropped to the ground, unconscious.

Two arrows flew from the treetops where Ynara was hidden, aimed at the big man holding Miera. They flew true, one hitting him in the chest and the other catching him in the throat. But instead of dropping to the ground, like anyone with such a wound would do, he looked calmly into the trees and said, "You'll regret that," his eyes glowing white hot.

Rimbal gripped the horn tightly and threw Miera to the ground. The arrows that had buried themselves in him shuddered, then seemed to dissolve into thin air. Raising his hand to the sky, there was a loud *crack* from the horn in his fist that rushed outward, sending everyone else flying backward like straw in a windstorm. Ynara hit the ground hard at his feet as she fell from the branches above.

"An Athrani and a Kienari all in one day?" Rimbal laughed. "This is too good to be true." Putting his boot on Ynara's back, he said to his companion, "Twig, tie them up."

Kneeling down, he grabbed Ynara by the back of the neck and raised her face to his. Then, through a mouth full of rotten teeth, said, "Let's show our guests some hospitality."

The last thing Miera saw was a thick, scarred hand coming right at her face.

Chapter 13

Athrani Prison, Outside of Lusk

Gift of the Shaper

Rimbal

Lying motionless on the ground was the young blacksmith, his arms tied around him with a good length of rope. The blonde girl—not a full-blood and not a half-eye, yet somehow Athrani blood flowed through her veins—was tied to his back. The two of them were planted on the ground, legs out, in front of the huge stone building.

Rimbal had bridled the horses nearby so they wouldn't run off, and he'd done the same with the Kienari, who was on the ground below them, bound hand and foot. Dried blood covered her face and eyes. Behind him a short distance was Bunch, who was doing his best to contain his sobs, but to no avail.

"By the Breaker, you're loud," Rimbal growled.

"He nearly took my leg off!" the smaller man shouted hoarsely.

"Well, you'd better hope these three don't have friends, because you just let them know where we are. Now keep it down, or I'll knock you out and tie you up myself." Turning to the small man with the wild red hair, he barked, "Twig, give him something that will shut him up."

"I'll see what I can do, Rimbal, but I really think we should leave," Twig answered. Fishing around in one of his packs, he produced a strip of leather and passed it to Bunch. "H-here. Ch-chew on this."

Bunch took it and bit down. He sat down with his legs spread out and sobbed for a few more moments but didn't say another word.

"You think we should leave after this just falls into our laps? No, Twig. I say we stay. There's no way D'kane won't be happy to see what we bagged here," he said as he motioned to the girl.

"I was afraid you were g-going to say that," Twig responded.

"Now get that door open," Rimbal said. "We need to get them inside and this one down to D'kane."

Twig, who was aptly named, walked over to the huge double doors of the stone structure and pulled on the iron handle with every ounce of strength that he had. "I don't know why I'm the one p-p-pulling this door open, Rimbal. You're the m-m-muscle."

"You need the practice," he answered sharply. "Do you remember where the Gwarái is?"

With a final heave, it came open.

"I th-think so," he replied.

"Then meet me there."

Twig looked petrified but nodded and disappeared inside. As Rimbal turned again to face the captives, sizing them up and trying to figure out the logistics of moving them inside, he heard Twig's high-pitched voice coming from behind him.

"On second th-thought, why don't I just go with you," the small red-haired man said as he bounded back out, eager to help, and just as eager to not have to face the Gwarái alone.

"Fine. Then help me get them in," Rimbal said. He reached down and loosened the rope that tied the two captives together. "Take the girl first," he said. "I'll get the Kienari."

Twig walked over to the girl and slid his hands under her armpits while Rimbal walked over to Ynara and grabbed her legs, dragging her inside like a fresh kill. The two men took them just inside the large entryway of the stone building and dropped them on the floor. Rimbal walked back outside for the blacksmith, moving him inside and closing the door behind.

The three captives were laid down side by side, with the girl in the center.

"You keep watch in here," Rimbal said. "And make sure Bunch stays quiet. I'm taking this one down to D'kane."

He knelt down and draped the girl over his shoulders, standing up with only the slightest effort and leaving Twig behind to watch the others while he made his way through the darkened interior.

Finally reaching the hatch that led to D'kane's makeshift quarters, Rimbal unshouldered his cargo and knelt to open the wooden door in the ground. He let it crash against the stone floor as he picked up the girl again and descended the staircase. When he rounded the corner into the large, circular room, D'kane was standing in the middle, holding the Gwarái horn that was chained to his neck. The Khyth seemed mesmerized by it.

"I've never felt the pull more strongly," he said as Rimbal entered the room. "I don't know how, but it's almost as if it . . . hungers." Glancing at Rimbal, he noticed the girl. "This one looks like she might not give you as much trouble as the last ones you brought me," he said smoothly.

"How was I supposed to know he could knock down walls?" Rimbal said defensively.

D'kane did not acknowledge the excuse. "Prepare her," he said.

With a nod, Rimbal pulled out a knife from a sheath hanging from his waist. He knelt down and cut loose her hands, then grabbed her hair and lifted her head off the ground. Two savage slaps wrested her from unconsciousness. She gasped and sat upright, her eyes going immediately to the knife.

"Where am I? What are you doing?" she asked in a panicked voice.

"Be a good girl and keep your mouth shut," Rimbal said threateningly as he pointed a finger at her face. "The less you struggle, the more you might live through this." He gave a yank on her hair and began dragging her by it to the center of the room. With a sidelong glance, he added, "But I wouldn't expect too much."

Rimbal seized her by the shoulders and slammed her down onto the altar. Grabbing her jaw with one big hand and holding her head still, he pressed his face into her hair and breathed in sharply. Moving his lips to her ear, he whispered, "You'll probably be pretty weak when he's done, but don't worry—I'll take care of you."

"That's enough, Rimbal," D'kane said. He moved gracefully across the floor, clearly relishing the thought of taking the power of yet another Athrani. "Now," he said, "the Gwarái."

Rimbal grinned as he heard those words and lumbered off to fetch the beast.

D.L. Jennings

Miera

Miera could hardly contain her panic as she realized she didn't know where she was—and Thornton and the two Kienari were nowhere to be found. She wasn't sure when she had lost consciousness, but her head hurt nonetheless.

The room she was in was large and cold, comprised mostly of gray stone, and the only light she could see was provided by rows and rows of candles that flickered in the darkness.

Her face stung where she had been slapped by the big man with scars—the same one who had grabbed her in the Talvin Forest, and the same one who had attacked her and Thornton in Lusk. She could still smell his breath from when he had leaned in too closely. "Be a good girl and keep your mouth shut," he had said. The words had made her skin crawl.

But there was a second voice. One that had scared her more than the ugly man with the foul breath.

"Now, the Gwarái," it had said.

Looking around to find the source, she recoiled in horror as she met the eyes of a Khyth. They were swirling and wild and sunk deeply into a face so charred that it looked as though its flesh would flake off.

When the Khyth caught her eyes, he seemed to be noticing something for the first time. He looked down to the large white horn that hung glowing from his neck, then back to her. "Ah, now I see. Only your mother was Athrani," he observed. "It let you pass as human, maybe even let you think you were one of them."

Trembling, Miera asked, "What do you mean? What do you want with me?"

"Call it a test," the Khyth answered smugly. "If you pass, you live."

The hair on the back of Miera's neck stood up, but not from the words—something else was responsible.

The air around her seemed to thicken as she turned to watch a great black terror being led into the room, bound by chains. Guiding it was the ugly scarred man who had dragged Miera in—*Rimbal*, she thought she had heard him called. The thing he led had a tongue that was lashing wildly as it sniffed the air with quick, violent snorts.

Miera managed to suppress her fear well enough that Rimbal took notice. "I don't think she's scared of him, Master D'kane," he shouted. "Can I let him go?"

D'kane smiled and the clank of chains was followed by sharp-toed reptilian feet dashing across the floor to satiate the Gwarái's taste for blood. A flash of fangs and yellow eyes streaked wildly toward their prey.

Miera felt a weakness unlike any she had ever known as the creature opened wide and dug its teeth into the flesh above her chest. The pain was so sudden and so severe that it nearly blinded her. She tried to pull away in an impulse to survive, kicking her feet and pushing on the neck of the creature that towered over her, but its jaws were much too strong. Relenting, she felt herself being lifted into the air as the creature began to feed.

A soft glow from the center of her chest was followed by a sudden and violent burst of light that streamed from her and into the Gwarái. The color drained from her face as she gasped desperately for air while the life was being squeezed out of her and into the creature standing over her.

D'kane held his hand just above the creature's head, hypnotized by its power as Miera's essence flowed out. She made a hoarse attempt at a scream that echoed throughout the stone structure, weakening quickly as the room was bathed with light and power. The intensity almost knocked Rimbal to his knees.

"I was right," the Master Khyth marveled. "She has the Blood."

With his hand on the horns of the Gwarái, D'kane caressed it like a child, and the creature lowered its head and put Miera back down.

"After years of searching," he breathed, "we've found one."

Miera was bloody and drained but still alive, and the Khyth looked at her like a tiger stalking its prey. "Khala Val'ur must be informed. Rimbal," he said, turning to his hired muscle, "I have no further use for you. Take your men and go."

"With pleasure," Rimbal sneered.

"I will use the Gwarái to take the girl," said D'kane.

Rimbal gave a nod and a grunt as he stooped down to scoop her up. Miera felt nauseous as the big man's hands wrapped around her, and she swore she could feel him smelling her hair again. He was strong, though, and he tossed her onto the Gwarái like a sack of potatoes.

"That's too bad," Rimbal said, dusting his hands off. "I was hoping she could stay a little longer."

D'kane turned to the stone wall and displayed the power that made him and all Khyth so feared. With a simple gesture, he threw the stones apart as simply as Rimbal had thrown Miera, revealing a path to the surface that had not existed mere seconds before.

Miera watched Rimbal grin as she was led out on the back of the great Gwarái. She was too weak to protest, but as the walls of rock reformed behind them, she could almost feel relief as his awful face disappeared behind the stones.

Rimbal

With a few slow blinks, Rimbal coughed and looked around the room that was suddenly thick with dust. As he placed a big hand over his mouth, he scanned the room but found no sign of D'kane or the girl. He shook his head. *Khyth Breaking. Sure would be nice to be able to do that,* he thought.

His coughing continued as he reached into his shirt pocket for the horn he'd stolen away. It was a small one, but he knew that D'kane would be angry if he discovered him with it. He struggled to focus his eyes on it, mustering a smile.

"You're gonna make me a rich man," he said out loud.

So focused was he on the horn that he never even saw the dagger that had forced its way in between his ribs and into his heart. He felt the cold sting, though, and the pain that coursed through his body while long and spindly fingers suddenly closed around his mouth. Looking up into the deep black eyes of a Kienari, he could muster no more than a stifled cry

Gift of the Shaper

as his life and breath fled quickly. He felt the knife go in again, this time to his liver, as waves of nausea washed over him like a tide.

As shock started to set in, his body seized up, and the horn fell from his hands, bouncing a few times on the stone floor before lying still. Rimbal's wide eyes followed it as he lurched forward in desperation, knowing it could save him yet lacking the strength to reach it. The Kienari swiftly kicked it away and beyond Rimbal's reach, standing up to strike again if needed.

But the Kienari's sharp knife had done its job.

Slumping forward to the ground, Rimbal coughed up a bit of blood as he felt his throat close up and his life bleed away. A body with one too many scars would one day pay the price for its dance with death. Now it was simply his turn.

The gurgling from his throat announced the end of a man who would rather be dead than wrong.

And now he was both.

Chapter 14

The Talvin Forest, Outside of Lusk

Gift of the Shaper

Kethras

Kethras stood up to put another squirrel in his pouch. He had gone further than he intended to but had no problem keeping them in his sights. He looked over to where he had left his sister and the two humans and shook his head in disappointment as their torches flooded the forest like beacons.

Then he froze. Something was not right. He felt like something was reaching out, like a hand groping in the dark for something it knew was there.

He narrowed his eyes as he heard sounds coming from further away. He put his nose to the air to get an idea of what it was. *Humans*, he thought as he breathed in, *three of them*. Their heat signatures were dim compared to the torches that Thornton had insisted he keep lit, but he could see them regardless, one big man and two smaller ones.

When he heard Miera shriek, he unsheathed a dagger and ran toward them, cursing Ynara for allowing the humans their light.

His padded feet hit the ground softly, despite his speed. Leaves gave way as he rushed through them, whispering against his body as he readied for battle.

But he was too late. A blinding flash of light filled the forest that caused him to cry out in pain as he dropped to his knees. The feeling of something reaching out was gone; whatever it was, it had found what it was looking for. He clawed at his eyes, blinded, as they ached from the influx of light.

"Let's show our guests some hospitality," he heard a voice say. Then came the sound of flesh hitting flesh and Miera yelping in pain.

They are taking them alive, he thought, as he winced again at the pain in his eyes. Slowly, he rose to his feet. He could track them. The smell coming from one of the men made sure of that.

Opening his eyes again, he found that his sight was beginning to return. He watched as three barely visible heat signatures made their way west to the edge of the forest.

Now to see where they go, he thought.

He followed them to a large stone structure that looked like there was much more below ground than above. *A prison,* he thought. *This was most likely where they were holding Thornton's father.*

He looked at a set of tracks near the entrance of the building and realized that it had seen some recent traffic. All signs were beginning to point to this being the place. He looked back to the men he was tracking.

They seemed disorganized as they dragged the bodies around, hastily tying Thornton and Miera together while leaving Ynara tied up and unconscious on her own. The horses were there too.

Thornton would be relieved, he thought.

The biggest of the men barked orders while the other two scrambled to listen.

Though he had caught up to them, Kethras knew he couldn't make a move yet. He would have to wait until they went inside. One of them was making an awful noise that sounded like crying, until the big man had yelled at him to keep quiet. *Thank you, loud one,* Kethras thought with a grin.

Finally, they retreated inside—all but the loud one. He had remained outside, but the sharp smell of blood was draped all over him like a cloak.

He's wounded, he thought as he readied his blade. *If the pain doesn't disable him, I will.* The sound of light snoring, however, had made the choice for him.

Silently, Kethras made his way past the man and through the wooden double doors of the prison.

Walking inside, he felt the cold of the stone floor below. He hated being indoors—it felt just like being trapped. No branches to escape to, no leaves to conceal him. He wondered how humans could do it at all. But in the midst of his wonderings, he felt the pull again. Something was reaching out, like back in the forest, but with astoundingly greater force.

The eerie, groping hand had found something.

On the floor, unconscious, were Ynara and Thornton. *Whatever it was that was pulling was after Miera,* he thought. Looking around the room, he saw a small man with red hair look up at him in terror as the distinct smell of urine hit his nostrils. Still holding his dagger out, Kethras did not even need to use it as the man collapsed to the floor.

He listened to echoing footsteps as he followed their sound further in, sheathing his dagger and slinking away. The walls seemed to go on forever, and all the doors looked the same. There was no way to tell exactly where he was. Naked stone was nearly impossible for him to navigate, he realized, as he instead relied on sound and smell to go after Miera. He froze as he caught another scent in the air. It was dark and heavy, like a nest of snakes, but different somehow. *Was it . . . blood? Athrani blood?*

Just then he heard Miera cry out. She was awake. Good. The panic in her voice was evident as he fingered the end of his dagger.

He was moving toward the sound when it hit him, a hundred sensations at once. His mind and body were bombarded as light filled the air, pulling him forward like a river current as a sudden jolt surged through him. He sensed panic, elation, and horror as they mixed together in the air beyond.

"She has the Blood," he heard a voice say. It crackled through the air like wildfire.

Kethras pressed his back against the smooth stone wall. Just on the other side of it was Miera—and whatever was causing the pulling sensation. He heard shades of a conversation between two rough, low voices and the sound of thousands of pounds of rock suddenly being shifted, then groaning back into place. Puzzled, he realized that there was only one scent in the air now. The others had all gone.

Slowly, he moved his head into the large door frame where he saw that his senses did not betray him. Miera was gone, along with whatever else had been in the room with her. Now, standing in the dust of recently shifted stones was a wide, well-muscled man in a black tunic who faced slightly away from him and held something white aloft.

"You're going to make me a rich man," he said.

He was distracted.

Perfect.

D.L. Jennings

Slipping into the room with as much sound as a breeze over a stone, Kethras covered the distance between them swiftly and silently. When he was nearly upon the man, he drew his dagger that by now was longing to spill blood. He reached out to slide it in easily, right into the rib cage of the big man, who hardly seemed to notice at first. Realization finally flashed in the man's eyes when Kethras closed his fingers around his mouth to mute his cries and cut off his breathing.

Knowing that just one cut would not do the trick, Kethras pulled the knife back out and aimed below the heart and above the stomach, slamming it back in with determined force. He stepped back as he recognized the look of fear in his prey's eyes, the look an animal will give when it knows it has been beaten, when it knows that death has come at last.

He watched the man drop the white object that he grasped, a horn of some sort of animal. Kethras kicked it away while the man slumped over. He would die soon. *Punishment for taking Miera.*

He was silent as he pulled out a cloth from his pack to wipe the blood from his dagger.

Now his attention was focused on the horn. He stepped over the collapsed body of the man as he got closer to it. Stooping to pick it up, he used the blood-covered cloth to grasp it. Glowing faintly, the horn was warm to the touch, even through the layer of cloth. He frowned at it, then tucked it away in a pouch as he looked back to the spot where Miera had lain only moments ago. He approached the altar and saw nothing but a faint outline, a shadow that served as proof she had been there at all. With a quick turn, he made for the entrance where he had left Thornton and Ynara.

When he returned, they were just as he'd left them—unconscious and bound hand and feet. "I told you I'd find you again," he remarked to himself. With his dagger, he deftly cut the bindings that held Thornton, then did the same for the Ynara.

He pulled back some of the cloth that covered the horn in his hand and thought of Miera. *I do not know what they have done to you, but I imagine we should keep this.*

Gift of the Shaper

His nose crinkled as he continued to eye the horn. He covered it back up to put it in his pack, then moved to check on Ynara. She was breathing but still unresponsive and had no doubt been rendered so with great effort. Thornton, on the other hand, was beginning to stir.

With Kethras eyeing him curiously, the boy opened his eyes. "My head," Thornton groaned.

"Yes, I told you the lights were a bad idea," Kethras said as he flashed a smile. It showed off his top row of sharp teeth—the only part of him that stood out as, even inside, it was like his surroundings were trying to blend with him.

Thornton looked at the gates of the stone structure, and a look of recognition flashed on his face. "I've been here before," he said groggily. "I brought chains."

"Then you most likely forged the ones used to hold your father," Kethras said wryly.

Thornton's eyes widened. "My father? He's here?"

"He was," Kethras answered as Thornton's shoulders sunk. "Thornton, there is something you need to hear," he began, making sure the weight of his words would sink in. "It's Miera."

"What about her?" Thornton asked.

"They have taken her," he said. The words made Thornton jump to his feet.

"Taken? Where?" His words were shaky and panicked.

"I can think of only one place—the Sunken City of Khala Val'ur."

Thornton

Thornton stormed out of the large stone building to see two men tied up on the ground—*Twig and Bunch*, Kethras had called them. Bunch, the one whose leg he'd broken with his hammer, was unconscious, either from the pain or from the fright of seeing Kethras. Twig, however, was conscious and alert, and his eyes were darting wildly back and forth, like he thought someone was after him. When he saw Thornton, he let out a yelp of fright.

"P-please don't hurt me! And keep that . . .that thing away from me!"

"That thing is more concerned with your safety right now than I am," Thornton said angrily as he approached the ground where Twig was tied up. He knelt down next to him and looked him in the eye. "Tell me what they did with my friend. Why did they take her?"

Twig winced. "D-don't hurt me. Puh-please. This was j-just a job."

"A job?" Thornton echoed. "Who were you working for?"

"Well, I n-never really got paid, because, because, because one of the men we kidnapped knocked me out and took my coins, which I guess I c-can't really blame him for because we d-did knock him on the head pretty hard and drag him all the w-way out here and lock him up in a cell which wasn't built all that well, because all he did was, was, was, was lower his shoulder and break out of it," he spouted.

For a man with a stutter, he sure can talk, Thornton thought.

He narrowed his eyes and put up a hand to stop him. Leaning in close, he asked through his teeth, "Who paid you?"

"A-a Kh-Kh-Kh-Khyth. He called himself D'kane," Twig answered. He took a breath as if to expound upon his short answer, but Thornton slammed his hand on the ground to stop him.

"What do they want with Miera?" he shouted. "Where did they take her?"

"They never told us! L-l-like I said, this was a j-j-job—my boss, Rimbal, was just another guy the Khyth hired as the m-muscle. You know, pick up heavy things, move heavy things, p-p-p-put heavy things down in different p-place. Not very friendly at all and, and, and he's much more muscle than b-brain and much more b-brain than good nature, w-w-which is to say, he's not very good-natured." When Thornton's eyes started to narrow again, he jumped back on track. "The Gwarái! They didn't tell me a lot about them, like where they got them from or, or, or what they do or why they're c-c-called Gwarái, but I did see them come and go a few times. I th-think the Khyth was looking for something."

Gift of the Shaper

"Okay," Thornton said, finally feeling like he was getting somewhere. "Looking for what?"

"Well, I'm not sure. It p-probably involves the Athrani, since we've, we've, we've only used the Gwarái on them."

"Used them?" Thornton said, standing up and growling. "Used them how?"

Twig shrunk away in fear, raising his hands to shield his head. "P-p-p-please d-d-d-don't hurt me," he begged.

Thornton looked at him impatiently. "Answer the question or I'll feed you to the Kienari."

"No!" Twig shrieked, doubling over into sobs. "I'll, I'll, I'll t-t-t-talk."

"Then tell me what you know." He looked the man in the eyes, careful to convey the consequences of telling him anything short of the truth.

His fear was apparent, but Twig managed to compose himself. Barely above a whisper, he said, "It's how they feed." He stopped, as if considering whether or not to mention the next part. "The Gwarái, they . . . drain the Athrani," he gulped, "until they're g-g-gone." He spit out the last few words and buried his head in his hands, letting out a whimper of fear. "It wasn't my idea!" he mumbled through his hands, slowly parting his fingers to peek out of one eye to look at Thornton.

"You killed them?" he asked with a frown.

"No, no, no, no, no. They died," he said, waving his hands in defense. "It's an important distinction because we never really m-meant—or I never m-meant—for anything to happen to them, but Rimbal g-got a little overzealous a few times and k-kept some horns for himself, which I told him wasn't a g-good idea because the Khyth m-might find out because they always seem to find out, and then it would be him who was d-doing the dying and not just the Athrani prisoners," he spouted, a tinge of fear still in his voice.

Thornton, horrified upon hearing this, turned his head to Kethras and Ynara who were still inside. Looking back to Twig, he said, "One last thing—we're looking for someone, a man. He would be a little taller than me and much heavier, with brown hair and a beard. Have you seen him?"

Twig winced at the description and nodded slowly.

"When?" Thornton asked.

"Not long before you sh-showed up," he answered. "B-but he's gone now."

"Where was he going?"

"I don't know," Twig squeaked, closing his eyes as if awaiting a beating.

"Stay here," Thornton said to Twig, who was still tied up. He opened his eyes and gave Thornton a confused nod.

Walking back to the stone structure and sliding through the door, Thornton moved over to Kethras, who was tending to a recently awakened Ynara.

"Did you learn anything?" The Kienari asked.

Thornton nodded. "He doesn't know much. The tracks almost certainly belong to my father. I'm still not sure what they want with Miera, but it somehow involves her blood." He made a sour face as the words came out. "And he doesn't know where they took her."

Kethras did not respond to this, which troubled Thornton even more. Miera was still alive, that much he gathered. But for how long? He moved his palm over his face and rubbed his eyes in thought, then looked to Kethras, asking, "What do you think?"

"Wherever they took her, we can follow," the tall Kienari said as he stood up and looked out at the sky. "But your father's trail will not last forever, and we may lose it if we change our path." He sniffed the air like he did when he was hunting prey.

Thornton paced the room in thought, torn between helping his lifelong friend and finding his father. He thought of Miera and how frightened she had been that day they were attacked in Lusk, and growled in frustration. Before he could say anything, Ynara appeared from behind.

"I will find her," she said.

"Yeshta bo'tharan, Ynara," Kethras objected in their mother tongue, but the younger Kienari waved it off.

Gift of the Shaper

"Kethras, you must help Thornton find his father," she said, turning her eyes to the west where Kethras had been looking. "Miera is my responsibility."

Thornton furrowed his eyebrows in worry; his thoughts were on Miera, but he was so close to finding his father.

Kethras put his hand on his shoulder. "Calm yourself, Thornton. Ynara is an experienced hunter and more than capable as a warrior. She will find your friend, and we will find your father."

Thornton looked at Kethras and forced a smile. "Thank you, Kethras. I needed to hear that."

"We can waste no more time," Ynara said bluntly. "Kethras speaks true: your father's trail is still fresh, and you have a greater chance of reaching him if you leave now." Her tail flicked sharply when she spoke, as if accentuating her words.

The big Kienari nodded curtly as Ynara walked toward the door.

"I will ready the horses," she said as he headed outside, her long black tail flicking behind her as she walked.

Chapter 15

Athrani Prison,
Outside of Lusk

Gift of the Shaper

Ynara

The sun had begun to set in the sky, lengthening the shadows of the trees that surrounded the big stone building and splashing the tops of the clouds with reds and oranges.

Ynara walked over to Matilda and gently patted the horse's nose. The old brown mare seemed a little nervous, shaking her head and whinnying. Ynara swept the backs of her fingers over her muzzle a few times like she had seen Miera do, and the horse looked noticeably calmer.

Then, with a look of contempt, Ynara's onyx eyes settled on Twig and Bunch, still tied up on the ground, alert and awake. She eyed the ropes that bound them and glanced back at Matilda. Crinkling her nose at the thought of taking the horse, she soon realized that she had no choice, as she would need some way to transport Miera when she eventually tracked her down. She approached the two men to untie them.

"S-stay away!" Twig screamed. "I taste terrible!"

Ynara's disgusted frown put the men at ease. "Quiet," she growled. "I'm letting you go." She knelt down to reach for the ropes.

Even stooping, she towered over the men as they sat quaking in silence, watching the lithe black terror come close. Twig stared hard with his one good eye while Bunch looked like he was reciting a silent invocation to the Breaker. Ynara bared her teeth when she realized what he was doing, and he quickly turned his head to avoid being seen.

Her long, nimble fingers untied the rope with ease as she looked at them through narrowed eyes. In as little time as it took for the two men to breathe a sigh of relief, she let the rope drop to the ground and stood up. She backed up, never taking her gaze from them as she stared with her large black eyes.

Twig helped Bunch to his feet and acted as a crutch as the two men made their escape. Looking over his shoulder at Ynara, he said, "Best not be following us."

A hungry, low growl leapt from Ynara's throat as she started to change her mind about letting them live. Alarmed beyond reason, Twig grabbed at Bunch's arm and dragged him into the forest and out of her sight.

D.L. Jennings

She found herself holding a dagger that she did not remember unsheathing. Turning her attention back to the matter at hand, she slammed it back into the leather sheath as she collected the ropes and laid them neatly on the ground. Rising again, she slinked through the towering doorway and onto the cold stone floor of the building.

If anyone else were to look at the body resting just inside, they might have mistaken it for a corpse, seated on the floor with no sign of breathing. But as her vision shifted from light to heat in the darkness of the stone fortress, Ynara could clearly see the life that emanated from Thornton's body. She tilted her head, unsure of what he was doing. "Is something the matter?" she asked.

Thornton shook his head. "It's Miera," he answered softly. "I can't stop thinking that she's hurt—or worse." He stood up and looked the Ynara in the eyes. "She's strong, but she's always hated being alone. Ever since we were small, we've had each other to lean on." With a sigh, he added, "I'm just afraid we might not find her in time."

Ynara was unsure of how to react to human emotions—they were still so new to her—but she had watched her brother and learned from him. Softly, she put her hand on Thornton's shoulder, like she had seen Kethras do before. "I will do everything I can to bring her back." After a pause, she added, "I promise."

Thornton looked up at her and smiled weakly. "I know you will," he said. "I just hope it's enough."

She withdrew her hand and looked right at the young blacksmith. "It will be," she said as she turned to walk away.

Exiting the stone building for the last time, Ynara found Matty once again. Placing one hand on her mane and clutching it softly, she swung her right leg over in a mount so effortless and graceful that it would have left Thornton stunned had he been watching. Her feet almost touched the ground, resting atop Miera's prized mare.

The horse seemed to sense Ynara's uncertainty and tossed her head about. Tightening up, Ynara tugged on the reins and pointed her east, then mimicked the clicking noise she had heard Miera and Thornton make when they rode. Surprisingly, it worked. Matilda trudged forward slowly, barely seeming to notice her payload. Ynara's tall frame was much lighter than it looked—no surprise to anyone who had ever seen a Kienari move—and did not seem to add much of a strain.

The Kienari were the furthest thing from horse riders, though, having no need for the animals and even less interaction with them. Everything that Ynara knew about riding, she had learned since meeting Miera and Thornton; lucky for her, she was a quick study. She'd taken note when Miera had clicked her tongue inside her cheek to spur Matty forward and watched as she pulled back on the reins to slow her down. The worn leather strips looked small in her night-black hands, but she carried them with the experience of a seasoned rider.

The ride ahead will be long, she thought, *but it must be done.* With a surge, she was moving to find any trace left behind of Miera. Turning her face to the sky, she closed her eyes and breathed deeply, soaking in the air as she rode.

Ynara stalked her prey silently, a huntress in her element, using all of her senses to guide her along the path of pursuit.

She had picked up the tracks just outside the prison. They led eastward, and their owners did not appear to be in a hurry. There were two pairs: one set that was decidedly human and a second set that looked like it belonged to something big—bigger than a horse, but with claws instead of hooves. It was heavy too. That much was obvious by how deeply the tracks had sunk into the ground, even having made an imprint when the surface was nothing but hardened dirt. She could think of no creature living that fit the description and wasted no more time thinking about it. Instead, she went about her tracking, determined to learn the answer when she caught up with them. She patted her bow out of habit in an unconscious reassurance that she was never truly alone.

She walked beside Matilda now, reins in hand, taking in what she could of the area she walked through as she counted herself fortunate that it was all still so green and alive. The vegetation in this part of Derenar was thick, and it reminded her of home. The trees that lined the roads grew well here, outside the greedy reaches of men, and provided a rich and bountiful ecosystem for all kinds of animals to thrive within. She knew that one of them would be providing her with a meal and nodded her silent thanks to the forest.

It had been night when she left, but by now the sun had risen high in the sky, giving shadows to the trees around her and the lazily drifting clouds above. She estimated that it was just before midday, as she began fighting off the pangs of hunger. The tracks were getting fresher, which meant she was gaining ground on them, having made better time than expected by walking beside the mare instead of riding. Soon both of them could stop to rest.

Finally, after almost a half day of tracking, she caught a glimpse of what she had been following. The sight grabbed her in the chest and froze her in her tracks.

It was still quite a ways off, but her sharp eyesight meant that she had no trouble making out the features of the towering beast that caught her gaze. With scales darker and blacker than the fur that lined her own body, the creature she had been following appeared to have stepped right out of a nightmare and onto the path in front of her. It looked to be resting, perched on the ground with its shorter hind legs out to one side and its longer, muscular forelegs folded underneath its body. Chains protruded from the collar around its long serpentine neck jutting out from its body only to curve back toward its hind legs where it rested its head. The creature's neck was easily twice the length of its body, making it appear incredibly top-heavy, but nimble nonetheless. Its head was small compared to the body and looked just like that of a snake. Even at rest it looked deadly.

Ynara left the road immediately. She had never seen one of these things before and would take no chances on being spotted. If she could see it from here, it could most certainly see her. She pulled Matty after her as she slunk silently to the tree line, seeking shelter in the shadows that clothed her better than any animal skin ever could. Crouching, she flicked her wide black eyes back to her quarry to continue her surveillance. Her keen vision spotted movement from up ahead.

Beside the massive beast, the two-legged figure that emerged from behind it looked tiny. She was too far away to make out much else, but it looked human. Approaching the creature, it spoke.

Gift of the Shaper

"Up with you," the voice came. It was a man's voice, low and gruff, and matched his demeanor. He was wearing a black robe, which told her that he was most likely Khyth or at least part of the Hand. He had the creature's chains in his hand and gave them a violent tug. It groaned in defiance but took to its feet. When it did so, Ynara immediately spotted what the creature was hiding: there was Miera, in the flesh, lying on the ground beside it. She was alive—the heat emanating from her told Ynara as much—but not moving. Her body shifted almost imperceptibly as it grew and shrank with her shallow and steady breaths.

Relief surged through Ynara the moment she laid eyes on Miera. They had taken her, yes, but it was obvious that they needed her alive. *If they had wanted her dead, they would have fed her to the serpent,* she thought.

There would be no way to snatch her from the grips of these two, Ynara realized be-grudgingly. Even if she managed to get close enough to the creature without being detected—a longshot, she surmised—she knew the power that belonged to the Khyth and how quickly the one standing before her would be able to put her in the ground for good.

With a breath of resignation, she determined to simply follow the three of them for as long as she could. The important thing was that Miera was alive, and if she was alive, so was the hope of getting her back. She waited for them to start moving before she spurred Matilda on ahead.

Another quick, unconscious pat of her bow preluded her pursuit as she headed down the path of her newly discovered prey.

Chapter 16

Gal'dorok, West of Khala Val'ur

Gift of the Shaper

The land of Gal'dorok was beautiful once. Even the name reflected that, meaning "great pinnacle" in the first tongue. But the Khyth had blanketed a once-great land with ugliness and decay as they sacrificed more and more of their humanity in their lust for the power of the Otherworld. A land once sought for its enlightenment now held nothing but darkness.

In the greatest act of audacity and in a desperate attempt to push back the Athrani during the Shaping War, the Khyth had used the mountains themselves as a shield. Through excruciating effort of Breaking, they lifted a mountain and dropped it on Gal'dorok, changing the face of the world forever and cutting themselves off from the outside. This self-imposed exile all but ended the Shaping War, with the Athrani leaving Gal'dorok for Derenar to the west and most humans forgetting the Khyth even existed. But it did little to extinguish the hatred the Khyth felt for the Athrani, and that hatred was focused into the formation of the great halls of Khala Val'ur, built upon the ruins of the once-towering mountains of Gal'behem, the Great Serpent.

The process of bringing a mountain to its knees, though, left everything else around it transformed as well: new peaks jutted out where the land had once been flat; streams and rivers were redirected; fields where trees once grew were now rocky, barren mounds.

Now, staring up at those peaks was the young blonde girl that D'kane had dragged half-way across Derenar and over the border to Gal'dorok.

D'kane

"What is this place?" the blonde girl asked. Her eyes were on the mountains that surrounded the city of Khala Val'ur—new mountains that were built upon the corpses of the old. Like a water droplet ripples a pond, the Khyth had rippled the very land of Gal'dorok, with Khala Val'ur as the epicenter. Now, from above Khala Val'ur looked like a central point—the city itself—with a ring of rock surrounding it and another larger ring surrounding that one.

"The mountains of the Great Serpent," D'kane answered coldly, "a constant reminder of the sins of the Athrani and a stronghold for those who wish to see them destroyed."

It was indeed a perfectly formed fortress, defensible from all sides and all but impenetrable. The only way in was to walk a path that was carved straight through the mountains. The Khyth had designed it so that the only path through the outer ring was to the north and the one through the inner ring was on the south. This ensured that any army bold enough or mad enough to march on Khala Val'ur would be forced to walk the circumference of the inner ring of mountains, leaving them vulnerable to attacks from the peaks above. The way between the rings was narrow as well, so they could march no more than five across, removing any advantage they might have in sheer numbers, as they would bottleneck at the entrance to the inner ring. The defenders in the city could pick them off, five by five.

There was a good reason Khala Val'ur had not been marched on since the end of the Shaping War.

Since leaving for Lusk at the behest of the High Khyth, it had been too long since D'kane had seen the mountains surrounding Khala Val'ur, but they were just as he remembered them: towering, imposing monuments to the greatness of his people. They were both a testament to the power they had achieved and a reminder of their hatred for the Athrani.

"Stop gawking and keep moving," D'kane said with a push to the girl's back, causing her to stumble. "We're nearly there." He looked at her, still weak from being drained by the Gwarái, as she walked beside the great black behemoth. They had come a long way, but the end was now in sight, and he wanted her to be able to cross the threshold of the Sunken City on her own.

"You don't have to push me," she protested. "It's your fault I can barely walk in the first place," she said with a glare to D'kane, who watched her every move.

"It was necessary," he answered. "And it would have been foolish to have gone on assumption alone. Now move," he said with another push. "We are close."

Gift of the Shaper

Miera

It seemed like they had been walking forever.

After some time, the two of them—with the awful Gwarái lumbering at their heels—approached the entrance of the outer ring, a massive arching tunnel blasted straight through the mountain.

Miera peered into its recesses as far as she could, but it was futile; under the mountain was nothing but black, as the daylight was swallowed up by the darkness.

"I'm not going through there," she said as she planted her feet firmly on the ground. She hated the dark as much as she hated her traveling companions.

Looking up at the Gwarái, whose yellow eyes were focused on the invisible path before them, D'kane seemed to have other plans. "You can walk through, or he can carry you through. The choice is yours." He looked back at Miera. "But he does look hungry."

Miera's face bore a worried frown as her fingers went to the marks below her neck where the creature's fangs had buried themselves. She allowed the Khyth to walk past her, relenting as she followed him into the dark. She would not allow D'kane the pleasure of seeing her tremble in fear.

Leading the beast through, the cracked fingers of D'kane's free hand touched the sides of the tunnel as they dragged slowly across the cold and jagged rock. Miera found herself, to her great revulsion, clinging to the Gwarái beside her as she fumbled her way through the dark, fighting back fear as she did. This deep in, the tunnel was pitch black, and touch was the only reliable means of navigation. She forced her eyes closed as she grasped the creature's scaly skin and tried to block out the loathsome sound of breathing, reawakening the horror of having her lifeblood drained. Distant drops of water echoed as they hit the ground, seeming to come from halfway across the world as the vastness of the mountain tunnel became apparent to her.

Together, they moved in silence, forward through the black until, finally, light from the other side crept in and brought with it relief in the form of an exit. Miera shuddered as her hands fell away from the Gwarái, free to once again move by sight. The warm sunlight on her face was a small consolation for the brief but awful journey.

D'kane

At the exit of the cave, D'kane looked up to see a watch tower that was manned by humans drawn to Khyth power like flies to a corpse. Atop the tower, the black flag of Khala Val'ur waved lazily in the breeze, with its skeletal white hand in the middle—the same hand that he wore on his left shoulder and one that the girl seemed to recognize.

"That hand," she said quietly. "What is it?"

"That hand," D'kane echoed, "is the Hand of the Black Dawn. It represents the brotherhood of all Khyth and followers of the Breaker, He who showed us power and bides His time in the Otherworld to strike at the Shaper of the Ages." He did not look back as he spoke, but he knew his words had the impact he desired.

Unlike the Athrani, whose Shaping abilities presented themselves in all males of Athrani blood, not all Khyth were born with the power of Breaking. Yet ever since the revelation by the Breaker that the power of the Otherworld could be controlled by other means, they dedicated their lives to learning its mysteries. They spent their waking hours in training, hidden away from prying eyes, concealing the secrets of the Hand. They toiled, they sweat, and they bled, all for a glimpse of power. And when it finally came—when the power first manifested—it was excruciating. The Otherworld poured into them and through them, filling every fiber of their being, soaking into them and saturating their bodies like water in a sponge.

For some, the power was too great, and it burned the life from them completely, hollowing them out and leaving nothing but a husk. For the lucky few that were not killed by it, they may as well have been. They existed in a state of constant pain that only seemed to diminish when they would Break. But there was not one Khyth living who regretted the power gleaned from their transformation. D'kane was certainly no exception.

Gift of the Shaper

They walked past the tower and down the path that ran south between the two rings of mountains. Besides the occasional watchtower, the path was largely empty.

Reaching inside his robe, D'kane could feel the power of the Gwarái horn pulsing against his hand. *The nearlimitless Shaping power of an Athrani, captured in a package about the size of a large dagger.*

The Athrani, who still retained the tiniest shred of their humanity, who did not have to suffer and sacrifice everything for their Shaping ability . . . The thought stirred up emotions that were as old as their split from humanity.

As they approached the entrance of the inner ring, D'kane saw two figures standing outside. Drawing closer, he recognized them.

The taller of the two was General Aldis Tennech, a cunning strategist who was as ruthless as he was brilliant. Age and wars had taken their toll on him, as the wrinkles in his face showed, and the streaks of white in his close-cropped black hair and mustache had become more prominent since the last time they met. On his right hip he wore a long black scabbard that hung casually at his side, complementing his panoply of silver and black platemail armor.

At his side as always was Seralith Edos, the general's advisor. She was tall, almost as tall as the general, and her long hair was a light shade of brown. She could have been called beautiful if not for the scar that ran the length of the left side of her face from forehead to chin. No one knew how she'd gotten it, and no one dared ask. But her height and her hair color were not what made her stand out here in the bastion of the servants of the Breaker—it was her heritage that set her apart. An Athrani, she was born and raised in the city of Ellenos; and like all female Athrani, she possessed no inborn capacity for Shaping. There were whispers that the reason for her departure lay in the lure of power that the Khyth promised. After all, anyone could learn their secrets—human or Athrani, man or woman.

But what made her turn to the Hand was of no concern to D'kane or to the general—her loyalty was unquestioned.

"Good day, General Tennech, Lady Edos," said D'kane.

The two of them nodded in return.

"What brings you back to the city, Master D'kane?" The general peered around him to the girl whose hands were bound in a short length of rope. "And who is this?"

"Both of those questions will be answered in the presence of the High Khyth," he replied. "And I would think that you should like to be there when they are."

The general looked skeptical. "If you insist," he replied. Turning to his advisor, he said, "We will put off the inspections for another time."

Sera nodded, and they fell in line to follow D'kane, who was already making his way inside the gates.

Chapter 17

Derenar, East of Annoch

Gift of the Shaper

Olson

The next morning, Olson awoke to find Dailus already awake, and he did not appear to have slept at all. Despite this, when the Athrani saw that Olson was up, he stood up wordlessly, ready to travel.

"Are you rested?" Olson asked.

"No, something happened last night. I feel different—empty," Dailus said, dusting himself off.

"I'm sorry about your friend," Olson began.

"He was not my friend, Olson, and that's not what I meant," Dailus said sharply. "He was Athrani. That is the only thing that matters."

Olson furrowed his brows and looked at him but said nothing.

"I marked the site of his death," Dailus said, "and buried him as best I could."

He was standing over the mound he had dug in the night, his hands still covered in dirt.

"I would've helped you if you'd said something," Olson said.

"It was not your place to help, though I appreciate the offer. It was something I had to do on my own. He was a half-eye like me, an outcast, a man with no place to call home." He stood silent before speaking again. "His death must have affected me more than I realized, though. I couldn't even perform the Shaping ritual to give him a proper funeral."

Olson didn't answer, but the frown on his face spoke loudly enough.

"We should be going," Dailus said finally and walked toward the trail. Olson shook his head and did the same. A small path led back to the road they had been following the night before, carved right through the heart of the forest.

First light had just broken in the sky as the sun rose against their backs. After years of waking with the dawn, Olson's body had grown accustomed to starting early and was utterly incapable of sleeping in late. This came in handy, he found, when traveling. And although walking was easier than swinging a hammer, Olson couldn't help but think that he would rather be doing just that, as the two men trudged down what seemed to be an endless dirt road into Annoch. The sun above them was a poor substitute for the roaring fire of his forge, and Dailus was certainly a poor substitute for Thornton, but he would have to make do with what he had. Neither man had said a word since they left that morning, and the silence was starting to get to Olson. Eventually, he found that he could stand it no longer and decided to break the silence.

With his eyes still on the road, Olson asked, "How long have you been away from Ellenos?"

Dailus turned his head and regarded Olson coolly. "Long. Long enough that I've lost count of the years."

"I thought you Athrani loved it there."

"Don't lump me in with them. I had my reasons for leaving, most of which I would prefer not to recount for you."

"Fair enough," said Olson. "What did you do after you left?"

"A bit of this and a bit of that. I'm a wanderer, really. I find it hard to stay put for too long, and the world is just too big to wake up in the same place every morning."

Olson scoffed softly at this, but Dailus seemed not to hear and went on.

"I managed to find work despite my heritage—hard to do when you're an outcast," he said. "And I found other Athrani who had scattered after the Shaping War, settling in other parts of Derenar. It was fully exciting but only half-eye-opening." He looked at the blacksmith with a grin. "That was a joke."

Olson raised an eyebrow. *Athrani humor*, he thought, *an oxymoron*.

"So where did you learn that trick you used on the guards?" Olson asked.

Dailus's smile faded, and he paused as if the question was deeper than he had expected. Finally, after a breath he spoke.

"In Ellenos, you are raised in the art of Shaping; you are taught to respect it, to develop it, to let it grow inside you. You learn to feel the power of the Otherworld and let it flow in you and through you and feel how it interacts with this world." He came to a stop in the middle of the dirt road and looked at Olson. "But Ellenos is steeped in tradition, and tradition hinders progress. No one proved that more than my father."

"Your father?" Olson asked. "How so?"

"He was an important man in Ellenos, but he never really explored his ability the way I have tried to do. He contented himself with what amounted to parlor tricks: making stone sculptures out of water and conjuring flames. He had no ambition, my father," Dailus said with a sigh. "Lived and died in Ellenos."

They had been walking for a good while, and Olson's stomach was complaining the whole way. It had been more than a day since he'd eaten, and even that had been something barely recognizable as food that his jailers had thrown in his cell. "I don't suppose you know a trick to make me think I'm not hungry," he said.

"Afraid not," Dailus replied. "But you may not have to worry about that for much longer. Look," he said, pointing over the tops of the trees. "The spire of Annoch."

Olson looked up to see a tall white structure peeking out above the trees. As they got closer, he could see a figure at the summit, with its arms held high in the air, a hammer clutched in one hand.

"I've seen that before," he said, "painted on the inside of the doors of the prison."

Dailus looked up at the top of the spire. "It is the Shaper of Ages standing atop the Anvil of the Worldforge, where She crafted the chains that have held the Breaker since the Shaping War. She gave them to the Binder of Worlds, who continues to watch from the shadows. Quite a story, really," he said as he turned to Olson. "You're not familiar?"

"Only in passing," Olson replied, "though I'm finding out new things about you Athrani all the time."

"But this is not just Athrani lore, Olson. This is why the world is the way it is. It is as solid a truth as you'll find." He paused, as if considering. "And quite possibly the reason the Khyth have grown restless lately."

Olson's gaze was fixed on the figure at the pinnacle of the spire. "You think this Worldforge has something to do with it?"

"I will tell you that it would not surprise me in the least. The Khyth serve the Breaker, after all. And as you and I both know, people will do anything to keep from being locked up."

The two of them approached the entrance to the city, which consisted of a pair of massive iron gates guarded by a small number of armored men. They wore scarlet breastplates and were armed with long spears, and Olson could see at least two men in a tower overhead, no doubt with arrows aimed at them. As the two men walked toward the gate, one of the soldiers stepped forward and put out his hand.

"Hold it right there, strangers," he said. "I'm Jinda Yhun, Captain of the Guard. What brings you to Annoch?" He had his helmet off, but it wouldn't have mattered—his face looked as hard as the steel in his armor. He was clean shaven with close-cropped red hair and eyes to match.

"Jinda," Dailus said as he forced a smile, "my name is Dailus, of Ellenos, and this is my traveling companion, Olson. We seek food for our stomachs and horses for our journey and plan to be off as quickly as we can."

"Ellenos, eh?" Jinda replied. He sized up Olson for quite a bit and had his eyes on him when he addressed Dailus. "See that your friend here doesn't make any trouble for himself."

"Trouble is the furthest thing from our minds," Dailus answered, "I assure you."

The Captain of the Guard said nothing. He simply met the gaze of the two men before him, his red eyes flashing as they flicked from Olson to Dailus and back. Finally, he turned his head back toward the gates to yell over his shoulder, "Open it! Two coming in."

The two men started toward the gate.

"Just be careful in there," he called after them. "The city has been in an uproar since last night."

The doors clanked and groaned as their giant iron hinges worked to move the mammoth gates.

Gift of the Shaper

Turning back to Jinda, Dailus asked, "Why last night?"

Jinda gave a confused look and answered, "They say the Shaper took Her gift back."

Dailus stood before the gates of Annoch, looking like the weight of the world had come crashing down on him.

"I knew it," he whispered. "I felt it. I knew something had changed," he said out loud, more for his own benefit than for Olson's. After some time, he seemed to snap out of whatever trance he had been in and, with a surprising quickness, began walking. "There has been a change of plans, I'm afraid," he said. "We head first to the Anvil of the Worldforge."

Olson shook his head and followed silently.

Chapter 18

Khala Val'ur

Gift of the Shaper

D'kane

In stepped D'kane to the entrance of the Sunken City of Khala Val'ur, where the warmth of the sun did not reach and the will of the Khyth still lay hidden. The walls had not changed much since the day they were formed: cold, black, and unrefined, yet otherwise completely unremarkable. Their only purpose was to hold back the weight of the great mountains that served as both prison and stronghold for the denizens of the Sunken City—a purpose which they had carried out well for ages.

The minerals that were abundant throughout the city provided the basis for trade with other cities in both Derenar and Gal'dorok. And although it was intended to be a military strong-hold, Khala Val'ur had slowly been repurposed to support long-term living, attracting some of the greatest blacksmiths around, who would give anything to work with the metals found within its walls. Trade routes had been created and dwellings built, and the Valurians eventually established themselves as some of the best metalworkers this side of Gal'behem.

The greatest fortune, however, was not found in the rocks but below them. Starting just outside of Lusk in Derenar and flowing east through Gal'dorok to empty into the Tashkar Sea was a mighty river that carved its way through the city, providing drinking water to the Valurians and endless water for the quenching buckets of the blacksmiths. It was what allowed the first Khyth to stay in the stronghold, making it their home below the earth. It gave them assurance that they could find in this city everything they would need. For that reason, they called the river K'Hel, the Bringer of Life, and everyone who came to the city would forever know its name.

After walking a good distance down, toward the center of the city, the tunnel in which they had been walking terminated on a ledge that overlooked Khala Val'ur proper. It was an awe-inspiring sight for even the most seasoned of travelers. The city sprawled out below them, centered around a great spire, atop of which was perched a light source for the whole city: a huge fire that was kept burning day and night, fueled by an arcane combination of Khyth Breaking and Valurian minerals. Roads converged on it like spokes on a wheel, and the rest of the city had simply built itself around it. Though the Khyth were cold and cruel, they certainly had a mind for design.

"This had better be worth the walk, D'kane," said an agitated Tennech, "because I'm going to be making it again very shortly."

"I assure you, General, it will be."

The walk down was tedious and slow. Wide, winding steps lined the inside walls of the underground city, snaking downward in a massive spiral that circled the city twice before reaching the ground. Choosing to live in Khala Val'ur meant becoming as hard as the rock from which the city was carved. Even keeping a moderate pace, by the time they had reached the bottom, they needed a rest.

They continued on to the center of the city, toward the great spire that lit Khala Val'ur—the heart of the Hand of the Black Dawn and the dwelling place of the High Khyth.

The base of the spire was a circle half as wide as it was tall, rising several hundred feet into the air. The single door at the bottom was adorned with the sign of the Hand, huge and white, painted so all could see. Two guards were posted outside, and they gave the party a solemn bow of respect.

"I seek an audience with the High Khyth," D'kane said sternly. "I have something of value for him," he said, motioning to the Gwarái.

The guard on the right nodded and grabbed the brass knocker that hung from the door, giving it three sturdy raps. "Master Khyth D'kane to see the High Khyth," he announced. After a moment, a strong-sounding voice came through the door. "Come in," it bid, and the Master Khyth did as he was told. The guard grabbed the handle of the large metal door and pulled it open, allowing D'kane to step through, followed by the general and his advisor.

Inside the door with his back to the entrance was Yetz, the High Khyth, most feared of all and figurehead for the Hand of the Black Dawn. He was old but had none of the weaknesses that typically came with age. He wore the traditional robes of the Khyth of the Hand—long and plain, save for the skeletal white hand placed upon the left upper shoulder. But, unlike any others' robes, his were uniquely stained the color of deep sanguine red that would continue to be his hallmark until the day another Khyth removed it from his still-warm corpse.

The chamber of the High Khyth was lavishly decorated, even by Valurian standards. The focal point of the interior was the large stone fireplace that emptied above, into the fire that lit the city. Ornate candleholders lined the walls and provided the majority of light throughout the chamber. The floors were made of smooth granite, and Yetz had laid out several large rugs for both decoration and relief from the cold floor, as he preferred to be barefoot when he was by himself.

He led his guests into the sitting room in the entrance and motioned toward the chairs. D'kane complied, as did Seralith; General Tennech remained standing, his arms folded sternly in front of him. The two guards escorting the girl waited with her just outside.

Walking across the room, Yetz stopped in front of the fireplace, with his back to his guests, where the crackling fire made his shadow dance upon the floor in front of them. "Tell me what you have learned."

D'kane had his eyes buried in Yetz's back. "I saw it myself, High Khyth, though I could not get close enough to be sure, but I could feel its power. It was exactly as the stories described it."

General Tennech spoke up. "You mean to tell us you had it within your grasp? What was stopping you?"

D'kane looked at him incredulously, but before he could answer, Seralith spoke. "General, he is a full-blooded Khyth of the Breaking. Without Athrani power to help him wield it, it would have been impossible."

"Using the Gwarái was wise," Yetz said as he removed his hood and turned to look at D'kane. His own eyes were hauntingly white, and his face was scarred with power. "Where is it?"

"Outside Lusk," D'kane said simply.

"Then we are close," Yetz said. "Will you be able to retrieve it?" D'kane was hesitant and Yetz narrowed his eyes at his silence. "Speak, D'kane."

He did as he was told. "Master Khyth Rennick and a few of his men went after its bearer, a blacksmith's son from a nearby village . . . None of them survived."

Yetz's face was devoid of expression. "You are telling me that a Master Khyth was no match for a boy? Rennick is one of my strongest men. I refuse to believe that he was bested by some child with a hammer."

"He was no mere boy," D'kane replied. "And I am told he had Kienari help."

Tennech scoffed at this. "Kienari—nothing but a myth."

Yetz snapped his head impatiently toward Tennech. "Kienari are no myth, General—of this I assure you—and they are far more dangerous than mere stories suggest. There are some things in this world that are older than even the Breaker."

Tennech glared at the old Khyth, but D'kane was the next to speak.

"We did manage to locate his father," he started. "Even now, he thinks himself free. It was no easy task, but if we find ourselves in need of leverage, I can think of none better."

"Perhaps," Yetz said before falling silent, seeming lost in his own thoughts. Finally, he spoke. "Tell me of your plan."

D'kane produced the Gwarái horn he had brought with him. It was cloudy and gave off the slightest hint of a glow. He handed it to Yetz, who studied it closely. "The Breaker provided us the perfect weapon for finding the Hammer. It is the single strongest pull I have witnessed," he said as his master studied the horn. "This one broke free of its chains when the boy was near, it was driven so mad. Even now, I can feel its longing for the Hammer."

Yetz eyed the horn in silence, then flicked his eyes to D'kane. "So we use the beasts to find it?"

"Yes, High Khyth," he replied. "I believe it was what the Breaker intended. The horns are pulled strongly enough that we need only them to track it down. And we can use the creatures here to siphon away the Athrani's power." Pausing to peer out to where his captive was waiting, he said, "But there is something about the girl that I still have not figured out."

Gift of the Shaper

Yetz lowered his head at D'kane in scrutiny. "And what might that be?"

"Though she is Athrani, she shows no signs of being one," he answered. "And her blood . . . Something happened during the feeding."

"Pray," Yetz said with a hint of annoyance, "tell."

D'kane complied. "It happened when the Gwarái began to drink too deeply and I reached out to stop it. I felt something strange, something unknown to me," he said, examining the horn. "Suddenly, it was like I was looking through a haze, where the whole power of the Otherworld stretched out before me. In the distance I could feel the chains that bind the Breaker. I felt the pull."

The High Khyth eyed D'kane with an air of suspicion. He took the sharp white bone to a small marble table by the fireplace, again turning his back to his guests.

Tennech stroked his mustache pensively. "If the Gwarái can capture that kind of power," he said, nodding at the horn, "perhaps they would be useful to my army as well."

Yetz did not turn around as he spoke. "No, General." His words were emphatic and echoed throughout the chamber. "They are far too important to be used as fodder. Freeing the Breaker is our endgame, and to do that we need the Hammer—anything else is a distraction." He turned to face them, never once losing his composure. "It is the only way to ensure the Breaker's release. And the longer we can keep it from Ellenos that we know of its whereabouts, the better."

Tennech crossed his arms in aggravation and said calmly, "I assume you have a plan."

Yetz turned to look at the general. "A small group of riders will escort the Gwarái horn, with two Khyth of my choosing. If what D'kane says is true, it should lead them to the Hammer."

Tennech held eye contact for a moment, then looked away to Seralith. "I will reach out to Commander Durakas in Ghal Thurái. His men are good riders and better fighters; it will be in our best interest to include them."

The tall Athrani nodded, saying, "I can be there and back in two days."

"Good," said Tennech. Looking back to Yetz, he asked, "How does that suit you, High Khyth?"

"So be it," the old one answered.

"Then I will begin the selection of riders at once," Tennech replied. "When I am finished I will report to you." He bowed slightly and turned to his advisor. "Come, Seralith."

The brunette rose gracefully from her seat and curtsied deeply to Yetz. "High Khyth." She nodded at D'kane, who nodded back. They left the room and the door closed behind them.

***

D'kane was still in his seat when Yetz came over to join him. The old one's white eyes looked him up and down, causing him to shift slightly in his seat. The High Khyth was intimidating in both actual power and positional power, and his harrowing appearance did not make D'kane any more comfortable. Finally, the aged Khyth spoke.

"You have done well," he said.

"Thank you, High Khyth Yetz," he answered with a bow of his head. "I took it upon myself to do as much as I could."

"Certainly," he answered, his eyes studying D'kane's face for a reaction. "Which is why I think you should accompany the riders."

D'kane's eyes widened in surprise, and he bowed his head again. "I am honored," he said.

"You should be. It is no secret that you are next in line for my position." D'kane winced visibly, but Yetz continued, "So it is fitting that you lead the charge that will begin the reclamation of our glory."

D'kane raised his head and looked up at Yetz. "I will not let you down."

Gift of the Shaper

Yetz laughed softly at this. "It isn't me you'll be letting down, D'kane, but the Breaker Himself."

The idea made D'kane shift uneasily in his seat.

"Bear in mind: that will not be your sole purpose on this journey," Yetz continued. "You alone will ensure that my will is carried out and the Breaker is set free. I will humor the general by allowing him to send some of his men with you, but I trust him no more than I would trust an Athrani to shave my neck. And as for the girl," he said, looking out the door to where the young blonde woman was being held along with the Gwarái, "if she is as important as you think, I will keep an eye on her. Give me a moment, then send the guards in."

"Yes, High Khyth," came the crisp reply.

"Now go," he said, turning his back to D'kane. "You will leave as soon as Seralith has returned."

Bowing once more, D'kane backed away from Yetz and exited the High Khyth's chamber.

Chapter 19

Khala Val'ur

Gift of the Shaper

Yetz

For the moment, Yetz was alone and walked across the room to the fireplace to listen to the crackling of the fire. He put the backs of his hands toward the flames and let the warmth chase away the ever-present cold of Khala Val'ur. It was a cold that seeped out of the walls of rock that lay at the city's heart; a specter that crept through the houses and floated down the halls of everyone who lived there; a hand that hung just above their shoulders, poised to entangle them in its icy fingers. It was nothing like his home, the city that he had left behind. That was a distant memory that grew fainter every year.

He felt the heat of the fire spread through his face as it reddened his cheeks and ears. After warming himself for a time, he dropped his hands to his side and stared into the flames as his hand went to a pocket inside his robes. There, his fingertips found the smooth side of another horn, tucked away and almost forgotten. He pulled it out from the pocket and examined it. It was heavy and black and looked almost nothing like the horn that D'kane had brought him. He pursed his lips in thought.

Pocketing it once again, he heard the two guards come in with the girl. He turned around to see them trembling at the thought of being alone with the most powerful Khyth in Khala Val'ur.

"Are you afraid of me?" he asked the guards.

One of them nodded, and the other seemed too frightened to move. The blonde girl made no indication that she'd heard him.

"Good. Gather the girl and follow me."

They obliged.

He walked to the small marble table where he had placed the Gwarái horn, picked it up, and walked to the rear of the large room, into a smaller study with a plain wooden door at the back. With the horn in one hand, he lifted his other to the door and made a sweeping motion. Silently, it melted away to reveal a black, rocky staircase circling downward.

As he descended, he could hear a soft ringing from the horn in his pocket, becoming louder with every step. The stairs terminated at a floor made of the same rock that comprised most of the walls of the Sunken

City. The room was open and wide, with high ceilings to add to the illusion of space. And the soft babbling of the waters of K'Hel could be heard from a chasm below, carved out by centuries of erosion. At the far end of the room, perched on the edge of the chasm, was a table covered in bones.

"Place her there and restrain her," he said as he pointed to an empty spot on the table.

With a grunt, the two guards did as they were told, holding her down and chaining her in place.

"Now leave us," he said with a dismissive wave.

The two guards bowed and scampered back up the staircase, tripping over each other as if they feared for their lives.

Yetz walked over and set down the horn. "All these failed experiments," he said to himself as he traced a finger across the table. It looked to him like a graveyard: the end result of years of trying one thing or another to no success. But finally they had uncovered the secret.

Of the objects on the table, most were horns. There were some skulls from the earliest days of the trials when he had only begun to understand the Prophecy. They were arranged in lines, with the largest bones on the far left, smaller bones to their right, and the smallest on the edge. At the head of the lines were three indentations that were carefully carved into the table. He placed the first horn of the Gwarái in the middle one. Then, stepping back to admire the table, he forced a smile.

"You can't possibly know it," he said to the girl, "but your blood is worth so much more outside of your veins than in it."

Miera

Miera did her best to keep calm, but the old Khyth Yetz made her skin crawl. "Just let me go, please. Take whatever you need; just let me go."

Yetz laughed softly at her pleading. "It doesn't work like that, my dear. And as much as D'kane doesn't want to admit it, we need you—alive." He punctuated the last word with what sounded like regret. "And once we have the Hammer, your true value will become apparent."

Miera was confused at his mention of the hammer—she had thought she heard them shouting about it when she was in the other room—and wondered if it had anything to do with the three men who came after her and Thornton in Lusk. She decided not to ask, though, in case they felt like testing whether or not they truly did need her still breathing.

"What happens until then?" she asked.

"We keep you away from prying eyes," he answered. "I'm afraid there's just nowhere else to keep you. But for now," he said, moving back to the staircase that they had descended, "there are matters I must attend to."

Miera watched as he climbed the staircase and heard the sound of sliding rock as he sealed her inside, and realized that her panic had rendered her mute. Her heart was pounding against the wall of her chest even as she struggled to cry for help, but she knew deep down it was worthless. Here in the depths of the Hand of the Black Dawn, no one would come to help her, even if they did hear her cries.

For the time being, she gathered herself and tried to calm her nerves. She closed her eyes and shut out the blackness of the walls, trading it for the blackness of her mind. She used the silence to think of her home and of Matilda. Of Olson.

Of Thornton.

Anything but the silent, dark walls of Khala Val'ur.

She managed to shut out the world around her so well that she soon forgot anything was wrong. She found herself back in her bed in Highglade, surrounded by her flowers and the warmth of the fireplace.

She fell into the darkness, embracing it and letting it cradle her in its arms. And the darkness answered with dreams.

Chapter 20

Derenar, East of Annoch

Gift of the Shaper

Kethras

Tracking was never easy with the sun directly overhead, especially when an effort had been made to hide the evidence—an effort that would have been lost on any less-capable tracker. But as Kethras stared at the tracks that still glowed with the power of the Otherworld, any remaining doubt of his ability to follow them melted away like shadows under the noonday sun.

"The tracks lead this way," he said to Thornton, motioning westward.

Thornton looked where Kethras was pointing but made no indication that he could see anything. He furrowed his brow in confusion and looked at Kethras, then back in the direction he was pointing.

"I don't see anything," Thornton said after a silence.

"That is because whoever is traveling with your father took care to conceal their tracks. He is a *Shaper*," Kethras replied, "Athrani."

"Athrani?" Thornton echoed. "How do you know that?"

Kethras followed the tracks with his eyes, scanning down the road. "Because Athrani Shaping is different than Khyth Breaking," he answered.

Thornton stared at him, his brow still furrowed.

Kethras sighed. "Athrani Shapers draw upon the energy from the Otherworld and use it to change whatever they please, in whatever ways they can imagine. Doing so leaves faint traces of energy, much in the same way that sparks fly off a piece of metal that you hit with your hammer as you shape it."

Kethras bent down to scoop up some mud into one hand and molded the mud into a ball. He picked up a roughly equal-sized rock in the other.

"An Athrani," he continued, "could look at this piece of mud and see endless possibilities, because the energy that exists in it mirrors the energy that comes from the Otherworld. They can take it and shape it into whatever they like. They could turn it into water, fire, metal—anything." He held the mud in his hand and quickly switched it with the rock, making it seem as if it had transformed, then quickly switched them back.

"But a Khyth cannot manipulate the energy like an Athrani can," he went on. "They can only move it or change the shape." With this, he smashed the mud with his fist. He spread it out so it covered his palm, then rolled it back into a ball. "It is one of the reasons the Khyth hate the Athrani so intensely. They believe they are wasting their abilities, abilities that could be used to change the world as we know it—abilities they, too, might possess if the Breaker of the Dawn is set free."

Thornton looked at the ball of mud in his hand and back to the tracks. "I still see nothing," he said flatly.

"Because your eyes see only the light and dark of this world." He paused and looked again at Thornton. "Kienari eyes see much more." Standing, he said, "Come. These sparks will soon fade away, and then we will have lost them completely." He started walking west in the direction of the tracks.

They went on for hours, mostly in silence, as Thornton alternated between riding and walking to give Jericho a break. He made sure to mention that traveling was not easy on the old horse, and he always made sure to give him the rest that he needed. For a horse as faithful and even-tempered as Jericho, Thornton said he would do just about anything.

Kethras simply nodded in agreement.

By the time the sun had begun to set, Kethras could tell where the tracks were headed: the city of Annoch. It was close enough to Ellenos—a few days ride—to have a decently sized Athrani population to complement its large human number. It was a massive city, though, and large enough to warrant a guard contingent posted outside of its heavily enforced walls.

Kethras had never felt comfortable around humans, and his experience with them was limited. As he glanced over to Thornton, he remembered that they were not all bad. In a big city like Annoch, though, he was hesitant. Most humans did not believe that Kienari even existed, like Thornton had said, and thought of them as nothing more than bedtime stories to keep children in line. He could not even remember the last time he found himself in a human city and was uncertain of how they would react to seeing him. The thought of being surrounded by more people than trees made him uneasy. But by the time he spied the Spire of

Gift of the Shaper

Annoch, as the sun finally dipped below the tree line, he knew he would have to make up his mind quickly on what to do. At the very least, it was night time and he could hide himself if needed.

"The tracks are leading to Annoch," he said to Thornton, who had been walking beside Jericho for quite some time now. "I am not certain that I will be able to follow them inside."

A look of confusion spread across Thornton's face, who opened his mouth to talk. But before he could say anything, Kethras answered Thornton's unspoken question.

"Not all humans are as welcoming as you are, Thornton."

Thornton shook his head. "Let's not think about that until we have to. Right now we need to worry about finding my father." He placed his foot in Jericho's stirrup and hoisted himself into the saddle. Clicking his tongue to spur the horse on, he said, "Let's get moving."

Kethras watched as Jericho trotted by under the command of his well-muscled rider with the sizable hammer attached to his back. He looked again at the spire, then back to Thornton as he quickened his pace.

As the spire loomed closer and closer, Kethras's unease grew. He could already see the massive walls that spilled out before him. He knew that the spire was tall, but he had no idea that something man-made like the walls could be so imposing. As the trees gave way to an open path that led straight to the gates, Kethras was able to take in the walls completely. They dominated his field of view, and he had to turn his head in both directions just to take them all in. They disappeared on either side as they curved to accommodate the city. But without any trees to help him judge distance, he could not be sure just how far they went.

Ahead of him, Thornton had dismounted. In the darkness, Kethras could clearly make out the heat signatures of a handful of humans who guarded the front of the gates. His hunter's instincts kicked in, and he calculated the quickest way to dispatch of them, as his hands went calmly to his bow.

Two in the towers, a roll to the right to shake off incoming arrows, three at the front gate, a knife to the one in the middle, two quick arrows to the ones on either side.

Just as he finished his mental preparation, though, the heat signature of the man in the middle went cold. *No, not cold*—, he thought, *gone*. When he felt the tip of a knife being pressed into the back of his neck, his preparation left him as quickly as his remaining sense of ease.

"I don't know what you are, beast, but I'll not have you picking off my men from the dark," came a voice just above a whisper. "Take your hands off the bow, and I'll let you and your friend live. Though I'm not sure it will do him any good. Approaching the gates of Annoch with a weapon like that strapped to his back tells me he's not the brightest."

Kethras slowly moved his hands away from his bow. Whatever was holding the knife to his neck clearly had him outmatched. No human could sneak up on a Kienari like that, that much he knew. He hadn't even heard it coming. The only other thing that silent that he knew of was Ynara. He was much better off going along with its demands and living to fight another day.

"Easy now," came the voice again. "Get on your knees and put your hands behind your head."

Kethras did as he was told, without even the slightest hint of non-compliance. "May I tell my friend to unhorse?" he asked smoothly.

"Do what you think is best," came the reply.

"Thornton," Kethras said evenly, "get down off Jericho." As Thornton looked at him, his eyes widened with surprise. "And throw your hammer on the ground."

"My hammer? Why?"

"Because there are two archers with arrows trained on you, waiting for you to make the wrong move," Kethras said calmly. "And compliance is easier when you're unhorsed and unarmed."

Thornton slowly took his left foot from the stirrup and slid from Jericho onto the ground. When his eyes found Kethras's in the twilight, he reached for his hammer as non-threateningly as possible and placed it at his feet, then joined him in his kneeling, hands-on-head posture.

When Kethras heard the sound of a knife being sheathed behind him, he exhaled in relief. The sound of bowstrings being held taut, however,

Gift of the Shaper

kept him alert. He flicked his eyes up to the two hot spots in the tower and silently cursed himself for not firing at both of them right away.

"Answer my questions to my liking and I won't snap your necks," came the voice again, still behind him. "Why have you come to my city?"

Before Kethras could answer, Thornton spoke up. "We were following the tracks of my father. He was taken from my home a few days ago, and I was worried I'd never see him again." He paused, and Kethras thought that he heard a waver in his voice as he spoke, "His tracks led here."

Kethras listened as soft footsteps made their way out from behind him. Beneath the faint light of the moon, Kethras was amazed to see the man before him blazing hotter than a camp-fire. He looked human, as far as he could tell, but the glow of the Otherworld surged through him like a river. He had to close his eyes for fear of being overwhelmed—it was almost like looking at the sun.

"Your father—describe him to me," the man said.

"Big," Thornton said, "bigger than me—and you. A great brown beard and hair to match. He is a blacksmith and built like one."

Kethras heard a chuckle from the man and opened his eyes enough to see him pull Thornton up by his armpit. He looked the boy up and down, then said, "He fits the description of a man that came through earlier today. He was traveling with a companion—an Athrani half-eye."

The words confirmed it. "That's him," Thornton said as he whirled around to face the man. "Where is he?"

Kethras saw the bright man hold up his arms in a gesture for the archers to lower their weapons.

"He went inside, though I almost thought better of it. But this city has a good relationship with Athrani, and the one with him looked like he could keep him under control."

Kethras had still not moved from his submissive position on his knees. "Then what will it take to get us inside?" he asked in his guttural growl.

The man looked his way, and Kethras found himself closing his eyes again. He heard footsteps approach him and stop. "I can let him in," he said, "but I can't say the same about you, beast. I don't even know what you are."

Kethras made a disappointed sigh. "I was afraid of that."

"He's a Kienari," Thornton said loudly, "and he's with me." The hushed murmurs from the guards made Kethras wince.

"Kienari, eh?" said the man, who was walking a slow circle around him. "My grandmother told me about your kind. Described you very well, it seems." He stopped after the second circle and stood facing Kethras. "Stand up," he said calmly.

Kethras slowly did as he was told. He could still not fully open his eyes, so he looked at the ground instead. When he'd righted himself completely, the guards who were murmuring before had ceased their whispers. At least one of them had drawn another arrow.

"Settle, boys," said the man, who reached out his hand to touch Kethras's forearm. He grabbed it with one hand and raised it up, inspecting the top and bottom like a craftsman would inspect a piece of art. Kethras was much taller than him, so when he spoke the bright man's head was tilted upwards. He looked at the bow that was strapped to Kethras's back. "I suspect he's more dangerous from far away than I am from close up," he said as he let the long black arm fall back to its owner's side.

Turning back to Thornton, the man added, "Your father and his companion said that they were stopping here for the night, then moving on to Ellenos. If I were you, I'd start by checking the inns. A man who fits your father's description might not be easy to find, but one who is traveling with an Athrani should narrow it down."

"Good to know," Thornton said.

"And if you've got any coin on you, it might help to jog their memory," he added as an afterthought. Turning back to the gate he shouted, "Open it! One coming in."

Thornton stood there a moment, looking confused. "There are two of us."

"But only one of you is human," he replied. "Your friend here will have to content himself with waiting while you look for your father." He eyed Thornton's hammer, picked it up, and tossed it to him. "Fine piece of work," he grunted. "Now go inside before I change my mind."

Thornton's shoulders drooped a little. "I'm sorry, Kethras," he whispered. "I'll come back as soon as I can." With a look of determination, he turned and walked toward the gate, its great doors moaning and straining under the weight of all that metal. They opened just enough to let Thornton slip inside, then groaned their way shut again with a mighty *clank*.

The bright man has disappeared again, Kethras thought. But no sooner did those thoughts form in his head than he heard the words "As for you" and felt the tip of a knife in his back. "We're going into the tower until I figure out what to do with you."

Chapter 21

Khala Val'ur

Gift of the Shaper

Sera

Ghal Thurái lay just a day's journey to the east from Khala Val'ur, depending on the reliability of the horse. For Sera, who had no real love for horseback riding, only the quickest of breeds was acceptable. And while her own horse, Ruen, was stabled here, she knew that the aging stallion would not be swift enough for the ride. She would have to rely on the judgment of the stablemaster to provide her with the right mount for the trek.

As she ascended the deep stairway leading out of the mouth of the Sunken City, she rounded the corner to the stables situated just above the surface.

The massive wooden structure had been one of the first to be constructed when Khala Val'ur was settled. The men who built it had obviously favored function over form, using nothing more than a hammer, wood, and nails to build it and leaving no special markings or ornamentation. They built it just outside the mouth of the city with its back up against the sturdy stone walls, and it was large enough to hold over a hundred war horses.

Sera was hit with the sudden strong odor of animals as she stepped inside, where she was greeted by the stablemaster, Avero.

"Evening, Lady Edos," he smiled. A slender man with high cheekbones and long brown hair, he looked far fairer than a man of his post might be expected to look. But his outward appearance, Sera knew, was not at all a reflection of what lay beneath. Avero had a gift for breaking even the most unruly of stallions, a gift unmatched in all of Gal'dorok. There was a fire in his eyes that commanded respect, even from someone as revered as Seralith Edos. And she noticed that fire was especially intense whenever she walked in.

She brushed off the thought and nodded her greeting. "Avero," she began, "I will be traveling to Ghal Thurái and have need of a horse that will get me there quickly. The less time I spend riding, the better." Sera had taken her long brown hair and began tying it up behind her head. She glanced around the stables at the collection of horses, all ultimately placed there by Tennech, and crinkled her nose in displeasure.

"Of course," the stablemaster replied with a wry smile. He began to scan the room like a warrior choosing a weapon. "If it's speed you require, I have just the one. Wait here." He made off toward the back of the stables, past the rows of muscular war mounts bred for battle. A few of them whinnied at his passing, but for the most part, the stables were quiet. Even Sera could tell that the man commanded respect in here.

She saw him open a gate near the back of the wooden structure, almost up against the stone wall of the city, and heard it clang shut as he emerged with a tall, pale mare with a mid-night-black mane and eyes. She was perhaps fifteen hands and carried every inch of it gracefully, walking obediently alongside Avero as the two made their way to the front of the stables where Sera waited.

"Say hello to Lanfear," the stablemaster announced proudly. As if in response, Lanfear dipped her muzzle and blinked.

"Hmm," Sera scoffed indifferently—though, she would admit, the mare had a certain quality to her that she found appealing. "She certainly has the look of swiftness about her, but I'm not interested in appearances. Can she run?"

"For days," Avero replied without a trace of hyperbole.

Sera raised a finger to her own face, tracing the tail of her scar in thought. She held Lanfear's gaze for a few moments as the rest of the stable fell quiet, bearing witness to the silent battle of wills that had suddenly arisen. Lanfear had no reaction, never moving her eyes from the imposing Athrani woman, and only blinking after what seemed like an eternity.

"Fine," Sera finally said to Avero. "Get her ready to ride. I will depart when you've finished." She still had not unlocked her gaze from the horse's.

Avero made an amused grunt of acknowledgment as he guided Lanfear into the rear to be tacked. Sera watched with no trace of emotion as they walked away, though she seemed to be content with the selection. "Avero," she called as the stablemaster walked away. "Where is Ruen?"

Gift of the Shaper

The Valurian raised his hand, pointing a finger toward the back from where he had come. "He outgrew his old stall, so I moved him into a bigger one."

Turning to see where he was pointing, Sera's eyes fell on her aging brown companion, who had been with her since she was a little girl in Ellenos. She smiled and walked over to his stall where he greeted her with a whinny and a nod of his head.

"Hello again, old friend," she whispered as she stroked his mane. Ruen was the only creature in the world that had seen the soft side of Seralith Edos, and she intended to keep it that way. "Has Avero been treating you well?" She produced an apple as she spoke, which she had deftly pocketed when entering the stables.

With an excited bite, Ruen flicked his tail contentedly as Sera laughed and looked on.

She stood tall over the ground, dressed today in the simple garb of a messenger so as not to arouse any suspicion. She was known fairly well even outside the capital city, and her Athrani heritage made her stand out among most of the citizens anyway, but she preferred to take every precaution she could. There was a small chance that she could run into some Chovathi on the way, she knew; it was part of the reason that she wanted a quick horse.

With a final pat of Ruen's head, she stepped back into the open air where she could breathe again without having to cover her nose. She had no idea how Avero could stand working in there, figuring that he must have adapted to the smell or had simply learned to ignore it, but not caring enough to step inside again and ask. She closed her eyes and breathed deep the Valurian air. At her side was a knife, easily concealed beneath her long-sleeved black shirt. She patted it in confirmation just as Avero called her name from behind.

"She's ready," said the lithe stablemaster.

Sera took a second look at the horse. Now that she was clear of the discomfort of the stables, she realized Lanfear was, in fact, quite beautiful. Her silvery-pale body shone majestically as it caught the waning light of the evening, and her perfectly groomed mane hung gently off the right side of her well-muscled neck. She was also, Sera noted, rather stoic compared to other horses she'd been around. Even her own horse, Ruen, was given to the occasional hoof stomp or nostril flare. Lanfear, on the other hand, was notably mute and still. *No unnecessary actions,* Sera thought. The stablemaster had indeed chosen well.

"Good. Thank you, Avero," she said as she took the reins that he offered and put her foot in the stirrup. Before she stepped up, she looked him in the eye. "She'd better be as fast as you say."

She took her place on the back of her mount and nodded a curt thanks before knocking her heels into Lanfear's ribs, sending the two of them charging off, into the coming darkness.

At a loss for words, the horseman could only back up and watch pleadingly as they left.

The sun cast long shadows as it continued its slow descent to the edge of the world, dragging the night inexorably behind it as Sera looked east toward Ghal Thurái.

Nighttime, she knew, was the best time to travel when going east of the capital. Though the outlying cities were all very well-protected, the roads that connected them were not, and the opportunistic Chovathi loved to prey on travelers desperate enough to use them. And, though she knew she could handle herself in a fight, she would rather not take any chances when it was just her—especially not when the general was counting on her to make it back in one piece.

She listened to the rhythmic beat of Lanfear's hooves as they tore across the ground, leaving the stables behind and winding their way around the narrow passage carved between the mountains that surrounded the city. Before long, they emerged from the northern pass and out of the protection of the Hand.

By now, the sun had completed its journey into the west, and the early shadows of night took hold of the world. There was still enough remaining light, however, for Sera to see where she needed to go. After some searching, she was able to locate the path leading east to Ghal Thurái. It was an ancient road, though no one knew exactly how old it was. It had simply always been around and was one of the busier roads going out of the capital. Since it ran all the way east past Ghal Thurái and into Haidan Shar, it was known to Valurians as Khala-Shar pass. Sera simply knew it as The Pass.

But the name of the road was not remotely important to her now as she controlled the thundering pace of Lanfear. What was on her mind were the looming plans of not only General Tennech but also those of Yetz and his abrasive suckling D'kane. She was not entirely certain if they were all mutually achievable or even if they were feasible. But here was not the place to question orders, so she charged ahead at the night, hoping to avoid catching the ears of any Chovathi that might be lurking nearby.

Lanfear galloped on, showing no sign of tiring or even slowing down. *Avero was right*, Sera mused. *This horse really could run for days.*

A few times in the night, she thought she heard voices, faint and sharp, that reminded her of the sound of cracking bones. *Chovathi*, she thought. They were out there in the dark.

She had been riding all night without stopping, and the sun had just begun to crest the foothills of Gal'behem, heralding her approach into Ghal Thurái.

The Mouth of the Deep, as it was called, was in fact a massive mountain fortress carved into the sturdy rock of the Spine of the Great Serpent that rivaled even Khala Val'ur in its impenetrability. Its strength was its inaccessibility; the difficulty of navigating any of the narrow roads that led into the city-fortress was unrivaled in all of Gal'dorok. The treacherous slopes and dangerous inclines provided no easy route to the city. It was no wonder the Chovathi had chosen it as their ancestral home before they were driven out by its current residents.

While there were considerably less Khyth outside of the capital, the few that were here could trace their ancestry back to those who had helped carve it in the first place, after seeing the success their brothers had with Khala Val'ur. Because of this, they tended to think much less of the humans that inhabited the city and sequestered themselves almost entirely. The command structure was also comparatively smaller, with only one Master Khyth serving as its premier authority on matters relating to the Hand. There were no apprentices here, however; the only Khyth found in the Mouth of the Deep were those who had undergone the Breaking and been ordered to the city by Yetz. It was considered an honor to be selected to serve outside the Capital, as only the very best were ever chosen.

Sera knew that Tennech's selection of Captains Cavan Hullis and Farryn Dhrostain, sons of Ghal Thurái, was largely political in nature, as it would almost certainly guarantee the promise of troops from the city leaders. If they had one weakness, it was pride. Historically, Thurians thought of themselves as more capable than their counterparts in Khala Val'ur. The Sunken City, they reasoned, was full of apprentices and underlings. Only the best and brightest of warriors and Khyth were chosen to serve inside the great marble walls of the Mouth, and they would take any opportunity to prove it. It was only a matter of suggesting the idea that there would be a battle worthy of their prowess in order to make them interested. Like a stablemaster showing off a prized horse, the Thurians would seize any opportunity to parade around their feared Fist of Thurái—even if it meant sacrificing their lives.

Sera could already make out the distinctly linear architecture that distinguished it from the mountain itself. Everything was angular and sharp, chiseled and discrete—in contrast to the architecture of Khala Val'ur, which seemed to flow naturally with the rock instead of in opposition to it.

The closest thing to an entrance that she could remember—it had been years since she had traveled here—was a small path leading up the side of the mountain, zig-zagging its way across the face as it ascended. She would be able to make it as far as the entrance to the city before being stopped, and that was good enough for her.

She coaxed Lanfear to a halt as they approached the path, choosing finally to dismount, as she would much rather be seen walking than riding when she approached. Taking the reins of the still stoic mare, she began the climb.

The entrance to the Mouth of the Deep was extravagant: two rectangular stone pillars, smooth and perfect, guarded the entrance like silent sentries, reaching several hundred feet up and supporting a sprawling marble ceiling that had been carved hundreds of miles away in a quarry to the east. Veins of gold circled their way down the pillars in a gaudy display of opulence. Any army that tried to make its way inside would surely die impressed.

Finally reaching the top, she took a moment to marvel at the architecture of the city while she was sure no one could see her.

"Impressive," she muttered to Lanfear, who was silent as always. "Now to see if the Thurians live up to it."

Lanfear's hollow hoofbeats echoed throughout the Mouth as the two of them walked across the floor made of polished pink granite. As they got closer to the huge stone pillars that guarded the entrance, she saw two men with spears, standing watch just beyond them, attending the two great iron gates that led inside the city—wide open at this time of day. She raised her hands to show she was unarmed, and approached.

"I am Seralith Edos of Khala Val'ur, advisor to General Tennech and servant of the Breaker of the Dawn. I am here to speak with Commander Durakas."

The two men guarding the gate looked at the approaching woman, eyeing her from head to toe. Tall, with brown eyes over blue rings, she was very clearly an outsider.

"You say you're from Khala Val'ur," said the man on the right—bearded, with bad teeth and a crooked smile, "but how come you look like an Athrani?"

"Because I am," Sera answered sharply. "And my heritage is of no concern to you, guardsman. Send word to your commander that I come with a message from his general."

"His general?" echoed the second man, whose bald head and long, crooked nose made him look like a vulture. He was smaller than the other guard, and Sera was sure she could have taken them both but chose to stay her hand in favor of diplomacy. "The Fist of Ghal Thurái answers to no general," he said, as if he was personally insulted by the implication, "especially not one in league with Ellenos."

Sera's calm demeanor did well to hide the storm that was forming inside of her. She pictured herself grabbing her dagger and slitting their throats before they had time to scream but pushed the thoughts back again and took a breath. "Please," she said in the same gentle tone she used with Ruen, "I have traveled far and long and wish nothing more than to deliver a message. Surely, one Athrani woman is of no threat to Thurians such as you."

The two guards puffed out their chests at the implication of their superiority and, exchanging glances, seemed to come to a silent agreement.

"That's all well and good," said the taller guard, "but the commander isn't in the city."

"He isn't?" Sera seemed taken aback. "Then where is he?"

With a nod of his head, the guard compelled Sera to turn around just in time to witness a small raiding party in the distance, no more than ten men, with one man at the helm. "On his way back," he answered.

Sera's discontent showed on her face as she realized the commander must have timed it perfectly. He was expecting her and would want to remind her of his military prowess, of his strength, in typical Thurian fashion.

"Well, isn't that convenient?" she muttered loudly enough for both guards to hear. "I will wait, then."

"You'd do well to watch your tone. That's the Commander of the Fist you're speaking about," the bald guard warned.

Sera silently heeded the advice and watched as the raiding party drew closer. There was a wagon behind them filled with the corpses of their conquest: Chovathi bodies to burn, a reminder as to who ruled the halls of Ghal Thurái. And as they scaled the mountain path leading up to the Mouth, Sera had to admit that she could see why the man in the lead was made Commander.

Tall and sturdy, Caladan Durakas was Thurian through and through, wearing on his face the toughness and pride that was bred into each one of them at home under the mountain. His jaw was chiseled and rough, like the rocks he lived beneath, and his graying brown hair matched the hue of his thick eyebrows and beard. He rode with an air of confidence that bled over into superiority. As the party approached, the two guards saluted.

Gift of the Shaper

"What do we have here?" Durakas asked as he left his mount.

Sera moved to introduce herself before the guards had a chance to weigh in. "Seralith Edos, advisor to General Aldis Tennech. I come with a request from Khala Val'ur."

Durakas rubbed his chin. "And he sends a woman to deliver it? Were all the other messengers busy?" He threw back his head in laughter, and the rest of his men joined in.

Sera took it in stride. "The general trusts me with his closest secrets," she said.

"Does he now? Interesting." He raised his eyebrows at her. "Fine, then. What does the Dagger of Derenar ask of me?"

"He requests the aid of the Fist," she began. "He has asked for two captains by name."

"And they are?" Durakas asked impatiently.

"Captains Hullis and Dhrostain."

The commander laughed when he heard the names, causing Sera's eyes to darken. "I'm afraid I am not well-versed in Thurian humor," she said. "Would you enlighten me?"

Durakas eyed her up and down, taking his time, with a pleased grin on his face while he did so. "It just so happens," he said, "that those are my two best men." Turning his head and calling over his shoulder, he yelled, "Hullis! Dhrostain! Come here!"

From the rear of the raiding party walked two men very different in appearance yet dressed uniformly in the white armor of Ghal Thurái.

The first of the two, Cavan Hullis, was a slender, young man who was as handsome as he was clever. His gift for strategy, Sera had heard, rivaled even the general's. He had straight blond hair that hung just below his chin and a gait that spoke of confidence and maturity.

Behind him walked Farryn Dhrostain: strong of will, with a temper to match. His hair was completely shaved off, leaving his head smooth, the aspect complimented by his thick jet-black eyebrows and a beard that hung from his chin, the product of a half year's growth. Known more for his complete lack of mercy than for his military prowess, Tennech had said that Dhrostain would be the perfect complement to Captain Hullis, whom he sometimes viewed as soft. His short stature was also noticeable—he only came up to Hullis's chest—and was often cited as the source of his cruelty—but never, ever to his face. The last person to have voiced that opinion was shoved off his seat in a tavern and beaten to death with the legs of the stool.

"This Athrani," Durakas said, emphasizing the word as if it were a curse, "tells me that you are to report to Khala Val'ur."

The two captains exchanged confused glances, finally looking to Sera for an answer.

"Says who?" Dhrostain asked.

"General Tennech," Sera snapped. "Perhaps you've heard of him."

The back of Durakas's strong hand found her mouth quickly, tossing her head back and sending a small spatter of blood onto the marble floor below. "While you are in Ghal Thurái," he growled, "you will show my captains the proper respect. And though I'm sure your tongue has served the general well on many occasions, it is not welcome here." He glowered at her, poised to administer another blow.

Sera choked down her pride and bowed her head. *He's baiting me*, she realized. *Or he's just an asshole.* "Of course, Commander. My apologies." She could hear the guards snickering behind her. "If you have no further questions for me, I will ride back with the captains when they are ready."

The commander was staring at the crown of her bowed head, ready to boil over. Without a word, he shoved past her, waving his hand dismissively as he disappeared into the Mouth.

***

The well-worn and ancient road to Khala Val'ur felt much longer on the way back than Sera remembered. She listened to the rhythmic breathing of the two men from Ghal Thurái as they slept, having agreed that she would take the first watch. She felt comfortable enough with two experienced warriors such as them to rest for the night, knowing that if anyone came upon their encampment, the two men would not hesitate for even a moment before hacking their way through them and on to safety.

Cavan Hullis, the less imposing of the two, slept with his sword at his side, sheathed in a long black scabbard to protect it from the elements. Farryn Dhrostain, whose ferocity far outweighed that of the younger captain, slept sword in hand.

With a small fire going—more for her own mental comfort than for convenience—Sera let out the braid in her long brown hair and took a seat on the ground a fair distance away from the two men. She ran her fingers through her hair, untangling it and straightening it as best she could, and started to relax. The horses made no sound as they rested, and the silence around her reminded her of the deep darkness of Khala Val'ur.

Before she could lose herself any more in the fleeting thought, she heard a noise that caused her hand to fly instinctively to her dagger. From the edge of her vision came a flash of movement as something pale and white crept into sight near the sleeping captains, making not so much as a sound as it did so. She waited and watched and tried to figure out exactly what it was she was seeing, as her mind raced, trying to place it. A hunched and lumbering form, vaguely human but smaller, it approaching the fire walking on all fours, contorted like it was doing so out of choice rather than by design. Not far behind it was a second creature, just as pale, standing fully upright.

In truth, they looked more frightening than threatening. They were thin and colorless, the results of living for generations in caves and dark recesses away from the light of the sun, adapting their bodies to thrive in darkness and hunger. The one in front was bent over, inches from Dhrostain, as its nimble fingers picked their way through his pack, searching for a piece of food that it had no doubt smelled. Sera watched as it found what it was looking for, quietly pulling out some half-eaten squirrel meat that the Thurian had saved for later. With a flicker of a snake-like tongue through jagged teeth, the creature slipped the morsel into its mouth, crunching on it with satisfaction and tilting its head to the second one, making a guttural and awful noise that passed for communication.

D.L. Jennings

Just as it did so, Sera saw Dhrostain's eyes fly open and flash with fury as he flexed his fingers around the hilt of his still-readied sword. With a violent thrust at the creature, he was on his feet and yelling—more for intimidation than from alarm. The pale skin of the creature split like paper as his blade slid in easily, just below its shoulder, eliciting a screech that was high-pitched and sharp, like the cry of a blood bat. Clawing desperately at the sword, the fearsome-looking thing was reduced to helplessness as the screeching continued, much to the dismay of Dhrostain. Sera saw Hullis grab his sword and yell, "Kill it!" as he leapt to his feet, and the second creature, still free, hurtled toward him with an ear-piercing cry.

Dhrostain gave a look of contempt as he pulled his sword back and chopped haphazardly at the creature, yelling, "What do you think I'm trying to do?" As his sword connected, the creature's arm separated from its body where Dhrostain had first stabbed it, and Hullis uttered a quick series of curses when he saw it fall.

The writhing arm flopped around on the ground like a fish out of water, jerking spasmodically and seeming, to Sera's eyes, to be growing. The hand took hold of the ground in front of it, sinking its three fingers and thumb into the earth, and braced itself. All the while, the screeching continued from the injured creature before them.

"What's the matter with you?" Hullis barked as he sidestepped the creature running toward him. Stepping gracefully and with hardly a show of effort, he swung in a swift, deliberate arc with his sword, connecting with the creature's neck and cleaving its head clean from its body, leaving Dhrostain looking angrier than ever—he hated it when other people corrected his mistakes. "The head, Farryn. The head of the Chovathi goes first." With a swift kick of his boot, Hullis sent the decapitated body slumping to the ground.

The trembling arm that Dhrostain had severed had already begun reconstructing itself, fleshing out a pale torso and neck, with a second arm on the way. Bones appeared seemingly out of nothing, forming the road map for the quickly creeping flesh and muscles that would envelop them and house the new body. The one by Dhrostain, freed when its arm had been severed, had already grown a new appendage.

Gift of the Shaper

Sera was caught in a trance as she watched the newly forming body of the Chovathi finally start to reform a head, still lying on the ground where only an arm had lain just moments before. *It's no wonder that Thurian mothers tell stories of Chovathi to frighten their children*, she thought as the hairs on her neck stood up.

"Sera," Hullis yelled, snapping her back to reality, "any time you want to step in." His words had no effect, though, as her thoughts were not on killing the Chovathi—she was much more interested in what else they could do. Shaking his head, Hullis trudged over to the body of the newly formed Chovathi and pressed his boot on its head, causing cries from both of the remaining creatures. "Can you handle doing it right this time?" he asked, staring right at Dhrostain. A violent downward stab of his sword relieved the creature of breath.

The short, bearded man grunted angrily as he twirled his sword in his hand, trying to regain some sense of pride after having it chipped away by Hullis. "Enough out of you," he said as he squared off with the creature. Its eyes were cloudy and gray, looking almost useless in comparison to its huge nasal cavities, which were great symmetrical holes in the front of its head. Baring its teeth, it revealed jaws and teeth that were made for nothing more than ripping through flesh.

"I don't want to be dealing with a fourth," the blond captain said sternly as he sheathed his sword.

"It's good training," Dhrostain said with a heave as he lowered his shoulder and lunged at the Chovathi. Barreling into the creature, he sent it toppling to the ground with a cry as it slashed the air, trying desperately to grab onto something. "No, no," he said as he dodged the sharp claws that tipped the creature's fingers, pinning its arms to the dirt with his knees. With a smile of bloodthirsty satisfaction, he plunged a dagger into its throat and raked it across, showing no mercy.

The small gray eyes widened in hopelessness as the Chovathi lost focus and strength, letting its arms go still.

"You could certainly use more of that," Hullis mused as he turned to face the fire, judging whether he would be able to get more sleep. With a nod, he sat back down on the ground and turned around to look at Sera.

The tall Athrani was still caught up in her own world, eyeing the Chovathi that had spawned from nothing more than a severed arm.

"I was tired," Dhrostain offered in his own defense. "Wasn't thinking clearly." Wiping clean the dagger he had used to deliver the killing blow, he tucked it away beneath his shirt, where it slipped out of sight. "It won't happen again."

"See that it doesn't," Hullis said as he lay back down to try to catch a bit of rest before it was time to take the watch. Grudgingly, he shut his eyes and folded his hands over his chest.

Sera walked over to the Chovathi that had its arm torn off, approaching it as if she thought it might leap up at her at any moment.

"The Chovathi reproduction system," Dhrostain said from behind her, startling her, "is frighteningly effective. It uses little more than brute force to reach its ends. As long as something other than the head is torn from the body, nature takes care of the rest."

Sera's brown-on-blue eyes shifted their focus as they examined the body. There was no scar where the arm had been torn off. "You're saying they don't mate?"

Dhrostain grunted out a laugh and walked to his own spot by the fire. "Chovathi show their affection for one another by ripping each other limb from limb," he said as he rolled over to try to get some rest of his own. "Hell of a way to start a relationship."

Sera's eyes moved from the creature and back to the fire, whose naked, dancing flames moved like the pyre that burned in the center of the Sunken City.

Just a few more hours, she told herself, and she would be home again.

Not a moment too soon.

Chapter 22

Annoch

Gift of the Shaper

Thornton

The city was dark when Thornton heard the great gates close behind him, churning and rumbling like metallic thunder. They were much heavier than they looked, and he winced from the resounding *boom* that sounded when they shut.

Although it was nighttime, Annoch was far from asleep.

Thornton looked around to see a city that was large and loud, full of comings and goings, with tall buildings and bright lamplights that made Lusk look like a dull peasant's tale. He turned his head from side to side as he tried to comprehend where all these people could be headed at this time of night, wandering about in the dark. Farmers with full carts, fresh from the countryside, vying for a spot to sell their goods; noblemen on regal steeds who trotted by, oblivious to the problems of the less fortunate; men wearing capes of scarlet, the same color that the guards had on outside, patrolling the streets undeterred. It was like he was watching the city come alive all around him, calling out like it knew him by name.

He hardly even knew where to begin. Though, he reasoned, the path at his feet led somewhere, and he might as well find out where. He started along, taking in the sights of the thrumming metropolis around him.

The outsides of houses and inns held torches that lit the path, flooding the streets with shadows and keeping the night at bay. He walked, hearing his feet hit the stone of the paved street below him, and followed the road that took him closer to wherever it was that it led. Searching for a place that might have an ear or two to hear him, his eyes were drawn to an impressive multi-story building just ahead of him, with the words *The Driving Steed* carved on its face. He could see a few horses tied up outside and, remembering the words of the guard by the gate, thought it as good a place as any to try his luck. He tightened the collar of his shirt around him and walked closer.

The double doors that formed the entrance were simple and wooden, and Thornton opened them easily to reveal a warm entrance room filled with chatter and the smell of ale. The fire in the back of the sizable room was being tended by a young girl who stoked it and piled on a few more logs. He watched her for a few moments as she hurried back and forth, checking each of the lamps that hung on the wall and filling them with oil, then disappearing into a side door.

Round oaken tables were placed throughout the hall, a room bigger than any he had ever seen in Lusk; and ceramic mugs pounded loudly onto wood as fits of laughter seemed to come from all over, feeding into the fiery roar of conversation. Annoch could get cold at night, so the fire made the room comfortably warm, and the smoke that crawled up the brick chimney reminded him of home. He sat down at one of the stools and scanned the faces of the people in the room, taking them in as he marveled at the commotion.

Finally, his eyes settled on the man standing behind the long wooden bar.

"Welcome to the Driving Steed, lad," said the barkeep. "If it's ale you want, you've come to the right place." He had snow-white hair that came down to his ears, and his eyebrows were wild, with traces of blond, looking like two caterpillars had taken up home on his forehead. His nose was bulbous and red, and he rubbed it with his finger as he looked at Thornton. "The name's Wern. Shouting it will get you a drink as long as you follow it with some coin." He nodded to the girl who earlier had been tending to the fire. "Or Alysana can fetch you a bowl of stew if you're hungry."

Thornton didn't realize that was what he was until he felt his stomach growling before Wern finished the word *hungry*. He nodded and reached into his pocket for some coins.

"I'll just have the stew," Thornton replied, tapping a piece of silver on the bar.

With a nod, Wern turned away, and Thornton thought of the last time he'd had a drink with his father. It had come after a long day of working the forge, when Olson had been paid in trade for a job well done. He'd insisted on that form of payment, Thornton recalled.

A light touch on his shoulder surprised him, just as the smell of meat filled his nostrils.

"The stew is fine," came the voice of a woman, "but steer clear of the potatoes."

Gift of the Shaper

Turning around, Thornton was startled to see that the voice belonged to a woman who was no older than he was. She had raven-black hair braided into pigtails that fell gently over her dark skin and an apron that was covered extensively with food and drink, the casualties of the day. If she was tired or frustrated from all the running around, her face did not reflect it. She smiled as she handed Thornton his prize.

"Thanks," he managed to say. He wasn't sure how long he sat there staring at her, but hearing Wern clear his throat loudly behind him made him grab the stew from her and whirl around in his seat in embarrassment. He hunched over the bowl and dug in, hoping his cheeks didn't look as red as they felt.

"Where are ya from?" asked Wern, staving off the discomfort and waving the girl away.

"Highglade, just outside Lusk," Thornton grunted with a mouth full of stew, still hot from the fire.

"That's a decent ways away," Wern replied, obviously impressed with the pace at which Thornton was devouring his stew. "Looks like you worked up quite an appetite along the way."

Thornton made a sound that could have been laughter or simply an attempt to further cool off the meat. Either way, when he placed the empty bowl back onto the bar, the man with the snow-white hair was staring at him like he couldn't make heads or tails of it.

"You want another bowl, lad?" he asked with aplomb.

Thornton wiped his mouth and gave a nod.

"Figured as much," Wern said as he raised his hand, motioning with his pointer finger for the girl with the black hair, who saw it right away and took a quick turn into the kitchen.

She was in and out in a flash with a second bowl of stew loaded up on her tray, wasting no time as she hastened to the bar and placed it in front of Thornton with a sidelong glance. "Maybe give this one some time to cool off?"

An embarrassed laugh from Thornton revealed the dimple in his right cheek that only came out when he smiled. "No promises," he said, guiding a healthy spoonful into his mouth.

A smirk seemed to be all she had time for as she shook her head and turned her attention to a pair of impatient old men in the far corner of the bar. "I'm coming," she shouted at them, with a hint of good nature. "You're not the only ones here!"

Thornton savored the food this time as a tumult of thoughts gave way to the dull roar of the room around him. The splashing torrent of noise came out sounding more like a river than a conversation, and it occurred to him then that he missed the sounds of people. *Coming to Annoch might not have been such a bad thing,* he thought.

He let his mind wander, reflecting on his journey so far—on Ynara and Kethras, learning how to track and how to catch and skin an animal, and spending the night under the stars with Miera. In his mental meanderings, he almost opened the door to the dark recesses of his mind, the parts which held the memories of what he had to do to defend himself, but he buried it beneath his drive to find his father.

His father . . .

The thought made his shoulders sag. He suddenly realized that he wasn't sure when he would see him again. Putting down his spoon, he looked up at the barkeep.

"Wern," he said, "I'm looking for someone." He dabbed at his face with a napkin to clean up the gravy that had somehow found more of the outside of his mouth than the inside.

"Half the people in the world are looking for someone, lad," the old man said with a grunt as he wiped down a mug. "The other half are the ones bein' looked for." He laughed at his own joke. "So who're ya chasin'?"

"My father," he said. "His name is Olson, Olson Woods. He's a big man, taller than me, with brown hair and a beard to match." Seeing no signs of recollection in Wern's eyes, he added, "He would be traveling alongside an Athrani. The guard outside mentioned that a pair like that might stand out."

Gift of the Shaper

Wern nodded and placed the mug down underneath the bar. "That is certainly the case," he replied, spreading his arms across the front of the bar, "though I haven't seen anyone come through here that fits your description." After some thought, he added, "But, if he is traveling with an Athrani, I can tell you the first place I would look."

"I'm listening," Thornton said.

"The Anvil of the Worldforge," Wern said as he reached to pick up another mug.

Thornton placed another coin on the table, deciding after all that his mouth was too dry for his liking.

"Fill up that mug with some ale," he said with a point of his finger, "and tell me what I need to know about the Anvil."

Wern laughed softly as he finished cleaning off the mug. "There's not much to tell," he said, placing it on the bar for the young brown-haired man in front of him. "It's in the heart of the city, for one, and it's one of the holiest sites for the Athrani—outside of Ellenos, of course. I've been around enough of their kind to know that. And after what happened, any o' them within a few days' walk are going to be coming here to see it."

"Why?" Thornton asked.

Wern gave him a look of surprise that was directed more at Thornton than at his question. "Why?" Wern echoed incredulously.

Thornton had a helpless expression on his face as Wern gave him the same look as when he'd wolfed down the first bowl of stew.

"Maybe you're better off learning about it from one of the Athrani there."

Suddenly appearing behind the bar with a handful of clean plates was Alysana. Placing them underneath the bar with the rest of the dishes, she looked up with a guilty look on her face "I didn't mean to eavesdrop," she said softly, "but I heard you say you're heading to the Anvil."

Thornton almost choked on his stew as he nodded. "That's right," he coughed.

"I live out that way. I could take you if you don't mind waiting for me to finish up here."

Thornton looked to Wern as if asking for permission, and the white-haired barkeep rolled his eyes and sighed. "Finish your stew and go, lad," he said. "You'd better get started while the night is still young. Any later and you might never find him."

Thornton stood up and gave a polite nod to the barkeep. He placed a third piece of silver on the table. "For the meal and the ale, Wern. And the conversation."

"All in a day's work," the barkeep said as he stiffened a bit. "Now get going."

Nodding, the young blacksmith followed Alysana out the door and into the streets.

Chapter 23

Annoch

Gift of the Shaper

Kethras

Kethras hated the touch of steel on his neck. It made him remember why he avoided humans.

He was being led up a narrow wooden staircase that climbed about halfway up the gates and connected with a single wooden room built into the wall.

The wall itself was impressive, he had to admit. It had huge cross-sections of gray stone inlaid with some sort of dark metal, though he wasn't sure what kind. Annoch was the only human city he could remember seeing that had a wall like this.

He slowly climbed the stairs in front of his captor, until they reached the top. When they did, the man reached for the wooden door and gave it three quick knocks. "It's Captain Yhun," he shouted gruffly.

Kethras was hesitant when a door opened inward just above the top of the stairs. He climbed in, though, knowing that his best bet was to show little or no resistance. Inside, he was greeted by a tough-looking man behind the door. He could see a few others seated around a table, playing dice, two watching through a window that faced the forest and one woman in the back seated by herself using a sharpening stone on a dagger. Everyone was wearing armor—scarlet breastplates and plain gray platemail pants. The commotion he had heard before he entered had stopped, and they were all looking up at him. He stepped into the room, with his captor following immediately after.

Everyone left their seat, but Captain Yhun waved them down.

"As you were," he said, and they all took their seats. Their silence, however, continued. "I'm just bringing him in here because I didn't trust him outside."

"What . . . what is it?" said one of the men playing dice.

"A Kienari," said Yhun, still standing behind Kethras, just inside the door. A few men laughed nervously. "At least, that's what his friend claims."

"Then his friend was right," said the woman in the back. She put down the stone she was using to sharpen her dagger and stood up. Tall and slender, the woman reminded Kethras of Ynara. Despite her heavy boots and armor, her feet fell gently upon the wooden floor as she moved.

"Is that so, Mordha?" the Captain of the Guard asked skeptically. "What makes you so sure?"

"I saw one—once. When I was a little girl."

Kethras looked at her and was surprised at how tall she was for a human. Though he still towered over her, she did not seem as diminutive as most females appeared to him. She had dark eyes and matching hair that tumbled down past her shoulders, braided in the front to keep it out of her face. Her skin looked naturally dark as well, and her accent put her place of birth somewhere far to the south.

"Where?" Jinda retorted. "How?"

"It was outside Lusk, on the way to Ellenos to see the Athrani High Keeper. My sister was dying," she said quietly, "and no one else had any hope of saving her. Yet even in G'hen, tales of the Athrani healers reach our ears."

Kethras watched as the woman circled him, as if she were seeing an old memory.

"My father could not afford to leave our farm but steadfastly refused to let my sister and me go by ourselves. Our only hope was to go with a man that my father hired, Ghaja Rus, who was to take us to Annoch where we would look for an Athrani escort into the city." She looked at the floor. "But Rus had other plans. When we neared the city of Lusk, he told us he was meeting someone there and made us wait." She paused and took a breath. "So we waited, my sister and I, in a strange city surrounded by strange languages and people, as a strange man promised our safety. But we would not wait long, as two other men returned with Rus and gave him a pouch filled with coins. He told us we had a new family now, and these men would be taking us there. Confused and scared, my sister and I went with them."

Mordha walked over to the window to look out among the trees. She continued, "What Ghaja Rus did not tell us, though, was that these men who had just paid for us intended to do much worse than simply take us to a new family." She looked again at the floor. "I wish I could say that slavery was the worst of it, but the first night after we left Lusk, we learned that there was still evil in this world."

She turned to look again at him. "I don't know whether the Kienari heard our screams or if it was our crying that drew him near, but that question has never mattered to me. What matters—what has always mattered—is, when I thought I would never be safe again, when I screamed for my life night after night, the Kienari came."

Jinda Yhun was stone-faced as he looked at Mordha. Most of the other men would not make eye contact with her.

The only sound came when she stepped back to the table where she was sharpening her dagger. She picked it up by the hilt, held it up, and said, "I found this buried in the neck of one of the men the next morning." She held it aloft like a prize. The handle of the blade was simple hardwood bound in dark-brown leather, with a cross guard and pommel of solid steel. The blade was symmetrical and looked to be useful for slitting throats or skinning animals. *No surprise,* Kethras thought—it was of Kienari make.

"When the second man awoke to the sounds of his friend dying, he charged," she said. "I've never seen anything move so fast." Her eyes were distant now, and her grip on the dagger tightened. "It was like a flash of black lightning; the Kienari was on him in seconds." She looked at Captain Yhun. "The man was dead before he hit the ground."

One of the soldiers playing dice shifted nervously; a second reached down for his dagger to make sure it was still there. Yhun ran a hand through his red hair and took a step backward.

One of the soldiers near the window shakily produced his own dagger. "Should we have tied him up?" he asked.

Mordha's hand trembled as she loosened her grip on the blade and looked at the Kienari before her. "I was so scared that day. Until then, death and cruelty had been strangers to me, yet suddenly they appeared before me in the flesh." Her voice trembled with emotion. "Never before had I felt such relief and such terror at the same time. I thought the creature wanted nothing more than to slit my throat and the throat of my sister, as it had just done to our captors."

She closed her eyes in sorrow and turned her face to the ceiling. "It was a death I welcomed. I'd had enough of begging for my life."

Kethras stirred. He could stay silent no longer. "Humans are such fragile creatures. I will never understand how you can be so cold and uncaring to your own kind."

The guard who had drawn his dagger dropped it to the ground in shock. It clanked as it hit the ground, and for a moment it was the only sound in the room. Even Mordha looked surprised at the sounds coming from the Kienari, whose speech was rough and sharp, like the sawing of a tree.

Kethras moved his eyes slowly around the room. He stopped himself when he realized he was again calculating exactly how to kill everyone in it, then did something that surprised everyone, even more than witnessing a Kienari speak.

He sat down, crossed his arms and legs, and waited.

The silence went on for a few moments as the rest of the guards wrapped their heads around what had just transpired.

Jinda looked at Kethras through narrowed eyes and finally spoke. "Mordha has been my second-in-command for years now. I met her the day that she dragged her sister, dying, to our gates. And I've never once heard this story of the Kienari." He took a seat, facing away from Kethras. "Mordha, what say you of this one's fate?"

She did not hesitate. "I am alive and free thanks to the Kienari. I only ask for a chance to return the favor."

Jinda frowned and looked again at Kethras. "The Shaper smiles on you today, beast. You may go where you please."

Kethras flashed a toothy grin that looked more threatening than friendly. "My thanks, Captain. But my friend is already on his way inside the city, and my tracking skills are useless in a forest made of people. If it would be all the same to you, I would like to pass the time by talking to Mordha."

Gift of the Shaper

The captain exchanged a surprised glance with his second-in-command, shook his head, and left.

Chapter 24

Khala Val'ur

Gift of the Shaper

Tennech

The quarters of General Tennech were not as impressive as those of the High Khyth, but they were impressive nonetheless. Situated close to the heart of Khala Val'ur, they were just a quick walk away, over the rocky black streets of the city.

With the overall architecture of the city focused around the great spire, the city was laid out in concentric circles around it. The more important you were, the closer to the center you lived; General Tennech lived in the very first of those concentric circles, just to the north of the chambers of the High Khyth.

He had been somewhat young when he was first appointed a general, but it came as a surprise to no one when he was. Despite his lackluster performance at the rigorous Valurian Military Academy, he had turned out to be quite the officer. His leadership skills seemed almost preternatural, and his strategic ability had earned him recognition from those in positions of power. In a perversion of the government of the Athrani, which was run by a High Keeper chosen by the people, the Khyth had adopted a system that put the most powerful Breaker in charge. To them, rule was won by might. Therefore, the General of the Armies of Gal'dorok answered only to the High Khyth, who ruled without question or challenger.

Tennech was a man who knew the value of loyalty and ambition, and he surrounded himself with both. As he approached his own quarters, he admired the bronze work that decorated his door. The hinges and the handle were both well-polished and laid upon a large wooden door that was stained black to match the stone below it. He opened it to reveal a large interior lit with candles and smelling faintly of incense. The floors were made of wood, which had always bothered him, as he had no hand in the original construction. It was the house of the presiding General of the Armies of Gal'dorok and had been so since the Shaping War. Tennech had always believed that the floors, like the floors of the chambers of the High Khyth, should be solid like the rock of the city beneath them. He had no tolerance for warmth, and his demeanor continuously proved that.

D.L. Jennings

Removing the thin leather gloves below his armored gauntlets, Tennech placed them on a round wooden table just inside the entrance. Like all the houses in Khala Val'ur, his house had a fireplace toward the back. There was also a dinner room; a large and open foyer; a space for entertaining; and a private study toward the rear, to the right of the fireplace. A large and perhaps overly gaudy staircase lined with silver led to the second floor, which contained little more than the general's bedroom and the bedroom of his aide, Seralith Edos. The ceilings were high and supported by two marble columns in the middle of the foyer.

Tennech made his way back toward the study—a library full of scrolls and books on military strategy, with a desk in the middle carved from a single piece of oak and stained a rich, deep brown. Its shape was that of a crescent moon, and it was littered with papers and half- and fully melted candles, a testament to the long nights that the general spent poring over his work. He sat down on a matching oak chair and lit two candles, then searched his desk for the ledger he kept of his troops. Beneath a few loose-leaf papers was a thin, leather-bound book of a few dozen pages. It listed the names, locations, and service records of every man under him. He pulled it out and started to thumb through it.

After a few moments of idle thought, a knock came on the door to the study, followed by Sera's voice announcing her arrival with the two captains. "Captains Hullis and Dhrostain, as requested."

"Come in," Tennech replied, not looking away from the ledger.

Following Seralith out of the foyer were the captains, both garbed in simple black tunics and pants, who centered themselves in front of the general's desk and took a knee.

Tennech finally took his eyes off the ledger and looked at the men before him. Both of them had their heads bowed in respect.

"Rise, Captains," he said from his chair. They did as they were commanded and met the general's eyes. "The High Khyth has requested a small group of riders to go west, as far as Annoch. I would like to see you at the helm, representing the very best of Gal'dorok's armies."

The two captains glanced at each other, then looked back at the general. Hullis was the first to speak, nodding his head in a slight bow.

Gift of the Shaper

"You honor us, General. But . . ." he hesitated, "why call us here? Why not pick a Valurian captain?"

Tennech nodded in acknowledgement but said nothing. He looked over the faces of the two men as he rubbed his chin with his fingers as if considering whether or not to speak his mind. He took a breath and said, "I've chosen you both for good reason, and while neither of you is yet worthy of the title of Commander, I believe you will have the opportunity to display your potential." Both captains looked puzzled but did not interrupt as the general grasped one end of his mustache between his finger and thumb, rubbing it pensively. His eyes traced carefully around the room as the silence continued to thicken like fog.

At last his gaze fell again upon the captains as he looked them each in the eye in turn before speaking. This time his voice was low, as if he feared being overheard. "Dhrostain, you will ride with the Khyth to Annoch and will keep thorough logs of everything that happens—day and night, significant and trivial—and you will share them with no one until you return. And when you do so, you will bring them straight to me. No matter what happens, bring them to me."

Dhrostain nodded his understanding, albeit hesitantly.

The general continued, "You will be accompanied by at least two others of High Khyth Yetz's choosing."

Dhrostain flinched at this last revelation.

"As for the reason I called both of you here," the general continued, "what I am about to tell you must be guarded closely and surely, even with your very lives."

The eyes of the two captains were on him, unblinking.

"There is a power struggle beneath the skies of Khala Val'ur, and even the Breaker cannot see how it will play out."

Hullis blinked, trying to digest what he had just heard. "Then, General, what will our roles be in this?"

"I need you to lead, Captain."

"I'm not sure I quite understand, General. What must I do?"

"When the time comes, you will know what is expected of you."

Hullis took a deep breath and blinked again. "Then we will make preparations at once."

The general nodded. "Seralith will see you out," he said as he gestured to his advisor, who had slipped in silently while they spoke. The two of them turned to leave, but Tennech held his hand out. "Captain Dhrostain," he said, "a moment."

The older of the two captains had his hands clasped behind his back as he waited to be dismissed by the general, who had pushed his chair back to stand up. He walked to the rear of the study and plucked a book from one of the shelves that was carved into the wall.

"Do you know what this book is?" Tennech asked. The one he held was thick and bound in light-brown leather. Its spine had three raised bands, spaced equally apart, with two endbands on either side. The cover consisted of four square corner pieces made of dark metal and a centerpiece in the shape of a hammer crossed over an anvil.

"I'm afraid I don't, General," Dhrostain answered evenly.

"This is a very rare book—only one of a few copies known to exist." Tennech unhooked the clasp as he opened the pages gently. The spine creaked like a voice that had not spoken in years. "This, Captain, is the recorded history of the Shaping War. It tells of how the two sects of Shapers came to see the differences in their abilities and of the humans who were caught up in the middle." He placed the book down on his desk, carefully turning the pages to the beginning. "Did you know that both the Athrani and the Khyth were once human?" he asked, with a sidelong glance to Dhrostain.

Dhrostain frowned and replied, "I did not."

"That is perhaps the most interesting part in here. It is a heritage that both are hasty to dismiss, thinking of themselves as superior to their human ancestors because we lack the ability to Shape or Break. They see us as nothing more than pawns to be manipulated in their struggle."

He turned a few pages, eyeing them silently, as Dhrostain mulled over this newfound information. Finally, he looked up at the bearded man and asked quite sincerely, "Do you see yourself as a pawn, Captain?"

Gift of the Shaper

Dhrostain's eyebrows came to a point as he frowned again and shook his head in disagreement.

"Then I have indeed chosen the best man for the job," the general said as he slowly flipped through the book, glancing at faded pictures and some script too arcane to make out. "Seralith!" he called suddenly, jostling the captain.

Within a moment, Lady Edos was in the study again, awaiting her orders.

"Please escort Captain Dhrostain to the chamber of the High Khyth, with instructions to wait for the rest of his riding party to be assembled. I have a few loose ends that need tying, so I grant you leave." The general did not so much as look up from the book he was poring over, waving his hand dismissively.

Seralith understood and motioned Dhrostain to follow her.

When he heard the outer door shut, Tennech shut the book he was looking at and listened. Hearing nothing, he said, "They are gone, Rus."

From behind the great bookshelf, seemingly from the shadows, snaked a bare-chested man with dark skin and a scraggly black beard. Overweight but well-muscled, he had short hair that was thin on the sides and bald on the top, and his fine clothes and two gold teeth showed his wealth. "So they are, General," he said. His deep voice was thick with a G'henni accent.

"Now, what is it that you could not wait to tell me?"

Ghaja Rus walked with surprising grace for a man of his shape and size. Though the vast majority of his wealth was amassed through unscrupulous means, he knew how to carry himself. Approaching the general, he produced a small book that fit easily in the pocket of his blue silk pants and flipped through it. He licked two fingers to help it along, which made Tennech crinkle his nose in disgust.

"We've gotten a new shipment in from Derenar," Rus said. "Two from Lusk, one from G'hen, one from Annoch." He looked up from his notes to see if any of this was having an effect on the general. It was not.

"Is that all?" Tennech asked, grasping the end of his mustache and rolling it between his fingers.

"No, General. I've brought you something else, as well—from Ellenos."

Tennech looked up and locked eyes with the dark-skinned man who did not hide his smile.

"Ellenos? Are they . . ."

"Athrani?" Rus offered. "They are."

There was a long silence as Tennech ran his fingers through his jet-black hair and rubbed his eyes. "And why have you done that?"

"I would much rather show you than tell you," Rus said coldly. "I've already arranged the meeting place, a gorge outside of Lash'Kargá."

"Lash'Kargá," the general repeated, his voice unwavering. "You were always one with a flair for the dramatic." The general's eyes met those of the dark-skinned man with the golden teeth, showing off his direful smile.

"That I am," Rus replied. "And I assure you, you will not be disappointed. I've seen the results of Master Khyth D'kane's work some time ago. He has managed to keep it hidden from Yetz, but not from me."

Tennech nodded curtly. "Good work," he said, breaking his gaze to look at the fingernails on his left hand. "Your intelligence may prove more useful than I thought."

Ghaja Rus licked his lips. "In my line of work, usefulness is weighed in gold."

Tennech frowned and appeared to be admiring his bookshelf. "We shall see." He paced slowly around the room, allowing Rus to soak in the silence. Finally, he spoke. "When will we meet?"

"Tomorrow, General," Rus answered, "at dusk."

"So be it. I will meet with you then and judge for myself."

Ghaja Rus smiled a crooked smile and punctuated it with a deep bow. He slipped through the doors and out of the general's office, slinking onto the streets of Khala Val'ur and up toward the mouth of the Sunken City.

Chapter 25

Khala Val'ur

Gift of the Shaper

Dhrostain

"This way, Captain," Sera said as she led the Thurian captain through the foyer and back to the front door. Before they crossed the threshold, she stopped him. Turning to face him, she bent down and wrapped her palm around the back of his neck to draw him in, so that their foreheads were almost touching—an interesting sight, given that Dhrostain barely came up to her mid-chest. Her brown hair was pulled back, leaving her terrible scar fully visible.

"I'll tell you what I told the blond one, Captain: whatever you were told in there does not leave your lips." She spoke in a whisper, but her teeth were clenched so tightly that it sounded more like a hiss. "Only two other people know what the general knows, you and Captain Hullis. So if it ever comes to light that somehow a third person knows . . . the three of you will be added to the fire that lights the city. Depending on how generous Tennech is feeling, he may have you killed first. There are always Khyth apprentices looking to hone their skills on tearing apart human flesh."

When she seemed sure he understood the gravity of the situation, she patted him derisively on the cheek and continued to stride toward the chamber of the High Khyth.

Dhrostain walked heavily behind her and was sure he did not understand what he'd just been brought into. All he knew was that he hoped the general was correct when he said that he was the right man for the job.

He hated things that he didn't understand—especially when they could kill him.

***

The inside of the Chambers of the High Khyth was silent when Dhrostain stepped in. It was the first time he had seen it up close, and he hoped it would be the last. Until now, he had made every attempt to distance himself from the Khyth as much as he could, even going so far as to request a transfer into an all-human brigade. But to be ordered to report to a Khyth by General Tennech, especially one as powerful as Yetz, meant he would do as he was told, since he feared Tennech more than he feared anyone. He knew what awaited those who shirked off orders from the Dagger of Derenar.

There was a young Khyth apprentice standing just inside the door, absentmindedly handling a small Gwarái horn. Her wavy red hair looked almost orange in the light, and her pale skin was dotted with freckles. The gray robes she wore told of her low rank in the Hand of the Black Dawn and that her path as a Khyth was set. She turned as she heard Dhrostain enter.

"Oh! Are you coming with us?" she asked the captain as she put the horn back down. Her eyes were pools of deep green, swirling around like dye stirred into a glass of water. It meant that at least one of her parents was Khyth and was more than likely the reason she was here. For those who were born the son or daughter of a Khyth, there was little choice in their destiny. They were expected to claim the power that was their birthright, undergo the Breaking, and eventually take the title of Khyth themselves.

Dhrostain did his best not to scowl. He instead gave a quick nod and looked away.

It was easy to recognize those who descended from the bloodline touched by the Breaker. In fact, one need not look much further than the eyes to see that they were different. In them lived the beauty and fear that fueled the Khyth. In contrast to normal human eyes, which only had coloration in a small portion of the center, Khyth eyes were colored throughout and looked almost as if they were alive. There were whispers that, if you looked long enough, you could see right into the Otherworld. Whether or not this was true was of no concern to Dhrostain. He had no interest in the Otherworld or in its power. It didn't stop him from being unnerved, though. Their movement and coloration made it impossible to tell where they were looking.

It was no wonder they kept to themselves.

Gift of the Shaper

Though the Hand of the Black Dawn was made up almost entirely of humans, it was split into two factions: warriors and Khyth. Those who showed some affinity for the power of the Otherworld were singled out to become Khyth apprentices and eventually Khyth. Those who did not became warriors. It was considered a great honor to be selected to become an apprentice, and only a small number were ever chosen to be so, which meant a great deal of bitterness could be found in almost every corner of the Sunken City. And those who descended from Khyth blood, who were practically guaranteed to be selected as apprentices, faced the greatest envy of all.

"Glad to have you along, then," said the young woman in the robes. "Elyasha, second year apprentice," she said as she put her hand out. "But people just call me Yasha for short."

At the sight of this, the scowl that Dhrostain had been holding back had made its way onto his face. "Farryn Dhrostain," he grunted, "Captain." He made no move to shake hands.

Yasha smiled, which continued to unnerve the Thurian. Her face was pleasant enough, and her thin frame contributed to her non-threatening appearance, yet Dhrostain continued to eye her suspiciously until Seralith entered the room. Upon seeing her, Yasha bowed her head slightly. "Lady Edos," she said pleasantly.

"Elyasha," she replied curtly. "Where is the High Khyth?"

"In his study, speaking with D'kane."

"Very well," she replied. "We shall wait. Dhrostain," she said, turning to the captain, "remember what I said."

Dhrostain scrunched his face up in displeasure, then mustered a nod. This day's unpleasantries showed no signs of slowing.

The three of them found seats in the large room, which was warmed by a small crackling fire. The ever-present sounds of distant hammering pierced the air as blacksmiths and artisans wrought their craft that had made Khala Val'ur famous.

Dhrostain watched as Yasha took her seat. Like Lady Edos, she was smooth and gracious with her movements, and she did not at all have the air of just a second-year apprentice. At that point in their training, they were expected to be focusing on developing their Breaking skills a little more every day. To do so, they often went out by themselves, under the direction of a Master Khyth, to hone their craft. The youngest of the apprentices were always doing something trivial: fetching water, restructuring a rock formation, redirecting small wind currents. They had no freedom whatsoever and were beholden to the whims and will of the Master Khyth to whom they were assigned. Because of that, most apprentices looked defeated almost all the time, tired and ragged from the mental and spiritual battering.

Yasha carried herself differently, though, Dhrostain noted. She held her head up high, almost regally or perhaps defiantly. He wondered if that would change when she experienced the Breaking. He didn't know enough survivors to say for certain.

The Breaking: that looming, secret ceremony where the apprentice surrenders everything and opens up to the full power of the Otherworld, becoming a Khyth in both name and blood. The first of those to harness the power of Breaking, in order to distinguish themselves from their Athrani counterparts, took the moniker of Khyth as a symbol of their submission to the Breaker, forever linking their identity with the Otherworld. Now, whenever a Khyth apprentice survived the Breaking, he or she was called Khyth in their honor. Before experiencing—and surviving—the Breaking, one of Khyth ancestry was forbidden to even acknowledge his ancient heritage. So even though the blood coursed through her veins, Yasha had no right to call herself one until she underwent the ceremony.

It was a prospect both welcome and daunting to any apprentice, and one that would change them forever. Their skin would crack and blister from the raw power coursing through them, and their eyes would burn out completely, replaced by a swirling maelstrom of color and fog. Yasha, who already had the eyes thanks to one of her parents, would be trading in her fair skin for an exterior of toughness and pain. After the Breaking, there would be no mistaking what she was. And that, a Khyth of the Breaking, was what Dhrostain feared the most.

But no sooner had the thought fluttered through his mind when he heard D'kane stride into the room.

Gift of the Shaper

The tall Master Khyth looked around, acknowledging Seralith first, then Captain Dhrostain. Finally, almost reluctantly, he nodded toward Yasha. "Apprentice," he mumbled.

"Master Khyth D'kane," Yasha said, bowing her head. "It is an honor." Something in her voice told Dhrostain that she didn't mean it. D'kane held her gaze for an uncomfortably long time, like he was trying to burn a hole in the back of the young apprentice's red hair. Finally, he looked away to address Lady Edos.

"By the command of the High Khyth, we ride tomorrow. Have you made your preparations?"

As Sera nodded, Dhrostain was reminded of a well-sharpened blade: as hard as she was beautiful; with more than her fair share of battle scars; and proving her durability and utility with deeds, not words. If Tennech was the Dagger of Derenar, she was most certainly the Sword.

"The general has ordered Captain Dhrostain to accompany you," she replied. "He has been fully briefed as to his role and expectations." She gave a sharp glance to the captain and then bowed her head to D'kane.

"Thank you, Lady Edos. If there is nothing more . . ."

"That is all," the tall Athrani replied.

"Then you may go," D'kane said with a wave of his hand. Dhrostain saw a fleeting sneer on her lips, which all but disappeared when she raised her eyes to the Khyth.

"Thank you," she said sharply and was off. Even the walls of the room seemed to relax with her exit.

"Now," D'kane began, "to business. Our journey will not be a quick one. As of this moment, our prize lies in Annoch. That may change along the way, but there is no way of knowing if or when it will." He looked from the eyes of the captain to the young apprentice. "And it should go without saying that neither she nor I will be able to enter the city." His gaze settled firmly on Dhrostain. "Which is where you come into play, Captain." Behind his eyes was power, and it made Dhrostain fidget where he stood.

Dhrostain swallowed hard, betraying his nervousness and discomfort to everyone in the room. "Yes, Master Khyth. How may I serve?" The words were forced and brittle.

"Your instructions will become clear in time, Captain," he answered. "Be ready to set off with us tomorrow, and if there is anyone that you will miss, I suggest you say your goodbyes sooner rather than later." A smile formed on his lips, and Dhrostain thought it looked as comforting as a corpse.

"Thank you, Master Khyth, but I have no one."

In truth, Farryn Dhrostain was fully devoted to his work. He was a warrior through and through and had neither the time nor the energy to commit to anything—or anyone—else. Most of those who found themselves among the warrior elite were similarly alone, more by necessity and external pressure than choice. The mentality was that one who learned to depend on himself, with no other ties to the world, was a force to be reckoned with in battle. He would take risks other men would not. He could be trusted to leave everything on the battlefield, never holding back, never afraid for the children he might leave without a father. He could be called upon to leave at a moment's notice and would do so without hesitation. And, should he die, no one would waste their time mourning his loss.

As such, the captain had no time for loneliness, and that suited him just fine.

"Then gather what you must and meet us at the north gate tomorrow at sunrise. From there we ride on to Annoch and to glory."

The way the last few words rolled off his tongue made Farryn Dhrostain shiver.

***

The Thurian waited nervously by the mouth of the northern gate of the city. Between the threats that Sera had issued and the prospect of riding with a Master Khyth, Dhrostain could not imagine things being much worse. *At least Hullis will be along for most of the trip,* he thought. The two men were not close, but knowing that there would be a rider among them who had no loyalty to the Otherworld brought him a small bit of comfort. He knew he could rely on him if his life depended on it.

The Khyth, on the other hand, were unpredictable and dangerous. He thought of them like fire: powerful and useful when controlled, but capable of indiscriminate and savage destruction in the blink of an eye.

He moved his hand along the muzzle of the horse he'd selected. It was a smaller chest-nut stallion that suited his riding preferences—slow and steady. Whenever possible, he preferred to walk, but a journey out of Gal'dorok and into Derenar would take many days, and he knew he would be better off riding for the majority of it.

He went through his pack one last time to make sure he hadn't forgotten anything: a knife for killing and skinning animals for food, a flask for water, a flint for sparking a fire, a small mat to sleep on, a map, a length of cord for general utility, and a warm coat for the elements. He closed it, securing it in place on the back of his horse, and gave it a light tap. He didn't know how Khyth traveled or how they hunted, but he hoped that he wouldn't have to do it for them.

The night was still and dark around him, and he frowned as he looked to the east, checking for daybreak. He knew they would be heading out at first light, and he was not in the habit of being late. By his reckoning, there was still some time left, but the other riders should have been there by now.

He squinted into the shadows when he thought he saw something approaching. As the shape neared, he recognized it as Hullis, riding atop a night-black mare.

"Your death be quick," Dhrostain called.

"And your enemies' quicker," came the response from Hullis, echoing the Thurian creed. "If we're to share the road with Khyth, at least two of us can handle ourselves in a fight," he mused. Coming to a stop beside Dhrostain, Hullis slid off his horse and held out his hand in greeting, which was quickly returned.

"Mm," grunted Dhrostain. "That's something I excel at." The darkness was giving way to twilight, and he did his best to size up the younger man. "More than I can say for you and your fancy swordplay."

Hullis looked insulted. "I trained under Cortus Venn, Commander of the Lonely Guard of Lash'Kargá. The fact that I'm standing here before you speaks of my skill with a sword."

Dhrostain huffed and pretended not to be impressed. Lash'Kargá, a southeastern city on the edge of the Wastes of Khulakorum, was known for its precarious position. It had to be manned constantly because of its proximity to the border, making it a prime target for attacks from the warring tribes in the south beyond the Wastes. There was a reason the city was nicknamed Death's Edge, and Dhrostain personally knew a few men who'd lost lives and limbs in its defense.

Before he could say anything, though, the rhythmic sound of hoofbeats filled his ears. The Khyth were finally approaching, along with the morning light.

D'kane was the first one to come into view, seated atop a large gray stallion, followed closely behind by Elyasha, who rode a white steed with flecks of gray throughout. Both of them were wearing black and had packs fastened to the backs of their mounts.

A silent nod from Dhrostain was the only greeting offered as the two robed figures brought their horses to a stop. They carried nothing else but what was in their packs, and the two warriors exchanged curious glances, unable to fathom going completely unarmed into the possibility of combat. Hullis's hand went instinctively to the hilt of his sword in a search for reassurance.

"I see you are ready," was all D'kane needed to say. A quick tap of the heels to his gray mount's rib cage was enough to spur him forward into a trot, with the apprentice behind him following suit.

"A man of few words," said Hullis to Dhrostain. "I like it." He clicked his tongue twice, and his horse responded by matching the pace of the riders in front.

Gift of the Shaper

The short, bearded warrior who had been the first to arrive was now the last to leave. He shook his head and urged his mount onward, with the mountains of the Sunken City to his back and the long road to Annoch in front.

Chapter 26

Annoch

Gift of the Shaper

Olson

Brick after brick, stone after stone, the towering construct that housed the Anvil of the Worldforge was as massive as the city around it, and undoubtedly the best brickwork that Olson had ever laid eyes on. It was apparent to anyone with even the most rudimentary understanding of construction that this was no ordinary building, as the Spire of Annoch that topped it was the tallest structure in the whole city.

Each white brick was laid with incredible care and precision, culminating in a vast, perfect spiral that reached up and clawed at the sky. The circular base, impossibly broad, was lined with a ramp that wound up and along the outside of the walls. It was originally designed to allow a quick ascent to the top by a lookout in order to spot enemy movement. But now, in the peace that had come at the end of the Shaping War, it stood as a quiet reminder that war could touch even the mighty city of Annoch.

But there were no remnants of war today; there was only a gathering throng of desperate and panicked Athrani.

Olson followed closely behind Dailus as he marveled at the sight before him. Beneath the height of the great spire were hundreds of Athrani, loud and disorganized, and massed below the tower with about half as many humans spread throughout. There seemed to be no pattern to the splintered groupings, as some were composed of only humans, some only Athrani, and still others a mixture of both. Most of them were yelling, some to other groups, and some to the group they seemed to be a part of. Confusion reigned completely, and suddenly Olson understood how Dailus had felt when he heard that the Shaper had rescinded Her gift.

He put a huge hand on the Athrani's shoulder to get his attention. Dailus turned and faced him with his blue and blue-on-gold eyes that glinted in the sunlight.

"The plan, Dailus," Olson huffed. "What is it?"

"We get in there and we talk," Dailus shot back. "If anyone knows what happened, we will find them here." He turned again to face the masses that had gathered near the entrance of the spire—a polished marble arch inlaid with gold—and walked closer.

When they reached the edge of the crowd, Dailus wasted no time slipping his way between bodies as he sidestepped and weaved toward the arc. Olson tried to follow but immediately lost sight of the nimble Athrani, choosing instead to lower his shoulder and plow through the mob on his own. He pushed aside grown men like he was swimming through them. When he stumbled out the other end, he found that the crowd was formed in a semi-circle around three men who stood beneath the marble arc, overpowering the voices of everyone else around them. Standing with their backs to the entrance were two humans—a gray-haired man, tall and slender, dressed in clothes of fine cloth, and a younger man beside him, middle-aged, with a voice as deep as his frown. Facing the two of them was an older-looking Athrani in white silk robes, who towered over them both by a head. Olson moved in closer to listen.

"Once the Khyth catch wind of this, they'll be at our gates in an instant!" shouted the gray-haired man.

"Old fool!" the Athrani yelled back. "For all we know, the Shaper will restore Her gift as quickly as She took it. Do you think the Khyth so rash as to attack a city still bursting with Athrani?"

"But a snake with no fangs is nothing but a worm," snapped the middle-aged man. "We have no use for you anymore!"

"You would spit in the face of our alliance?" shouted the enraged Athrani as he buried his finger into the man's chest.

"The past is the past," said the third with a dismissive wave. "You and your people need to go back to Ellenos. You endanger us all just by being here!"

There were shouts of agreement and dissension among the crowd.

Dailus grabbed Olson's attention with a whistle, then gave a nod toward the bickering men.

With a nod of acknowledgement, Olson brought his hands to his mouth and took a deep breath. "ENOUGH!" he bellowed.

The crowd—and the three men—fell silent.

Gift of the Shaper

Nodding his thanks, Dailus took a few swift steps onto the ramp and elevated himself above the crowd. "I am Dailus of Ellenos, son of Jecko, of the same. I did not travel halfway across Derenar to see my people resorting to petty arguments and senseless squabbling."

The old Athrani, who was closest to Dailus, looked at him and sneered. "What would a half-eye like you know about pride?"

Olson saw Dailus wince in shame. Though he knew little of Athrani culture, it was clear that the insult hurt Dailus down to his core.

"If you can't bring yourself to look past something as petty as my eyes, old man, then we are all lost," he answered with cold conviction. "Only moments ago, you found yourself pleading with the humans not to reject you because of who you are. You can't help that you were born Athrani, and I cannot help that I was born a half-eye. But none of that matters anymore. You all felt what it was like to be powerless for the first time since the Shaper gave us Her gift. For once, even if it was only for a moment, we were all equal."

The crowd was silent in the wake of this truth. Some looked down in shame; others looked from face to face as if they were seeing each other for the first time. The old man had broken eye contact with Dailus and could not bring himself to look back up.

"Look around you, all of you," he went on. "These are your brothers." The crowd did as he asked, still shocked from the realization. "The one thing that made us different, for as long as any of us can remember, unites us now. Athrani come from humans; we would not be here without humans." He paused. "The Shaper's love affair with them is older than our race. And now look at you, bickering and squabbling like children." His face was filled with anger, the anger of a man who had been persecuted all his life. "Have you ever stopped to think that it was your own arrogance that led Her to revoke Her gift?"

His anger was met with silence. Finally, one of them spoke up. "They say it is the work of the Khyth," said a younger Athrani. His suggestion was met with murmurs; most were in agreement.

Dailus looked grim, then answered, "You are not the first to suggest such a thing." He glanced at Olson, then back to the crowd. "In fact, I have reason to believe that is precisely what happened," he said to their dismay. "I was held captive outside the city of Lusk only a few days past, and . . ."

Olson saw the pain behind his eyes and knew that the young Athrani was watching Aidren die all over again.

"What?" prodded the old Athrani, a hint of worry behind his words.

"I saw a Khyth take away the Shaping of an Athrani," Dailus said with heavy inflection.

Olson watched as Dailus wavered, no doubt reliving the memories of what he had gone through. A panic seemed to pass through him and work its way into the crowd as Olson was sure that Dailus might collapse. But before he could react, an Athrani taller and older than Dailus put a hand on the half-eye's shoulder. He stared out at the crowd, with eyes of blue under rings of gold, and raised one hand to call for silence.

"Brothers," he began, "citizens of Annoch, Athrani and human, I beg you, calm yourselves." He looked slowly over their faces as he spoke. "The worst thing we can do right now is run. This city was founded by the blood of our two people. And so long as we both remain here, united, no Khyth shall breach these walls." The crowd remained silent until he spoke again. "Go back to your homes. Go back to your families. In these uncertain times, no one can say what the future may bring. But one thing is clear: your city will need you. Look inside yourself and be sure that when she calls, you will be ready."

Silently, the crowd began to disperse, with Olson and Dailus looking on in awe.

"Who are you?" Dailus asked, stunned.

"I am Aldryd, Keeper of the Anvil," he answered. He was dressed in the traditional silver robes of the Order of the Shaper, the governing body of the Athrani in law and in worship. The wrinkles on his kind face belied a sternness that his position no doubt demanded, and his thick fingers told of years of working with his hands. He walked toward the marble arch that served as the entrance and pressed lightly on the solid brick wall.

Gift of the Shaper

Olson and Dailus watched in amazement as it slowly gave way, sliding into the wall and revealing a huge, grand entrance. "Please, come inside, Dailus of Ellenos, and tell me what you know."

Aldryd walked inside and did not wait for the other two to follow him. Dailus hesitated but made his way after the Keeper. Olson found himself standing underneath the sweeping marble arch and wondering how he ended up there in the first place. With a sigh of defeat, he went in after them.

Chapter 27

Khala Val'ur

Gift of the Shaper

Sera

General Aldis Tennech stood at the gates of Khala Val'ur, holding his helmet beside him and looking out beyond the entrance. Any time he left the city, Tennech dressed for war, and today was no different. The ends of his black mustache were visible below his chin when he slid his helmet on, open enough in the front to accommodate the corners of his mouth, with just a thin slit at the top for his eyes. He turned to Sera and said, "Ready the horses," while slipping on his armored gloves one at a time.

Sera nodded respectfully and turned toward the stables that she knew so well, where the general's mount and her own horse, Ruen, would be waiting for her. Rounding the corner to the stables, she met the stablemaster, who already had both horses tacked and ready, and guided them out by the braided reins that were attached to their bridles.

"Avero has done a good job taking care of them," Tennech said with approval as they approached.

"He always does," Sera replied. She came to a stop just in front of the Valurian general, both horses' reins in hand. "It's one of the reasons we keep him around."

The larger of the two horses was black as night, with white markings around the eyes that looked like war paint. The general took his reins and led him onto the path, lining up to the left of the horse, slipping his foot into the stirrup, and swinging his leg around with ease. "Follow me," he said to Sera, who was standing by the smaller horse.

Hers had a coat of chestnut, with a saddle to match, which she mounted just as easily as the general had. "Right behind you," she said, taking the reins in one hand and giving them two light shakes, spurring the diminutive stallion on to a trot.

From his earliest days in the Academy, Tennech had taken a keen interest in horseback riding and had gone out of his way to see that he had the best training and the best horses. He was well aware of the broad military application of horses as well as their profound value in transportation and had taken up breeding them as a hobby. The black one he rode now was one of the first he'd ever bred, and he had named it Calathet, meaning "horse lord" in the old tongue. Though there were horses that were bigger than Calathet or even faster, he was the clear favorite of Tennech due to the fact that he was fearless, obeying his rider without even a moment's hesitation. The general bragged that he could ride him straight off a cliff if he felt like it.

"We will meet Rus just north of Lash'Kargá," he said, "away from prying eyes." The sound of Calathet's even hoofbeats was loud and strong, echoing off the mountains as they passed through.

"You know I don't trust him," Sera answered with a frown. She was riding a few paces behind him on Ruen, the very same horse she had ridden when she fled the city of Ellenos. He was aging, it was true, but he also may have been the one thing in the world that she had ever cared for. And she would cut out the tongue of any man who voiced that fact.

"Then your instincts are still as sharp as the day you came to me," he answered with a hint of a smile.

The two of them rode on in silence through the inner gate. Turning north, they followed the thin, semicircular path toward the outer gate. The guards in command of the watchtowers that littered the paths made sure that their sharpest men were on lookout duty that day. One missed salute when General Tennech rode by meant that the watch officer would have to start learning how to speak without a head.

Calathet had slowed from a trot to a walk, and Ruen was slowly coming up on him. Abruptly, the general called his horse to a stop. Sera rode up alongside him. He held the reins in one hand and was looking at something off in the distance.

"General," she asked, "is something the matter?" She squinted in the direction he faced, seeing nothing of importance to speak of.

He turned to her and almost looked surprised to see her there. "No, Sera, it's nothing." The tension in his face told her otherwise.

"Why have we stopped?" she asked.

He put down the reins and removed his helmet. "I'm not one to question orders, am I?" he asked with a bit of doubt in his voice, scratching the end of his mustache with an armored hand.

Gift of the Shaper

"Certainly not in the years that I have known you, General."

"No. No, I am not," he said, as if reassuring himself. "But I am one to think of the consequences," he said, glancing back toward Khala Val'ur. "And if we move forward with this—when we move forward with this—there will be no going back."

Seralith hesitated, unsure if the general was seeking advice or if he was testing her resolve; neither one was unprecedented. In the many years she had spent working with him, though, she had learned to read him—his body language, tone of voice, and facial expressions. Everything that she was seeing now indicated that he was not testing her.

"It's a solid plan, General," she began. "One that we have spent much time preparing, vetting, and testing. And no one else knows about it, save those who play crucial roles." She paused. "Although I cannot speak to the loyalty or discretion of a man like Ghaja Rus, who seems to lend his services to the highest bidder."

Tennech looked at her sternly. "Rus is unwavering," he answered. "He is a man who values power more than anything, and those who wield it are the ones he holds in the highest regard." He gave Calathet one quick tap of the reign to spur him forward again. "He is as valuable to me as I am to him."

Sera nodded as if validating her decision to advise the general. She gave Ruen's reins a light tap and was matching the walking pace of the general's horse in no time.

Calathet, she admitted, was a pleasure to watch. His muscular frame was supported by legs that cycled seamlessly as they carried the weight of their rider, pounding the ground with every step and somehow still remaining graceful. Tennech had him at a collected trot, where most of his weight was toward the back, allowing for greater mobility. His endurance was impressive, and he certainly could have been put to a gallop for the duration of the ride. Tennech would have been exhausted far before Calathet.

It was only a short ride to the northern gate, where they would once again turn south, circumnavigating the entire mountain range that encircled Khala Val'ur. The ride south to Lash'Kargá would take most of the day, she knew, bringing them in around dusk, just in time to meet with Ghaja Rus.

Sera frowned at the thought of meeting with the G'henni so close to darkness, but she trusted that Tennech knew what he was doing. The Dagger of Derenar was not one who rode into battle unprepared. He always had a plan, and he always knew the risks. The only question was whether or not this was a battle from which he could walk away as the victor.

"Up here," Tennech said to Seralith as he coaxed Calathet to a stop.

Dusk was approaching in Lash'Kargá as the general guided them south. They were heading into a thickly wooded area that grew vibrantly and in stark contrast to the cold deadness of the underground city-fortress of Khala Val'ur. The Khyth were peculiar in their penchant for the dark and dead, a taste that perfectly suited their solitary tendencies and wore endlessly on the patience of General Tennech, who preferred real light over the one burning inside the city.

"We will leave the horses," he said. He tapped lightly on the side of Calathet's face in what was not so much affection but affirmation. Removing his right foot from the stirrup, he swung it around to an easy dismount, and Seralith did the same. Dusting himself off, he took the big black horse by the reins and led him to a nearby pine tree. "The rest of the way, we must go by foot."

Old habit had led Tennech to leave his helmet on, even when he was not in combat. He said that he found comfort in the weight of the steel on his head and solace in the knowledge that someone would have to swing very hard to bury a weapon in his skull. After years of wearing it, it was just as much a part of him as his own skin.

Sera took no such pleasure, however, and removed her helmet at the very moment her feet touched the ground. She did not enjoy riding at all, yet managed to find herself constantly engaged in it at the behest of the general. Shaking out her long brown hair, she put a hand to her stiffened neck. She would be sore in the morning.

"This way," said Tennech, who was making his way off the road to a small grouping of trees. Sera followed him over, leading Ruen to a tall, sturdy-looking pine. Seeing no better options, she clasped one of the lower-hanging branches and tied a slip knot, securing the chestnut stallion in place.

Tennech, who appeared to be searching the area for something, apparently found what he sought as he knelt down to look at the ground. He could see a small pool of blood on the road that was oriented northward.

"The trail starts here," the general said, eyeing the droplets. Blood was the calling card of Ghaja Rus.

The man from G'hen was obsessed with it and was known to use it as a signal for those he did business with. While Tennech admittedly did not understand his methods, he certainly did not question the results. "This way," he said, standing back up.

The path that Rus had chosen was short, surrounded by trees, and impossible to navigate on horseback. Why he had chosen to do this when he knew of the general's affinity for horseback riding was of obvious annoyance to Tennech with every branch that he swatted from his face. The two of them descended a steep, rocky path that took them into a small gorge.

Ages ago, there had been a river running through it, but the last drop of water had long since dried out, leaving nothing but a dusty, barren riverbed.

At the bottom of the path in the gorge stood Ghaja Rus, smiling with satisfaction, like a hunter over a fresh kill. On their knees behind him were three figures, bound hand and foot—two males and one female. Their hands were tied in front of them, and they wore brown hoods over their heads, that were cinched at the neck, cutting off their vision completely. Behind them loomed two big G'henni men that appeared to be Ghaja Rus's personal bodyguards.

"Good day to you, General," the fat man said with a flourish. "And to you as well, Lady Edos." Seralith acknowledged him with a sneer. "I thank you for coming all this way to meet me."

Tennech looked over the three figures and nodded, his lips taut. "I certainly hope it was worth the ride," he said flatly.

"I am confident," Rus smiled, "you will agree that it was." He walked over to one of the men and reached down to loosen the hood. Deft fingers pulled it off to reveal the terrified eyes of a brown-haired boy, not even old enough to tend stables.

"What are you playing at, Rus?" the general growled. "I need soldiers, not boys." He crossed his arms with a scowl.

"Boys are just as good as men for our purposes, General, and much easier to acquire," the dark-skinned man said coldly. "Besides, they are not the main course—simply something to whet the appetite."

Tennech frowned and looked at Seralith, who was equally unimpressed. "Very well," he said calmly. "I'm waiting."

The words brought a light to Ghaja Rus's eyes. He danced over to the other two and removed their hoods, collecting and cradling them in his left arm. Sera exchanged a curious glance with the general, but Rus was undeterred. He seemed to take perverse enjoyment in removing the hoods. Perhaps it was seeing the look of fear on their faces when the hoods came off that gave him pleasure or simply the joy of being in control. Whatever it was, Ghaja Rus reveled in it.

When he had finished, he laid the hoods neatly on the ground, taking great care to fold them and smooth each one. The whole time, he kept his eyes on the three trembling bodies, smiling like he knew the answer to the riddle that all madmen share. Then, gracefully, he stood back up and let his eyes wander.

"Did you bring what I asked?"

His words were meant for the general, who patted a Gwarái horn that was tied to his belt. It clanked softly against his chain-mail leggings.

"Give it to me," said Rus, his hand outstretched in a beckoning motion.

The general took it out with narrowed eyes and moved closer to the G'henni.

Rus, standing above the captive—an Athrani boy with short brown hair and gold-on-green eyes—suddenly unsheathed a dagger from inside his waistcoat. It was a small silver blade attached to a worn bronze handle, simple in design and purpose. "I'm going to show you some of what I've learned," he said as he grabbed the boy by the hair, his sharp cries of pain seeming only to encourage the rough hands of the G'henni.

"At first, I thought D'kane's use of Athrani was simply because of the inherited hatred he harbored for them. Who better to cut open than your oldest enemy to see how much they bleed?" He looked hungrily at the throat of the boy. "Then I thought it might have something to do with the difference in their Shaping. But it turns out, there was one piece I was missing," he said, motioning Tennech over. "Please, General, the horn."

Tennech furrowed his brow as he looked at Rus. He had no understanding of Khyth Breaking or Athrani Shaping—and no desire to learn. All he knew was that it was power, and power was meant to be controlled. He humored the G'henni and walked over to him.

With his hand held out to the general, Ghaja Rus asked, "May I?"

Tennech kept his eyes on the shadowy fat man as he relinquished the horn, handing it over by the thick end. His old white hands looked sickly next to the big, dark hands of the southerner.

Rus took the horn and examined it, smiling, and looked back to the trembling captive. "I know very little about Shaping, and surely there are others who know its secrets much better than I. But one thing I do know: it is driven by life force." He looked again at the boy, whose lower lip was trembling, perched on the verge of tears.

The older blond boy, whose scabbed right arm had been used to supply the blood for Rus's cruel display, shouted, "Get away from him!" He looked to be crying as well. "We haven't done anything!"

The G'henni stood up and savagely backhanded him across the face. "Still your tongue, child. Or I will make this much more painful than necessary."

The blond boy was silent through a mask of fear.

Turning again to the brown-haired Athrani, Rus grabbed him by the throat this time, picking him up just barely off the ground. The boy's desperate, choking attempts at breathing made the G'henni smile. "The secret is in the blood, where the life force is held," he began. "Athrani and

Khyth—it all springs from the same well." He took the knife and held it to the stomach of the boy, whose eyes quaked with fright, managing no more than a gurgle with a hand around his throat.

"And the life force is the most important part." His gaze steady on the boy's youthful eyes, he plunged the knife into his stomach and twisted it, watching as they opened impossibly wide and rolled back into his head. He lowered the boy just enough so that his feet touched the ground, sliding the knife out as the child collapsed onto the fallow riverbed. He held the knife up, smiling at the beautiful crimson-streaked blade.

The blonde boy beside him, growling with anger, lunged at Rus. Hands still bound, he screamed *No!* in a high-pitched cry of desperation, knocking the G'henni on his side and pounding on him with balled-up fists. General Tennech held out his hand to restrain Sera, who started toward them, knowing full well that the big man was not so easily overpowered.

With violent strength, Rus's meaty elbow caught the boy in the mouth and knocked him back onto the ground, where he landed with a thud. Rus kneeled over him with nothing more than a scowl and labored breathing. The boy did not move, and the dark southerner was appeased for the moment.

Speaking barely above a whisper, the girl broke the silence. "Why won't you let us go?" she pleaded in a small, gentle voice.

Rus whirled around to see the girl, eyes glistening with tears, on her knees and trembling. A thin layer of dirt subdued her freckles and wild red hair, and the clothes she wore were little more than rags.

"Because you're worth more to me than you are to your mother and father," the G'henni answered callously as he lumbered to his feet. "You should thank me, girl," he said, waddling over. "I'm giving you the chance to be a part of something great, something powerful. Something more than just a poor farmer who dies drowning in pig filth." He stood over her and smirked, then picked his leg up off the ground. Swiftly, he brought it down on her chest, slamming her to the ground with such ferocity that it squeezed the air from her lungs. She could muster nothing more than a whimper as Rus leaned his weight onto her and looked menacingly at the other captives.

Gift of the Shaper

"That's enough, Rus," Tennech said sternly. "Spare us the theatrics. I didn't come here to watch you torment children. I assume there is a point to all this?"

The G'henni lifted his boot from the young girl's chest and bowed toward the commander of all the forces of Gal'dorok. "Of course, General." He walked over to the boy with the fresh knife wound in his stomach. By now, the ground beneath him was saturated with blood. "That should be enough," he said.

"Enough for what?" the general inquired.

"You'll see," Rus said simply. He knelt down over the boy, horn in hand, and dipped into the crimson pool. When he stood, the earth trembled.

"What's happening?" Tennech asked, uneasily placing a hand on his sword.

Rus only answered with a smile as the horn of the Gwarái began to glow, submerged in the lifeblood of a son of the Shaper.

"One thing that has always fascinated me about the Gwarái," Rus began, "is their thirst for blood. But what most people fail to understand is that they are not after the blood; they are after what's inside it." He looked at the Athrani clutching his bleeding stomach on the ground in front of him. "They are after the power of the Otherworld."

He backed away from the boy, who hovered near death. As his warm, dark blood ran into the earth below, it seemed to funnel into the horn, drawn to it like water in a sponge. And from the horn came life—or what passed for it—in the form of a Gwarái. Slowly and insidiously it grew, forming bone and sinew, called to life again from nothingness, and stretching before them like a great black serpent.

In just a few brief moments, a fully-formed Gwarái stood before them, brought to life by the blood of the Athrani. Hungrily it lowered its head and lunged for the abdomen of the boy, now soaked through with blood. Tennech looked away in disgust as the creature's thick tongue lapped thirstily at the scarlet pool. One of Rus's guards put a hand to his mouth and looked to be choking something back.

All the while, the G'henni smiled. "There is nothing like the blood of the Athrani to the Gwarái," he said with a hint of admiration. "And they will do just about anything to get to it." He approached the creature slowly.

The Gwarái, its black scales smeared with blood, was looking at Rus with one wary yellow eye as the fat southerner crept closer to it. Still it drank.

"You're going to get yourself killed," warned Tennech, who went for his sword. A cautionary wave from Ghaja Rus stayed his hand.

The boy's struggling had finally ceased; and, with a few more sharp flicks of the tongue, the Gwarái stopped too. Its eyes, which still gazed warily at Rus, began to droop. Its powerful hind legs relaxed, bending down to put its knees on the ground. Rus was standing right next to it now and reached his hand out for one of the dagger-like horns that grew from its head. He took the horn in his hand, and the creature did not so much as flinch. "When they have drunk enough blood of the sons of the Shaper," he said, smiling, "they become as harmless as a child."

Tennech stared in amazement as Rus walked around the front of the creature, white horn in hand, and forced its gaze upon him. The Gwarái looked mesmerized. "Yuta, Mundi," he called to the two G'henni behind him, "the chains."

The two big men approached cautiously, regardless of how docile the creature appeared. It was still a frightening and formidable beast, with jaws and claws that rent flesh with ease. Yuta, the bigger of the two men, held a large shackle in his hand, and Mundi held the chains that it was fastened to. With a lunge, Yuta snapped the shackle onto the neck of the Gwarái, quickly backing away as if he expected to be torn to pieces.

Tennech, whose gaping mouth was framed quite well by his mustache, couldn't seem to find the right words. Sera, as usual, found them for him.

"So this is how the Khyth have resurrected the Gwarái," she stated plainly.

"With the very thing the Gwarái seek," Rus smiled, "Athrani blood." He stroked the long, scaly neck of the creature standing beside him, still appearing entranced and utterly calm.

Gift of the Shaper

"But how?" the general asked, his silence finally broken.

"It is not my place to question how, General," the fat G'henni replied, still admiring the scaled monstrosity. "I prefer to ask instead: How can we profit?" He turned to look at Tennech, who had wrapped one hand over his mouth in deep introspection. "And I believe that you are just the man who can answer that question."

Eyebrows raised, the Dagger of Derenar looked at the Gwarái with a mixture of awe and greed. "Are there more?"

"Only a handful that we know of," the G'henni said with a baneful smile, wringing his plump hands together in marked anticipation. "And if you'd like me to acquire them for you," he said with a smirk, "I can do it." The man sensed opportunity like the Gwarái sensed blood and would stop at nothing to seize it when it was within his grasp. "But not for free."

Sera moved for her sword, but Tennech held her at bay. "So it's true what they say about you, Rus. Everything comes with a price." He reached for his coin purse, saying, "Very well, G'henni. Name yours."

Rus shook his head. "I am a rich man already, General," he said curtly. "Yet there is one thing that continues to elude me."

Tennech narrowed his eyes at the fat man standing before him. "What, then?"

"Power," he said as he looked again to the Gwarái. "A partnership. An understanding." He swept his fingers gently across the great maw of the beast. "Even the mightiest of warships can find itself stranded at the mercy of the wind."

"My patience for your flowery speech runs thin," Tennech growled. "What do you want?"

The G'henni was unconcerned. "I have my connections to supply you with soldiers, and you have the wherewithal to lead them. I simply propose that we combine our efforts," he said innocuously, "and work exclusively with one another. I will bring you Gwarái—and the Athrani to awaken them—and you will think of me as a trusted ally and confidante." His wry smile made his gold teeth shine perilously. "I feel the arrangement could be beneficial to all parties involved, and perhaps the wind will blow in your favor." He had the look of a snake poised to strike.

General Tennech appeared almost amused, but the wrinkles around his eyes conveyed distrust and hesitation; both of which were qualities that allowed him to survive this long. He looked to Sera, who had not yet torn her scowl away from Ghaja Rus.

"Seralith," the general began, "you look as though you have a strong opinion on the matter."

"I do, General, but I would rather not speak it aloud."

Ghaja Rus regarded her with callous conceit. "I assure you, Lady Edos, I make a better ally than an enemy."

She was on him in an instant, clutching the collar of his silken tunic in one hand, with a naked dagger in the other, calmly leveled at the pudgy neck of the southerner. "That sounded like a threat, Rus," she hissed through her bared teeth. The eyes of the fat man flew open in surprise as he flung his hands in the air in confusion. Yuta and Mundi, the two bodyguards, looked hesitant.

Tennech tried to hide his amusement and reproached her sternly. "Seralith," he called, "I am sure our friend from G'hen did not mean it as such."

As quickly as it had come out, her knife found its way back into its small leather sheath, and Sera unhanded Rus's collar by shoving him backward. "Then I apologize for my haste," she said, not meaning a single word of it.

"Apology accepted," Ghaja Rus said with a look of annoyance to his bodyguards. "I would never threaten the fabled Dagger of Derenar."

Tennech raised an eyebrow at the mention of the nickname that was perhaps older than the G'henni. "My advisor does not think very highly of you, Rus," the old general said. "And she most certainly does not trust you. Then again, neither do I," he asserted. "But you have a skill set that is very valuable to me."

Gift of the Shaper

The words made Rus relax a bit as he attempted to straighten his vest. His excitement was masked in caution as he looked to Tennech and said, "I am pleased to hear you acknowledge that, General."

"Get me more of these," he said, looking up at the Gwarái, "and I can overlook my lack of trust in favor of your newfound worth."

Ghaja Rus bowed deeply.

"Do not make me regret my decision," the general added.

"I would never dream of it."

Chapter 28

Annoch

Gift of the Shaper

Olson

The inside of the Spire was older than anyone could figure.

The city of Annoch was built around it, and any records of its original construction were long forgotten—or never existed in the first place. As Olson walked inside, he was hit with just how cold it felt, and the sharp smell of aging marble overwhelmed him. It was dim, but his eyes adjusted quickly.

"Follow me," Aldryd said as he marched down the interior hallway.

There were columns all around the inside, which was spacious beyond imagining. A few stone steps led downward into a huge, circular interior with at least three levels that Olson could see. The architecture on the inside was similar to the outside: arcs upon arcs provided the support for walls and ceilings covered in carvings, both ornate and fantastic, whose meanings had been lost to time. But one need not be versed in ancient and forgotten tongues to recognize that this was a holy place. The air itself was heavy with power and import, and something about it made the hair stand up on Olson's neck. He trod carefully, trying to keep his eyes on the Athrani in silver.

"Keeper," Dailus said to the elder Athrani, "where are you taking us?"

"Someplace we can talk," he answered without breaking stride. His lavish robes flowed behind him as he walked, flashes of silver and white playing with the dim light inside the temple.

Confusion worked its way onto Dailus's face as he looked around. "Can we not speak here, in the heart of the Shaper's temple?"

With a smile, Aldryd turned his head to his guests. "Cold, dead stone stifles the mind and weakens the breath, young one. I'd much rather we talk somewhere warm and alive." Turning to the marble wall, he touched it with his palm. "We will speak in comfort—I insist."

The Keeper pressed his hand into the wall, which seemed to give way as he did so, almost as if he was pressing through it. With a grunt, he pulled away and stood back, looking at the wall like he was waiting for something. He crinkled his nose like he was trying to solve a problem, staring hard at the white stone that surrounded them, when his confounded look turned into one of satisfaction. He smiled and turned to his guests.

Olson was concerned at the old man's delight, unaware of what could have pleased him so. Then, imperceptibly at first, the temple began to change. It was subtle, in the way that sweat can be there one moment and gone the next, but it was enough for Olson to notice. He cocked his head in confusion as he tried to work out just what was happening, then stepped back in surprise when he realized the marble that made up the temple was beginning to disappear.

He looked from the walls to a reverently still Dailus, who either knew something he did not or was simply not seeing what he was seeing. With his eyes back on the temple walls, Olson watched them—like his sanity—melt away like ice from the sun.

It happened like a wildfire radiating from a single point, silent and gentle in its swiftness. The place where Aldryd had pressed his hand was by now fully absent from sight, replaced by a light that Olson swore he could feel more than see. From behind him, he felt the temple moving and had the momentary sensation of weightlessness.

"What's happening?" he shouted, but his words sounded like they were coming from inside a well, thousands of miles away. He looked around in fright, to the nothingness that had so easily intruded and showed no sign of stopping, continuing its creep across the wall in incalculable and elegant waves.

By the time his surroundings had disappeared completely, he had given up on ever regaining his sanity. He closed his eyes in the hopes that he would open them again to find that he had just imagined the whole thing. But the light that he felt persisting in his mind, even through his tightly closed eyelids, told him that what he was feeling was real.

Before he could cry out a second time, though, he felt the world come to a stop. Like a man who had fallen a great distance and finally hit bottom, he exhaled in a great puff of pain. The light that peeked through into his mind was still there, but now it was somehow soothing, somehow welcome.

Cautiously, he opened his eyes. And, precisely as he feared, the entire world around him had changed.

His mouth agape, he surveyed his surroundings. As little exposure to Shaping as he had, the fact that walls and worlds could melt with a touch was deeply unsettling.

By the look of it, the three of them were standing in some kind of a forest, made of trees and with a skyline that were unfamiliar in color and condition. Even Dailus looked surprised as his eyes traced the misty gray skies.

One thing was certain, Olson felt: this place was alive. He wasn't sure what made him so sure of it, but it somehow felt more vibrant, more energized. It was warm and bright and comfortable, despite its unfamiliarity.

"I come here when I need to clear my head," said the Keeper. "I find that a change of scenery helps me to relax."

Olson made a noise in disbelief.

"Where," Dailus stuttered, "where are we?"

Aldryd crinkled his forehead as if he was pondering how much of the truth he should offer.

"A refuge," he said at last, "that can only be found by those who know its secret." He looked around, admiring the view. "There is great power buried inside the Anvil," he explained. "And the forces that shaped our world still beat strongly in its heart."

Olson's mouth was still hanging open as he looked for some sign of the huge marble structure that had towered over them only moments ago. He gazed all around, thinking maybe it was somewhere in the distance, scanning for some sign of the gigantic spire of Annoch. He found none. Besides the strange trees that stood around them, there was nothing else.

He put his hand on one of the trees nearby; it was soft, and he pulled back in surprise. The ground beneath his feet, too, seemed soft. And though there was no sun above them, it was warm, like the place itself gave off light.

D.L. Jennings

The area surrounding them was filled with trees of all types, and there were ample places to sit. It looked as if portions of the ground had been molded into perfect seats. Aldryd picked one and sat down, legs crossed in front of him. "Join me," he said as he patted another seat beside him.

Olson, who was still marveling at his surroundings, wandered over to the Keeper of the Anvil to take a seat on the soft earth. Dailus had already sat down next to the older Athrani.

"Please," Aldryd said as he looked at Dailus, "tell me what you can." His soft, inviting smile seemed to put Dailus at ease, and the younger Athrani was visibly more relaxed. The sudden transportation from one place to another altogether had obviously jarred him more than a little.

Dailus took a breath and gathered his thoughts. He told Aldryd about his capture and captivity, about the Khyth, and about Aidren. When he told him how they had found him, Aldryd stopped him.

"Did you see what happened to him?"

Dailus shook his head. "I did not, but I saw its effects. I felt it, when he was dying. He was empty." He cast his eyes downward, clenching his fist in frustration.

"Empty?" Aldryd echoed. His wild white eyebrows were furrowed inquisitively.

"I don't know how to put it, Keeper, but there was nothing there. It was as if he was stripped of what it means to be Athrani." He paused, reflecting. "He had no Shaping power at all."

Aldryd grimaced. "That is not good, young one, not good at all."

Dailus still had his eyes on the ground when Olson spoke up.

"Of course it's not good," he said. "If they figured out how to hollow you out like that,"—he made a scooping motion as he talked—"everyone has a whole lot more to worry about."

"Well," the aged Athrani said, holding up a finger as if it somehow emphasized his point, "it's not that they figured out how to take it; it's what they used to do it." He stood up and clasped his hands behind his back, beginning to pace. "There is, so far as I know, only one thing in all of creation that would allow the stripping of Athrani power." He suddenly whirled around and pointed straight at Dailus. "Do you know what that one thing is, son of Jecko?"

Dailus's head jerked back in surprise. "I can't say I do," he muttered.

"Gwarái," the old man said, his finger in the air again. "The Shaper's Bane."

"Gwarái?" Olson repeated. The puzzlement on his face expressed his ignorance.

"A creature of legend known for its thirst for blood," Dailus answered, "and its taste for Athrani. The first one was believed to have been formed by the Breaker Himself as a means to hunt and kill our kind." He scratched his head in confusion. "But the last one died ages ago, hunted to extinction at the end of the Shaping War."

"Say what you will," Aldryd retorted, "but the Khyth have proven themselves resourceful and relentless when it comes to the hatred of Athrani." He paused. "Perhaps they have found some way of . . . bringing them back."

Dailus shuddered visibly at the thought. "But to what end?"

"We can only assume to this end," he said, holding his hands out to indicate their present position. "One we never considered, in light of the old prophecies." A look of pained confusion flashed across his face, followed by stone-faced stoicism. He closed his eyes and was silent.

Olson stood behind him with his arms folded, stroking his big beard with one hand and looking expectantly from the old Athrani to the young one. The two of them exchanged glances, unsure of what to say or how to proceed. Neither of them wanted to interrupt his thoughts.

It was only when Olson thought he heard snoring that he cleared his throat a few times.

"Huh?" Aldryd shouted as his eyes snapped open.

"You were saying something about the Gwarái," Dailus piped up.

"What about them?"

"You mentioned something about the prophecies," Olson added helpfully.

"I did?"

"Yes," said Dailus, growing impatient.

"Well, I suppose that can't be helped now. No matter." He waved his hand dismissively. "Very little knowledge survives of the Gwarái, but I have no doubt in my mind that, whatever the Khyth are planning, it involves them somehow." He turned slowly to the trees and crossed his arms. "The prophecy I speak of is called the Prophecy of Power and is so named because of what it entails. Much like the carvings you may have seen inside the Spire, its words have been long forgotten, but the meaning has endured. The creatures' nature revolves around the power of Shaping, but we of the Order had always assumed the prophecy was speaking of a different kind of power, such as the rise or fall of a great empire. But in light of recent events, it appears that we were wrong. Somehow the Khyth have found a way of draining not just one Athrani but our entire race."

He turned his head and looked sidelong at Dailus. "We must find out what they are after. I do not believe that the Shaper took Her gifts back from us; I believe that they were taken by someone else, and the Gwarái could be involved."

"So what do we do?" Dailus asked.

"If we could find some way of tracking down the Gwarái you saw, that would be a start," Aldryd answered. "But the only thing that could do so has been surrendered to the ages." He sat back down, looking defeated. "And without it, I fear we may be lost."

Dailus and Olson traded worried looks. Finally, the younger Athrani spoke.

"You said there was great power in the heart of the Anvil," he began. "Could we use that somehow?"

The old Athrani let out a deep sigh. "The Anvil is powerful, yes, but it is incomplete. When the Shaper used it to forge our world, She tempered it with the Hammer of the Worldforge, an artifact so powerful that She separated it from Herself in fear of the destruction it could cause if they wound up in the wrong hands. Perhaps used together again, they could provide us with an answer . . . But I'm afraid the chances of that happening, of us finding the Hammer, are not good. We made sure of it."

Gift of the Shaper

"I don't understand," Olson said. "You lost the Hammer of the Worldforge . . . on purpose?"

Aldryd grimaced. "We had to be sure no one would succumb to temptation to use them together—neither Athrani nor Khyth. So we did with it what we thought would do the least amount of harm, which was to give it to someone that would have no use for it, who would keep it hidden from the world. We gave it to you," he said, looking up at Olson, "to humans. We concealed its nature and passed it off as an ordinary hammer. For all we knew, it was turned to ash and smoke before it ever saw the sun again."

"So that's it?" Dailus grumbled. "There's nothing we can do? Seated upon the heart of creation, at the center of the greatest power in the world, and we're reduced to sitting around and pouting about it?"

The Keeper's lips flattened together in an uncomfortable frown. "I am the only one who knows this," he said as he began to stand, "and this must not leave your lips once I have told it to you. It was one of the reasons I brought you here."

Dailus and Olson looked at him with rapt attention, like they were watching the temple come apart all over again.

"The Anvil has always had a special connection with the Shaper. If you stand close enough, you can almost feel Her, like She is standing in the room beside you, singing softly in your ear." He closed his eyes and smiled, lost in memories of bliss. He was silent for long enough for Olson to contemplate clearing his throat again.

Before he could, though, the Keeper frowned and continued.

"Yesterday," he labored over his words, as if they pained him to speak aloud, "She went silent. And a song I had heard my whole life was cut off in an instant."

Dailus stood up in shock. "Are you saying . . ."

Aldryd finished his thought for him. "The Khyth have done more than suppress our power, my friends. They attacked the source." He trembled as he spoke. "If I am right, and I pray by the Anvil I am wrong, they may be in possession of the one power keeping the Breaker in check for all these long years."

At that moment, the old man narrowed his eyes and craned his neck. "My friends," he said, "we are not alone."

Thornton

"In here," Alysana said as she pushed gently on the stone beneath the arch of the Spire. It slid back with ease, scraping across the floor and opening to reveal the inside of the temple. The two of them walked inside, and Thornton felt like he had stumbled into the presence of greatness.

"What is this place?" he marveled, touching his hand to one of the great marble spires that held up the temple.

"The Temple of the Shaper," Alysana answered. "Inside is kept the Anvil of the Worldforge, where they say the Shaper Herself created the world."

"Here?" Thornton asked her incredulously as his mouth opened a little wider.

"That's what the legends say," she said as she led them inside. "You can ask Aldryd more about it if you want."

"Ask who?"

"Aldryd, the Keeper of the Anvil," she replied, her tone indicating that he should have known who he was. "It's a pretty important position in the Order of the Shaper, from what I hear, but he's always seemed like a kind old man to me. I've known him since I was a little girl."

The two of them walked deeper inside the temple, and Alysana called the Keeper's name a few times. Each time, she was met with silence. "He should be here," she started. "I've never known him to leave."

Thornton frowned at this, knowing full well that his chances of finding his father diminished with every passing day. "Maybe he stepped out?" he suggested with false hope.

"Never," she insisted. "I've been coming here for years, and he's always been here. This place is his home." Her eyes scanned the walls of the large marble enclosure, searching in vain for some sign of the Keeper. She looked just as baffled as Thornton.

Gift of the Shaper

"You don't think he could be in danger?" the young blacksmith asked.

"If Aldryd is in any danger, we are all in danger," she said solemnly. "He is one of the strongest Shapers I know." Turning to Thornton, she looked him in the eye. "I'm alive today because of him."

Before he could ask what she meant, the temple began to shake, and Thornton looked up, thinking he had finally come face to face with his end.

"Run!" he shouted as he broke for the door. "It's going to collapse!"

"It's not going to collapse," came a sturdy voice from behind him. "You'd think the son of a blacksmith would know a thing or two about construction."

Thornton stopped dead in his tracks. He knew that voice. Deep down he had convinced himself he would never hear it again. The deep baritone that could shake a room, the confidence and self-assurance that were harder than any steel he forged—that voice belonged to one man and one man alone.

"Father," Thornton said. The word leapt eagerly from his mouth, like a caged bird that was once again free to fly on its own.

Olson, looking a little worse for wear, was covered in scrapes, bruises, and blood, but he was in one piece. To Thornton, he may as well have been the Shaper Herself.

"It's good to see you again, son," the elder Woods replied evenly. In typical Olson fashion, there was no hint of the emotions that his son was so prone to displaying. But none of that mattered to Thornton, who dashed along the ornate marble floors into the waiting arms of his father.

Behind them peeked out the aged face of an Athrani. "Hello, Alysana," he said with a smile. "How thoughtful of you to bring a gift for my guest."

Alysana looked confused but smiled back regardless. Her dark G'henni figure stood out starkly against the snow-white marble of the walls.

"You disappeared. I didn't think I was going to see you again," Thornton said as he looked up at his father, who stood a half head taller than him. "I tried to follow your tracks."

"You did?" Olson looked amazed. "How?"

"I had help," his son replied.

"Well, you know your old man wouldn't go down without a fight," he said gruffly. "They were even thoughtful enough to give me some company," he said, motioning to his Athrani companion. "This is Dailus. He was in the cell with me."

"So you were in there," Thornton said. "Who took you?"

"We don't know much, but he was Khyth," Dailus answered, extending his hand to Thornton in greeting. "I wish we could tell you more, but we're not sure of what he wants or why he was taking Athrani prisoners. We can only guess at what Khala Val'ur is up to."

Thornton's ears perked up when he heard mention of the Sunken City. "Khala Val'ur—I've heard that name before." And then he paused, as he remembered the second reason for his grief. "It's where we think they took Miera."

Olson looked stunned. "What?" he asked in shock. "Who took her? When?"

"Only about a day ago," he said in a deflated tone. "A Khyth named D'kane."

Aldryd inhaled sharply at the mention of the name of the Master Khyth. "I know of this one," the old man offered. "He is one of the trusted advisors to High Khyth Yetz." The name came out as bitterness on his tongue. "And if Yetz is involved, I have no doubt in my mind what they intend to do. They aim to free the Breaker."

Dailus looked at him incredulously. "But the only way to do that is—"

Aldryd cut him off. "With the blood of the Shaper."

Chapter 29

Kienar

Gift of the Shaper

Ynara

Ynara breathed out, and the forest breathed in. The moment that she entered the boundaries of Kienar, she knew it. It was a tangible change—something in the air, like when the sun comes out from behind a cloud and bathes the world in light. It sent a warm shiver down her spine, and she knew she was home. The Mother always surrounded herself with life, and Kienar was the best example of how even her mere presence could have an effect on the land around her.

Though she had come a long way after leaving behind the mountains of Gal'behem, Ynara felt energized as she walked deeper inside the forest. At some point during the journey, her worry had melted away almost entirely.

It was just past dawn, and the light that streamed through the trees did well to illuminate her path, though Ynara knew she would not need it. Even if she couldn't navigate perfectly in the absence of light, she knew Kienar well enough to use any of her other senses to guide her to the Mother. She heard the familiar sounds of birds as they welcomed the morning with songs and flapping of wings. She smelled the sap that crept through the trees as it transported nutrients from root to leaf. The sensations were as familiar to her as an old friend, and she could pick out each individual tree that made up the bouquet as plainly as a man could pick out the fingers that made up his hand.

Even the earth beneath her feet was familiar. The soil that gently gave way as her feet met the ground seemed somehow softer than any other soil in the world. It had been too long since she had been back. Oh, how it pained her to leave! But she had returned and would soon be face to face with her Mother again. Her spirits rose with every step.

She thought again of the frail girl she had tracked all the way from Lusk to Khala Val'ur, who seemed so delicate, even for a human. She was not dead, Ynara knew, but it still troubled her that she could not follow her any further than the outer ring of the Sunken City. She was placing a great deal of faith in her guess that the Khyth needed her alive.

She walked along a dirt path that was not carved but seemed to grow out of the forest itself, or rather, the forest grew around it. The trees were thick on both sides of the path, and what little light managed to steal through fell on the smaller plants that lined the trail. Sunshine barely had a chance to touch the ground here, where the vegetation was the thickest. But even in the absence of light, there was no question that life was flourishing.

As she basked in the rich and familiar scents that filled her nose, Ynara became conscious of the fact that she was walking with her eyes closed. The thought pleased her, and she resolved to keep them shut, letting herself be guided by the forest of her childhood. She walked with one hand outstretched to gently caress the leaves and plants that filled the woods.

After a bit, she opened her eyes again and felt a familiar presence. It was like stepping in front of a fire after being caught in a winter storm for days. Ynara felt the warmth surge through her body, and for a moment it seemed that the whole forest trembled around her.

The path by now had opened into a clearing, and the road sloped gently upward toward the tallest tree in the forest, around which the entire clearing was centered. It was a massive oak tree that towered over all the others, said to have been old even when the world itself was young. Humans had named it *Naknamu*, "the old one," as it had stood taller than any tower they built, for longer than they could remember.

Ynara knew it well. She had climbed its branches when she was small, and from the very top, the whole of Kienar was visible—and beyond. She remembered the first time she had looked out from its highest branches and realized there was another world out there, beyond her forest. She had vowed back then to see it when she was old enough to leave. Thinking about her intentions back then, she allowed her lips to curl into a slight smile of satisfaction.

Undaunted, she walked toward Naknamu once again, filled with purpose and determination. And as she neared the great oak, her heart leapt with each step until she was sure she could stand it no longer.

"My child," came a voice, soothing and light, which seemed to resonate through her entire being, "you have returned to me." Though the words were gentle, there was power woven into them like patterns in a cloth.

Gift of the Shaper

"Mother," Ynara said as she dropped to a knee, relief filling her voice.

From an arch in the trunk of the great tree emerged the First Kienari, the one that generations before Ynara had called *Mother*. She was impossibly tall—easily twice the height of an average human—and exuded the strength and grace that her children were renowned for. Her huge eyes were deep, solid pools of black, and her body was lined with the fine, smooth fur that made her disappear in shadows. Any creature that did not know better would have looked upon her in fear. But as she stepped out into the sunlight, Ynara was filled with nothing but reverence.

The Mother wore a simple crown upon her head, made of gold and inlaid with a single jewel, and a plain white necklace hung around her throat. The clothing she wore was, like Ynara's, made from the skins of animals and favored function over form.

Ynara continued to kneel as the Mother approached. She waited patiently, head bowed in fealty, for the object of her unfailing devotion to draw near. Joy spread through her as the Mother placed a hand under her chin and, smiling, said, "Rise, daughter. It is good to see you again."

Ynara stood up and embraced her creator, head pressed against her chest and arms wrapping around her waist. Beside the First Kienari, she still looked like a child, despite being fully grown and almost half-again taller than some humans.

"It is always good to see you, Mother," she said as she pulled her head away, craning her neck upward to look her in the eyes.

"I am sorry that it has to be under these circumstances," the Mother said as her eyes turned far west, toward Khala Val'ur.

Ynara stepped back and let her arms fall to her side. "Then you know," she said with only a hint of surprise. "I have failed, Mother. They have taken her."

"I know they have taken her, my child," the Mother said gently. "I felt it the moment it happened. But you have not failed," she said as she placed a hand on her daughter. "I had always known that this day would come. I just wish it had not come so soon." The First Kienari turned back to Naknamu, admiring its branches as if she was recalling a memory from long ago.

"I do not understand, Mother," Ynara said under a cloud of confusion. "I could not stop them."

The First Kienari smiled warmly at her daughter, who was wise, yet still a child in so many ways. "You do not understand. But you will," she said as she strode toward the great tree. "Come, my youngest. We have much to talk about."

Chapter 30

Annoch

Gift of the Shaper

Thornton

Thornton felt like he had just been hit by a ton of bricks. "I don't understand. What could they want with Miera?"

Aldryd turned to the young man from Highglade and asked, "I have my suspicions. When did you say they took her? When exactly?"

"It was nighttime, one day past," he said after some thought. "We'd been . . . overtaken by three men. They took Miera inside." His shame from the retelling was obvious, and his shoulders sunk a bit as he spoke. "I haven't seen her since."

"I do not believe this to be mere coincidence," Aldryd said softly. "The same time that your friend was taken by D'kane, it was as if the Shaper cried out in anguish. I felt it, here in the heart of the Anvil."

"I don't understand," Thornton repeated.

"Your friend Miera," Aldryd began as he looked at him, "has she ever displayed any talent for Shaping?"

"Not in the years that I've known her," Thornton said. He looked to his father for confirmation, and he gave it with a nod.

"Was her father Athrani? Or her mother?" the Keeper asked.

"Not her father," Thornton replied, "but I never knew her mother. He said that she died giving birth to Miera."

Aldryd turned his head slowly to size up Thornton, like one does when discerning lies from truth. "How much do you know of Athrani lore?" the Keeper asked in a somber voice.

"None," he admitted.

"Then this next part may be confusing." He took a breath as if determining where to start. "The first Athrani was a male child, born the son of the Shaper and Her human love, here in this very temple. It was the Shaper's plan, knowing that She must hide Herself from the Breaker, to give up Her power of Shaping to this child and use him as a vessel, allowing it to spread for generations to come and ensuring that She would be safe among Her children. Thus, the power of Shaping has always passed to the men, which is why we are all called sons of the

Shaper." He said this part with a bit of pride, then turned to walk to the enormous Anvil, fixed by design as the focal point of the temple, and motioned for Thornton to follow him. He pointed to the middle of the Anvil, to writing that Thornton didn't recognize, and said, "But the next part is a little more difficult, thanks in part to the ambiguity of ancient Athrani, where some words can have more than one meaning."

When Thornton crinkled his forehead in confusion, the Keeper went on. "This sentence here contains the best-kept secret, written by the Shaper Herself, and passed down from Keeper to Keeper since the first Athrani walked these halls. It is a phrase which is simple, yet confounding. Its perceived meaning is 'Through my daughter, I live.'" His voice quaked as he read the words. "But its true meaning is much deeper." He turned to the others, elated, and said, "'As my daughter, I live.'"

Thornton's eyebrows arched in puzzlement. "I'm not sure I follow."

Aldryd frowned. "At the very moment of birth, the Shaper became Her daughter." He studied Thornton with unsure eyes. "While every male Athrani inherits Her power, Her spirit is passed down, until the end of days, through Her daughter."

Olson crinkled his forehead as he heard this. "So every female Athrani is the Shaper?"

Aldryd sighed. "No, no," he said, scratching his head. "When the Shaper gave birth to Her daughter, Her life force passed to her that very instant, and so on, to every daughter born in that line." He put his finger up in emphasis. "There is only ever one Shaper, and She is reborn again and again, with no knowledge of who She is and with no way for the Breaker to ever track Her down." Even as the words came out of his mouth, he seemed to realize their inaccuracy.

"Until now," Olson said with a grimace.

"Hm," muttered the Keeper, "I suppose you are right." He put his hand on his head, wiping away at imagined sweat. "But we can take solace in one thing: without the key, the Breaker will remain chained in his prison in the Otherworld forever."

"Key?" Thornton asked. "What key?"

Gift of the Shaper

"The Hammer of the Worldforge," answered Dailus, pointing to writing further down the Anvil. "'By the Shaper, the chains were forged, and by the Hammer must they be broken.'"

"Correct," Aldryd nodded. "So, while She is the only one who can open the door, the key has been hidden from Her for ages."

Thornton's hand went to the smooth handle of his hammer. "So without it, the Shaper is . . . useless?"

The old Athrani raised his eyebrows in surprise. "Young one," he began, "She is the Shaper. Above Her, there is no more valuable being in this world—this one and the next."

The words gave Thornton pause. "You really think Miera is the Shaper?" he asked. His voice was high pitched, as if he did not believe the words himself.

"I think there is more evidence pointing to her being the Shaper," Aldryd said, "than to her just being an ordinary girl, caught up in extraordinary circumstances."

Thornton was dizzy and put his hand on the Anvil to steady himself. As he did, it took on a white-hot glow that was instantly matched by the head of his hammer that caused him to leap backward in surprise.

The eyes of Dailus and Aldryd were as wide as the entrance to the temple.

Chapter 31

Gal'dorok, Northwest of Khala Val'ur

Gift of the Shaper

D'kane rode on ahead of the rest of the company, his gray stallion seeming to be most comfortable when he was ahead of the others—a born competitor. Elyasha flanked him, about twenty paces behind, followed by Hullis and Dhrostain, who rode side by side and well out of earshot of D'kane, exchanging war stories and making small talk.

The road they traveled was an old one, coming north out of the mountain pass of Khala Val'ur, then turning northwest to head all the way to Lusk. It was mostly a dirt trail, said to have been made around the time of the Shaping War, and was well traveled by merchants and soldiers alike. When it was first traveled, by ancestors long since dead, they had called it *Thorad bo Thagran*, meaning "the path that leads to the sun." But in the many years that had passed, the unwieldy words in the name wore away like the dirt beneath it, and it became known simply as the Sun Path.

The countryside around them was flat and mostly empty, save for the occasional patch of trees punctuating the landscape, allowing riders on the Sun Path to see for miles. Because of that, as soon as they crossed the border from Gal'dorok into Derenar, they tended to stay off the road a ways in the hope of avoiding any patrols from nearby villages—Khyth were neither welcome nor expected anywhere west of the border.

Hullis

Leaning over in his saddle, Hullis got closer to Dhrostain. "We've been riding all day," he said, "and he hasn't said a word. I can't tell if he's quiet or resentful."

"Probably both," Dhrostain quipped as he scratched his beard. "But that's fine with me—never could stand Khyth. They make my skin crawl. The only reason I'm on this road right now is because the one man I respect more than anyone, General Tennech, ordered me to be. If not for him, I'd be back in Ghal Thurái training with my men." The older captain exhaled a quick puff of air through his nostrils in frustration.

Hullis scratched his head. His blond hair was tied up, jostling in time with his trotting mare. "I don't care one way or the other," he said. "But I'd much rather die on the battlefield than in the Breaking."—he shuddered—"Nothing is worth that."

The two of them looked forward to see D'kane holding up his hand and signaling them to a halt just off the road ahead.

"Night will fall soon. We will make camp here and wait," the Khyth stated.

The two captains looked at each other with smirks on their faces after seeing the wide open area beside the Sun Path that the Master Khyth had chosen to rest.

"Has he ever had to make camp before?" Dhrostain snickered quietly.

"Master Khyth," Hullis said loudly, "wouldn't we be better off finding someplace . . . less open?" He tried to phrase it as delicately as possible.

"No," D'kane answered sternly. "Apprentice," he said to Elyasha, never dignifying her by using her name, "that spot over there." He pointed to an area about fifty feet from the road, rocky and barren, with none of the makings of a proper campsite. Yasha nodded and slid from her horse.

Dhrostain scoffed at the impropriety of it all. "Best of luck to you," he said to his compatriot. "I'm off to find a better spot," and tugged on the reins of his horse to turn it around. Just as he did, though, Yasha lifted her hands and, with a great amount of strain and exertion, raised a small bit of the earth in a jagged, makeshift wall. It stood no higher than her ankles, and she had broken into a sweat, turning in defeat to her stern mentor, who was frowning at the effort.

"I expected more from you," D'kane said. With a quick flick of his hand, the wall surged upward, reaching nearly ten feet in height before it rumbled to a stop. "Especially from one so close to her Breaking."

Yasha winced. "Yes, Master D'kane."

"Show me you aren't completely useless, and go gather some wood for a fire," he growled.

"Yes . . . Master D'kane." Her words were soft and defeated. She turned to a small copse nearby to carry out her task.

"Apprentice," said Hullis suddenly as he held up his hand, "I'll help." His words made the other captain eye him incredulously as he swung his feet off his horse and walked over to the red-haired woman.

Gift of the Shaper

"Thank you," Yasha said quietly as the young captain approached. "I don't know what I'm doing." Her pale skin announced her blushing emphatically as she turned away.

D'kane had already dismounted and walked over to the campsite, and Dhrostain sighed and followed suit. Hullis chuckled to himself, knowing that Dhrostain was probably losing his mind being so close to the Master Khyth.

"It's no trouble," Hullis answered. "I expect that you haven't left the gates of the Sunken City too often." He was at ease around her, in glaring contrast to Dhrostain, and it seemed to have a calming effect on the young apprentice.

"I haven't," she replied. "This is my first time leaving the city, in fact. I was raised there and never had any reason to leave."

Hullis walked up to a medium-sized oak tree that looked like it had been dead for a few days, and started looking around on the ground. "Well, I can show you a few things if you like," he said, eyes fixed on the ground.

Yasha looked at the captain, then to the spot that he searched. "Please," she said. "Anything to keep me from disappointing him again," she said with a huff.

Hullis laughed at this while he looked around. "They really treat you like dirt, don't they?" He reached out for a few clumps of dried grass and held it up for her. "Tinder, to catch a spark."

"It's expected," she sighed, "especially for someone like me, forced into it because my mother was Khyth. There's no room for mistakes, and their eyes are on you constantly." She knelt down to help, seeing that he had moved on to gathering small sticks.

"Oh," Hullis said, suddenly looking up at her. "It wasn't your choice to become an apprentice?"

"Not at all," she answered quietly, wary that D'kane could be within earshot. "But if I say no to my heritage, to my birthright, I couldn't set foot in the city again. There would be no place for me." She tucked her hair behind her ears and looked at the captain. "Could you imagine me, looking the way I do, trying to be a warrior?" She pointed to her eyes, swirling green spheres, and scoffed, "It's unheard of. They'd laugh me out the door."

With a grunt of realization, Hullis agreed: "I'd never really thought about it like that. I always assumed it was an honor to be chosen." He handed her some twigs as short as his pinky finger and half as thin. "Here—some kindling to catch when the tinder burns."

"Only for those chasing power," she said. "So here I am, doing what the world expects from me."

"Well," Hullis said, "if you want to learn how to swing a sword, I understand that Captain Dhrostain is handy with a blade." He'd moved on to normal-sized sticks now and was using his arm to hold them against his body.

The young apprentice laughed. "Him?" she said, turning her head to see the short, bald man seated as far away from D'kane as he could reasonably get. "He wouldn't spit on me if I was on fire."

"We could test that theory," Hullis said as he rose, hands now full of sticks and branches. "Here," he said, handing her a few, "take these back, and we'll make one more pass."

With a nod, she grabbed what they had collected and walked it over to the camp, giving a nod of acknowledgement to both men. Neither reciprocated. She grimaced and turned and headed back to Hullis, who was rummaging around on his knees in his search for more firewood.

Chapter 32

Annoch

Gift of the Shaper

Thornton

"How can this be?" the Keeper said, unable to peel his eyes away from the hammer, which glowed white-hot from handle to head. "We've not heard so much as a whisper of its whereabouts since the Shaping War." He shielded his eyes from the ever-increasing strength of the light. "We had all thought it lost."

"Just like the Gwarái," Dailus mumbled, similarly captivated. Aldryd frowned uncomfortably at the realization.

As the antechamber was bathed in light, Thornton glanced incredulously at the hammer that his own father had given to him. He searched the faces of those around him, hoping for an answer from one of them, but was met with awe-struck silence.

The white marble walls of the inside of the Temple of the Shaper seemed to react to the light as if welcoming back an old friend, opening up and making the room as bright as the sun on a clear day. Thornton held the hammer away from him as if he feared what it was capable of—as if he was holding a venomous snake rather than his greatest boyhood treasure. The power of his habit, though, dispensed with his fear as he continued to hold it tightly, despite every impulse inside him begging him to do the opposite.

"What's happening?" He squinted through the rays of light streaming before him. "Why is it doing this?"

Aldryd was the first to speak up. "You've brought it home." His words were soft but heavy with veneration. "The Hammer of the Worldforge has been reunited with the Anvil."

"For the first time since the Shaper breathed life into our world," Dailus said, poring over the weight of the words, "the key is found."

Aldryd flashed a sidelong glance at the younger Athrani, as if noticing him for the first time. "Indeed it has," he said quietly. "And now, more than ever, it must be protected."

Dailus's eyes were focused intently on the Hammer as he nodded his agreement.

"The Khyth already have one piece of the puzzle," the Keeper was quick to remind everyone. "I cannot bear to think what would happen should they get their hands on the second."

Olson nodded in understanding. "Then, what?" he asked. "We destroy it?"

The corners of Aldryd's mouth curled up in amusement as he set his old, weathered eyes on the man from Highglade. "That would be the best course of action if any of us possessed the power to do so," he said, looking at the big blacksmith. "But, just as with the Breaker of the Dawn, it is not ours to destroy—only to contain." He looked again at the Hammer. "The powers that made it are far, far greater than the ones we possess. This very hammer was used in the forging of our world," he said with reverence. "How could we ever hope to destroy it? It would be easier for the world to extinguish itself than for us to break what made us."

Dailus, tearing his eyes off the Hammer, looked away. "Perhaps it is fate that brought it here."

"What do you mean?" the wizened Athrani asked as he looked at his younger countryman.

"The city of Annoch is one of the best protected in the whole of Derenar. Perhaps only the walls of Khala Val'ur are more formidable, and even they are considered nigh impenetrable." He looked again at the Hammer, then to Thornton. "The Hammer is exactly where it needs to be."

Thornton looked to Aldryd, whose face showed a deep mental anguish. The old Athrani touched a long finger to his parchment-thin lips and turned again to the Anvil of the Worldforge, clasping his hands behind his back and sighing deeply. "Though every Keeper is honored with the responsibility of the position, each one secretly hopes that he will never need to exercise it." He turned again to face them. "We have always known that the Pieces would be reunited, and each of us has feared the consequences." The pain on his face seemed to grow with each moment that passed. "Events have been set in motion that are now out of our hands." He turned to Alysana, who had been silent the whole time, saying, "Have Mordha put the guard on high alert. The Khyth are coming, and the Hammer must be protected."

Gift of the Shaper

The confusion on the faces of those in the temple seemed to spread in a wave, raising eyebrows and widening eyes as easily as the cold causes shivers.

"What makes you think they're coming?" Olson asked.

"The Khyth will breach the gates before the Breaker is set free," he answered. "So it is written." Turning again to Alysana, he said, "Swiftly, dear. Hurry!" He shooed her with his hands to emphasize his point.

Alysana's raven-black braids bobbed quickly as she nodded and made her way out of the temple, off to warn her sister who was standing guard at the city gates. Turning back to the others, Aldryd let his tranquil facade melt away to reveal the importunity that faced them all.

"Few living know of the existence of the Hammer, and fewer still of its location." He looked at each of them in turn. "Every one of you now carries a burden heavy enough to unravel the world. Pray that you have the strength to uphold it."

Thornton frowned and looked at the solid black head of the hammer, which had reverted to its old, familiar form. He was thinking of Miera, hoping—knowing—that she was still alive, and knew that he held in his hands the best chance of ever seeing her again. So focused on her was he that he barely felt the blow to the back of his head that brought him to his knees and into the black, hollow darkness where dreams hold sway.

Olson

Thornton laid face-first on the ground. He was bloody and bruised but still breathing as Olson knelt over him, now painfully aware of the burden of which Aldryd spoke. His first instinct was to shield his son from any further harm, but this was one threat he feared he might not be able to overcome.

"Here?" Aldryd's eyes undulated with power and rage. "In the very temple of your goddess?"

"She's not my goddess," Dailus shrieked at the old Athrani. "And she hasn't done a thing to deserve to be called so." He was standing, hands trembling, within reach of the Hammer, and the anger on his face recalled every Athrani who had spurned him for his half-eyed heritage and every human who had feared him for it.

"Even so," the Keeper retorted in stride, "the Hammer does not leave this temple. I will not allow it."

But as Dailus grabbed for the Hammer, they all knew it was already too late. The Khyth had indeed come, and without ever setting foot inside the city walls.

Metal scraped against stone as the young Athrani gripped the smooth, pale handle of the Hammer of the Worldforge and dragged it toward him. The energies in it, like the ones contained in the Anvil, were ancient and mighty. A human, like Thornton, would have no use for them, but an Athrani like Dailus, whose very existence was woven into the fabric of extra-worldly power, could capture them like sails harnessing the wind.

Dailus stood up, both of his eyes now fully golden, and laughed.

Through him now ran the primordial power that had shaped the world, the power that would one day break it.

"You won't allow it?" Dailus echoed mockingly. He tightened his grip on the handle, and the marble of the temple walls seemed to bulge outward. "I've had enough of being told what to do, being told I'm not good enough, because of, what—my eyes? Because of my heritage? Because I struggle with power that people like you take for granted?" He was clutching the Hammer with both hands, handle to the sky and head facing the floor, and in a swooping clockwise motion he raised the head above him like he was poised to strike an anvil. He gritted his teeth in frustration and fury, and brought the Hammer down in an arc, sending a shockwave surging outward from the floor, knocking down everyone around him and leaving him as the singular standing soul, steeped in stolen superiority.

"No more," he asserted, making his way to the temple door. A wave of his hand served to congeal the air around him, barring the way behind for anyone careless enough to try to follow him. "No more," he repeated and was gone.

Olson coughed blood onto the ground below him, hunched over and clutching his side. He looked at Aldryd, who was on his back a few feet from his son, tossed about in the exchange but only shaken up. He did not appear to be injured.

Thornton, on the other hand, seemed to be in much more dire straits.

"Olson," croaked the Keeper, "your son."

"He's alive, thank the Shaper," the big man grunted as he helped himself to his feet by placing his thick hands on one knee to help him stand. "Takes after his old man—stubborn, and doesn't know when to quit." The big blacksmith walked over to Aldryd and offered his hand, which the elder Athrani took thankfully.

When he was standing again, he looked to the temple's exit, where Dailus had strode only moments before, and frowned.

"The further away he gets," said the Keeper, "and the closer he comes to Khala Val'ur, the graver our situation becomes. But I fear that the power the Hammer grants him is too great and anything we do to try to stop him will be met with merciless and overwhelming ferocity."

Olson's eyes were not on the Keeper, but he didn't need to see him to know what he intended to do. The decision he was faced with was a difficult, if not impossible, one: risk the lives of the citizens of Annoch now or risk the lives of everyone who would see the Breaker confined to His prison.

"You don't plan to follow him, do you?" Olson asked, though his words sounded more like a statement than a question.

The silence of the temple reflected the mindset of the Keeper: passive, heavy, and conflicted.

Chapter 33

The Sun Path, East of Annoch

Gift of the Shaper

Dailus

Dailus crept toward the orange glow of firelight, barely discernible in the distance. He had been prepared to travel all the way to Khala Val'ur by himself, but if he was being met this close to Annoch it must mean that things were moving more quickly than anyone had anticipated.

Besides the sporadic popping of burning logs and the crackling of flames, there were no sounds.

He massaged the white ash handle of the Hammer as he neared the campsite, nervous but unafraid, yet still mindful of the power contained in the skillfully crafted relic he held in his hands. Walking closer, he froze when he heard movement.

"I thought I heard something," came a low growl, barely above a whisper.

"Then satisfy your curiosity, Captain," came an equally quiet reply.

He was motionless, questioning his decision, wondering if it was in fact the right one. *There are many paths to power*, he reasoned. Why shouldn't he take the one that was right in front of him? Having power is one thing, but being surrounded by power is another.

Wrestling with last-second doubts had distracted him more than he realized, as the sharp sound of drawn steel and the point of a sword against his back barely registered. It was only when he heard the words "Throw down the weapon or I'll put a hole in your back" that he realized he might be in over his head.

His fingers reflexively loosened their grip on the thick wooden handle, and the Hammer dropped heavily to the ground. He felt a strong hand on his arm, grabbing him firmly and whirling him around to face his captor—a hard-looking man much shorter than him, with a bald head and a jet-black beard, holding up a sword to his throat.

"It's an Athrani," the man called over his shoulder. The sound of another sword being drawn pierced the air. "He's armed."

A second man, blond and tall, walked over to them with quickness in his step and a look of determination on his face. "What is an Athrani doing on the road to Khala Val'ur?"

"Please," Dailus said with his hands held aloft in surrender, "I can explain."

"There will be no need," came a third voice. Dailus looked over to see a Khyth, draped in black robes, walking toward them. "He is one of ours." A look of confusion washed over the faces of the two men as the Khyth approached and motioned their swords down. "Dailus," he said, "there is only one reason I can think of to see you standing here, and I hope for your sake I am right."

When D'kane had agreed to let him keep his Shaping power in exchange for keeping an eye on Olson, he'd had no idea the trouble he would have to go through. He had just hoped it would be worth it.

"I brought it, Master D'kane," he said, shaking a little, "just like you asked."

"Show me."

Dailus indicated the Hammer lying on the ground, and the eyes of D'kane, swirling and strange, flashed with hunger. "So you did," the black-robed Valurian said as he gazed upon one of the pieces of creation. "And you have my thanks."

Dailus felt like a scared child who wanted nothing more than to please his father. "Will you take me to the Sunken City, then? Like you promised? I've done what you asked." His words were full of hope but underscored his fright, as he wanted only to find himself in the company of those with power.

"Yes," D'kane said as he looked down his nose at Dailus. He turned to the one who had held the sword to his throat, saying, "Captain Dhrostain, his reward."

The armor-clad warrior nodded and approached Dailus. With the quickness and precision that only years of handling a blade could bring, Dhrostain thrust out his sword, sending it straight through Dailus's chest, and pulled it back out to wipe it on the Athrani's robes before he could even fall to his knees. A cry of surprise came, not from Dailus but from a hooded woman nearby, who seemed to be witnessing violent death for the first time.

Gift of the Shaper

The battle-hardened captain looked at his sword, mostly free from blood, and forced it back into his sheath as he turned back to the campsite as casually as if he had done nothing more than relieve himself in the woods.

Shock and confusion covered Dailus's face as his last-second doubts were inexorably justified. He felt his life slipping away as the thought of Aidren crept into his mind, surrounded by strangers and left to die; and he couldn't help but think that things might have been different somehow, some way. His eyes rolled back in his head as he fell forward, feeling the words "have the apprentice bury him out of sight" sting just as deeply as the captain's blade had stung. A thought flittered into his mind as he felt unconsciousness creep in around him: at least he had not given up the secret of who the girl was.

***

A whimper of acknowledgement came from the young woman with the teeming green eyes. With help from the taller of the two captains, she put Dailus on the back of her horse to move him away from their campsite and into a shallow grave.

"We have what we came for," D'kane said coldly, "and must not waste any more time. The moment she returns, we make for Khala Val'ur."

Chapter 34

The Sun Path, East of Annoch

Gift of the Shaper

Elyasha

Elyasha looked back at the bleeding body of the Athrani—someone she had been raised to hate since birth—and felt nothing, not hatred, not pity, not fear—nothing. She was as empty as the Valurian sky, and just as cold.

The shock of seeing Dhrostain so swiftly and effortlessly take another life made her question everything she knew and everything her people stood for. It had rattled her to the core and had made her realize that she could not be a part—could never be a part—of what they were trying to accomplish, because of the cruelty, the thoughtless killing, but most of all, because of the inability to choose anything for herself.

She wasn't sure exactly when she had made up her mind to leave; she had just continued to ride instead of stopping to bury the body. After a while, she feared that she may have been pursued by one of them, coming to claim her again and take her back to Khala Val'ur, where she would be made an example of, as a lesson to the other apprentices who had any thoughts of leaving the ranks of the Hand. But no one came, not D'kane, not Dhrostain, not even Hullis—which, she had to admit, made her a little disappointed. The blond captain had been the first human—the first person—to treat her like she was an individual and not just another apprentice to be Broken. He looked upon her not with fear but with . . . Was it respect? She suddenly felt like she had lost all sense of the word's meaning as she remembered the cold, thoughtless orders that had sprung from the mouth of D'kane or any other Master Khyth who had once lorded over her. She rid herself of the thought and focused on the path ahead.

The heavy hoofbeats of her horse pounded hypnotically below her as she rode on, a black-on-white streak beneath a cloudy gray sky. Day had broken a while ago, and she wondered how long the three of them had waited campside before realizing she would not be coming back. Apprentices of Khyth blood hardly ever left the city, since they were too precious a resource to be allowed off by themselves. And none of them ever left for good. Her mother had almost managed to escape, years before she was born, even managing to settle down and raise a family—

but even that came to an end. While Yasha was still growing in the womb, her mother had been tracked down by agents of the Hand and brought back to Khala Val'ur, where she eventually gave birth. If she had not been carrying the life of a Khyth inside her, she would have been killed on the spot. Luckily for Yasha, they waited until the moment she was born to do it instead.

The path she trod was made of dirt, stretching all the way from Annoch to Lusk, and was the primary road connecting the two cities. As such, the footsteps of forebearers too numerous to count had flattened the passage into a uniform and well-worn route along its length that was familiar to those who traveled it, one time or one hundred.

Sharp coughing from the Athrani startled her as she realized her efforts to bandage him were not in vain. Shortly after she had left, she had done what she could to stem the bleeding, knowing full well that she would not make it into the city of Annoch without a large bargaining chip to grant her asylum. A Khyth in the City of the Forge was as unheard of as an Athrani in Khala Val'ur. And of those, she knew only one. *Improbable but not impossible*, she told herself.

She turned her head to the man she was transporting. He was alive but not awake. His breaths came sharply and labored, no doubt thanks to the wound that ran deep within his chest and just below his heart, meant to bleed him slowly to death in the cruelest way possible. She thought again of Dhrostain and how he had looked at her—with fear and contempt. *Given the chance, he would have done the same to me without hesitation,* she thought. Of this, there was not a doubt in her mind.

The thunderous hoofbeats of her mare charged steadily on toward Annoch, which she knew was her best and closest refuge from the riders of the Sunken City. If she could make it to the gates, she knew she would be safe. She knew she would be protected beyond its towering walls.

She also knew there was no turning back. Her fate had been sealed the very moment she had decided to flee.

At the edge of her vision, the surging crest of the spire of Annoch rose like a beacon of hope, signaling freedom and escape and promising respite. She trudged on with her valuable encumbrance in tow as she pulled back the hood that covered her light orange hair, revealing a face far too fair to be called Khyth. As she drew closer, her heart began to race even more than it had when she left. She feared death, like any living thing should, and she feared punishment. But the thing that kept her going was stronger than both of those: the fear of turning back to leave freewill behind her. So, unwaveringly, she pressed on. Her mind had been made up, and her path had been set—two things that she had never thought could be said of her life.

When she finally approached the gate, imposing and impenetrable, she dismounted, gritted her teeth in uncertainty, and raised her hands high in the air in a clear display of surrender.

"Greetings," she called out to the tower beside it. "I . . . I want to come in."

The deep voice of one of the guards boomed back to her as he approached. "What brings you to Annoch?"

Her answer came clearly and without fear, like she had practiced it a thousand times before. "An Athrani who needs to be brought to justice."

The fiery red eyes of the guard stared at her like she had three heads. What may have confused him even more than the unconscious Athrani before him was the fact that there was a Khyth staring him right in the face, out in the open.

"You're a long way from Khala Val'ur," he said gruffly. "We don't see much of your kind this far from the Sunken City."

Though she looked like a normal human in almost all respects, Elyasha's eyes were a dead giveaway. They marked her for what she was; and what she was, was not welcome anywhere west of Gal'dorok. She could see that the guard was already uncomfortable with the sight of her, despite the fact that he was nearly twice her size. His skin was savage and bruised, and he carried himself like a man who had no fear, but something about his demeanor had changed when he saw her.

"Your accent—" Yasha said, "you're from beyond the Wastes."

Though she'd never before left the confines of Khala Val'ur, she'd had more than her fair share of run-ins with travelers from beyond the great desert of Khulakorum passing through the Sunken City on their way to a better life. The ones she'd spoken to had all said the same thing: they braved the unforgiving land south of Lash'Kargá, the last remaining outpost among the sands, because to have stayed would have meant death. The man standing before her, his hair as red as fire, would undoubtedly say the same.

"I am," came the simple reply. "But that was long ago, and I have left the tribes behind. My place is here, in Annoch, where wars and kings are both tales for children."

She studied him, his dark features and his hard face. He was a wanderer, like herself, looking to escape from the path that had been chosen for him and the violence and cruelty that it spawned. "Then you, better than anyone, should understand why I need to get into the city."

"We are all running from something, Jinda," came the voice of a woman, startling Elyasha and causing her to look past the guard in surprise. A tall woman—G'henni, judging by the darkness of her skin—was walking toward her. "This one seems to be no exception. I will take her to Aldryd. No doubt he will at least be interested in this half-dead Athrani."

A feeling of hope and relief washed over Elyasha—then quickly disappeared when she felt cold steel slap onto her wrists. Looking pleadingly at the G'henni woman, she was met with a stare as cold as the shackles.

"My thanks, Mordha," said the man from beyond the Wastes. "And take the Kienari with you. He's making the rest of the men uneasy, and I'm afraid we'll have an uprising if he stays any longer."

"Kienari," Elyasha whispered breathlessly.

"You heard him, Kethras," Mordha seemed to say to the darkness. "Inside with you, while it's still dark enough for you to move around."

"Very well," came the reply.

Elyasha could only reconcile the words as some sort of death growl from a mountain lion about to make her its prey. She screamed and ducked but didn't get far. Mordha still had a firm grip on the chains that bound her wrists. And when the G'henni threw her head back in laughter, it only served to confuse her even more.

"I think she's just met her first Kienari," Jinda said with amusement.

"Perhaps," Kethras snarled. "But this is not my first time meeting a Khyth."

The words seemed to come from nearby, closer than the growl just a moment ago, but Elyasha could not tell from where. She strained her eyes in the darkness to try to pinpoint the source of the noise but came up empty. Just as she was about to give up, she saw a flicker of moonlight that seemed to form . . .a head?

When it finally came into focus, she thought she had managed to bring a nightmare to life as it stared her in the face. The creature's cloak of darkness blended seamlessly with the night—so dark that it seemed to make the surrounding blackness even darker. She thought that his face resembled that of a cat or a wolf or some strange mixture of the two, but his eyes, huge and dark, were completely alien.

Elyasha, with more fascination than fear, stood up and looked at the avatar of night before her. Though her rational mind now told her that she was safe, the hairs on her neck were standing on end, and a shiver like ice water ran down her spine. She gulped and asked, "What are you?"

Kethras looked at her and blew a puff of air out though his nostrils but would give no further response. He turned to Mordha, saying, "We should go. My friend will be waiting for me."

Chapter 35

The Sun Path, East of Annoch

Gift of the Shaper

Dhrostain

Hullis and Dhrostain exchanged nervous glances, like they had figured out the answer to a question that neither would voice aloud.

Dhrostain frowned as he looked over to the Master Khyth, who had his back turned to them, facing the light of the rising sun. Finally, after a long silence, he spoke: "She's not coming back."

D'kane did not turn around, but his anger was evident. "No matter. We have what we came for." His words were victorious, but they reeked of defeat. "I will deliver the Hammer to Yetz personally."

Dhrostain was unsure if his tone implied anger or embarrassment. He'd heard that D'kane was not one to be defied and had no tolerance for disobedience. But, even more than this, he had never had an apprentice leave his control. He looked nervously to his companion as he wondered how exactly the wrath of a spurned master Khyth might manifest itself. He would find out, as the black-hooded Valurian turned to face them, anger flowing in his otherworldly eyes.

With his hood off, D'kane was a fearsome reminder of the power of the Breaking, as his cracked and blackened skin pulsed with inner rage, swelling with power and looking less human than Dhrostain thought possible. He had seen traitors burnt at the stake before and was sickeningly reminded of them when he looked upon the Master Khyth.

Hesitantly, Hullis inquired of the black-clad servant of the Hand, "Are we to return to Khala Val'ur without her?"

D'kane looked evenly at the young captain. It was evident that the desire to return to his city and his men was greater than his fear of any power the Khyth wielded. A twisted grin of amusement crept across D'kane's lips as he answered, "I am, Captain Hullis. And I will answer for her absence."

The captains exchanged puzzled glances when he spoke only of himself, as if he intended to leave them behind.

D'kane wrapped his long fingers around the smooth handle of the Hammer as the horn around his neck glowed. He had the look of a man who was staring his salvation in the face. "Once word has reached

Annoch that the Hammer is gone, there is no doubt in my mind that the Athrani will try to take it back." He glared into the eyes of the captains deliberately, in turn. "See that you at least slow them down."

Dhrostain's skin crawled from just looking at the Khyth, and he averted his eyes onto the ground. A mixture of fear and disgust convulsed through him as he tried to maintain his bearing.

"What is it you would have us do?" Hullis asked, still mostly in control of his faculties.

The ghastly eyes of D'kane probed the young captain as they appeared to be looking for weakness, but finding none. "Surely, your general has given you instructions," he said as he turned and walked to his mount, placing one foot in the stirrup and effortlessly climbing atop, with one hand firmly grasping the Hammer. "I suggest you follow them."

With those words and no further explanation, the Master Khyth thumped his feet into the animal's rib cage to spur it forward, leaving the two Thurian captains steeped in silent confusion.

They watched, dumbfounded, as he rode away without so much as looking back, leaving them with nothing else but the horses they rode in on and the packs on their backs.

Dhrostain, overcome by the stress of the whole ordeal but relieved to finally be rid of the Khyth, promptly took to a knee and vomited.

Chapter 36

Annoch

Gift of the Shaper

Dailus

The inside of an Athrani prison was not a pleasant place to be, and Dailus found himself cursing his half-eyed heritage—rather than his own foolish decision making—that he should wind up in one.

He sat with his legs and arms crossed, elbows resting on his knees. The cell was barely big enough to lie down in, and the ceiling was built low enough that he could not stand comfortably—part of the allure of the celebrated Athrani prison building. The walls, in contrast with most prisons, were wood—splintered and dried from years of disrepair, but thick and sturdy enough to securely hold their prisoners. The sulfur smell of urine stung his eyes and nostrils as he looked at the corner and frowned, noting the lack of cleanliness that the last occupant seemed to have had. There were no windows, and his cell was wrapped in darkness.

As near as he could tell, he was somewhere below the Temple of the Shaper, judging by the cell. Ellenian prisons were typically larger and loud; Annochian prisons had their own flavor to them, and this reeked of it. The stone beneath him was cold, and the air was stale—neither of which surprised him—but the fact that he was still alive left him puzzled.

His hand went slowly to his chest where Dhrostain had run him through, and he flinched at the pain of the slow-healing wound. He wasn't sure how he had ended up here, but he remembered hearing the voice of a woman. His head ached, and he was almost certain that he had come in on a horse, though he had no recollection of how or when.

Just as he was about to delve deeper into thought, the iron bolt securing his prison clanked open and the door swung out. Olson, arms crossed and frowning, stood in the door in front of a well-armored Athrani jailer, who turned and left at Olson's insistence.

The big blacksmith took a breath and looked down his nose at Dailus. "How is it," he said gruffly, "that we always manage to meet in a prison cell?"

Dailus cupped his face in his hands in shame, offering no answer. Whether it was actual shame or just stubbornness that held his tongue seemed to matter little to Olson. The big man was wont to speak his mind.

"You could rot in here until the world ends for all I care," he said, looking at the Athrani. "And after what you did, that might be sooner rather than later. But we need to know what you know." He stared sternly at Dailus, who still had his face buried in his hands. "And what you told the Khyth."

For the first time since Olson had entered the cell, Dailus looked up at him. "Nothing, I swear. I didn't tell them anything," he said. Defeat hung heavily from his words as he frowned. When a surge of pain reminded him of his fresh wound, he closed his eyes again to speak. "I didn't even have a chance to. They were on me in seconds . . ."

Olson rubbed his chin with a scowl, shifting his weight from front leg to back. "Aldryd didn't even want to come see you," he said, eyeing the Athrani that was huddled pathetically in front of him. "You're lucky. You've at least earned a stay of execution until this whole thing blows over." He thought he heard a sigh but wasn't sure if it was from relief or disappointment. "So all they have is the Hammer?" he asked. "Nothing more?"

"Nothing more," Dailus confirmed.

The big man considered this with a frown, shook his head, and turned to leave. As he crossed the threshold of the cell, though, he stopped. Without turning around, he voiced one word.

"Why?"

Dailus looked up at the broad shoulders and back of the blacksmith from Highglade. Those shoulders had gotten them out of the converted Khyth prison where he had first met D'kane, days before Olson showed up, just like the Khyth had said. They had carried Aidren, the Athrani whom he had barely got to know before his life was cut short. And they had carried the burden—albeit shortly—of the true identity of the Shaper. He wondered if his own shoulders could continue to carry that burden or if they would even have the chance after the Athrani justice system dealt with him.

"I'm an outcast, Olson," he answered. "I never fit in with the Athrani and didn't fare much better with the humans. I never found a place to call home, despite a lifetime of searching." He looked to where a window would have been had it been any other prison cell. "I thought if I gave them what they wanted, the Khyth might find a use for me."

He sighed and looked back to Olson to find that he was alone again.

Closing his eyes, he told himself that it was for the best. His shoulders ached enough as it was.

Olson

As he shut the door to Dailus's cell, Olson thought he heard the beginnings of a sob, but he didn't intend to give it any acknowledgement. He nodded to the Athrani soldier beside him, who closed and locked the door.

"Please," came the soft voice of a woman, sounding as if it were miles away.

Olson stopped as he tried to figure out if he had indeed heard anything at all.

"Please. Is someone there?" the voice came again.

Olson looked to the jailer. "Is there someone else down here?"

The jailer nodded, saying, "A Khyth they captured at the gate. She was the one that brought in the half-eye,"—the word was filth on his tongue—"so we put her down here until we get word from the Keeper on what to do with her."

Even though the jailer was tall, Olson still had to look down when he talked to him. "Could I see her? She might know something," he said with a shrug of his bulky shoulders.

The jailer looked past Olson to his commanding officer, who gave a nod. "This way."

The two of them walked down the thin corridor that wound through the underground jail. The cells were spaced far apart—a design intended to make prisoners feel even more secluded—and the only light to guide them came from torches on the wall. Deeper inside, Olson noticed that the torches were not lit; the jailer started lighting them as they got deeper in. Whoever was being held down here was doing so in total darkness.

"Please, I haven't done anything wrong," came the pleading voice, nearer now.

"Quiet, Khyth," barked the jailer from behind Olson. "You know what your people have done. You're lucky to be alive at all down here." He mumbled a few choice words in Athrani as they neared the source of the voice.

Right away, Olson could tell that the cell was nothing like the others. It was small, maybe half the size of the one housing Dailus, and cramped. What's more, there was not one but two locked doors between her and her freedom. The outer door was lined with thick, vertical bars made of iron, and the inner door was made of solid stone, with a single round hole in the middle for air and food. Olson was amazed that they were able to hear her at all.

The guard took out a key to unlock the padlock of the great barred door, swinging it open with a metallic *clank*. For the second door, he did what only an Athrani jailer could do, changing part of the stone in the middle into a metal keyhole through a small effort of Shaping. When he had finished, he used the same key to unlock it, swinging it open past a mystified Olson.

There, on the floor of the cell, was a girl no older than Thornton, with untamed red hair falling down past her shoulders. She was curled up in a ball and shielding her eyes with one hand when Olson walked in. It was still dark enough inside that Olson could make out little more than an outline.

"Please," she repeated, "I was born a Khyth, but it's not who I am."

Olson watched as she lowered her hand, uncovering her face, and almost jumped backward when he saw her eyes, brightly visible despite the darkness of the cell. They were green and wild, dancing in the shadows on her face, and reminded him of a memory long-forgotten, yet one that was still painful enough to make him flinch when it came bubbling back to the surface.

"Then who are you?" he asked, his gruff demeanor fighting its way through.

Gift of the Shaper

"My name is Elyasha. I was a Khyth apprentice, but . . ."

"But what?"

"But I ran," she said. "And I'm not going back. I can't," she said between breaths. "They'll kill me."

"Who?" Olson had his arms crossed over his chest and gave no mind to the fact that he probably looked terrifying to the young girl. "Who's going to kill you?"

"Master Khyth D'kane," she answered meekly, "and anyone who will listen to him."

Olson knew that name and knew that nothing good came from being associated with it. He also knew that the girl was telling the truth: they would kill anyone that fled the city. He knew it far too well.

"Then tell me what you know, Elyasha. I might be able to get you out of here," he said. His words were met with an angry look from the Athrani guard. "It might be in chains, but I'm sure that's better than being stuck in this hole."

The young woman sniffed and wiped her eyes. In the dim light, Olson saw that they were red and puffy from crying.

"Yasha," she said. "Call me Yasha."

Olson stood in silence for a moment. Then, like a bear coming out of hibernation, he moved again, slowly. "Alright, Yasha, tell me what you know."

His eyes were fixed on the girl, whose fiery red hair took him back to Highglade and back to the only woman whom he'd ever loved.

Aldryd

The Keeper of the Anvil's long gray hair hung loosely at his shoulders as he peered out a small window that was cut into the marble wall of the second story of the temple. From it, he could see over the gate and out into the great Talvin forest that lay between Annoch and Lusk. Staring at the treetops that blotted out any view of the ground, he frowned as he felt his hope slipping away like the fading rays of light from a sinking sun.

The inside of the temple was empty save for him and one other man, a dark-haired Athrani garbed in blazing orange and red—the robes of the archaic order of the Fires of Ellenos, whose members were as few as they were elusive. This one, whose title was that of Speaker, was known to Aldryd as Deyhan.

A remnant of ages past, Deyhan's was a position deemed necessary, even sacred, when the world had been plagued with war. But the halcyon days that followed had caused their number to dwindle and fade, and the once-mighty Fires of Ellenos became no more than dying embers spread across a barren land, leaving a mere handful of men to desperately fan the coals of a smoldering ancient tradition. Now they were all but ceremonial, much like the Keeper of the Anvil had always been since the time of the Shaping War. But that, Aldryd knew, had changed the night the Shaper was taken.

The aged Athrani turned to the Speaker to address him. "I hope your skills are as sharp as they say, Deyhan. I have words that must reach Ellenos, and swiftly."

The young man grinned with a slight bow, softly touching his left shoulder with two fingertips of his right hand. "They are, Keeper. My father taught me well." Looking up again to see worry creased across a normally placid face, Deyhan rose. "But may I ask what troubles you?"

Aldryd closed his eyes and winced, as if saying the words out loud pained him. "Khala Val'ur moves to break the chains that bind the Breaker." He looked into the eyes of the Speaker, deep brown inside an azure ring, and spoke his urgency with weighty dismay. "It may already be too late, but I will not remit myself to that assumption. I will do everything in my power to see that they fail." He paused, considering his words carefully. "Anything and everything."

Deyhan's face was stalwart as the Keeper spoke. "You mean to awaken the Three." The words were as thin and frail as a man on his deathbed.

"What choice do we have?" Aldryd threw up his hands in defeat. "I would burn Annoch to the ground if I thought it would help. We must

𝔊ift of the 𝔖haper

loose every last man in defense of the chains and do so quickly before it is too late." He sucked in air through his nostrils, fueling a solemn prayer. "Shaper be with us," he said, "and Ellenos too."

With a curt nod of acknowledgement, the Speaker knew his task. "I will begin at once."

"Thank you, Deyhan. It will be good to speak to Sh'thanna again." A sigh escaped his lips before he spoke again. "I only regret that it must be under these circumstances."

With a final bow, the young Athrani turned to the window to do what very few others could. His brow was furrowed in steady concentration as he summoned a power now nearly forgotten, tucked away in only the stories of what once was.

A pallid glow emanated from his forehead, just above and between his eyes, spilling onto the floor like liquid light filling an invisible container. It coalesced as Deyhan willed it into being—a luminescent mass of indeterminate form and features that served to remind Aldryd that not all of the ancient ways were lost.

Slowly, the light formed a pillar, fluctuating weakly in the middle of the room.

Conjuring the pillar was no easy task, and it certainly showed from the effort on Deyhan's face as he struggled to gain control, like a dreamer roughly roused from sleep and made to command an unwilling body. The motions of his hands, however, were intricate and easy, and they came by instinct, the result of long years of practice and tradition, passed down by his father, and perfected in secret long after his passing. A wave of one hand preceded the sweep of another, as each performed a hypnotic and rhythmic dance that seemed equally independent yet somehow synchronized. His left hand rolled over as he fanned his fingers out, copying the motion with his right hand and bringing the backs of his hands together so they barely touched before thrusting them apart again. So much of the conjuring was mental, but the gestures were every bit as important. For this reason, every Speaker practiced them endlessly until they became second nature.

He pressed his hands together in front of his chest, with the heels of his hands resting against his sternum, his fingers together and pointing straight out. Moving his hands forward in synchrony, he thrust them into the column of light that wavered before him, bringing his hands apart and commanding the pillar of light to do the same.

As he did this, Aldryd felt the air around him rush suddenly toward the light as a void was opened and something else hurried to fill it. The pillar pulsed and jumped, and a whispered boom cracked like distant thunder. Aldryd knew that a similar pillar of light had also opened far away in the Temple of Ellenos.

Deyhan, teeth clenched in effort, turned his palms to the ceiling and made a final, silent grunt of exertion as the room flooded with light and sound, culminating with a tremendous clap like thunder as a steady hum of energy burst in and engulfed them. He lowered his hands and was silent, taking a deep breath of relief as the room seemed to relax along with him. The portal was stable, and his work was done. Wearily, he smiled at Aldryd, who returned the gesture.

"You have not lost your touch, son of Yaden," said the Keeper. "Your father taught you well indeed." Turning his head, he looked through the portal of light that had been conjured up and stared into the face of a beautiful Athrani woman, who looked as intrigued as she was pleased to see him.

"Aldryd," she said, her voice shaky and low as it passed through the tear in the world that now linked Annoch with Ellenos, hundreds of miles away. She was garbed in an elegant robe of purple and white inlaid with gold, with a small but opulent crown seated atop her head. *"Nif haca me'le fada'thu."* The words of the old tongue came forth like honey and were just as sweet.

"It is good to see you too, Sh'thanna," the Keeper replied warmly. "How long has it been? Five years? Ten?"

The woman on the other side smiled coyly as she closed her eyes and shook her head. If not for the licks of gray that weaved through her hair, she would have shown no sign of aging at all. "Twenty, by my count," she said, "though I cannot fault you for it. Annoch needs a Keeper just as Ellenos needs hers. It is just a shame you have not left the protection of your gates in all this time."

Visible through the portal was the throne room of Ellenos where its Keeper sat. It was as majestic and refined as the woman who occupied it. Lining the alabaster walls were tapestries depicting lore and legend sacred to her people, ranging from the moment of creation to the birth of the first Athrani. They hung from high walls that surrounded the throne room, which was seated inside an equally impressive temple whose sole function was to glorify the Shaper. The Athrani owed everything they had to their goddess—and they knew it.

Sh'thanna's pale blue eyes were inlaid with a ring of deep blue that made her stand out even among the Athrani, which had played no small part in her being chosen as Keeper at an unprecedentedly young age. She had presided—though some might say ruled—over their capital city of Ellenos for nearly sixty years. Her word was law, and her reach was immense.

"So why is it," she continued, "that you appear to me now?"

The smile of familiarity faded from Aldryd's face as he seemed to suddenly remember the reason he had beckoned his old friend. The heaviness of his heart was almost visible as he spoke. "No doubt you felt it, Sh'thanna." He was loath to speak the words aloud, as if keeping them silent would somehow unravel their truth.

The Keeper of Ellenos grimaced, hiding pain behind her now-fading smile. Denial was written on her face as she shared in Aldryd's attempt to suppress what they both knew to be real. "I did, old friend. Is it as I feared?"

"They have her," was all that Aldryd managed to whisper before turning his head to try to regain his composure. With a voice as stern as stone he said, "Khala Val'ur seeks to free the Breaker, as we have always known and feared. But now they have the means to do it."

Sh'thanna frowned, more out of disappointment than unhappiness, as she stood up to pace the room. "What is it you ask of me, Aldryd?" The unearthly tear in the world followed her as she moved.

"The chains must be protected, Sh'thanna," he answered. "I have no doubt that the Khyth know of their whereabouts in this world. I ask for the full might of the Athrani Legion to defend them."

Sh'thanna stopped in her tracks and looked at Aldryd, whose face showed no emotion. "No," she said, "not the full might. I will not awaken the Three." Aldryd started to speak, but she cut him off: "Not as long as I live. I fear we may succeed in destroying the world we intended to save. It is simply too much to ask."

Aldryd's eyebrows narrowed as he thought briefly of protesting, but he bit his tongue instead. Collecting his thoughts, he said, "Military might, Shaping or otherwise, will be the key to stopping the Khyth. We need troops—there is simply no way around it."

"Then I will send you what I have," Sh'thanna answered, "down to the last man."

The old Keeper nodded his thanks. "Annoch is mustering troops as we speak, though their number will not be as great. I have not reached out to Lusk, though I fear the influence of the Hand of the Black Dawn may be greater than anyone realizes."

"Is it worth the risk?"

"I cannot answer that now," Aldryd said. "I will wait until I can speak with the commanders and weigh their input. I have no mind for military affairs; I am but a keeper of secrets and traditions."

This made Sh'thanna smile through the wavering portal. "Of course you are," she said, knowing full well that he was much more than that. "I will call for the commanders, then; and as soon as they can be ready, I will have them depart."

"Thank you, Sh'thanna. Annoch will welcome the Athrani Legion."

He turned to Deyhan and nodded, signaling the end of the need for the link between the two cities. With a nod in return, Deyhan turned to the shimmering portal and thrust his hands forward. Balling them into tight fists as if grabbing onto pieces of rope, he gritted his teeth and pulled his hands apart, cinching the break in the world into a flat, horizontal line. Then, with no small effort, he clapped his hands together and the breach disappeared, leaving the room silent and cold as ever.

With a reverent bow to the Keeper, he turned to exit, leaving him alone to tend to his thoughts—thoughts that were yet plagued with uncertainty.

The gray-haired Athrani once again peered out the window overlooking the woods beyond the gate, as he had done countless times throughout his long life, and wondered. He wondered how his brother had turned so far from the city they loved as children and if there had been something he could have done that might have made him stay. Perhaps all of this could have been avoided.

Or perhaps this all was preordained.

A pallid hand covered his eyes in frustration as the sting of tears deepened his pain. *None of that matters,* he thought. *The only thing that matters is the road to Khala Val'ur, which will once again be flooded with Athrani boots and human swords.*

If it's war Yetz wants, Aldryd thought, *then he is certain to have it.*

He knew his brother too well to think differently.

D'kane

There was urgency in every hoof beat as D'kane pushed his mount onward down the Sun Path. He knew time was of the essence, and it would not be long before Annoch—and Ellenos—knew that the Khyth were close to their goal. Who knew what that foolish apprentice had gone off and done?

Charging down the road, he flexed his fingers over the wooden handle of the Hammer and felt the power pulse through him like a current. Its allure was palpable, and the desire to use it burned in his hand like hot coals. The last time he felt this much power . . .

He remembered very clearly the day the Otherworld had first coursed through him—savage; thunderous; overwhelming; the very energy of creation, present when the Shaper first breathed life into the world, filling every fiber of his being. He had cried out in agony when it first happened; it had taken him by surprise. He had known it was coming—every apprentice who underwent the ceremony knew—but he'd had no idea it would be so painful. It was the gift that the Breaker imparted to them, but it came at a price.

The intensity nearly blinded him, forcing him to his knees and wrenching the breath from his lungs. As the power of the Otherworld washed through him and over him, he was suddenly aware of the powerful smell of cooked meat, and his screams only worsened when he realized it was his own self, his charring, burning flesh, that battered his senses. Even now, it made him gag just thinking about it.

It had only been him and one other apprentice—D'kane could no longer recall his name—and he had not been so lucky. The power was too much for him, this apprentice who was not even of Khyth blood. He was a human off the streets of Khala Val'ur who hoped to find for himself the power of which others only dreamt. *No wonder he did not survive,* the Master Khyth thought wryly.

He shook his head to rid himself of the memory and focused on the path ahead. The road back to the Sunken City was long and would take more time than he was comfortable with, but as long as he kept a steady pace, he could make it in time to begin the ceremony of opening the way to the Otherworld.

He no longer cared about being seen out in the open, he realized. Handling the Hammer of the Worldforge had not only filled him with power but it had also seemingly pushed out any inhibitions, such as fear and caution, and replaced them with recklessness and defiance, as if he was daring the world to come at him. It was that same impulsiveness that caused him to ride off without the two human captains accompanying him.

No matter, he thought, *they would only slow me down. And there are much more pressing matters to attend to.*

He felt a burning inside of him, though, almost a hunger lingering in the back of his mind like a wolf stalking through a heavy fog. He knew it was there, but it was impossible to tell what it was. He could feel that it wanted something. He glanced down at the Hammer as if he expected to

Gift of the Shaper

find an answer, but the ashen handle and black steel head remained ever silent.

As his mount carried on down the Sun Path, the beginnings of a thought crept into D'kane's mind: he could use the Hammer. He didn't have to turn it over to Yetz.

The mountains of the Great Serpent crept up the horizon like a lumbering giant as the Master Khyth ventured onward, seeds of doubt already taking root and planting themselves firmly in his mind.

Chapter 37

Ghal Thurái

Gift of the Shaper

Durakas

Commander Caladan Durakas stood on the outstretched marble slab of Ghal Thurái, listening to the synchronized breathing of his troops behind him. He had received the summons from Khala Val'ur, just like Lady Edos had said he would, and was determined to march to the Capital and on to glory. But glory, as he knew, always came at a price.

"They are ready, Commander," came a voice from behind him.

He turned to see his own advisor, Duna Cullain, approaching him on horseback, having just emerged from the depths of the mountain city. The young blonde woman was outfitted for battle and looked every bit the part of a commander's advisor—stern, gritty, and showing no weakness. The column of armored men in front of her parted to let her through, doing so in perfect synchronicity like an armored wave of water.

The army of Ghal Thurái had built its reputation on being mechanically sound and ruthlessly efficient, as the scores of dead Chovathi would no doubt point out if they could. Their movements were drilled into them night and day, over and over, until they acted as one. There was no other army, outside of the Lonely Guard of Lash'Kargá, that could claim to be so well-trained and efficient. Commander Durakas knew that their reputation would precede them, though it would do little good anywhere west of Khala Val'ur. To the Athrani, or even to anyone living in Lusk, they were no more than ghost stories. They had not marched west of the mountains of the Great Serpent since before the Shaping War.

"Then we march," Durakas answered. His deep voice carried effortlessly, thundering throughout the marble enclosure that made up the entrance to the Mouth of the Deep. His white breastplate, upon which was etched a copper fanged mouth—the crest of Ghal Thurái—shone dully in the morning sun, matching the luster of the rock that had made the city famous. His own horse, standing beside him, was every bit as imposing as the army that stood behind him: sixteen hands high, with fierce black eyes and a coat of copper. It was bred from the sturdy stock of those horses found beyond the Wastes of Khulakorum, favored by the many tribes of Khadje Kholam for their hardiness in battle and their endurance.

The commander turned to face his troops, crowding the entrance to the Mouth. They were uniformly garbed, wearing chain mail that had been colored white so as to identify them as the Thurian army—possibly saving any potential attackers the trouble of needlessly throwing their lives away. Anything less than a fully calculated and well-organized attack against the Fist of Thurái would be an exercise in futility. One might as well cut a stone to see if it bleeds.

"Ready yourselves, men," the commander boomed. "We make for the Capital today. From there, after we have rested and resupplied, we will head on to Derenar. Any information beyond that is limited to the inner circle of the High Khyth Yetz. However," he added, "the Fist of Thurái is never requested lightly. Where we go, death follows. So I urge you: gaze upon your city now, for it may be the last time you stand at her gates."

If the words had any effect on the men of the Fist, there was no indication.

"A rousing speech, to be sure," hissed a black-hooded figure standing beside him. Kunas, the Master Khyth of Ghal Thurái, was sneering at Durakas with contempt. "A return to the Mouth with anything but total success will likely be viewed as a failure. And if what I hear about Tennech is true, your men would be better off dying victoriously down to the last man than even one of them limping back in defeat."

"If I have need of your input, Khyth," Durakas spat, "I'll smack it out of you with the back of my hand." The tall Thurian scowled at the white-hooded servant of the Breaker as he tightened his own grip on the hilt of his sword. Turning to Duna, he said, "Give the order."

With a nod, she whirled around to address the swarm of soldiers. "Ready!" she shouted, raising one hand in the air like an axe waiting to swing. The Legion obeyed immediately, with the sound of thousands of chainmail-armored feet snapping together as one, in preparation for the march. Durakas turned sharply and walked to his own horse, grabbing the reins to lead it down the twisting path that would take them away from the city.

"March!" Duna barked, slashing the air with her knife-edged hand. A thousand left feet picked themselves off the ground and struck the marble floor below in a flawlessly executed step, echoing throughout the entrance of the Mouth and displaying the frightening precision that made them so well-respected in every battle they fought. Even Durakas's mount was a model of consistency, striking the ground with its hooves in time to the rhythmic steps of the Fist behind him.

Forward they marched, toward the steep and winding descent of the path that streaked across the face of the mountain. Effortlessly, the soldiers adjusted their lines as the path thinned, cutting the number of columns from twenty to ten, then five, and finally two. The white armored snake of soldiers flowed its way down the mountain and onto the Khala-Shar pass as quickly and easily as Duna Cullain had issued the command to begin. They had many, many miles to go before they would see the mountain passes surrounding Khala Val'ur and just as many more before the dirt roads of Derenar would be tread upon by Thurian boots.

***

Back beyond the marble walls closed the great, sturdy gate that protected Ghal Thurái from peering eyes and pilfering hands. With his back to the wall and peering into the darkness that enveloped the inside of the Mouth of the Deep, Kunas began the slow descent back into the heart of the city. No Chovathi had ever been foolish enough to try to make their way into the city before, but there had always been a Fist standing in their way. He did not like having to entertain the idea that they might choose this time to mount an attack. But if they did, he would be ready.

Chapter 38

Derenar, Southeast of Ellenos

Gift of the Shaper

Endar

The thundering footsteps of the Athrani Legion shook the world as they marched southeast from Ellenos to Annoch, while Endar, son of Olis, looked over his shoulder at the multitude of soldiers marching behind him. When he had received the summons from Sh'thanna ordering him to report to Aldryd, Keeper of the Anvil, he wasn't sure what to expect.

For his entire life, and the lives of his forefathers, the Athrani Legion had been nothing more than a ceremonial collection of soldiers. Among them were some decently respected Shapers, this was true, but no more than half of them could be trusted to swing a sword with any amount of precision. In times of peace, even a war machine could become rusty as the need for violence waned.

Mostly due to the fact that Shaping was so prevalent among Athrani men, there were not many who chose to train with a sword and shield rather than developing their powers, as swordplay was considered "less refined" by Athrani society. Rarer still were those who preferred both, and Endar was considered chief among them in skill. Holding tight his mare's reins with one hand, he rested his hand on the hilt of the sword that had made his name famous inside of Ellenos and feared beyond it.

The Legion, comprised of much more than just citizens of Ellenos, was a modest defense force that came about during the time of the Shaping War, conscripting every Ellenian citizen into its ranks and granting citizenship to those who volunteered, even raising some half-eyes to a respectable level in Athrani society. And none knew this better than Endar himself, who had inherited his human mother's green eyes, with a single ring of deep red infecting his right. Joining the LegionLegion had been his one and only chance at gaining respect, and it had been an uphill battle the whole way. Perhaps because of this, he fought tenaciously for everything that he achieved, always setting his sights on becoming better than the man beside him.

He sat atop a stocky gray mare, which was clad in light chain mail that matched his own. His gold epaulets were engraved with the symbol of the Anvil that clearly marked him as Ellenian, and the purple cape he wore that hung halfway down his back identified him as one of the four Legion commanders. Each commander was assigned a specific function. One was in charge of the Athrani Shapers, a second in charge of the close-range combatants, and a third in charge of the ranged combatants. The fourth, which happened to be Endar, son of Olis, was in charge of those three. He oversaw the deployment of troops to each region and worked closely with the other three commanders to decide tactics, troop strength, conscription demands, and army placement. So when the word came down to assemble the full strength of the Legion, down to the last man, he'd had to reach out to his sub-commanders in Ghalís and Théas for an emergency mobilization of the forces in their cities, as the number in Ellenos had fallen uncomfortably low.

"While I am thankful for these many years of peace," he said to the rider on his left, "I can't help but regret not maintaining a combat-ready force."

"You did not get to where you are by second-guessing your decisions." The words came from a grizzled old Athrani with a thin blond beard and broad shoulders, whose brown desert eyes sat on dark rings of mahogany that Endar would have killed for some years ago. "And I didn't get to where I am by listening to them," he added with a smirk. "Lucky for you, I still think you're a fool and I kept my bowmen on a short leash."

Endar chuckled at this and shifted his body to face his companion. "That's why I keep you around, Thuma. You've always been sharp enough to know when to skin the wolf and when to tame it." With a glance back at the soldiers behind him, he added, "Hopefully, these wolves can pull their own weight."

Thuma scratched at his beard. "I think they will. It depends on what we're up against, though. What reason did the Keeper give for the summons?"

Facing forward and looking off into the distance toward Annoch, Endar frowned. "She gave none."

"Well, it has to be important," the blond man retorted. "And I think you and I both know that it has something to do with what's been going on with Shaping lately. Even a half-eye like you can see that something is wrong," he grinned.

Endar acknowledged the jab with one of his own: "These eyes will see you shipped off to the Wastes if you're not careful." A wink of his red-backed eye capped off the riposte.

The Legion had been marching for some time now and was nearly a quarter of the way to Annoch, keeping a pace quick enough to get them there within two days while not wearing out the men entirely. It provided the perfect pace for reflection, which was the real reason Endar had chosen it. He was unfamiliar with Aldryd, the Keeper to whom Sh'thanna had transferred control of the Legion, but there were whispers that his own brother had run, long ago, into the depths of Khala Val'ur in search of power. While it was not unheard of for Athrani to be drawn to the Breaker, it was certainly unsettling, especially when he shared blood with someone as powerful as Aldryd was said to be.

In the many, many years of peace that followed the Shaping War—and Endar knew that "peace" was simply a cloak drawn around the shoulders of the Khyth, ready to be thrown off at a moment's notice—Ellenos had regularly sent scouts into Gal'dorok to determine things like command structure, troop strength, and whether or not the Sunken City was massing troops for an invasion. There had been a few occasions when it seemed like war was inevitable. Khala Val'ur, while certainly an adequate city, was nowhere near as rich in resources as Ellenos or even Annoch, and it was clear that an animal could only stay caged for so long before it outgrew its restraints.

Add to that the fact that the commanding officer of the armies of the Hand were led by none other than the Dagger of Derenar, Aldis Tennech, there was certainly cause for concern. Word had spread about his ruthless use of troops outside Ghal Thurái to cull the growing population of Chovathi, driving them nearly to extinction.

And now, Endar thought, *the blood conflict that has simmered for generations may be coming to a boil—and the Khyth have their hands in the flames.*

With the sun high overhead, Endar steadied himself atop his mount and clicked his tongue to spur her onward. He was picking up the pace, as his curiosity began to eat away at him. What was it that Aldryd needed with the full strength of the Legion? And why so suddenly? Did anyone know what they were walking into?

He certainly hoped someone had the answers; and even more, he hoped that the feeling of dread that he felt in his chest had nothing to do with the disruption of Shaping that had every Athrani turning his eyes to the sky in a silent prayer to the Shaper of Ages.

Onward they marched, into uncertainty and unease.

Chapter 39

Annoch

Gift of the Shaper

Olson

Olson climbed the steps leading up from the prison below the Temple of the Shaper, glancing up at the magnificent architecture that was its hallmark. He admired the swooping and perfectly smooth arcs that made up the inside, knowing that it must have taken years and years of labor to get something like this right. Even with everything he had seen in these last few weeks, he was most impressed with this construction.

Turning the corner into the heart of the temple where the Anvil of the Worldforge was kept, he was surprised to see Aldryd standing there, a look of contemplation on his face. Thornton was beside him, unmoved from when Dailus had knocked him out with a single blow to the head. He was still resting—stirring but not yet awake.

"Keeper," Olson said in a quiet voice, hoping not to startle the old Athrani.

Aldryd was facing away from him, his eyes on Thornton, who looked considerably better than before. The Keeper made a quiet noise of acknowledgement. Hearing this, Olson approached.

"I went to visit Dailus," he started. "You were right: he didn't have the Hammer. He was quiet, defeated."

Aldryd sighed, still not facing Olson. "Normally, I would be happy to hear that, but I can only guess that whoever took it from him did so with a purpose." He tilted his head upward to the ceiling, looking at the grand and intricate artwork that graced the inner temple. "And I stood by and let it happen."

Olson scoffed loudly. "I wouldn't call what you did 'standing by,'" he insisted. "He overpowered you. I was there. I saw him do it."

Finally, the Keeper turned to look at Olson, his golden eyes looking pained. "I should have seen it coming, Olson. I should have done something more." Though he had no doubt tried to regain his composure as best he could, it was apparent that he was under a great deal of stress. He looked like he had aged ten years in the last few hours.

"But how? What could you have done?" Olson demanded.

"These walls hold many secrets, my friend," the old man conceded. "And I am their keeper. I should have listened before. But I am listening now. I know what I must do and where I must make my stand."

"Your stand . . . ?" Olson began. But before he could finish his thought, the sound of heavy footsteps behind him made him turn around.

"My sister told me you were looking for me," came a sturdy female voice. Into the room stepped a woman, tall and dark, who Olson thought looked like a muscular version of Alysana, dark-complected with hair and eyes to match. She wore a plain brown dress that did well to hide her shape, with long white sleeves that hugged her arms. The belt that hung loosely around her waist held the leather sheath of a rather large dagger; Olson thought she looked more than capable of handling it.

"Mordha," said the Keeper. When he had seen her, his expression melted into one of relief. "Thank you for coming to see me."

She moved gracefully across the floor to him, smiling at the old Athrani and barely acknowledging Olson. When she reached him, she curtsied slightly, leaning in to give him a kiss. Her height—unusual for a woman, even a G'henni—meant that she did not have to strain to reach his cheek. "Of course, Keeper. How can I serve?" Her voice was soft and friendly, despite her tough exterior. She didn't speak like a servant to a master, though, but more like a daughter to a father.

Before the Keeper could answer, Olson heard a second voice, low and rumbling like the sound of a tree falling in a forest. "What have you done?"

Olson watched as a streak of black moved like an arrow under the white marble ceiling of the temple. He blinked a few times to try to make sense of what he was seeing, but it did not avail him. All he saw was a pillar of darkness pouncing at Aldryd. Toppling the old man over, the darkness came to rest on top of him, brandishing a dagger inches from the old Athrani's throat.

"I'll ask again: What have you done?" The creature's sharp teeth were bared, and he was pointing with a long, wiry arm to Thornton, who still sat unmoving. "If I don't like what I hear, you meet your goddess tonight." He took Aldryd by the hair, inching him ever closer to the steel of his knife.

"Kethras!" Mordha boomed. "Release him."

"Give me one good reason," the Kienari growled.

"Because he can help. He had nothing to do with your friend's current state."

Olson stared as the great black wonder before him let go of Aldryd's head, making a silver blur of his dagger as he twirled it around in his hand and back into its sheath. He took to his feet swiftly and firmly and crossed his sinewy arms across his chest. "Then who did?" he demanded. His black eyes looked empty and huge, blinking a few times in defiance.

"It was Dailus, an Athrani," Olson answered, staring right at the creature he was still trying to figure out. "He took the Hammer and fled. We think he is working for Khala Val'ur."

Kethras looked coolly at him, eyeing him from head to toe, then looking to Mordha for confirmation. When she nodded, Kethras spoke again.

"Then there is much I do not know." He turned to the Keeper, who was still on the ground, looking stunned. "My apologies." He reached out a hand that looked very human, save for the fine black fur that covered it completely.

When Aldryd took it, Kethras helped him to his feet as smoothly and effortlessly as the wind moves a sail. "I am Kethras," he said to Aldryd, adding, "of Kienar."

The old Athrani looked at him with a bit of surprise, nodding to hide how shaken he was. "Yes, of course. A Kienari," he mumbled. "Cut first, ask questions later. Then cut again if the answer does not suit you."

Kethras frowned but could not deny the truth of the statement. "It was hasty of me. I will try to be more careful," he apologized again.

Olson narrowed his eyes in suspicion at the Kienari. "How do you know my son?"

For a moment, Kethras was still. He looked at Olson as if he was sizing him up, taking him in from head to toe. He glanced from Olson to Thornton, then back again, as if trying to reconcile the differences between the two men. "You are his father," he said, more as a statement than as a question.

Olson, holding eye contact, nodded carefully. He was unsure of what to make of this creature that had leapt out of legend and into their midst, brandishing teeth and daggers. He was unpredictable and unimaginably quick; Olson liked neither of those things.

The blacksmith's own weapons were his fists, and he readied them at his side, prepared to defend himself if the need arose. When the Kienari bared his teeth again, Olson brought his hands up and squared himself with the beast, determined to go down swinging. Adrenaline flooded his veins, and he braced for a fight.

"You have raised a fine son," Kethras said, much to Olson's surprise. "Not much of a tracker, but he learns quickly." His black, expressionless eyes were focused intently on Olson. It took a few seconds for him to realize that the Kienari was smiling.

Out of the corner of his eye, he noticed Mordha slipping her dagger quietly back into its sheath. He had no intention of asking how she planned to use it, but he made a mental note that she was apparently willing to. Unclenching his fists, Olson dropped his hands to his sides and exhaled. Allowing his pulse to steady again, he let out a laugh that echoed through the halls of the temple. "Now I see why Thornton was so jumpy earlier," he said, still trying to figure out the Kienari. "He couldn't tell if you were going to coddle him or kill him."

Kethras looked like the last part had wounded him slightly. "That seems to be my problem with most humans," he said with a frown. "I try to avoid them."

Mordha's almond eyes fell softly on the Kienari. "But the ones who know you can vouch for you. And if that does not work, I've always found that a sharp knife is the best ambassador." She patted her own dagger once again, looking right at Olson.

Gift of the Shaper

"Friends," Aldryd said gently. The other occupants of the room looked like they had forgotten he was even there as they jumped at his utterance. "We are short on time, and the hour grows late. I have sent word of our need to the Keeper of Ellenos, and the might of the Athrani Legion will be passing through Annoch on its way to defend the chains from Khala Val'ur."

At the mention of the chains, Kethras shifted uneasily. Noticing this, Aldryd turned to address him.

"I know you must know of their secrets, Kienari."

Kethras nodded, remaining silent.

"And you know what is at stake," Aldryd added.

"I do," Kethras replied. "It is a story that my Mother has told to me since I was small. Has the time truly come?"

The aged Athrani looked at Kethras despondently, nodding slowly. "I'm afraid it has. Khala Val'ur will begin their march soon—if they have not done so already—and will aim to break the chains that lie in this world. Then all that stands between them and freeing the Breaker lies in the blood of the Shaper." He looked defeated under the burden of guilt that he refused to share with anyone else. "And we must do whatever it takes to see that they do not succeed."

Chapter 40

Annoch

Gift of the Shaper

Aldryd

The mighty gates of Annoch groaned open as Aldryd came out to greet the army that had marched down from Ellenos and set themselves outside his city's walls. Looking over the faces of the men, he saw a huge number of humans and Athrani, with no apparent distinction between them. They were soldiers of the same army, regardless of birth.

They were well-organized and well-equipped, looking every bit as professional as their reputation suggested. Despite being an army made up largely of volunteers, they had the look of a well-seasoned fighting force, with the confidence and mannerisms to match. They were uniformly dressed, as well, wearing the purple and gold chain mail so commonly associated with Ellenos.

At the forefront of the formation were the pikemen, with their impossibly tall weapons—some, more than twice the size of the men carrying them—tipped in the sharpest of Ellenian steel. Their heavier chain mail covered more of their bodies than the other soldiers, and they were the largest men by far, being the first line of defense for a reason.

Behind them were the bearers of swords and shields, men who would wade into the fray of combat after the front line of the pikemen had been overrun or ordered back. Their heavy steel shields were large and rectangular, covering most of their torsos, and appeared to be useful for fending off arrows just as well as swords. The same design graced the front of each and every shield: two white swords forming an X over a night-black anvil. And the background—the dark red of fire—made the white of the swords stand out as if they were real.

Finally, behind them were the rows of archers. They were the least physically imposing of all the soldiers. *No doubt earning them their place in the back,* Aldryd thought. They were lightly armored in little more than padded leather, allowing for maximum movement and minimal noise. They were highly mobile and served as a first attack or a last defense, depending on how desperate the situation was. Each man carried two bows: the first, a longbow made of light polished yew; and the second, a smaller handbow that hung from their backs, was useful when rapid-fire shooting and evading were called for.

Each of these elements of men formed the whole of the Athrani Legion, which stood now outside the gates of Annoch like a viper ready to strike. Each man, however, was focused not on the walls of the city but on one man on horseback, seated calmly at the front of the Legion.

His piercing green eyes held a trace of Athrani heritage, with a scorching red fire blazing behind one, and his salt-and-pepper hair told of age and experience—and of the great effort he had expended to get this far. To his left sat a silent Athrani, bearded and blond, who was admiring the guarded city before him.

"You must be the Keeper," said the first one, a look of indifference masking his concern. He looked to be in good shape for his age, and his face showed flashes of a keen intellect that had no doubt helped him climb into this lofty position.

"I am," Aldryd responded, moving toward the man on horseback, who was now dismounting. "Forgive me," he said, "Sh'thanna did not give me your name."

With a grunt of amusement, he answered, "Endar, son of Olis; Commander of the Athrani Legion and servant of the Keeper of Ellenos," he said with a small flourish, "at your service, I suppose." He was tall—his Athrani heritage shining through—and well-built. If the soldiers did not follow him for his leadership, surely his imposing physique had something to do with it.

"Indeed," Aldryd said as he swept his eyes across the multitude of soldiers. "I hope it will do." Ignoring the puzzled look from Endar, the Keeper turned toward the guard tower that sat atop the wall and called for the Captain of the Guard. "Jinda, could you come down here please?" His words were no louder than a conversational tone. "We have a few things to discuss."

A faraway grunt of annoyance was heard, followed by a bright flash of light in their midst and a low *boom* reminiscent of thunder. By the time the light faded into the shape of a tall man with red hair and eyes, the pikemen had their weapons at the ready.

"So discuss," Jinda said, paying no mind to the forest of razor-sharp blades bowed in his direction. He was standing with his arms crossed as if he had been there the whole time.

Gift of the Shaper

Aldryd watched as Endar, clearly a man who disliked being taken by surprise, dealt with Jinda's sudden appearance with aplomb. Endar's hand clutching the grip of the sword at his side, he calmly demanded, "Who are you, and how did you get here?"

"This is Jinda Yhun," said Aldryd, "Captain of the Guard of Annoch. And he is a Farstepper. If there are no more questions for your idle curiosity, I suggest we get to the point."

Farstepper—the word clearly meant something to Endar—men born with the power to move seamlessly between this world and the Otherworld, renowned for their prowess in battle and feared for their skills as assassins. It was said the only thing that could kill a Farstepper was another Farstepper. The battle-hardened Ellenian did his best to keep his eyes from getting too wide. He nodded, unable to tear his gaze from Jinda.

"Good. Every moment we waste is one that Khala Val'ur could use to move closer to the chains. How much has Sh'thanna told you?"

Still looking at Jinda, it took a quiet moment for Endar to process the question. "Just that I would report to you," he said, finally able to look the Keeper in the eye, "nothing more."

"Then what I am about to tell you will not come easy." Aldryd looked from Endar to the Legion of men behind him. He knew what awaited them no more than a sunset from now. "And you may wish to hear the news yourself so you may tell your men the way that you see fit." His steady gaze met Endar's, and the reflection of the burden that he had been carrying shone heavily in the other man's eyes.

"No," Endar replied firmly. "In the Legion, we are all equals. Anything you say to me, you say to them."

Aldryd pondered this for a moment as his gaze went from commander to troops and back again. "Very well," he said at last. "Khala Val'ur has located the Hammer of the Worldforge and most certainly has the means of opening the way to the Otherworld by using the blood of the Shaper." He left the last part purposely ambiguous, as the knowledge that Miera was the Shaper could do unthinkable harm if it reached the wrong ears. The more closely guarded it remained, the better. "We do not have long before they begin their assault, and I fear that they may already be on the move."

Endar flinched as the words hit him like arrows. Softly and mostly to himself, he muttered, "No wonder she did not tell us why we were being sent. She was sending us to our deaths." The murmurs of the men behind him told him that they were thinking the same. Eyes back on the Keeper, he asked, "What must we do?"

"We ready ourselves as best we can and make for Kienar," Aldryd answered. "Jinda here will accompany you," he said, nodding to the red-haired captain, "as will the city guard. You will not be doing this on your own, Endar, son of Olis, though it will certainly not be easy. We must defend the chains by any means necessary."

The Commander of the Legion nodded to Aldryd. "Thank you, Keeper," he said. "But if I know my men, nothing will make them feel more at ease than a few hundred barrels of Annoch's finest. It will certainly help with swallowing this news."

Looking over the faces of the army once more, the Keeper saw men who were prepared to give their lives in defense of something greater than themselves. The least he could do was make them happy. "In that case," he said as he turned, "I must see Wern at the Driving Steed regarding some ale."

Endar

Endar breathed in the weight of responsibility that had been placed upon him and frowned. All his years of experience, his climb to the top, his development as a feared warrior and brother of the Athrani Legion—all of these things would now be put to the test. Running patrols and keeping the peace were one thing. Riding into battle—against Khyth, no less—was another thing entirely. Most of these men had never even seen one in person, let alone in combat. He turned to his second-in-command, Thuma, who had the look of a man ready to accept his fate.

"We will rest while we can. Thuma, have the men ready the tents and fires. Tomorrow is a new day, and we must be ready when we greet it."

Gift of the Shaper

The bearded blond man nodded and turned around to start spreading the word.

Endar watched the Keeper retreat back into Annoch, saying something about requisitioning barrels for the Legion. He watched him as he went, confident and calm, seemingly unaffected by the prospect of their task. He knew that he should be doing the same for the sake of his men but quickly tossed the thought aside. He had been fighting alongside some of these men for most of his adult life. They knew him and they knew how to read him; it was useless affecting a false front.

No, tonight he would be himself. He would eat with his brothers, share stories and slaps on the back, and think nothing of what the dawn would bring. That was a problem for tomorrow. And tomorrow could go to hell for all he cared.

Chapter 41

Khala Val'ur

Gift of the Shaper

Durakas

Just past the horizon, Commander Durakas could see the guard fires of Khala Val'ur that littered the mountains encircling the Sunken City. Turning to Duna, who rode just behind him, he said, "It looks like we're not the only ones ready for a fight."

Duna nodded, saying, "Then I certainly hope they know we're coming. One skittish guard is all it takes to be met by arrows instead of handshakes."

Though she was young, Duna had been chosen by Durakas for a reason. It was not her looks, as she could hardly be regarded as attractive, with her larger-than-average forehead and drab green eyes that looked to be set just too far apart. Indeed, physical traits had nothing to do with why she was selected as advisor; it was her fierceness and perseverance that made her stand out. She beat out every other male candidate for the spot because of her inability to take *no* for an answer and her absolute unwillingness to back down, even in the face of hostility and adversity. These traits were what made her attractive.

"No doubt Seralith has spoken to the guards and told them of our coming," Durakas replied. He had his sights set on the mountains again as the Fist of Thurái neared their destination. "She seems too good at what she does to overlook something as simple as preparation."

The thousand footsteps of the Fist continued to pound as one, not even relenting over the hundreds of miles they had marched thus far. Fatigue did not show in their faces or in their cadence, as their training and instincts took over the moment Duna had given the order to march. As it neared darkness, the long line of white stood out starkly against the world around them.

"And once we make it there?" Duna asked.

"We see how willing Tennech is to share his battle plan with us—or even why we are marching in the first place. Otherwise," he said, turning again to his advisor, "we go on like we always have, obediently and in order."

As they neared the northernmost point of the outer wall of mountains, Durakas spotted a lone figure on horseback riding out to meet them. As the figure approached, he noticed long brown hair trailing behind, tied tightly into a long braid. It was Seralith, he realized, as her aging brown mount carried her closer.

The Fist marched on with no change of pace.

"Well, if it isn't the Dagger's messenger girl," Durakas called out. "How nice of you to come out to meet us." Beside him, Duna raised her hand in silence to signal the halt of the army. A synchronized clap of thunder sounded as their feet met the ground as one.

The tall Athrani's face was cold and indifferent as she eased her horse to a halt. "Nice has nothing to do with it," she began. "High Khyth Yetz doesn't trust a foreign army marching inside the walls of the city."

"Foreign?" Duna sneered. "You're one to talk, Athrani."

The fire in Sera's eyes could have melted steel, but she clenched her jaw and struggled visibly to keep from lashing out. Before she could speak, though, Durakas put up his hand as if holding a wolf at bay.

"Ladies," he said, "please. We have marched a long way and bickering does not behoove us." His eyes narrowed at the Athrani. "But I hardly think that the Fist of Thurái should be made to stand outside like dogs," said the Thurian, "especially after coming at the direct request of General Tennech."

"General Tennech is not High Khyth of Khala Val'ur, Commander," Sera answered sharply. "Though, if he were, I suspect he would have ordered the same." Her blue rings made her brown eyes stand out sharply, and they concealed a smugness that came from humiliating an entire army. "But you will not be waiting long," she continued. "Valurians long for battle as much as you do, and they can smell the coming conflict." She looked over the imposing army of Ghal Thurái that seemed to be carved from the same single piece of stone. "Do your men need rest?"

Durakas set his jaw, and the pride of Ghal Thurái bubbled to the surface. "No," he asserted.

"Good," she replied, as the sound of thousands of footsteps began to fill the air behind her, "because their march is not yet done."

Gift of the Shaper

Emerging from the rocky mouth of the mountains of the Great Serpent was General Aldis Tennech flanked by thousands of riders from the Sunken City, dressed for battle and for glory. They poured out of the craggy pass like ants from a nest, garbed in night-black chain mail, with the white Hand of the Breaker cresting their left shoulders.

"Durakas," Tennech said over the sound of his army, "you made it intact, it seems. Any problems with Chovathi on the way?" His smirk betrayed his disingenuousness.

The Commander of the Fist of Ghal Thurái nodded a curt greeting and answered, "None to speak of, General. I think they are still licking their wounds from their defeat at the hands of the Dagger of Derenar."

The old general grunted his approval as his army continued to emerge from the protection of the walls of Gal'behem. "Good. Bastards had it coming." He turned to Seralith, who still had her steely gaze locked on Duna Cullain. "It was practice for what is to come. Are they ready?"

Sera looked at Tennech, then back to Durakas, who was still composing himself after having his pride stepped on by Khala Val'ur. "The commander assures me that the Fist of Thurái is tireless and that they are prepared to march to Derenar behind the might of the Sunken City."

Durakas flinched when she implied their inferiority but would not let her know that she could get to him so easily. This Athrani woman was turning out to be more trouble that he had expected. He looked back to General Tennech, who kept glancing around, past the armies around him, scanning the horizon for something.

"Are we waiting on another army?" Durakas asked with more than a subtle tone of mockery.

"Blasted G'henni have no sense of timing," Tennech mumbled. Ignoring the confused look from Durakas, he barked, "Follow me! The road to Kienar is a long one, and the might of the Athrani wanes. If we are lucky, we will reach the chains unopposed." He pulled on the reins of Calathet and turned toward the Sun Path, taking his place at the front of the gathering multitude of men and Khyth. "And I pray to the Breaker that we are not lucky."

D.L. Jennings

With one last look at the mountains of the Great Serpent, Tennech commanded his mount onward, down the long and uncertain road to greatness. Following him closely was the full strength of the armies of Gal'dorok and the crushing weight of inevitability.

Chapter 42

Annoch

Gift of the Shaper

Thornton

Thornton awoke to the dancing green eyes of a young woman whom he did not recognize, sitting at his bedside, waiting. He found himself covered in a blanket, and the feather-stuffed mattress he slept upon had likely cost more than his entire home back in Highglade.

Seeing that he was awake, the woman jumped back in surprise, saying, "His eyes are open!" to nothing but the four walls that surrounded them.

Thornton heard the heavy footsteps of someone rushing into the well-lit room inside the Driving Steed.

"It's about time," came the deep voice of Olson Woods. "Thank you, Yasha."

Sizing up the woman standing next to his bed, Thornton was caught up in silence as he looked at her eyes, frenetic pools of emerald green that danced wildly behind her ruffled orange hair. He'd only seen eyes like that one other time in his life, and the recollection sent him into a panic. Frantically, he flung his blanket off and leapt to his feet.

"What's she doing here?" he shouted, pointing a finger at her accusingly. "She's Khyth!" His fingers quickly balled into fists, and his legs bent defensively.

"Thornton," his father said, reaching out with a calming hand, "she's with us."

"But," he sputtered, "how?"

Coming into view, his lumbering father had a frown on his face. "It turns out that things are more complicated than we thought."

"Much more," added Kethras, who appeared behind Olson.

Thornton looked at his father in disbelief as he once again eyed the Khyth, who looked to be even more frightened than he was. She wore a simple hooded gray robe, with no other features that set her apart from any other woman, and her smooth, freckled skin looked nothing like the cracked and horrid body of the Khyth the night they were attacked.

"Your skin," Thornton blurted, "it's . . . Why isn't it burnt?"

Elyasha looked hurt but relieved as she scratched the back of her hand with her fingertips. "It's because I'm only an apprentice," she said. "I haven't undergone the Breaking yet." When she saw the confusion in Thornton's eyes, she offered what she could. "My mother was Khyth, so I'm Khyth," she said with a sigh.

The explanation did little to quell Thornton's curiosity, but it did help him to relax. He had his back to the wooden wall of the inn as he approached her, guessing he wasn't even that much older than her.

Olson was still just inside the doorway to the large room, moving closer to Thornton, eventually standing behind the young Khyth apprentice. "Elyasha fled her home city of Khala Val'ur in hopes of starting a new life," he explained.

"In Annoch?" Thornton asked incredulously. "But Khyth hate the Athrani."

Elyasha looked at Thornton and grimaced. "Most of us do," she started with a nod. "But not all of us. It's not my fault I was born the way I am." Her pallid skin flushed easily as she turned to hide her burning red cheeks. "And I didn't like what I would have to become, so I left."

Thornton could barely believe that the woman in front of him, who seemed so gentle and meek, could share the same blood as someone as cruel and ruthless as the Khyth that tried to kill him.

She looked at Thornton, her green eyes swirling like a storm. "And when your father saw that I'd been thrown in prison here for nothing more than my heritage, he did something about it." She turned to the big blacksmith. "Thank you again. I don't know how long they would have kept me down there."

Crossing his arms, Olson gave a gruff nod of his head in response and looked at the young apprentice with a hint of sadness in his eyes. "When I heard that you'd patched up Dailus and brought him back to the city," he said, "I had to do something. Anyone who would do that, even to a blood enemy, deserves a fair shot at freedom, in my eyes."

Thornton felt himself staring at the girl and thrust his eyes downward in embarrassment. "I'm sorry. I think I hit my head; I'm still a little dazed." He rubbed the back of his neck as he searched around the room

Gift of the Shaper

for his familiar steel companion. Finding nothing, he said, "Where's my hammer?"

When his confused gaze met that of his father, he knew something was wrong.

Olson scratched at his beard as he frowned, saying, "Dailus took it."

"And handed it over to D'kane," Elyasha finished.

It seemed to take an eternity for the words to register as Thornton tried to comprehend just how much he had lost in such a short span of time. "I think I need to sit back down," he said woozily, nearly losing his balance. A nimble Elyasha was there to catch him, though.

"Oh!" she said, grabbing him above the waist and helping to steady him. "Careful!" A hint of a smile flashed briefly on her lips as she walked him to the bed.

"He knocked you out almost a day ago, son," Olson said as he watched Thornton climb back into bed. "Ran off with the Hammer and gave it to the Khyth straight away." His hands were on his hips now, and he was looking out the window at nothing in particular.

Thornton rubbed his eyes in frustration. "So all that stuff that Aldryd said about needing to protect it and how it's the key to setting the Breaker free . . ."

"Only makes it that much more valuable to the Khyth," Kethras answered.

"So that's it," Thornton said, palms up in a shrug. "They have Miera, and they have the Hammer."

Olson nodded slowly, trying to deflect the weight of the words.

"Then it's over. They've won." Thornton was too tired to be angry, but his rage showed nonetheless. "They've won, and they're going to set the Breaker free."

The silence that embraced the room was neither comforting nor welcome, and the words that followed shortly thereafter were even less so.

"There is a way to stop it," Elyasha said quietly, "but you might not like it."

Before Thornton could muster a response, another set of footsteps echoed their way into the room.

"Ah," came the weathered voice of Aldryd. "You are awake. Good." Stepping into the room, the aged Athrani looked around, addressing all of them, even Elyasha. "The Athrani Legion will soon begin their march to the forest of Kienar to defend the chains, and we will need help from every last one of you,"—Aldryd had his eyes fixed on Thornton—"especially you."

"Me?" Thornton asked. "How?"

"Yes," the old man began, "if the unthinkable happens and the servants of the Breaker make their way through, we have one last hope. But I must ask you: What are you willing to do to save your friend?"

Thornton sat up in his bed, obviously mustering a great deal of strength in order to do so. "I'll do whatever I can." He looked at his father and back to the Keeper and thought of the citizens of Annoch, human and Athrani, and realized that Miera's importance was greater than just the friendship they shared. She didn't belong to him anymore; she belonged to the world. "Whatever it takes," he said firmly.

Aldryd studied his face for a quiet moment, as if turning over each word and weighing its worth. Finally, he spoke: "Prepare yourselves for the journey ahead, then, all of you. The Legion marches soon." Turning to Kethras he said, "And you, Kienari, come with me. You know the forest better than anyone, and I want the Commander of the Legion to meet you on neutral ground so there is no confusion about your intentions."

Kethras grunted, sounding more like a growl than an acknowledgment, and followed the Keeper out of the room. Elyasha, looking like a lost puppy, kept at his heels.

Thornton looked around the room to see his father standing, arms crossed, with a frown heavier than any hammer he was used to swinging. His head was turned to the door, with his eyes trailing the bouncing orange hair of the Khyth disappearing through the threshold. Olson looked as though he had words perched on the tip of his tongue, waiting to be set free. Knowing that they could very well have stayed there until the end of time, Thornton spoke first.

Gift of the Shaper

"I wish we were back in Highglade," he said with a hint of a smile, trying his best to lighten the mood. The words seemed to chisel away at the granite frown that was carved across the big man's face.

"Me too," Olson said at last, eyes back on his son. "Nothing exciting ever happens there." He waved his hand parallel to the ground dismissively. "And that's fine with me."

Thornton managed a laugh, which served to further relax his father. The towering blacksmith almost seemed at ease for the first time in a while, and he had a look that Thornton recognized.

"You're thinking about her again, aren't you?" Thornton said.

Olson rarely spoke of Thornton's mother, and when he did, he was distant. "I can't help it," the elder Woods answered. "I just wish she could see the man you turned out to be." His normally gruff exterior had softened, and Thornton thought he saw the early stages of a smile.

There was vulnerability in his father's eyes, something Thornton was not used to seeing, and it was enough to make him struggle to his feet and walk over to stand next to him. His father was not one for being comforted, Thornton knew, but the look of appreciation that the big man flashed when he drew closer was good enough for him.

"I did the best I could raising you," Olson said. "I made some mistakes, but it wasn't from lack of trying." Thornton opened his mouth to speak, but his father went on: "I just want you to be able to take care of yourself."

Thornton sat there in his bed looking as puzzled as when he'd seen a Khyth beside him. "You make it sound like you're leaving," he said.

Olson cracked a smile that looked more like a grimace. "The Keeper needs me out there,"—he gestured absently toward the outside, doing nothing to solidify the abstract concept—"And he needs you here."

Thornton felt as pained as when he'd learned that his hammer had gone missing.

"Now come on," Olson said. "The Legion is waiting for us at the gates."

D.L. Jennings

Endar

The last of the fires had been extinguished, and Endar Half-eye stood watch over his army as they gathered their things for the march ahead.

"Think they're ready?" came the voice of Thuma. The blond, bearded man approached from behind, facing the rising sun with his back to the gates of Annoch.

Turning to his old friend, Endar answered, "It doesn't matter what I think." The Commander of the Legion was resplendent in his Ellenian armor, dressed for battle and nothing else. "It matters what they think," he said with a nod to his men.

The vast army of the Athrani Legion was slowly coming to life. Requiring the smallest amount of preparation for battle, the archers were the first to awaken, so they were the first to be ready, as well. The pikemen and shieldbearers, in contrast, were heavy sleepers and slow to get ready. Some of them who had been up since dawn were sparring with the flats of their swords or the shafts of their pikes. The majority of the big men, though, took a while to get moving, despite the shouts and excited rumblings from their squad commanders to get them going.

The march would not be long compared to the one from Ellenos, but emotions would be mixed and minds would be clouded with thoughts of battle, so it could feel like an eternity. Endar knew this and had prepared for it accordingly. With his left foot in the stirrup, he swung his right leg over the saddle and sat atop his war horse.

"I know for some of you, this will be your first time seeing combat." His voice rose over the disjointed chatter and clatter of morning preparations, and most of the Legion stopped to listen to what he had to say. Even for those still moving about, it was not much of a challenge to hear the strong voice of the commander. "But even a hawk must be pushed from the nest before it can fly." His glance swept over the soldiers as he spoke, meeting their eyes. It was hard for each man not to feel like he was addressing them individually. "And today each of you leaves the comfort of the nest in favor of open skies."

Gift of the Shaper

Behind him, from the open gates of Annoch, walked Kethras and Jinda, along with a few members of the city guard. Following them was Aldryd, Keeper of Annoch and perhaps the single greatest Shaper alive. Endar turned to acknowledge them, extending one muscular arm out toward them. "And here to lead you into those skies are some of the greatest warriors that Derenar has to offer."

Jinda, with his second-in-command, Mordha, behind him, was stoic as always, his blazing eyes burning like the smoldering coals of the fires from the night before. Turning to Kethras, he whispered, "I think he means us."

With a sidelong glance, Kethras grinned.

Seeing that his men had finished the last of the preparations, Endar turned to the three who had just joined them. "Are you ready for the journey ahead?"

Kethras cocked his head to listen to something behind him. "Not yet," he answered. "There are more to join us."

"Very well," Endar replied. "I'm almost out of speech, though." Endar flashed a toothy grin at the Kienari. Turning back to his army, he looked them over once again, pursing his lips and nodding with satisfaction. He looked to Thuma as if to say, "Yes, they are ready."

"I hear we'll get the chance to see some Khyth," came a booming voice from behind. Turning to see who it came from, Endar almost fell out of his saddle as he watched a bearded mountain stroll from the city gates, followed closely by a young woman wearing gray robes and a broadshouldered young man dressed in simple blacksmithing attire. "If that's true, then count me in. I've got a few things to say to them," the big man said, grinning as he cracked his knuckles.

Endar nodded, relieved that they were on the same side. He didn't see any weapons on him, but that didn't seem to matter. He looked more than capable of taking down half the Legion with his bare hands. "It is true," said Endar. "And we can use all the help we can get."

"Hear that, Kethras?" said the brute with the beard, slapping the Kienari on the back. "Looks like you'll be useful after all."

D.L. Jennings

The whole of the Athrani Legion seemed to hold their breath as they tried to read the face of the Kienari, who seemed far more deadly than he let on. "Thank you, Olson," came the low rumbling through the sheer white teeth of the son of the forest.

Endar, visibly relaxing as his hand crept away from his sword, looked at Kethras and asked, "Are you ready?"

The Kienari gave him a smile that looked like a predator closing in on prey. "Now we are ready."

"Very well," said Endar. He turned to Thuma, who was standing by his own mount, ready to command the Legion. "We march." With those words, Endar Half-eye dug his heels into the rib cage of his muscular steed and gave an emphatic *hyah!* that spurred them forward, into the parting sea of men and Athrani.

"Legion!" shouted Thuma. "Ready yourselves!"

The chaotic collection of warriors that only moments ago had been listlessly lingering outside the gates of Annoch almost instantaneously assembled itself into an organized mass of men. As the Commander of the Legion bore toward the front of the army, Thuma thrust his fist into the air in his direction, shouting, "March!" in a growling voice that sounded more lion than man.

Thornton

Thornton watched in amazement as the biggest collection of soldiers he had ever seen took to the wide road leading from the City of the Forge, marching heedlessly down the path that would eventually take them to Kienar.

"Impressive," Olson said, not taking his eyes off the marching Legion before him. "At least I have a big target to follow." The blacksmith took a breath as deep as if he were trying to take the city with him.

Thornton knew that he was needed in Annoch with the Keeper, but obligation didn't make goodbyes any easier. He knew that his father wouldn't like it, but he reached over and gave the big man a hug, letting his arms drop away before the elder Woods could protest.

Gift of the Shaper

Olson's eyes were narrowed in a display that did well enough to fool any onlookers into thinking he was as cold and hard as the Annochian Forge. "We're going to talk about that when I get back," he insisted.

Aldryd, who was still watching from the gate, added his own piece: "And that will not be long, Olson." The Keeper, in his white robes, was standing with his hands clasped behind his back, looking like a statue guarding the night-black gates of the City of the Forge. "But the first step is to make it there with the rest of the Legion," he said, nodding toward the disappearing multitude of soldiers that marched away toward Kienar.

With a scratch of his thick brown beard, Olson gave a nod to the Keeper and took to the road behind the great army, looking like a giant bearing down on a crowd.

Aldryd approached the last remaining souls this side of the gate, Thornton and Elyasha, and put a hand on each of their shoulders. "Their part will come later," he said in a voice that was soothing despite the words. "And yours may come sooner than we expect." Turning to the gates, he began to walk inside. "Come," he said, without turning back. "We are needed in the temple."

Thornton heard the groaning of the gates that heralded their closing and gave Yasha a quick glance to spur her along. He sprung forward toward the Keeper, staying at the heels of the one man who seemed to know what the future held in store.

Chapter 43

Kienar

Gift of the Shaper

Kethras

Kienar was quiet when Kethras stepped through the threshold. His Mother was near, and he knew it. Even more, he could feel it. He knew she was waiting for him, and his eagerness must have shown.

"You are pleased to be back," Jinda said. The large man from Khulakorum rarely spoke unless he was certain his words would have an impact.

"I am," Kethras answered. He felt the weight of the air, which was different somehow, and looked at the thriving vegetation that surrounded them. Tall trees with broad leaves filled the sky, towering over grass and flowers that lined the dirt path leading to the center of the ancient forest. "It has been some time." He inhaled sharply through his nostrils, taking in the familiar smells that took him back to his childhood.

He was home.

Behind them marched the might of Ellenos, bolstered by the fearsome guard of Annoch, who had served the city for generations, protecting the walls just as much as the walls protected them. Kethras turned to watch the scores of men and Athrani that now poured into his home, a home he missed yet had hoped he would not have to return to for fear of what was to come.

Endar rode up to him and saw the conflicting emotions playing out on his face. Kienari were tough to read, but raw emotions translated well across the faces of any living creature. "Kethras," he began, "what is it?"

Behind him, the Athrani Legion came to a slow halt, just within the confines of the great forest.

"I did not expect to be back so soon," he answered. His tone was as dark as his great black eyes, and Endar, son of Olis, seemed to notice.

"Things never seem to play out exactly as we plan them," Endar said with a raised eyebrow. "But the events that brought me to Annoch have landed us here, in your forest." The great half-eye threw his legs off of his mount and slid to the ground. "The sun is still high in the sky, and we may have some time before the servants of the Breaker arrive. We should do what we can to prepare."

Nodding, Kethras turned to the leader of the Legion. "I will give your archers the lay of the land. They will be our most valuable asset in defending against any attackers that try to breach the forest." He flashed a sharp, toothy smile. "The trees hold many secrets."

"I'm almost afraid to see what the Kienari are capable of." He looked at Kethras and gestured toward the heart of the forest, saying, "Should we make our way in?"

Kethras nodded, answering, "I will lead the way from here. But do not follow too closely. I want to be alone when I greet my Mother again."

Endar extended his arm as he let the Kienari pass. "After you."

Kethras calmly took to the path that led toward Naknamu and to the Mother. It had been far too many years since he had set foot in the forest, but not much had changed from the image that he had sealed away in his mind. The sounds of the forest put his restless spirit at ease.

Endar

Thuma was riding beside Jinda, who marveled at the sight of the forest.

"Do you know where we are?" Thuma asked the man from beyond the Wastes.

"I do," Jinda replied. "It's why my hand is still on my axe."

They walked the ancient path that led deeper into the forest, with the Legion falling gravely quiet. Whether it was out of respect for the senescent land or from fear of the unknown, Endar wasn't sure, but he noted their silence with a turn of his head to Jinda.

"It's not the trees you have to worry about, you know."

The Farstepper acknowledged him with a grunt. "One Kienari is trouble enough, and now we come knocking on their door? I just hope they knew we were coming."

Endar cracked a smile that was barely noticeable on his weathered lips. "They know." Jinda tightened his grip on the axe he was carrying, and

Gift of the Shaper

Thuma shifted his eyes to the trees. The two men took solace only in the fact that they were coming into the forest to defend it.

If they felt this uneasy as its protectors, Endar could only imagine how the Khyth would feel marching in as conquerors. He did not envy them, not in the slightest.

Chapter 44

Annoch

Gift of the Shaper

Thornton

Thornton walked behind Aldryd as they made their way through the city, with Elyasha bringing up the rear.

By now he had been able to take in the sights of the city, but he was no less impressed by its size than when he had first set foot inside the gates. *It's even more impressive during the day*, he thought.

Towering houses of wood and stone each seemed to have a place in the sprawling city, circling and protecting the ancient citadel that stood at its center, standing higher than any tree he'd ever seen.

Elyasha had been silent beside him and looked just as awed as he was. He studied her face and almost laughed at the absurdity that she could be Khyth. Though he had to admit, she had a point: she was more than just her heritage.

As if feeling the eyes of the young man from Highglade, she turned to him and spoke. "You don't have to be afraid of me, Thornton," she said, causing a flush of embarrassment across his cheeks. "Look all you want. I won't bite."

Thornton grimaced and sucked in a breath through his teeth, making a sound like steam from a hot coal. "I'm sorry for staring," he said as he turned away. "It's just . . . the last Khyth I met tried to kill me."

Yasha looked over at him with her wild green eyes, calm as a summer morning, in sharp contrast to her muted white skin. "I'm not them, Thornton." The words were sharp and carefully chosen. "Your father saw that. I was hoping by now that you would too." She was stern but not overly aggressive. Thornton took the opportunity to apologize again.

"You're right. I shouldn't have brought it up." He took an audible breath as the three of them walked on toward the spire.

"You mentioned the Breaking earlier," Thornton said, causing her ears to perk up. "What is it?"

The rigid sternness that had cloaked her face earlier seemed to melt away as Yasha cocked her head in thought. "It's a ritual that apprentices go through to become Khyth," she began. "Not all of us are born into it. The power of the Otherworld is one that anyone can harness if you know where to look."

Thornton saw that, at these words, Aldryd had come to a stop in front of them.

"And a power that is just as dangerous as the ritual of the Breaking," the Keeper said, "where even those who manage to harness it are branded and scarred for life." He paused. "Yet still they seek it out—in droves."

Thornton remembered the man who had bought the chains from him and how his skin was burnt and charred. It looked like he had been in some sort of fire.

Yasha went on: "Those born with Khyth blood are born with the power of the Otherworld already inside them. People like me don't have to go through the Breaking," she admitted hesitantly. "But if I ever wanted to be as powerful as someone like D'kane, I would have to. My power doesn't hold a candle to what he's capable of."

"D'kane shed the last of his humanity a long time ago," Aldryd said with disgust. "He will do anything for power, which is why he must be stopped." The Keeper turned on his heels and started again down the path to the spire, passing scores of humans and Athrani going about their business on the busy roads of Annoch.

"He's right," Yasha said, her lips taut and restrained. "I studied under D'kane, and I know how relentless he can be when he wants something." The two of them started walking again, following in the footsteps of the Keeper. "And I know that he was the one who had my mother put to death for fleeing the city, too."

The words made Thornton jolt to a stop as a frown spread across his face. Suddenly, he regretted ever questioning why she would leave. "I'm so sorry," he mumbled. "I know what it's like to grow up without a mother."

Yasha turned to him and sighed, grabbing him by the arm to spur him forward. "It's alright," she said. "It was a long time ago, and I've had plenty of time to get over her loss." Dragging him behind her, she added, "But I've never forgiven him for it."

Gift of the Shaper

The two of them caught up to Aldryd, who seemed oblivious to the outside world as he strode toward the tallest point in all of Annoch. The towering height of the spire overlooked the sprawling city like a mother watching over her children, silently guarding and waiting.

Waiting for what? Thornton wondered. The answer seemed as distant and cloudy as the smoke that had enveloped his home on that night when his father was taken.

As they drew closer to the spire, he felt a tightness in his head, like an invisible hand was gripping it, slowly squeezing. He thought about his hammer and flexed his fists nervously, idling in its absence. Yasha, who still had her arm around his, didn't seem to notice.

Closer and closer they walked to the mighty spire, and the tightness in Thornton's head became heavier and heavier, feeling like a ripe tomato that would burst at any moment. But neither Aldryd nor Elyasha seemed to notice as they pressed onward, with Thornton grimacing to hide the pain that he thought would soon pass, a remnant of the blow to his head by Dailus, the half-eye.

"I can tell you more inside," Aldryd said as he put his hand on the ancient bricks of the spire, opening the way to the Temple of the Shaper.

Thornton could manage little more than a nod, as he was now relying heavily on the forward motion of Yasha to carry him inside. "My head," he whispered.

"What's that?" Yasha said without looking back. She was eagerly following the Keeper, and neither of them noticed that Thornton's eyes were starting to change.

A wave of nausea washed over him as he stepped inside the temple where a piercing headache crashed through his skull and into the back of his eyeballs. "Where's my hammer?" he breathed.

"Your hammer?" Yasha asked, finally coming to a stop. When she turned around to look at Thornton, her ever-present smile faded into a frown as her mouth fell open. She managed not a single word as Thornton's fingers tightened around her, gripping her like a drowning victim clinging to a raft.

"My hammer—Where is it?" he asked woozily. Stumbling forward, he let go of Elyasha and fell to the floor.

Elyasha

"What's going on back there?" Aldryd asked, his light footsteps echoing more loudly as he approached.

Ignoring the Keeper, Yasha stared at Thornton.

She could not find her words, yet she recognized his eyes—eyes that swirled with the power of the Otherworld; eyes that looked like they were filled with liquid smoke, dark brown and thick; eyes that, she knew, were the product of one thing and one thing only.

There was no mistaking it: Thornton's eyes were the eyes of a Khyth.

Chapter 45

Kienar

Gift of the Shaper

Tennech

The trees of the forest of Kienar stood sturdy and tall as they greeted General Aldis Tennech, Dagger of Derenar and leader of the armies of Gal'dorok. He knew they were the only thing standing in the way of the gateway to the Otherworld and to the chains that bound the Breaker.

Atop his chosen mount, Calathet, the general came to a halt, prompting his second-in-command to do the same.

"Send a scout ahead, Sera," he said. "I want to know how many there are and what else to expect." He looked at the brown-haired Athrani as her blue-ringed brown eyes stared back at him. "There will be much that we cannot plan for, but for what little we can control, I want to be well-informed."

Lady Edos nodded her head and answered, "I will have Durakas send one of his men." She pulled lightly on Ruen's reins to turn around.

"No," Tennech said, reaching out an armored hand to her elbow and drawing her close. "Send one of ours." His gaze swept over the multitude of men that followed behind them, still out of earshot. "I don't trust them. Ours is a hasty alliance, and I'd rather not stake the survival of my army on the words of a Thurian."

Sera's eyebrows rose slightly, but she nodded in agreement. "Of course, General. I'll see that it's done."

He watched her disappear into the thick fray of soldiers and exchange a heated glance with Caladan Durakas, who was riding toward the general with his own advisor on his heels. The two Thurians looked tired, despite their reputation, and it showed in their eyes and on their faces.

"General," Durakas nodded, bringing his war horse to a halt. The big Thurian removed his helmet, allowing the sun to glint off his sweat-laden salt-and-pepper hair. "Why are we stopping?"

"Because we've nearly reached our destination, Commander," Tennech replied. As was his habit, he did not remove his armor, especially not this close to combat, but the ends of his graying mustache hung below the opening of his helmet. He looked at the Thurian through his narrow eye slits and gave an empty smile. "Now comes the time for strategy."

The Commander of the Fist of Thurái looked surprised, perhaps even a little relieved, as he followed the general in dismounting. "I see," said Durakas. Turning to his second-in-command, he said, "Leave us, Duna. Women's minds were not built for strategy. Go tell the men that now is their chance to rest."

"Yes, Commander," she said, tapping her fist to her opposite shoulder and turning to leave.

With a smirk, Durakas turned back to the general. "Almost as obedient as your Athrani bitch," he said. "Now we can speak, man to man." He tapped a finger to his temple. "To strategy."

Tennech, who looked at Sera less as an advisor and more as a pupil, did not acknowledge the Thurian's coarseness, taking it in stride as easily as a shield deflecting an arrow. "To strategy." He held out his hand, inviting the commander to walk with him.

The two men walked the perimeter of the woods. It was clearly delineated from the outside by the rich vegetation that seemed to spring from an invisible border. The lands outside the forest were thin and drab; inside the forest, they were lush and alive.

"I've sent a scout ahead," Tennech began, "one of our best. Though the Kienari are fierce hunters, even their best cannot find a Khyth who does not want to be found."

"So I gather," Durakas answered. The Fist of Thurái, down to the last man, was an entirely human army, as the commander's contempt for Khyth was well known and taken out almost daily on Kunas, the Master Khyth of Ghal Thurái. "What do we know so far?"

Tennech stood at the edge of the forest looking in. The trees were thick and tall and provided excellent cover for whatever waited inside. Stroking the ends of his mustache, he spoke: "In the depths of the forest, at its heart, lies Naknamu, The Old One, no doubt guarded by the Binder of Worlds defending the chains that bind the Breaker." He turned to Durakas, looking the Thurian in the eyes. "That is what stands between us and the Otherworld."

Gift of the Shaper

"The Otherworld?" Durakas echoed. "You mean for us to enter . . . the Otherworld?" The commander's tone was incredulous, as was his expression.

Seeing his unease at the concept, Tennech smirked. "No, Commander. That is for D'kane to accomplish. All we have to do is clear the way."

Durakas mopped his forehead, still lined with sweat. "Leave that to my men," he said. "Combat is what they were bred for. Just give us a direction."

The sounds of the forest of Kienar lurked darkly in the distance: leaves rustling, twigs snapping over thick soil and under the padded feet of the Kienari that no doubt waited inside. Besides that, the forest was deathly still. *Like the herald of a storm,* thought Tennech.

"Soon, Commander, after the scout has given his report. Until then," he said, turning back to face his army, "we wait."

Durakas frowned. "As you command, General. But how should we proceed? I have no knowledge of this forest."

Tennech raised an eyebrow at Durakas. "Of course. The bulk of their defense will come from above," he said, pointing to the trees. "The Kienari prefer to strike silently and from a distance. But luckily for you," he said with a slight grin, "my Khyth will be able to deal with their arrows."

Durakas flinched visibly. "Then why bring my men?" His Thurian pride had worked its way to anger.

"Because we will need to take the Tree," Tennech replied. "And the Athrani are not stupid. They will be guarding it because they know what is at stake."

No sooner had the words left his lips than Sera approached them from behind.

"General," she said, taking a knee, "the scout has returned. He awaits your presence to pass on the word." As her eyes moved from the general to Durakas, she stood.

With a glance from Sera to the well-armored Thurian, Tennech said, "Thank you, Sera. Commander Durakas will be accompanying us." He walked off toward the gathered multitude of soldiers from Gal'dorok. "And so will you."

He didn't wait to see how angry it made Durakas to have included Sera, and frankly, he didn't care. He was doing it for her benefit, not the commander's. Besides, the commander was only as useful as the army of Thurians, and right now all those Thurians were under his command.

Kethras

As they approached the center of the forest, the stillness in the air was compounded by its weight. There was a certain quality to it, a blanket of depth, this far in. And Naknamu, the tallest tree for miles, was teeming with life. Kethras made his way toward the clearing that spread out in front of the mighty oak. "Wait here," he said as he put his hand out to the Athrani men behind him.

He wanted to be alone when he greeted his Mother; he knew it would not be an easy reunion.

Kethras watched Thuma and Endar exchange nervous glances as the men of the Legion scanned the trees. *An exercise in futility*, he thought with a smile. A Kienari that did not want to be discovered could remain hidden indefinitely, especially in the forest they called home.

"Of course," Endar finally replied. He lifted his heavy thighs off of his mount and stepped firmly onto the ground. Those on horseback behind him did the same. The clanking of metallic stirrups was the only sound in the air as the Athrani Legion dismounted.

"I won't be long," Kethras said, already making his way toward the opening.

The forest had not changed; that at least was some small comfort. The smells and sounds were all familiar to him, and he would have smiled under any other circumstances. But today there was little room for happiness.

The base of the mighty oak was wide and sturdy, and the arch that was carved to accommodate the Mother lay high over Kethras's head.

Gift of the Shaper

Stepping inside, he felt the change: it was cooler here, below the ground, where the moisture from the roots and soil crept slowly and heavily into the air. The smell of familiar flora filled his nostrils. Those that did best in darkness had dank and heavy odors that blanketed the senses. Stepping into the cavernous entrance of Naknamu, he followed the path downward, below the ground, where he knew his Mother waited. His padded feet made no sound as they tread softly on the dirt, a deep black indicative of the rich nutrients inside.

As he walked deeper in, his eyes adjusted to the darkness behind the fading light by switching to the vision that helped make him the deadly hunter that he was. Down here, there was only heat to guide him, and the cold blackness of the walls made it that much easier for him to pinpoint the heat signatures of not one but two Kienari.

The recognition of his sister, Ynara, brought a brief smile to his lips, though they all knew it would not last.

"My two youngest children, under the branches of Naknamu once again," the First Kienari said almost wistfully. "It has been too long, Kethras. It is good to see you again."

Kethras felt like a child again as he crossed the dirt-covered floor, so far below the surface of the forest. "Mother," he said with a smile, "it is good to see you, as well." Turning to Ynara, he added, "Sister, I am glad you are safe."

The two youngest Kienari greeted each other briefly and gently, touching one hand to the face of the other in silent recognition.

"You as well, brother. Our Mother said your journey to Annoch would be . . . tense."

Thinking of his run-in with Jinda, Kethras grinned slightly and nodded. "There were a few moments when I may have wondered if I would make it out alive," he said. "But luckily for me, one of the humans I met had seen a Kienari before." His voice went up as he smiled a sly grin. "She said she was saved by one on her way from G'hen."

A smile spread across Ynara's lips. "A spared life for a spared life, then," she said. "I even left her my best dagger."

"She still has it," he replied, a mix of surprise and clarity in his voice. "The woman's name is Mordha, and I think you will be pleased to see how she turned out." He breathed a laugh through his nose at the thought of his sister willingly leaving behind one of her prized daggers. It was one of a pair, he knew, and perhaps that was why she could spare one to leave with the G'henni girl.

"I saw strength in her eyes," Ynara said. "Even in her helplessness, there was defiance. I am pleased to hear that I was right."

In the silence that followed, the First Kienari took her hands and placed them on the tops of the heads of her two children in comfort. "My youngest ones," she said, "the time to protect the chains draws near, and I will rely on the strength of both of you to ensure that they are not broken."

Kethras looked up at his Mother, who towered over him as she always had. Though she was old, older than any living thing in this world, she still looked as young as she did when the world was first formed, when she had first taken the mantle of Binder of Worlds. "Just tell me what I must do, Mother, and I will do it."

The First Kienari smiled warmly at her youngest son, gently caressing the back of his head with her wide hand. "Your job is to protect the forest, Kethras. The archers of men will need your guidance, as well as that of your sister." With that, she allowed her hands to drop to her side as she looked him in the eye. "Though they may lack your stealth, their strength and courage will be crucial in the battle to come."

"Of course, Mother," he answered. "And Ynara?"

The Mother, the Binder of Worlds, had seen the forthcoming battle a thousand times, over a thousand years. She knew how it ended and what would follow. She had seen it play out countless times, and it never got any easier. "Ynara knows what she must do," she answered. "We have had long to talk."

The youngest Kienari fixed her gaze on Kethras and gave a firm nod. "I am prepared, brother. Our lives have led up to this point, under the guiding hand of our Mother, and now we play the parts that we were born to play."

Gift of the Shaper

Kethras could see the heat coming from Ynara and could have sworn that her eyes had gone cold. But he trusted his Mother's wisdom and did not question. "Then I will take my leave," he finally said.

"Go with the wind, my son" his Mother said. "The time draws near."

Upon hearing those words, Kethras bowed his head to his Mother. "I will make you proud," he said, turning again to the entrance that lay above them and finding his way back out into the light.

The smile that graced the lips of the First Kienari was broad and sincere. "You always do," she answered, "you always do."

As Kethras walked out of the cavernous space below Naknamu, his eyes met those of Endar Half-eye, Commander of the Athrani Legion.

"I hear whispers that the Khyth are near," said Endar. There was a fire burning behind the green eyes of the Ellenian, and he looked like a starving man about to sit down to a feast. "Have you done what you need to?"

The smooth black fur that lined Kethras's body caught flashes of the sunlight that shined overhead, and he cocked his head to the side as he listened to sounds that only he could hear. "I have," he said after a silence. "Have you?"

Endar turned to Thuma, who was grinning from ear to ear, gripping a sword that looked like it belonged in the hands of a man twice his height. Looking back to Kethras, Endar answered.

"We have. My archers have spread themselves out and hidden in the trees, like you instructed. The pikemen and swordsmen have armed themselves and are ready as well." He turned his head to the tops of the trees that arched over them, boughs of green obscuring the sky, and took a breath. "We are ready for whatever comes."

"Good," Kethras answered, "because they will be ready for us, too." His words were nearly lost as the leaves above them in the trees began to quiver as a tremor—small at first, like waves rocking a boat—ran through the forest. Then the earth began to shake with all the violence of a lightning storm. Planting his feet, Kethras knew that the sons of Khala Val'ur had just announced their arrival.

Chapter 46

Annoch

Gift of the Shaper

Elyasha

Aldryd was kneeling over Thornton, barely able to make sense of what was happening.

"His eyes," he said. "I don't understand."

Thornton was awake. His eyes were open and his lips were moving, but no words were coming out.

Yasha was just as perplexed. "How . . ." she started to say as she rubbed her temples in confusion. "He was using the Hammer all this time. It's not possible." She looked up to the aged Athrani, whose eyebrows were furrowed in thought. "He is Khyth."

A moment of pondering left the air of the temple silent and heavy. "Perhaps that is the answer," Aldryd said at last, standing upright again. "The Hammer kept his blood at bay. But now that it's gone . . ." His voice trailed off as he began to pace.

"It comes out," Yasha said. Her words were draped in disappointment. Watching the Keeper, she stood as a feeling of sickness welled up in the pit of her stomach.

Aldryd noticed her frown and walked back, standing beside her and over Thornton. "What is it?"

"I guess I just feel bad," she said softly. "I know what life is like for someone with my blood." When she heard the words spoken aloud, she looked at the young man from Highglade. "With our blood," she said. "Knowing that he didn't choose this, that he didn't want it—knowing how afraid he was of me when he first saw me . . ." She shook her head. "This is awful."

The Keeper stroked his eyebrows with his forefinger and thumb, cupping his eyes and rubbing them in frustration. He grimaced and looked at Elyasha. Then his eyes narrowed. "No," he said, "maybe it won't be."

"What do you mean?"

"It means he has a better chance of surviving in the Otherworld," Aldryd answered. Motioning her to follow, he said, "See if you can get him to his feet."

Yasha, perplexed as ever, did as she was asked and put her hands around Thornton's arms and pulled. With a small amount of effort, and much to her surprise, the young blacksmith stood up. His movement was heavy, almost like a sleepwalker, and his eyelids fluttered as they danced between open and closed.

The two of them followed the silver and gray robes of the Keeper as they wound through the corridors of the ancient Temple of the Shaper. Looking around, Yasha remembered where she was. The last time she was here, her wrists had been shackled. She rubbed them involuntarily as she kept walking, dragging a barely conscious Thornton behind her.

As they moved deeper in, her eyes went to the walls—magnificent and white under the high, sturdy ceiling of the temple. It was certainly more welcoming than the walls of the prison below, but there was still a deadness about it. She wasn't quite sure what the feeling was.

"In here," Aldryd said as he turned a corner.

Opening before them was the resting place of the Anvil of the Worldforge, a vast and towering circular chamber whose center point was an anvil much larger than Yasha had ever seen. The room that enclosed it went high up into the air—she guessed that they were standing under the highest point of the Spire of Annoch—and was at least three levels tall. Each level had an ornate railing carved of white rock encircling each floor. There were no windows, yet the chamber was as bright as day. She knew what power felt like, and she knew that it was concentrated strongly in this room.

"You are the first Khyth to ever see this place," Aldryd said as he looked at Yasha. "Well," frowning at Thornton, "you and him."

Ever since she had left the dark, stifling walls of Khala Val'ur, she had been continually impressed by what she had seen, even by things that passed as normal or routine for other people. But this, she had to admit, was the most impressive of all. The enormity of the room around her—she had never seen such space inside—and the massive iron anvil that sat in front of them was almost too much for her to take in. Even the air felt impressive. She breathed it in and looked at Aldryd. "I'm honored," she said, and she meant it.

Gift of the Shaper

"Good," Aldryd answered dismissively. "Now help me move him over here," he said, pointing to the Anvil of the Worldforge.

"There?" Elyasha asked with a tilt of her head. "Why?"

The old Athrani took a moment as he looked at Yasha, his face devoid of expression. His blue eyes looked like they were boring into her as he tried to read her. Finally, having silently come to a conclusion, he answered, "Because we are taking him through."

Yasha looked stunned. "Through? Through to the Otherworld?"

With a nod, Aldryd spoke again: "Yes, because it has been made clear to me now that Thornton is the one the prophecy spoke of. I thought it might have been you when you first entered the gates of the city, which is why I asked that you stay behind." The ornate robes of the Order of the Shaper hung loosely on his arms as he crossed them. "But I was wrong. And it's a good thing I was."

"How is you being wrong going to do us any good?" The young apprentice had let go of Thornton and now had her hands on her hips.

"Because he's going to need someone to guide him on the other side." Aldryd's eyes flashed what may have been a look of sympathy, but he whirled around to face the Anvil before Yasha could be sure. "Now, help him up. This won't be easy."

Yasha did as she was asked and walked Thornton over to the massive piece of the Worldforge that was older than even the stone that housed it. The Anvil was seated in a circle carved into the ground, with the leading edge of the Anvil flush with the floor so that one merely needed to step across a small gap to stand on top of it.

When the two of them were close enough, Aldryd put his hand on her shoulder.

"Thank you, Elyasha."

Her puzzled expression had not changed much since she came inside the temple. "Thank you for what?" she asked.

"You'll know soon enough. Now," said the aged Athrani, "take his hand and step onto the Anvil. I'm going to help you through."

"I don't understand." Yasha's swirling green eyes were fixed on the Keeper. "Why am I going with him?"

Aldryd smiled at the young woman for the first time since they met, and she felt that it had been kindness, not obedience of a prophecy, that had led him to free her. "Because I cannot," he answered, "and he will need someone there to help him."

"Help him with what?"

Turning toward the entrance, Aldryd waved a dismissive hand. "You ask too many questions," he said loudly. "Step on the Anvil. We don't have much time."

With a glance at Thornton, who still looked like he was caught halfway between dreams, she shook her head and took his hand. She muttered to herself as she stepped off the small gap and onto the Anvil of the Worldforge. Thornton followed.

The Anvil was roughly the size of a small boat and was certainly larger than any that Yasha had ever seen on the underground K'Hel River. Her feet touched the ancient metal, and she thought she felt something surge through her when she did. She had yet to undergo her Breaking, but she had heard the stories of what it was like. She was sure that there was power contained in the Anvil that rivaled that of the ancient ritual.

Spread out before her was sprawling and indecipherable writing. Each symbol was perhaps as large as she was.

"Alright," she said as she moved the two of them toward the center, "here we are."

"Good," Aldryd said. He took his hand and pressed it against the wall of the entrance, and the world began to shake. His eyes flashed with power as he looked at Yasha and the boy. "Take care of him."

As his words floated through the cavernous halls, everything else fell away. Yasha watched as the white walls of the temple melted from existence like wax on a burning candle, cascading down and out of sight to reveal a staunch gray nothingness that took its place.

Gift of the Shaper

Somehow, Aldryd's words seemed to echo in her ears as if they were the last remnants of a dying world. She was afraid and didn't seem to notice how tightly she was squeezing Thornton's hand.

"Ow! Let go!" Thornton shouted, causing her to leap backward in surprise. He shook his hand and grabbed at his wrist, rubbing it vigorously. "What's wrong with you?"

Yasha was taken aback by not only his sudden return to lucidity but also his apparent apathy for their current surroundings. She stared at him, words failing to make their way from her brain to her tongue.

"Well?" Thornton asked, still massaging his hand. He hadn't taken his swirling brown eyes off of her since he spoke. Slowly, though, he blinked and turned his head. The gray mist of nothingness that surrounded them finally grabbed his attention. "Oh," he muttered. "Huh."

In her two short years as an apprentice, Yasha had only caught glimpses of the Otherworld. She had heard stories of its power and of how it could be entered by using an artifact strong enough. But never in her life did Elyasha imagine that she would one day stand inside of it. She felt the surging energy that had been there when she stepped on the Anvil of the Worldforge, energy that flowed through her when she trained in the art of Breaking.

Now, that energy was all around them, permeating the air and their bodies, almost to the point of discomfort. She found herself suddenly pushing it away, forcing it back, rejecting its allure. Something in the back of her mind told her that if she let it in, it might never stop.

She was worried that Thornton might not be able to resist the pull like she could. Trying to shake the thought, she got him talking.

"You blacked out earlier," she said. "Are you . . . feeling alright?" She was unsure of how to break the news to him—about everything—but she also felt like now was not the time. *There might never be a time*, she thought.

"My head hurts," he answered and rubbed his eyes. "And so do my eyes. Ever since Dailus knocked me out and took my hammer, I've felt . . . strange."

Yasha was turning around, trying to get a fix on something, anything. All around them was gray, and the entire place seemed to be empty. The floor below them was an ethereal cloud that floated at their feet, somehow suspending them in its impossible haze. "I can tell you about that soon," she said, "but first I need to figure out why Aldryd sent us here."

Thornton looked around, seeming just as lost as the young Khyth beside him. "Aldryd? What did he say?"

Squinting, Yasha fixed her eyes on a dim point of light on the horizon. "He said to help you, whatever that means. Come on," she said as she waved him toward her. "I think I see where we need to go."

She couldn't quite tell, but it almost looked like the light was reaching up and clawing at the sky, waving around like the branches of a tree. "Maybe we can find some answers there."

With Yasha in the lead, the two of them headed toward a speck in the distance, beckoned by an invisible force that seemed to pull them in, away from the Anvil and toward whatever it was that lay on the other end.

Chapter 47

Kienar

Gift of the Shaper

Durakas

"To the trees!" General Tennech shouted. "Cover our ingress!"

Durakas watched as the general thrust his sword toward the heart of the forest to spur his men forward. They all knew that the Kienari could sense their coming, and the general would do everything to counter that advantage. At his side stood Seralith, who nodded at one of the Khyth, giving the signal to unleash the power that had lain dormant since their departure from the Sunken City.

A group of them closed their swirling eyes in concentration and lifted their hands skyward, beckoning the earth of the forest floor to do their bidding. It groaned and shook in response, lifting dust and rocks into the air like a swarm of insects, far too numerous to count. Huge chunks of rock hung in the air as the Khyth moved their hands to channel the power of the Otherworld. As they did, the rocks began to move. They shook and shuddered, picking up speed and coalescing into a dome around the army that protected them from the eyes of the forest, rocky and impenetrable.

"Forward!" shouted the general, as the massive, swirling vortex of dust precipitated their march toward Naknamu and the chains.

The Khyth were stone-faced in their focus as they walked, using their power to cloud their approach by commanding the earth itself. What little sunlight that had made its way through the thick boughs above was now completely shut out by the whirling tempest of dust and debris. It surrounded the Valurian army that was bolstered in strength by the might of the Fist, tearing a vicious circle through the air that grew thicker as they crossed the threshold of the forest.

The outlines of trees were barely visible through the cloud as the army carried on. They were nothing more than shadows, silhouettes of looming monsters that towered above their heads.

Durakas, who was already distrustful of the Khyth and their power, had a grim look of fear lining his face as he stared at the encircling cloud, blinking furiously to keep out the dust. He exchanged an uncertain glance with Duna, walking beside him, who had her own look of concern chiseled in her eyes.

"What have we aligned ourselves with?" Durakas asked aloud as he gaped at the circling dome.

"Strength," Duna answered simply. She squinted, covering her nose and mouth with a hand as she tried to stave off the debris.

Durakas knew that she was right, but that didn't seem to matter. A wolf on a chain was still a wolf, and it was only a matter of time before it would devour the hand that sought to control it. He watched Tennech, who marched on fearlessly, as if he felt that he was completely in control of these men—these things—who told the earth what to do. *It cannot last forever*, Durakas told himself.

Endar

"What is that?" Endar asked as he pointed to the edge of the forest. Though the vegetation was thick at its heart, it was still possible to see a fairly good distance away. And coming slowly toward them like a lumbering giant was a thick haze of brown, a malicious dark fog that was slowly devouring the trees before it.

"The Khyth," Kethras said gravely. "They are using the earth to close our eyes." He turned to Endar and Thuma, who gripped their weapons uneasily. "They are smart."

"Well, so are we," Endar replied. Turning his head to the side, he shouted, "Yorvath! Bellarin!"

At the half-eye's command, two Athrani men clad in silver robes of the Order made their way to the front of the army. When they emerged, they touched two of their fingers to their opposite shoulders in a salute. "Reporting," they said at once.

"The Khyth are on their way," said Endar. He was holding his sword out in front of him, absently admiring the blade as he spoke. "Make sure you and your men are ready."

Yorvath, the taller of the two, answered, "We are. Shall we march out to meet them?"

Gift of the Shaper

Endar moved his eyes from his sword to the eyes of Yorvath. "Go," he said, as he slammed his sword back into its scabbard. "The battle has begun." He nodded to Thuma, who understood the unspoken request. With a grin, the bearded Athrani let out a booming cry: "Legion! Awaken your iron!"

A thundering multitude of voices answered as one: "The Shaper awaits!"

Durakas

The first volley of arrows had already started falling through the swirling dome of dust that heralded the coming of the Khyth.

"The trees!" Tennech shouted over the sound of the vortex. "They're in the trees! Get rid of them!"

Durakas looked at him incredulously and shouted, "What do you expect me to do about it?" The noise from the dust storm was loud enough to necessitate yelling, despite the fact that the two men were nearly side by side. "My men can't see anything down here."

"A little dust is enough to stop the mighty Fist?" Tennech growled. "Get us through, Commander."

Durakas scowled and turned around to face his men, raising his hands up over his head and making them into fists. He thrust them apart and spread out his fingers, signaling the order to his men, who understood immediately. The Fist of Thurái, quickly and silently, scattered throughout the trees in an effort to keep them clear. Durakas didn't know how successful they would be against the waiting Kienari, but he had to at least try.

The general did not tolerate failure.

D.L. Jennings

Endar

"Now!" Thuma shouted.

With a nod, Yorvath started moving his hands in synchrony with Bellarin, and the dust storm moving toward them started to change. They could not stop the wind, but they could transform it.

The chaotic whirling of dust and rocks that had obfuscated the army of Gal'dorok suddenly began to melt away at the power of the Athrani. Yorvath concentrated on the rocks, picking them out individually amidst the debris, and began to change them. He felt the air around him and, one by one, began to shift them to match it. Bellarin, standing beside him, worked in concert with his fellow Shaper, strengthening his efforts and bolstering the power they beckoned.

"Legion!" Endar shouted, "Forward! We will be there when they break through!"

The pikemen had their weapons at the ready, parallel with the ground and pointed toward the swirling pocket of air that loomed in front of them. They knew that waiting on the other side was the army that had marched across half of Derenar to meet them. They did not know how many there were, nor did they care. All they knew was that they were charged with the defense of Naknamu behind them, and they would stop at nothing to keep it safe.

Slowly, the Legion crept forward toward the approaching army. Bellarin was still weaving his will into the air when the first of the pikemen saw it: the army that was gathered in front of them was much, much larger than any of them had imagined.

"This is what you trained for," Thuma boomed. "Stand your ground!"

The big human blacksmith walked behind them, clutching a hammer that Thuma had given him knowing that he would feel comfortable with it. "What should I do?" Olson asked. For a man who had never been in a battle, he was exceedingly calm.

"Nothing now," Endar said. "We lean on the strength of our Shapers to hold them back." He nodded toward the encroaching Dorokian army. "But we know that we can't hold them forever. The most we can hope for," he said, glancing at the blacksmith from Highglade, "is to give the Kienari a chance to cut down their number before they make it to us."

Olson nodded grimly. "When they break through, I'll be ready."

"I hope so," Thuma grinned, "because it's going to get messy."

Durakas

"What's happening?" Durakas shouted. The dome of dust that was concealing their approach, serving to weaken the effectiveness of the Kienari arrows that were raining down over their heads, was suddenly changing. "Why are your men stopping?"

"They aren't," Tennech answered. "It's the Athrani. They're trying to counter our approach."

The whole of the Dorokian army watched the dust and rocks above their heads turn to translucent air, swirling harmlessly and uselessly overhead. Just as it did, the Kienari arrows began to fall again.

The men of the Fist raised their shields over their heads to block the incoming projectiles, but some of them were too late. Though more disciplined than any men this side of Derenar, the men of the Fist screamed just like any other when catching arrows in their flesh.

"Do something!" Durakas yelled. Their subterfuge had been removed, and they were fully exposed. "And do it quickly," he added.

The Valurian archers had arrows of their own, but they were all but useless in their position on the ground. And even if they could see the Kienari in the trees, they would be hard pressed to shoot one with any accuracy.

"We're exposed, and our approach has been compromised," Tennech said as he turned to Sera. "We need to meet them head on."

Sera nodded, adjusting her helmet and drawing out her dagger. "Perhaps it is time we rely on brute force," she said as she patted Ruen's neck from her place in the saddle. The old brown horse responded with a toss of his head at the gentle touch of the tall Athrani.

"Indeed," Tennech said. "I don't know what is keeping Hullis and Dhrostain, but every moment they delay is costing us lives. We'll have to press on." The general's long mustache barely covered his frown. "And if they fail, they will have failed all of us."

Sera nodded at this and eased her horse forward. "I will take a group of men and circle around," she said. The screams of fallen Thurians continued around them as she raised her dagger into the air.

"Do it," Tennech said.

With a nod of her head, she eased Ruen around to face the men behind her. "Riders!" she shouted. "With me!" Her voice was rife with command and carried well, even in the forest. "Let us show them what a well-trained army is capable of!"

A resounding yell of determination thundered from the lungs of the army, as the sound of hoofbeats filled the air.

The riders followed her in the direction of Naknamu, which was barely visible from their position in the forest.

Endar

"We're thinning their number, but it's as useless as weeping into a fire," Endar said. "They just keep coming."

Thuma rubbed his beard and nodded. "Should we advance? Meet them now and catch them off guard?"

Endar's short, purple cloak trembled like the leaves on the trees above, and he considered it for a moment. He frowned and furrowed his brow. "No," he said finally. "We hold them. The longer we can do that, the weaker they will be when they break through. And that will be the key to their defeat." He turned to Yorvath and Bellarin, who were steeped in concentration. "Wall them in," he commanded.

The two Athrani Shapers acknowledged the order silently, altering their movements slightly, and the air around the approaching Dorokian army began to harden. They were still far enough away that their screams were distant, but the distinction as they turned from panic to terror was obvious.

"Are you sure there's nothing I can do?" Olson asked. He was gripping the hammer that Endar gave him. It was big, which he liked, and he said that it reminded him of the one he grew up using. His gaze was fixed on the pillar of air in front of them that was, for the time being, the only thing separating them from the armies of Gal'dorok.

"Unless you have some hidden Shaping power that you've neglected to mention," Endar started, "there's nothing you can do but make ready." The towering Athrani half-eye had pulled out his helmet from his saddlebags, placing it on his head to make sure it still fit. It did, and he gave himself a contented smirk, knowing that his head had not grown too big with all his accomplishments. However, looking over the blacksmith from Highglade, he frowned a bit. "You'll be hard-pressed to find some armor lying around that might fit you."

Olson had a high choke on the hammer, gripping it just below the head, and casually used it to scratch his beard. "I was afraid of that." He glanced around at the forces of the Legion. They were an eclectic collection, to be sure, but they were dedicated. "I'll see what I can come up with."

Endar watched as the blacksmith parted the sea of men and worked his way to the rear to the makeshift camp to see what he could scrounge up. He wasn't sure how much combat the man had seen, but he certainly fit the part physically—and they needed every able-bodied man they could find.

He moved his eyes back to the trees ahead, where the Shapers had focused their attention, as well.

Tennech

"Pathetic," Tennech growled. "The best-trained army in Gal'dorok is being humiliated by amateurs." He whirled around to find Durakas. "What the hell is taking your men so long? Those arrows should have stopped by now."

The stoic Thurian had no answer. "They're the best, General. They'll get it done."

Even as the words were leaving his mouth, the slew of arrows came to an abrupt end.

"It would appear you are right," Tennech said, his eyes moving skyward. After a moment, though, they narrowed as a creaking sound filled the ears of every soldier from Khala Val'ur. "Or perhaps I've spoken too soon."

"What now?" Durakas groaned.

The men watched as the air above their heads went from clear to cloudy in a matter of seconds, taking on the texture of ice, solid and opaque, and forming in almost no time at all.

Tennech looked over to where Sera had galloped off and hoped that she and her riders had made it out. "They're trapping us," he said. "Damn it, Hullis, where are you?" He clenched his fist nervously as he scanned the edge of the forest, hoping to catch a glimpse of one of the Thurian captains.

A few Valurians looked at the wall of air forming around them and approached the edges. One of them reached out to touch it with his palm, resting it flatly on its surface and pressing down. It was as solid as a block of ice, but without the cold. A few of the men exchanged glances with each other as they pulled out their swords and tried chipping away at it.

"It won't work," Tennech shouted, causing the men to stop. "You'll never break through—the Athrani will just reform it. They're using the air against us." He was seated atop his horse, Calathet, and still focused on the air above them.

"So what, then?" Durakas said as he walked over and took a swing at the surface of the air. It produced a loud *clank* as his sword connected. "We wait?"

Tennech lowered his eyes and looked at the commander. "We wait." He urged Calathet around as he surveyed his men. "And it had better not be long."

Chapter 48

Outskirts of Kienar

Gift of the Shaper

Dhrostain

Dhrostain was not afraid to speak his mind. "I don't like these things one bit," he grumbled. "Ghaja Rus might say that they're tame, but I don't see him riding one all the way across Derenar."

The two captains were nearing the forest of Kienar, each seated atop their own Gwarái, which Rus had personally procured for them at the behest of the general. It was just past midday, right when they were told to be there; and the beasts were lumbering on heedlessly, unaware of—or apathetic to—the riders commanding them.

"I don't trust him either, Farryn, but do you want to be the one to disappoint the Dagger of Derenar?"

Dhrostain let the words tumble around in his head a bit before frowning and cursing his luck. "No, I don't," he finally said. "But that doesn't mean I have to like it."

The blond Thurian captain laughed. "Fine, Farryn. I won't tell anyone how much you enjoyed it."

Dhrostain glanced at Hullis with a look he normally reserved for Chovathi right before he removed the head. But before he could say anything, Hullis put his hand up.

"Listen," he said. "Do you hear that?"

The two captains had brought their beasts to a halt with an ease that surprised both riders.

"Hmm?" Dhrostain mumbled, straining to listen. "I don't hear anything."

Hullis looked annoyed with his traveling companion. "Then you're not listening."

Dhrostain pulled on the end of his dark black beard and shifted atop his ghastly mount. "I give up. What is it?"

"It sounds like a wind storm," Hullis started. His left ear was tilted to the sky, with one hand cupped around it.

"Now I know you're joking," Dhrostain said with a laugh. "It's calmer than a Valurian wedding out here." He tapped the leather strap that served as makeshift reins for his Gwarái. "Let's keep moving."

"I'm not joking," Hullis snapped. The young captain had an angry look painted on his face, and his scowl told Dhrostain just how serious he was. "I think they may be going in."

Dhrostain raised his head skyward in dreadful contemplation. "That's not good," he said without looking back.

"No," the blond captain replied.

"The general won't be happy."

"No, he won't."

"Then we'd better see just how fast these things can move." He turned to Hullis with a look of concern, knowing full well what he had to do and liking it even less.

"Your secret will be safe with me," Hullis smirked as he dug his feet into the ribs of the mighty black leviathan. With a terrifying grunt, the creature responded with quickness, both unexpected and unbelievable, surging forward past Dhrostain and his mount, who scowled and did the same.

"It had better be," he shouted.

***

The two captains had passed Lusk hours ago, and now only Kienar lay before them, its lushness creeping up the horizon like ivy over stones. The two Thurians knew they were close and that they would have to sustain the frenzied pace for just a little while longer. Regardless, it didn't seem to affect their mounts at all, who actually seemed like they were chasing something.

The Gwarái sped across the land with incredible velocity. Their gait, nowhere close to that of other mounted creatures, was as efficient as it was rough. The two Thurian captains found themselves clinging to the long necks of the creatures as they galloped on, reins gripped desperately in one hand, like fleas latched onto charging wolves.

The long necks of the creatures were extended fully forward as they pounded the ground with their clawed feet, resembling enormous black panthers as they charged, legs stretching out in front of them in impossibly quick strides and swinging under their body after pummeling the ground beneath them. Their wild yellow eyes were wide open as they ran, but they did not need to see where they were going. Their powerful sense of smell was what guided them now, and even their riders couldn't hold them back, even if they tried.

For what drove them was stronger than any human.

What drove them ensured they would not slow.

The great black streaks tore across the land as relentlessly as the predators they were, edging closer and closer to something that neither Hullis nor Dhrostain could sense, but it was definitely there: the blood of the Shaper.

Their master, the Breaker, was waiting. And they were coming to set him free.

Chapter 49

Kienar

Gift of the Shaper

Miera

Miera fought him every step of the way.

Her hands were bound behind her, together at the wrists with a long, thin rope that was fastened around her waist. The only thing keeping her from running was the watchful eye of D'kane, whose vigilance in keeping her close bordered on obsessive. Once again she jerked her arm away as he tried to place his hand on her.

"I keep telling you that you're just going to wear yourself out," the Khyth said. His pulsating, swirling eyes were locked onto her, and his hideous face was warped into a sneer.

Miera ignored him as he tried again, wrapping his pale fingers around the upper part of her arm to maintain his grasp. *I won't let him get to me*, she kept telling herself. She hadn't said a word since they left Khala Val'ur.

"It's not much further. Look," D'kane said as he pointed, "the forest of Kienar lies ahead. Tennech and his army will be waiting for us there." He was staring right at her now. "And I can finally rid myself of you."

The words were a sharp dagger to her chest. "What?" she gasped, realizing too late that her reaction was exactly what the Master Khyth had been digging for.

"So you have not forgotten how to speak," he said. "Good. You'll need your voice when we arrive."

One thing was certain: everything about D'kane made her nervous, from the way he looked, to the way he sounded—even his words were ominous and deliberate. She hoped that he was only trying to get a rise out of her again. Relenting, she spoke her mind.

"I'm not going to help you free the Breaker," she said. Her words were defiant, and the weight of truth gave them purpose. "There's no point in even trying."

D'kane didn't need to look at her to see that she meant what she said. Perhaps that was why his sudden and fitful laughter sent a shiver down her spine.

"You think you have a choice," the servant of the Breaker said with wild eyes. "I'm not even sure I need you alive, but I'd rather not risk it." He tightened his grip on her arm. "No, you're going to help me," he hissed through his teeth. "It's just a matter of how much of a fight you put up."

Miera looked away as the two of them continued walking. Her thoughts, as they had been for the last few days, were on Thornton. She hoped that he hadn't forgotten about her, and something in the back of her mind told her that he hadn't. The way he had looked for Olson when he went missing was the one reassurance she had that he would never give up. Despite the fact that she had seen no sign of him—or the Kienari—since D'kane had carried her away, she would not surrender her last bit of hope. Instead, she clung to it like a piece of driftwood in an ocean of doubt, keeping her head just above the reach of the pounding waves, in desperate determination not to drown.

The two of them continued walking toward the forest, and as they got closer, the sound of swirling wind filled their ears.

"It seems that the general has chosen not to wait," D'kane said to himself. "Come," he said as he tugged on Miera's arm, urging her forward, "we've no time."

Miera stumbled as she tried to dig her heels into the ground in a feeble attempt to slow them down. When she did, she felt D'kane's hand heat up as he pulled her in to face him, and the cracked lines in his face glowed a muted orange that looked like fire.

"Don't test me, child," he growled. The flash of power behind his words was only a hint, Miera knew, of what a Khyth fully enraged and bent on destruction was capable of. Her legs nearly gave out beneath her, but the strong hand of the black-robed Valurian was enough to keep her upright. "I'm beginning to question my decision to let you live."

Their progress was halted, though, by the sudden sound of thunder—thunder, it seemed, that was coming closer.

Closer on four legs.

Gift of the Shaper

D'kane

No, D'kane thought—*eight*. He saw the familiar forms of Hullis and Dhrostain perched upon massive mounts of black galloping closer.

"So it was you they were after," Hullis said as his Gwarái slowed to a stop. Its forked tongue traced the crests and valleys of its razor-sharp teeth as the creature moved its head to Miera's, heaving moistened air in and out of its great nostrils with enough force to move her hair.

"Control your mount, Captain," D'kane snarled. "It's not yet time."

Hullis acknowledged the command with a yank of the makeshift reins that fed into the creature's mouth, causing its long neck to snake backward and allowing it to stare the Thurian right in the eye.

"I don't think he likes that," Dhrostain said as he struggled with his own Gwarái.

"Clearly he doesn't," Hullis answered, maintaining eye contact with the Shaper's Bane. His hand crept toward his sword in silent reaction to the guttural growl that came rumbling from the long black throat of the Gwarái.

"Stop fooling around," D'kane barked. He reached behind for the Hammer strapped to his back, taking it out of the sling and holding it in his hands for the first time since Khala Val'ur. He spun it in his grip like a dance partner as he felt the surge of the Otherworld flow through him more strongly than ever. He knew that their proximity to the chains—and to the Otherworld—had everything to do with it. "Now come. We have an army to meet."

With the Hammer present, the two Gwarái seemed to suddenly shut out the world around them and raised their heads to the center of the forest, to Naknamu, where the door to their master lay. Theirs was a look of possession, of intense concentration, that knew no equal.

"Looks like they know it too," Dhrostain remarked. "I don't think we have a choice."

The creatures moved forward with no urging from their riders, like spiders crawling back into their webs—insidious and purposeful, careful and deft, and with the feel of struggling prey within their slowly closing grasp.

Endar

Yorvath's eyes were closed as he worked the air around him, bending it to his will and forcing it to change, becoming something it was not. His blood brother, Bellarin, stood beside him doing the same, intensifying the effort of Shaping and making the effect even more powerful. They were like a pair of dancers who knew each other's steps inside and out, moving seamlessly across a ballroom floor with effortless grace and poise. Their hands knew the motions as they worked together in time, weaving and waving in a peregrine display. After years of working together, it was no wonder the effects were so precise.

So when both of their eyes shot open in panic, Endar knew right away that something was wrong.

"No," Yorvath whimpered as a specter of fear began to permeate the forest, moving in like a shadow to blanket the Kienari homeland. It was a weight crushing down on the chests of every Athrani under the branches of Naknamu, and it brought with it the realization that an ancient terror thought by everyone to be long dead had returned at last.

The arms of the two Athrani men fell fecklessly before them, as useless as their Shaping had just become.

"It cannot be," Bellarin said, his own voice hoarse and barely above a whisper.

Endar felt it too. In the hairs on his neck and in the depths of his heart, his terror grew. "Yet it is," he said as he drew his sword. The fear in his eyes was real, but he did not let it last long enough for his men to see it. He shook it off, knowing that now more than ever they needed strength.

"Brothers!" he shouted, raising his sword high into the air. "Where Shaping fails, our swords and spears will find victory!" He turned his head, shifting in his saddle, to make sure his voice was heard by the whole of the Athrani Legion. "You've marched the length and breadth of this land, protecting it, and now the time has come to fulfill the oath you swore

Gift of the Shaper

when you first joined the Legion. For the Shaper," he yelled.

"And for Eternity!" the Legion boomed in response.

As he thrust his sword forward toward the advancing army of Gal'dorok, he caught a glimpse of sunlight shining and shimmering throughout the trees. *No, not shining*, he thought—*reflecting*. It was the tips of the arrows, nocked and ready, that were poised on the edges of Kienari bowstrings, waiting like the teeth of tigers to engulf their prey.

With the strength of the forest behind him, he charged at the army before him. And with his attention focused so far in front, he had no way to see the flanking group of riders, led by a tall brunette dressed in Valurian steel, that was closing in to split his army in half.

Durakas

"The Gwarái have arrived," came the voice of one of the Khyth standing behind the general. "The Athrani will have felt it."

Commander Durakas turned around to marvel at the two black beasts that made their way through the rear of the army, dwarfing his men and towering over the multitude. He had never before seen such monstrosities, and the tales he had heard as a boy did them no justice, as they rumbled like mountains through a valley of men. They held their heads aloft as they walked, grazing the treetops with their impossibly long necks; and they were guided by the unearthly glow of their two yellow eyes, shining like beacons on a hill.

"By the Breaker," he whispered, "the stories fall so short."

His men could barely register the sight, and some narrowly missed being trampled as they stood in amazement at the creatures of legend, brought to life before their eyes.

The war-hardened Dagger of Derenar made no indication that he was so moved. "Now is not the time for fear!" Tennech shouted. His words barely registered in the ears of the awe-struck soldiers. "Now is the time to become fear!" He dug his heels into the ribs of Calathet, spurring him on. "To the tree!" he shouted.

D.L. Jennings

Breaking out of their trance, the army of Gal'dorok was slow to awaken. But beneath the shadows of the advancing behemoths, they felt the urgency and the beckoning of war, calling them forth to the chains.

D'kane

D'kane watched as the swarm of soldiers surged forward to clear the path to Naknamu, smiling a sinister smile to the girl as he clutched her arm in one hand and the Hammer of the Worldforge in the other.

"It won't be much longer now," he said as he watched the battle begin to unfold. "Come," he said as he grabbed her arm and pulled her toward a horse that Tennech had readied for them. "The Breaker awaits."

Chapter 50

Kienar

Gift of the Shaper

Endar

When the first of the swords struck armor, Endar felt alive. The two armies met like waves crashing over rocks, a cacophonous clattering of skin and steel, blood and soil. Hoarse war cries sounded as both sides advanced beneath a hail of arrows, surging forward, spears and fists meeting bone and flesh. The ghastly yellow eyes of the Gwarái towered above them, boring straight into the heart of his army.

"Kethras, if you're listening," Endar shouted to the trees, "get those things out of here!"

The mere presence of the Gwarái was enough to tie their strongest arm behind their back, that of Athrani Shaping. Outnumbered and outpowered, he watched their narrowing chances become slimmer and slimmer.

Then from behind him came the sounds of steel on steel as the shouts from his men told him that they were being outflanked. He turned in time to see the one leading the charge and was shocked to recognize a fellow Ellenian, perched atop her war horse, commanding a group of riders.

"Shieldmen!" Endar shouted. "Turn and attack!"

The Legion was visibly shaken, and a large number of them were quickly realizing that they were not cut out for this. As the threat of death by a blade to the throat became increasingly more real, panic began to set in and Endar knew he had no choice but to take matters into his own hands. He grabbed the reins of his mount and climbed on.

Turning to Thuma, he said, "Press the attack. We've been flanked and have no choice but to split the forces."

His second-in-command looked at him, perplexed. "Why tell me? You are the leader of this army."

"Because," Endar replied, "I must do this myself." With a nod to Olson, he said, "Blacksmith, come with me."

With a quick kick to his horse, he was off, to the rear of the Legion, hoping to regain control of a quickly spiraling situation.

D.L. Jennings

Thuma

Thuma watched his commander ride away with Olson in tow. Then, wasting no more time, he turned around and began yelling commands to the soldiers within earshot. While he did not have Endar's gift for speeches, he made up for it in military prowess.

"Spearmen, advance! We will meet them head on. Swords at the ready!" Thuma was already formulating the right approach to meet the enemy and keep them at bay. "Archers, spread out and use the trees as cover. It's our best shot at slowing them down."

The volley of arrows continued steadily as both armies tried to pare down the number of soldiers remaining.

Standing silently by his side was Jinda, the quiet yet imposing Captain of the Guard of Annoch. He looked up at Thuma, who had been suddenly thrust into command, and asked simply, "Where am I needed?"

Thuma looked him over. He was rugged and strong and looked like he had seen his fair share of battles. Being from beyond the Wastes of Khulakorum, this was almost certainly true. Thuma looked back to the clashing forces behind him, nearest the Tree, and then again to the ones bearing down in front of him. He frowned and pointed forward with his chin. "We need to reinforce the front line. We're already outnumbered, and now we are in danger of being overtaken."

"Then I will cut down their number," Jinda said. From a strap on his back he removed an axe and produced a dagger from his boot. With a wild look in his eye, he looked right at Thuma. "Best of luck," he said and vanished.

Miera

D'kane galloped on toward the Tree as Miera struggled to free herself from her fetters.

"It won't do you any good," the Khyth said, turning his head slightly so that he could see her. "We've nearly arrived."

Gift of the Shaper

As they slowed to a stop, Miera could hear the sounds of war all around them.

The bulk of the skirmish was concentrated in the middle of the forest—practically a straight line out from the entrance to Naknamu. It looked like there was a group of riders coming in from the south to flank the Legion, which meant there was almost no resistance for a lone rider and his cargo riding in from the north.

"Where are we?" she asked.

"Quiet," D'kane shot back. He was constantly scanning the trees, watching for any sign that they had been detected—though it was not doing him much good. So far there had not been a single arrow fired in their direction, and most likely any Kienari that would have been able to spot them was otherwise engaged. Regardless, as they neared the Tree, D'kane swung his legs off his mount to make the rest of the journey on foot. After slipping to the ground, he turned to the horse and quickly shoved Miera off. The gasp as she fell worked its way right back out of her lungs when she hit the ground. All she could do was look at D'kane with a mixture of anger and confusion. Even if she asked the question that was on her mind, she knew she wouldn't get an answer.

"Get up," he barked. "For once in your life you're going to be useful."

Forcing herself to her knees, Miera stood slowly—no easy task with her hands bound. She knew she had no choice.

"What is this place?" she asked.

"None of your concern," D'kane answered. "All that you need to know is that you hold the key."

He was staring at the largest tree in the forest, a great solid oak standing in the middle of a large clearing. It was mostly concealed behind the smaller trees that lay on the outskirts of the clearing, but Miera knew without asking that it was where they were headed.

The Khyth had his head tilted, listening to the sounds of battle. "If Tennech does his job right, we will see minimal resistance," he said. "And the Gwarái will make things much easier. How he managed to convince Yetz to let him bring them out here, I'll never know. But he has." He

394

turned to Miera and took her by the rope that tied her hands together, looking her in the eyes.

"When we make our way to the tree," he said, "I will either lead you or drag you." He was grabbing her arm in the way that he knew bothered her. "How quiet you are when we walk will determine which. Do you understand?"

Every time he looked at her it made her squeamish. His eyes were vile pools of green that reminded her of algae floating on top of stagnant water—a sure sign that something lurked beneath the surface, possibly dangerous, and certainly unwelcome. Wincing, she nodded through her discomfort.

"Fine," she said, "I'll be quiet." She wasn't sure if she meant it, though, as she scanned the trees for Kienari. Kethras, Ynara—it didn't matter to her; anything covered in fur at this point would be a welcome sight. And when she noticed D'kane doing the same thing, she started hoping vehemently that he would find one—or one would find him. Her heart skipped a beat as she saw a shadow flutter across some branches high above.

"Move," D'kane said as he grabbed her, pulling her after him and toward the edge of the clearing. The Khyth's eyes were still on the trees as Miera's heart sank back into her stomach. Whatever she had seen had not seen them—or it had but had chosen not to do anything about it. An arrow loosed from the bow of any Kienari, even at that range, would surely find its target, she knew.

The sounds of battle grew louder and closer as they walked, and Miera felt a looming sense of despair, like she was being forced into a corner against her will, unable to back out and incapable of fighting forward. And whatever it was that she felt seemed to be coming from up ahead. Whatever it was, it was coming from the tree.

Gift of the Shaper

Olson

The first thing Olson noticed was the blood.

It was everywhere, covering everything, like a sanguine snow dusting the forest floor. Even with all the armor surrounding every soldier, the swords and spears still seemed to find a way to pierce through, spilling their crimson prizes onto the ground.

Olson had been in fights before—as had any man in Highglade who liked to drink—but this was his first time seeing real combat. And for a moment he was caught up in the chaos.

"Blacksmith!" Endar shouted, bringing him out of his daze. "Use that hammer of yours!"

Olson looked down to his hands and saw that he was, indeed, still holding the hammer that Endar had given him. He wasn't sure exactly how he should use it on a person—he'd only ever hammered steel—but he thought that the principle must be the same. With a nod to the half-eye, he waded into the fray.

Endar

The first Valurian to find out exactly how hard Olson Woods could swing a hammer was also the loudest, as the mountain from Highglade brought it down on the man's chest, crumpling him to the ground. Endar nodded approvingly as he parried blows from two men at once. "You catch on quick," he said with a kick to the chest of one of them.

Olson barely acknowledged the compliment as he continued to fight.

The group of riders that had caught them by surprise was a small one—led by an Athrani woman, no less—but the fact that the Legion was flanked and unaware of the attack meant that they were disorganized and vulnerable. They were fighting an uphill battle, and their footing was slipping. They had to find some way to regain it, and Endar knew that they needed it now. It was the reason he chose to command this particular group of soldiers himself, in fact. He thought that, with a push from him, they might regain the traction needed and perhaps swing momentum back in their favor. As his sword cut flesh, he pressed on, hoping that his presence was what they needed to turn things around. He shouted at a handful of retreating archers, compelling them to stay and fight.

A few moments and well-placed arrows later and they had nearly turned the tide of the battle. But just as he was about to shout for the killing blow, he was nearly blinded as a roaring flame filled the air just beyond them, accompanied by a surging tremor that rippled through the battlefield.

The Athrani woman on horseback was heard shouting to her troops: "Only a moment longer." Her troops acknowledged her words and pushed back, fighting with renewed vigor.

Endar didn't like any of it. Looking over to see where the blast had come from, he called to Olson. "Blacksmith," he shouted, "that came from the Tree. Find out what it is and report back to me."

Swinging his hammer and connecting yet again, Olson looked at him. "I can't leave now. We've nearly turned this around."

"Go," Endar shouted, barely dodging the blade of a Valurian. "We can clean this up." Grabbing the spear of a fallen pikeman beside him, Endar hurled it at the woman who had led the charge, catching her in the chest and tearing her from her mount.

Begrudgingly, Olson threw his elbow into the face of an oncoming soldier and headed toward the source of the blast. "This had better be good," he said.

Sera

Sera would be the first to head into the fray, and she preferred it that way. A smirk crept its way onto her face as she charged forward, with the bloodcall of Gal'dorok urging her on.

Her quorum of riders was few in number, but every one of them was a seasoned warrior, with countless years spent fighting off the Chovathi that were intent on reclaiming their homeland of Ghal Thurái. The lone

Gift of the Shaper

Valurian with them was a Khyth that Tennech had insisted ride along. Despite the general's mistrust of their power, he knew it was necessary. The rest of them—to the man—were a force to be reckoned with.

The gap between Sera's riders and the Athrani Legion was rapidly shrinking. She waved her hand above her head to silently grab attention and pointed at soldiers on the left- and right-hand sides. Most of them were archers, she could see, which made them easy targets.

They should hear us by now, she thought. She couldn't imagine what reason they would have for focusing their attention ahead of them when there was such an obvious threat bearing down behind them.

Then she saw it.

There was not one good reason why the Athrani Legion should be so preoccupied. *No,* she thought with a smile, *there were two.* And each one was topped by a son of Ghal Thurái, Captains Hullis and Dhrostain.

"The Gwarái are here," Sera shouted to the Khyth behind her. "Do what you will."

With a nod of understanding, the black-cloaked rider began to weave his power as the onslaught began.

Sera and her riders could not have asked for a better distraction as they smashed into the flank of the Legion. Their swords met skin and bones almost immediately as the Athrani were caught too off guard to even lift their shields. She watched as the lone Khyth elevated scores of boulders, dropping them one by one on the heads of soldiers from Ellenos.

The Legion was in chaos. The archers in the rear were practically defenseless against the close-range cavalry breathing down their necks. They turned and scattered, exposing the meaty underbelly to the sharpened blade of the Fist of Ghal Thurái.

"Only a moment longer," Sera shouted. "The way must be made clear!"

Then, from the roar of retreat, sounded a different call. It was sturdy and bold and had the power of command behind it. "This is what you swore to defend," it shouted. "With me!"

She watched as a burly man in gold epaulets and a purple cape—a commander, she realized—muscled his way toward her group of riders, quelling the retreat of his men and whipping them into a frenzy. *They listen to him well,* she thought.

She watched as he leapt from his horse and grabbed a Thurian rider, dragging him off his horse and planting a dagger in his throat. Looking up to his soldiers, he shouted, "They're men, just like us! And all men will bleed if you press hard enough."

Sera motioned to the rest of her riders to continue their assault. With the Gwarái bearing down on the front lines and the Athrani Shaping power cut off, Tennech and D'kane would not need long.

She never saw the spear that knocked her off her mount, but she certainly felt it. And as her world went dark, her only thought was how she had failed General Tennech and that he would surely be upset. She hoped that her death would be a good enough distraction for D'kane.

Chapter 51

Naknamu

Gift of the Shaper

Miera

Naknamu stood silent and tall among the trees of the forest with its heaven-thrust branches clawing at the sky above. Miera realized its enormity as they closed in, and wondered how, in a forest filled with trees, one of them could stand out so starkly against the rest. The bark of the thick oak was darker than most of the other trees, and it looked like it could withstand even the strongest of storms.

D'kane was cautious as they approached, but his eagerness to get to their destination was beginning to show. Shouts of battle were coming from just beyond the clearing.

"Just keep moving," he said to Miera as he prodded her onward. "It won't be long now."

The words did not put her at ease. In the back of her mind, she was worried that she truly was expendable and when D'kane finished whatever it was he needed her for he would dispose of her as easily as he would a piece of rotten meat. But she tried to push those thoughts aside for one of hope instead: this deep in the heart of the Kienari homeland, there was the smallest chance that she might be found. It was a thought she had kept tucked away, a faint light inside her dark cell of captivity, and with each step deeper into the forest it had become brighter.

And when they approached an arch at the base of the great tree, the biggest Kienari she had ever seen emerged from beneath it, turning her light of hope into a roaring pillar of flame. Before D'kane could react, the creature spoke.

"I know you, son of Khala Val'ur. Servant of the Breaker." Her voice was a windstorm, thrashing wild and threatening ruin. "And I know why you have come."

D'kane froze in his tracks like a wild animal suddenly aware of imminent predation. The power behind the voice of this creature was surely enough to give him pause to reconsider trying to make his way past it and to the waiting chains of the Otherworld. With steady determination, though, he approached with his hands on the Hammer of the Worldforge.

"And that," the Kienari said, pointing, "is not for you to wield." The words hissed through her sharp teeth like steam from a kettle. "Its power is older than this world and was not meant for the likes of you, Khyth."

The Hammer in the hands of the Khyth had taken on a faint glow of sorts as they had gotten closer to the tree, and its muted blue sheen had now become more intense, like the coals of a furnace.

"I know very well about its power, Binder of Worlds," D'kane answered, steeling his gaze on the First Kienari. "And I plan to use it. I'll not have you stand in my way."

"Yet here I am," answered the Mother. Her words rumbled forth in a torrent, shaking the trees and the forest floor.

The hooded Valurian tightened his grip on the ashen wood handle of the Hammer. The Master Khyth, capable of tearing apart mountains and bringing armies to their knees, would not be cowed, even in the presence of something as great as the First Kienari. With one free hand, he beckoned the earth to do his bidding and used the rocks as his voice. "If you will not move," he said, "then I shall make you move," as a great boulder flew from behind him, right toward the base of Naknamu where the Mother stood.

The Binder was unwavering, standing as sturdy as the trees that held her children. "Your hubris is great, Khyth," she stormed. "But I have locked eyes with the one you call 'Master,' and I know his power." She reached out a hand and struck down the impelling boulder with a flick of her wrist, crashing it to the ground in a starburst.

Miera looked over her shoulder to the clashing armies behind them. The Athrani forces were occupied for the time being, but the moment they realized that the real threat had slipped past them and to the Tree, they would come crashing down around them with neither mercy nor restraint.

Or so she hoped.

She turned back just in time to see an explosion of air knock D'kane backward to send him sliding onto his back.

Above him stood the Mother, hands raised high, with deep black eyes effulgent with fury.

Gift of the Shaper

"Abandon your path," she warned.

Defiantly, D'kane raised his gaze to hers and stood, using the Hammer as a crutch. "No," he said as the cracks in his skin began to burn. "You have stood in the shadow of this tree for too long, Binder, and have forgotten what power means."

Miera watched in horror as she relived the night that she and Thornton were first attacked. D'kane's skin was fire, and that fire extended to the Hammer he now wielded—the one thing that had defeated the Khyth on that night.

With a sudden burst of flame he grew in size, matching the height of the first Kienari and screaming toward her furiously, swinging his blazing hammer at her head. The two titans clashed in an explosion of strength, sending a shockwave through the forest that shook the trees and awakened the earth. D'kane swung again as a wall of rock surged upward from behind the Mother. He connected, sending the towering pillar of darkness staggering backward and smashing into the boulders that he commanded.

Melting into the shadows, she disappeared, materializing instantly behind the burning Khyth and sinking her clawed hands into his molten skin. He cried and thrashed about, trying to pry her off, but she was stuck fast, and a frenzied bite from the Mother's razor-sharp teeth nearly brought D'kane to his knees.

With a yell, D'kane willed the inferno into a furious blaze that threatened to scorch every tree in the forest, engulfing the inky black figure that clung to him. The grass beneath them withered and burnt away, leaving nothing but blackened soil on the forest floor. The brightness of the flame flickered and surged as smoke began to pour out, leaking onto the ground and rising to the tree tops. Miera coughed and choked as it stung her eyes, and she suddenly realized she couldn't see a thing.

"Fool!" boomed the voice of the Mother. It was coming from all around, echoing off branches like they were the walls of a cave. What had been bright as day only moments before was now draped in shadow, sealing off the light of the forest and extinguishing the roaring flame that had come from the Khyth. The voice of the Mother resonated powerfully throughout. "You attack me in the heart of my forest?"

The burning figure of D'kane had shrunk and retreated, bending to the power of the First Kienari as a tortured groan escaped his lips. He was slowly being crushed, as the very trees seemed to give the Mother strength.

"I will show you what it means to fear pain," she thundered.

Then, dimly at first, the blue light of the Hammer began to sing at the center of the cloud. It surged and brightened, cutting through the smoke as easily as the sun melts the fog. In its wake was D'kane, standing once again and holding the Hammer of the Worldforge above his head.

"The Breaker will see me claim that which is His," he shouted. Slamming the head of the Hammer into the ground, the forest shook again as a scream pierced the veil.

Miera watched as the smoke cleared away to reveal a trembling black figure, fragile and huge, bent on one knee and clutching her chest.

"Shaper," she heaved. Sadness filled the Mother's eyes as she looked at Miera, staring deep into her soul. "You must follow him through."

A confused Miera gasped as the Hammer came down again on the Mother, crushing her to the ground and expelling the breath from her. The blue light of the Hammer turned to red as it burned, engulfing the Mother where she lay and sending a twisting pyre skyward that raged as it rose. A sudden shock burst forth as the corporeal form of the Binder was erased, leaving only the Khyth, stooping over the spot and trembling with power.

"Come," he said as he stood, his voice like thunder. Walking over to Miera, he grabbed her by the arm and dragged her after him, to the entrance of Naknamu, into what once stood as the throne room of the Binder of Worlds. "Nothing stands in the way."

And as she was being dragged inside the giant tree, Miera could have sworn that she saw Olson burst through the clearing to run after them, with a scowl on his face and a hammer in his hands.

Gift of the Shaper

Olson

The inside of Naknamu was dark and pungent, smelling strongly of the soil that housed the tree and the water that fed it, and Olson scowled as he walked deeper inside. He did not even remotely enjoy being below the ground. Trees were useful for nothing more than being fed to fires, he always said. But he was sure that he had seen Miera disappear beneath the roots, and he wasn't about to turn back now.

With the sounds of war completely muted behind him by the layers of dirt dampening the noise, he carried on. Cursing himself for not bringing a torch or something by which to see in the dark, he fumbled about by feeling the walls with his hands. The soil was soft, cool, and damp, and he hated it.

For all he knew, he had been down there for hours, wandering in circles through the dark.

But just as he convinced himself that he was never leaving this underground burial chamber, he heard Miera's voice. It was distant and quiet, and he couldn't make out any words—several feet of dirt made sure of that. Then he heard a second voice, lower and deep, but raspy like metal scraping across a stone.

The two voices hit his ears from the right, and he swiveled his head out of reflex. It was almost entirely pitch black and the voices were like a small spark to lead him through the dark. Still keeping his bearings by dragging his fingers on the wall, he walked after the sound.

The voices grew louder.

He was getting close.

He followed the wall for what seemed like ages, keeping the voices ahead of him and trying to ignore the heavy smell of dirt that flooded his nostrils. It was only when he heard the shrill sound of a scream that every other thought fled his mind but one: save her.

He could make out words now.

"Please, you don't have to do this."

Miera!

"That's where you are wrong."—the second voice, the one he didn't recognize.

"Can't you just take me through with you?" Miera pleaded. "Why do you need my blood?"

"Because it's the key," the voice answered. "It's always been the key; you're just the vessel for it. Once I've opened the way, the vessel is useless."

Olson heard Miera sob softly as he continued working his way toward her. His pulse pounded in his head as he walked, sweating despite the cool air around him.

"Crying won't help," the voice snapped. "And if you don't stop, I'll find out just how much blood I can get from a corpse."

Olson didn't know what was happening to Miera, but he knew that he had to hurry. A light from up ahead told him that he was close. It streamed onto the floor like molten steel, illuminating the night-black passageway below the earth. Quickening his pace, he heard Miera stifle her cries.

"There," said the raspy voice, "the process is complete. Now to open the door."

Olson had his eyes on the light that was bathing the hallway. It was dim, but it was enough. As he sped toward it, he felt the earth shake and heard the old familiar sound of a hammer striking steel. He heard it again and felt the earth quiver along with it. He rounded the corner just in time to see the back of a robed figure standing before a huge, shimmering portal that was draped on both sides by loose-hanging chains, looking like they had just been broken. They had apparently been draped across its face as if they were supposed to keep people out, but Olson could see straight through it to the other side of the wall. As far as he could tell, it looked just like an arch standing harmlessly in the middle of the room.

Then he watched as the hooded man turned around and was horrified the moment he did so, suddenly realizing why Thornton had been so perplexed by Yasha's smooth skin. This Khyth was horribly scarred all over, like a burn victim, with a voice to match.

From a hidden pocket inside his robe the Khyth produced a Gwarái horn that was almost as long as his forearm. "Now, as promised, I have no use for you anymore," he said with a smile.

Olson had no time to think and knew what the Khyth intended to do. He had to save Miera, and he had to act now. So he did the only thing he could: he charged at the man at full speed, catching him by surprise and tackling him and sending both of them straight through the portal to the Otherworld.

Miera

Miera watched, stunned, as she saw Olson fly into D'kane, seemingly out of nowhere, only to disappear into thin air right through the portal. She blinked a few times to make sure her eyes weren't playing tricks on her and finally realized that what she had seen had been real. Olson and D'kane were gone, nowhere to be found. And she was alone and still trapped.

The realization hit just before the panic did.

She looked up at her bonds. Her hands were shackled together at the wrists, and her wrists were chained to the wall. D'kane had made sure she would not get out. So unless she found a way to free herself, she thought that she could be stuck down there forever.

Both of her forearms had been sliced down the middle by D'kane, using the Gwarái horn, and she was slowly but surely losing blood, adding to her panic.

The only thing that calmed her down was when she remembered the last and desperate words of the Mother before D'kane had struck her down: "Follow him through."

She determined to do just that, but before she could do so, she had to get free.

The shackles around her wrists were tight, and her struggling had done her no favors in getting them loose, but she was not ready to give up just yet. The Gwarái horn, knocked from D'kane's grip when he had tumbled into the portal, lay just beyond her reach. She looked up to her left wrist, the smaller of the two, and made up her mind.

Closing her eyes and biting her lip, she wiggled her wrist into position at the edge of the shackle so that the base of her thumb and outside of her pinky were pressed tightly up against it. With a deep breath, she yanked down—hard.

The pain made her bite her lip with enough force to draw blood, and she thought for a moment that she might have broken a bone in her hand. But she had not pulled it through.

Biting down again, she yanked down even harder. This time, though, her hand broke free, leaving skin and blood in its place on the shackle. She groaned and immediately brought her hand to her lips to try to alleviate some of the pain by sucking on her wound. The taste of copper splashed onto her tongue as she held it in her mouth, letting the warmth distract her from the stinging.

When she felt the surface bleeding die down, she held her free hand up to inspect it. *All there,* she thought and went back to work, leaning forward to stretch toward the Gwarái horn.

With all her weight pulling down on her right wrist, she feared for a moment that it might snap off. But the fingers of her free hand worked their way slowly onto the horn as she desperately clawed at it with her fingertips. She exhaled the remaining breath in her lungs, providing her with the tiniest bit of extra reach, and found that she had just enough traction on the horn to inch it closer until she was finally able to grab it, victoriously, and stand back up. Relieving the pain in her wrist, she took a breath and gathered herself.

Now for the hard part, she thought.

When she was younger, she had seen Thornton pick his way out of some shackles that Olson had made, using nothing but a metal splinter, in an attempt to show off for some of the other girls in the village. She was hoping that she could use the horn to do the same.

She examined the lock mechanism and the point of the horn and hoped that the two would soon become good friends. She placed the end of the horn in a small hole in the shackle and started working it back and forth, up and down, hoping for the best. She rocked it around in a circular motion and then back again the other way. Not really knowing what she was doing, she tried everything as the blood from her arms continued to ooze.

Gift of the Shaper

Finally, after what seemed like an eternity, she heard a *click*. She gasped audibly and tried to move her hand, and the shackle came apart easily.

She was free. She moved her hands to the bottom of her dress and tore off two pieces of cloth to wrap the slashes in her arms in an attempt to halt the bleeding. Most of the blood had flowed down to the crook of her elbows and dripped onto the floor below. It was a gruesome sight for someone who made her living by selling flowers.

Now, she thought as she rid her head of the sight of her blood, *for the other hard part*.

She looked at the arch in the middle of the room. It was simple and plain and didn't look like much. *All that fuss over this*, she thought.

Since Olson and D'kane had gone through with no problem, she reasoned that she could do the same.

She took a breath, hoped she was doing the right thing, and stepped through the portal, after D'kane and the Hammer of the Worldforge.

Chapter 52

The Otherworld

Gift of the Shaper

Elyasha

Yasha tensed as they walked. She took a deep breath, carefully considering her words. Her mind had been spinning a thousand times a second trying to figure out just how to breach the subject with Thornton—and exactly how to phrase everything. It was the delicate surface of a frozen lake, and if they walked too hard or too fast, they could both fall through.

Before she could speak, though, she found herself relaxing a bit as the young man from Highglade spoke first.

"This place isn't how I pictured it," he said.

She felt a flutter of hope at being afforded a bit longer to think. Turning to Thornton, she asked, "How did you picture it?"

Thornton shrugged his broad shoulders. "More colorful I guess. Vibrant. This place feels so . . . dead." His large strides looked effortless, and Yasha's shorter legs were overcompensating to keep up.

He was looking around, but Yasha knew it wouldn't do any good. The landscape was far too foreign. It was like being trapped in a dream.

"In a way, it is," she replied. "They say that's where the power comes from: from the dead. When someone dies, their energy is pulled here and it works sort of like—"

"Like logs on a fire," Thornton finished the thought for her. He had a frown on his lips.

Yasha screwed up her face. "I was going to say like the sun, burning for the benefit of everyone. It doesn't have to be used for destruction." Blinking, she suddenly realized she had an opening.

"How much do you know about the Khyth?" she asked, gently testing the ice. She was looking ahead of them as they walked, not making eye contact with Thornton.

The young blacksmith pursed his lips in thought. "Not very much," he admitted. "I'd never even met one until that night outside Highglade. I know that you can be one through birth or become one by the Breaking. Either way, it's obvious that you're different."

Yasha nodded her head. "And by now you know that not all of them are . . . well, bad?"

Thornton grimaced a bit. "I've never heard of one leaving the Sunken City, so I kind of lumped them all together as hating everything and everyone that was different. But," he said, looking right at Yasha, "meeting you has made me reconsider things."

His answer placated the butterflies in her stomach, but only a bit; they had stopped fluttering around, but she knew they were still there. "I'm glad. Because not all of us hate humans. And not all of us want to be associated with the Hand of the Black Dawn, either. Some of us just want to live normal lives," she said.

"I can respect that. But how do I know who they are? As far as I know, you're the first one who's ever tried to leave."

"I'm not the first," Yasha snapped.

Thornton stepped back and held up his hands in mock surrender. "Whoa, calm down. I didn't mean anything by it."

"Sorry," she said as she shrank away. "It's just . . . the last Khyth to leave the city was tracked down and put to death as an example, and she also happened to be my mother. I guess it's still sort of a touchy subject for me."

Thornton stopped walking. "Oh," he said after a pause. "I'm sorry."

She brushed it off. "How much did Olson tell you about your mother?"

Yasha was careful here. She knew that she would have to cushion her words or Thornton was liable to crash right through the ice.

"Almost nothing," he said, "but that every day of his life he misses her." His words were quieter. "He told me she was beautiful, that she had hair like fire. He says that working the forge reminds him of her, and it's why he still does it."

"What about where she came from?" Yasha was verbally tiptoeing now.

"He never said. And whenever I bring her up, it's like he just shuts down." He turned to Yasha. "I've pretty much come to grips with the fact that he's told me all he cares to about her. 'Mother' is just another word to me; it's a label for a concept I just don't understand. And I'm fine with that."

Yasha took a breath before speaking again. She'd been dancing around it long enough.

"Thornton," she said. The two of them were stopped, and she'd taken one of his hands in hers. "Do you remember how you said your head hurt? After Dailus took your hammer?"

"Yes," he said. "Why?"

"Aldryd thinks it's because you were connected to it in a way. That it was a part of you, somehow. And when you were separated, something changed in you. Something," she looked him up and down, "came out."

"What do you mean 'came out'?"

"There's no easy way to put this."

"Then just say it." The look in his eyes told her that his patience was wearing thin.

Yasha knew that her next words would determine whether Thornton would be able to cross the frozen lake or if he would panic and fall through. "Your mother," she began, "I don't think she was human."

"What? That's not funny, Yasha."

"I'm not joking." Her tone was grave, and Thornton paused as he seemed to weigh her words.

"Then what are you saying?"

Yasha reached into her robe and pulled out a smooth stone that had been polished to perfection and offered it to Thornton saying, "Here. It's better if I show you."

Thornton

Thornton's head had been swimming ever since they came into this strange and empty place. His entire body felt odd, somehow lighter, like his bones had become feathers. Then there was the troubling sensation of a ghostly finger running down the back of his neck, one that he caught himself trying to brush away more than a few times. But each time he would look around, he found nothing more than himself and Elyasha.

He had tried to pay attention as she was going on about Khyth and bloodlines—even his mother. But the strange feeling in his head made it hard for him to concentrate for too long. He tried to blink away his bleariness when he found Yasha staring right at him.

He looked to her now, to her outstretched hand, and saw that she was holding a flat, round stone about the size of her palm. He wasn't sure what to expect or what to say, so he reached out and took it. It was smooth, cold, and well-polished.

Yasha gestured at him to look at the stone more closely.

He held it in his hands and moved it upward, where, to his surprise, his own reflection was staring back at him. He looked hesitantly back at Yasha, who had a look of sympathy on her face, while Thornton looked like a prisoner who was about to have his sentencing read to him. Looking back to the mirror, he squinted as his face came into focus. His eyes darted around, trying to anchor themselves on something, scanning frantically. They stopped suddenly, widening in surprise and confusion.

He blinked a few times, attempting to process the information, as the rock slipped from his hand, hitting the floor below with a *clink*.

He stood there, mute, unable to comprehend what he'd been shown and unable to move or react.

He had seen eyes like that before. He had seen them the night he was attacked, and he had seen them when Yasha had waited by his bedside.

His head spun.

No, he thought, *it isn't possible. It couldn't be. Father would have told me. He had no reason to keep this from me my whole life.*

Or did he? came the afterthought.

Maybe there was a reason he never mentioned her, never said where she was from.

Maybe there was a damn good reason, he thought, a reason that he had stumbled upon, somehow, when deprived of his hammer.

He fought to keep a grip on his sanity as the identity crisis he was experiencing started to drive him over the edge.

Olson

The massive figure of Olson Woods came tumbling into the Otherworld, grappling with the Khyth who was clinging desperately to a hammer—*Thornton's hammer?*

With a glance around, he realized that they had left Naknamu far behind for some other place entirely. Olson brushed off the thought and swung hard.

When he connected with the face of the Khyth below him, it felt like banging his fist against a brick wall lined with sandpaper. He sucked in air through his teeth as he shook out his hand, sure that his knuckles were bleeding. Despite the pain, he swung again, and his big, meaty fist did just what it was built for.

"Wipe that smirk off your face," Olson said between swings.

"I'm afraid I can't," the man answered. His voice was deeper than before and had an edge to it. "Now move." Olson suddenly felt an invisible force rocket him backward and onto the ground. It felt like getting kicked by a horse.

He watched as the Khyth stood up, pulsing with power, driven by something unseen that seemed to permeate the air.

"I suppose I should thank you," the Khyth said.

"Thank me?" Olson responded. He spat on the floor—blood, mostly.

He looked around, taking in their surroundings. The air around them was cloudy and shifting, barely more than shadows in a gray and shapeless expanse.

"Yes," the Khyth said, "I wasn't so sure I'd survive the journey through. But you've shown me that not only can I but a human can as well. You're likely the first to ever come through—but not the last, once my work is done. Then our two worlds will be forever connected, and my people will take their rightful place as rulers of both."

"Is that what you're after?" Olson asked as he stood. "Power?"

A cry of pain wrenched its way past his lips as it felt like all of his ribs had been broken. Breathing in sharply, he looked at the Khyth.

"It is the only prize worth pursuing," he said with a smile. "And as for you," he said, turning to face him, "the Breaker awaits."

Olson narrowed his eyes at the words.

They were words that had echoed in his mind for nearly twenty years now, words that haunted him. Words that he'd heard in the middle of a dark night in Lusk, looking on helplessly near his infant son, while the love of his life was taken away by the Khyth that she had tried so desperately to flee. He could hear her screaming for him to help but could do nothing but watch as two Khyth apprentices held him down. *"Come,"* he remembered the voice saying, *"the Breaker awaits."*

He no longer saw the figure in front of him—his vision was far too cloudy for that. It was replaced instead with a burning rage that had taken decades to ignite. Any semblance of sanity he had left went up in smoke that instant.

Leaping at the Khyth before him, Olson swung harder than he'd ever swung in his life, a swing of desperation and pain, borne on the back of a life he never got the chance to live. All the sorrow and emptiness he'd felt, all the anger and longing—he put all of that into his swing, and then some.

It was enough.

As the black-robed figure staggered backward, Olson surged forward, swinging madly, and knocked him onto the ground. The thick fingers of his worn hands found their way around the man's throat as they clamped down and began squeezing with every ounce of strength they had, driven by eyes that were blinded and twisted by fury. Olson screamed through a mask of contempt as he slammed the man's head on the ground, over and over and over. His last bit of control had vanished.

He never saw the hammer that caught him on the side of the head.

Gift of the Shaper

It jarred him, knocking him off balance, but he kept his hold on the throat of the Khyth. Through the blood and the pain he squeezed, wanting with every ounce of strength to inflict the pain that he'd felt since his wife was taken.

"Shahandra," he cried.

A second crack to the side of his head was enough to make his fingers start to loosen.

"Shahandra?" the Khyth laughed. "That worthless apprentice that ran away all those years ago? She was a fool for leaving! And you were a fool for thinking we would never come for her. Had it not been for the life inside her, we would have killed her then and there."

The words hit Olson harder than any hammer ever could. "Life?" he croaked. Blood was seeping from his ears and his eyes, and he struggled to move his broken jaw. "What life?"

"You mean you never knew?" The words were iced with cruelty.

Olson frowned and clenched his teeth. "You're lying," he said, his voice strained. He had propped himself up with one muscular arm and was resting on his side.

"I'm afraid I'm not," the Khyth replied. He reached inside his robe, pulling out a small dagger and inching his way closer to Olson. "I wish I were. She turned out to be more trouble than her mother. It's just such a shame that young Elyasha will never know her father."

His eyes a maelstrom of chaos, the man closed the gap between them and knelt down to plunge the dagger into Olson's chest, working it sharply in between his rib cage and into his heart. "And just so you know, this is how I killed her," he hissed.

D'kane

Instead of the shock and hatred that he expected, D'kane was confused to see that the big man was smiling.

"Yasha," he whispered, spilling blood and spittle onto his chest. "She's beautiful . . . just like her mother."

D.L. Jennings

The last gasping breath from the big man's throat barely made it to D'kane's ears as he retracted his dagger and stood up in a flurry. He had already wasted enough time. He kicked the large body of the man one last time as he tried to get some semblance of where he was or how he could get to his master.

He picked up the Hammer and started walking.

Miera

The very moment that Miera passed through the portal, she knew something was different. Every fiber in her being, every cell inside of her, was singing, ripe with power. It was a cataclysm of sensations, some new and some old, but all of them fiercely intense. She had never felt anything like it before—not in this lifetime.

Looking around, she saw the Otherworld alight with power itself. She could trace the lines of energy that seemed to ebb and flow as miniature distortions worked their way through the air. It was an ocean of energy and strength, filled and fueled by the life force of the dead, who all eventually found their way here. Currents of light seemed to form before her eyes like lines connecting two points; they trailed off into the distance, crisscrossing and intertwining in a chaotic, blazing dance.

Whatever the lights were, they seemed to tell her that she was not alone. A chorus of unseen voices whispered their agreement.

She took a few steps into the strange world that was dense like morning fog, drawing in a deep breath as she did so. The power of the air filled her lungs and burrowed into her blood, sending pin pricks across her skin like freezing rain. Something inside her was moving, pulling her like her body knew something that she did not. She glanced over to a strangely colored path of light that was a dark purple mixed with hot orange that seemed to be the source of the pull and began to move toward it.

She wasn't sure how she knew it, but she could tell that the light was two separate strands that somehow mingled together. They had come out of the very portal that she had just stepped through, then moved together, for a time, away from it. They weaved their way through the air

Gift of the Shaper

like translucent vines of smoke, compact enough to give the illusion of solidity but comprised of nothing more than echoes of light. Reaching out to touch it, she watched as her hand passed right through like there was nothing there at all. The trail was undisturbed, frozen in time like it had always been there, would always be there.

She followed, walking beside it and through it as she played with the light, letting it pass hauntingly into and out of her body. Up ahead, it seemed to balloon outward, like the bulge in a snake's stomach after it swallows its prey. She traced the lines of the crystallized light as she got closer to the disturbance, made mostly of the orange-tinted light. The purple traces had untangled themselves shortly afterward and headed off in another direction. Her eyes moved back to the orange light, which was growing fainter as she followed it down, curling and circling its way through the air. There, where the light was the thinnest, she saw something on the ground. She squinted, as the trail had left her night-blind. She stared for a moment as the shape came into focus. It was a boulder of some sort.

No, not a boulder. A . . . body?

A few blinks rid her eyes of the last of the trails of light as the form came into focus. There, sprawled out on the floor of the Otherworld, was the body of Olson Woods, blacksmith of Highglade and her second father for years.

Miera gasped as she froze in shock. Maybe her eyes were playing tricks on her, still confused by the strange liquid lights that had brought her here. She rubbed them and shook her head to try to make it go away, but it was no use; no matter how many times she closed her eyes, the body was there each time she reopened them.

She dropped to her knees as the knot in her chest worked its way up to her throat, choking her as it grew and spread throughout her body. She felt sick as she looked at the pool of blood below him that still looked fresh, soaking through his shirt and staining it black.

"Olson," she whispered, knowing it would do no good. She reached out a trembling hand to his body, recoiling when she felt how cold it was.

He was gone.

All the times in her life when she had come crying to him when she was a girl, with skinned knees or scrapes on her elbows.

All the years she spent in the light of his forge watching him and Thornton as they worked their iron and their steel, hammering away into the night and filling it with sounds.

All the times he scratched his beard in thought, all the times she brought them flowers.

All of them.

Gone.

Dried up and dead like the blood that pooled beneath him on the ground.

She knew that tears were wasted on him, but she let them come anyway, a stinging reminder that she was alive, and alive because of him.

Olson had not even hesitated when he saw D'kane raise the horn that the Khyth intended to use to end her life.

She had always suspected that Olson was the kind of person who would give up his life for someone if he had to, but she never thought that he would actually get the chance. She blinked clear the warm tears that clouded her eyes and flooded down her cheeks, standing to distance herself from her friend.

Her mind snapped back to the Khyth that had brought her here.

D'kane.

The word made her scowl as it tumbled around in her head. *He did this*, she thought. There was no question he did, and the idea sickened her.

The purple light, she thought, *it must be him.*

She clenched her fists and turned, finding the light that led away from the body of Olson and deeper into the Otherworld, going who knows where—though deep down she felt that she knew. D'kane had talked about it enough. He was obsessed with setting the Breaker free, and now that obsession had robbed her of one of the things that she cared for most in the world.

She would not let him.

Gift of the Shaper

Her fury ignited as she blazed with rage, letting her anger consume her and burn away any remaining doubts she may have had.

Without knowing it, her legs had already started her along the path. She was floating now, being pulled along by her body with no direction from her brain, as the numbness in her face and thoughts had dulled her senses. She felt like she was looking up from the bottom of a warm pool of water, with everything around her wavy and unclear, as muted sounds made their way to her ears. They undulated in, pulsing against her eardrums like waves.

Ah.

Eera.

Heera.

Heera.

Miera.

Miera.

"Miera!"

The word registered slowly. She knew it, recognized it. Her body turned in answer, aligning her eyes to the noise as she suddenly felt arms drape around her and lift her off the ground, with a squeezing sensation slowly bringing her back from the numbing fog.

The noise thrummed against her eardrums again as she felt herself coming back, her eyes now able to focus on the world around her. Her head had breached the surface of the water that she felt like she'd been submerged in, and reality snapped back into place.

She recognized the figure in front of her.

"Miera," he said, "I can't believe it's you!"

Her mind told her that it was Thornton, yet somehow he was different. She had not fully shaken off the haze that had overtaken her as she stared ahead with empty eyes. He seemed happy to see her, though, and was squeezing her tightly.

He was smiling.

Without knowing just how, she smiled back.

"Thornton," she finally said. The word rolled lazily from her lips.

"Part of me thought I might never see you again," he said, embracing her a second time.

She looked him over and saw that he was draped in his own orange glow, similar to the one she had seen coming from Olson, a glow that was made even brighter by a second crown of light that shone behind him, stepping forward to reveal a young red-haired woman clothed in gray, giving off the same shade of orange that Thornton was. Miera could see from the woman's eyes that she was Khyth.

"Miera," Thornton said, "this is Yasha."

The hooded girl reached out a timid hand to Miera, who smiled and shook it, pleased with the warmth it provided.

"I'm sorry," Miera said as she suddenly took back her hand, "I haven't felt right since I set foot in this place." She began to rub her temples with a wince.

"It's fine," Yasha said. "This place does strange things to all of us." She was looking around as if searching for the reason why, her eyes wandering aimlessly.

Thornton didn't seem to mind. "I'm just glad to see you," he said, smiling.

It's good to see him smile, Miera thought. She managed to keep her frown suppressed when she thought of Olson again, determining not to tell Thornton until she could be sure it was the right time. And now, certainly, could not be further from then. "It's good to see you, too," she answered. "But we can't linger. I followed D'kane through," she said, turning to her friend. "And he has your hammer."

Yasha had her back turned to them, pointing off somewhere in the distance. "If that's true then I have a feeling that's where we need to be going," she said.

The two of them looked where the young Khyth was pointing. There, in the deep distance, was a great pillar that seemed to rise forever into the sky, surrounded by a great number of smaller pillars all equal in height and thickness. The clouds and haze of the Otherworld kept most of it from view, but as Miera looked at the pillars, she could see that spiraling toward it was the unmistakable trail of purple crystallized light that she had followed from Olson's body.

Whatever was at the base of those pillars, D'kane was certainly after it.

"Then that is where we must go," Miera said as she stepped into the path of the light. "We don't have long. D'kane has a head start on us already."

Yasha and Thornton followed, trailing the blonde woman who seemed to be glowing with a strange and uncertain strength that covered her in a way that neither of them could quite explain.

Chapter 53

The Otherworld

Gift of the Shaper

D'kane

D'kane was moving through the emptiness of the Otherworld with ease, using the Hammer of the Worldforge as his guide. He could feel the pull of the Breaker, inexorably tied to it, as it called to him.

He was close.

Every now and then he would feel something in the back of his mind, like someone was following him. He was being pursued, but by whom he could no longer remember. He knew that it was important, but he would not let it deter him from his goal, as he knew he was almost upon it. The Breaker awaits: this much he knew.

Through the fog and the gray he looked and saw a great, burning pillar. *It must be there*, he knew.

The Hammer was pulsing now, like a heartbeat. It felt alive.

He could see the pillar clearly now. It reached up forever into the sky—or what passed for a sky in this place—disappearing into the abyss above. Surrounding the pillar were a dozen other pillars, smaller than the one in the middle but similar in appearance. And attached to each one, at the base, were the chains, bigger than any chains on earth and wider around than ten men. They were like spokes on a giant wheel that converged on the center, holding in place their ancient keepsake that had remained there since the Shaping War.

D'kane knew what he had to do, and he was so very close now.

The path to the crux of the chains was clear, yet still distant. The plane he was standing on had a slight decline to it that dipped down impossibly far. If it had existed in the physical world, it would have been a valley or perhaps a trench, but one thing was certain: it would have been the largest of its kind by a factor of ten. But on he walked, undaunted, following the pull of the Hammer as it urged him onward. The closer he got to the chains, he noticed, the stronger it pulled until it started to take nearly all of his strength just to keep it in his grasp. It was hungry, and he knew for what.

Yet still he couldn't shake the feeling that he was being followed.

With every footfall on the ethereal surface of the Otherworld, D'kane drew closer, on and on and on, downward, ever closer. He wasn't sure how long he had been walking, or even if he had been walking at all, but it seemed like ages, decades, centuries perhaps. Time in this place had little meaning. But finally the pillar came into view.

And chained to it, for ages untold, was the very reason that the chains existed in the first place. Towering above the horizon like a mountain, burned and scorched, and stirring once again in his ancient prison, was the Breaker of the Dawn.

His form was blackness, only vaguely human-like, with arms that made Naknamu look like a sapling. His shoulders topped an impossibly broad torso which could have borne the weight of all the peaks of Gal'behem; and his legs, shackled to the ground, could step over the mighty spire of Annoch with a single stride.

The Breaker craned his massive neck in order to see what it was that was coming toward him, awakening inside him the ancient fire that had long since been extinguished. With the might of a gale-force hurricane, he spoke.

"Long have I awaited your arrival, son of Khala Val'ur, and heavy are the chains." His words rumbled like an earthquake. "The time has come," he said. "Release me."

D'kane stood his ground in the face of his ancient master, cloaked in the power of the Hammer, the only thing keeping him from crumbling into dust before the Breaker. He felt it pulsing in his hands, flowing through him and filling him, focusing every iota of power in the Otherworld. He felt the power that was present at his Breaking, power that paled so dimly in comparison to the firestorm of energy that now engulfed him.

He held the Hammer high in his hands, grasping it with fingers interlocked, and called upon its ancient energy. A torrent more powerful than anything he could have ever foreseen ripped through him as he was lifted up and into the air.

He spread out his arms, welcoming the power, as his lungs nearly burst with a cry of excruciating pain. A burning sun above the surface of the Otherworld, D'kane felt his body try to give way to the power, threatening to disintegrate—but he would not let it.

He was a hundred feet in the air now and rising; in front of him was his master, and around his master were the chains that had been forged by the very hammer he held in his hands, the Hammer that had played a part in the creation of the world and would be instrumental in its end.

The one thing that could destroy the chains.

The one thing that could destroy the Breaker.

D'kane held it out by the handle, its sturdy black head facing the behemoth before him. He was now a conduit for all the power of the Otherworld as he reversed the pull that the Hammer had been inflicting on him and began to drain the power of the Breaker into himself and his implement of destruction.

With a cry that shook the foundation of the Otherworld, the Breaker pulled against the chains that had held him since the dawn of humanity. And just as they had done thousands upon thousands of times before, the chains held fast.

"No!" roared the Breaker, with all the fury of a volcano. He was struggling against the might of the chains, pouring every ounce of strength into resisting the power vacuum that was draining His essence into the Hammer of the Worldforge. "This power is not for you to wield!"

But D'kane did not listen.

He had survived the Breaking.

He would survive this.

The power burned through him like lightning as he felt it permeate his entire being.

He had destroyed the Binder of Worlds, so there would soon be nothing to stop him. He would have the power of creation and destruction in his hands—and the power to move freely between both worlds.

He had been waiting for this a long, long time.

D.L. Jennings

Miera

"There!" Miera was pointing ahead of them, to the pillar that seemed to be the center-point of the entirety of the ghostly plane of the Otherworld. She felt the warm waters coming over her again, like she had when she first set foot in this place. She didn't know what it meant, but she felt herself losing control. "We don't have much time."

Thornton and Yasha were following behind her, not saying a word. Breath did not work the same in this world, and they were both surprised to find that they were able to run as fast as they could without having to stop and recover. The three of them had covered a huge distance since first finding each other and showed no sign of slowing as they made their way toward the pillar.

None of them had to say anything. They knew exactly what was at stake and what D'kane aimed to do. They knew that he would try to set his master free, and when he did he would rain down destruction upon the world, the likes of which no one living had ever seen.

The closer they got, the cloudier Miera's vision became. The purple trail that led toward the pillar, though, did not lessen its glow in the slightest; no matter what happened, she was sure that she could follow it. She felt herself being pulled, like a current had caught hold of her and was slowly dragging her out to sea.

Weightlessness followed as her body seemed to disregard any cues from her mind that might have slowed their progress. As the fog surrounding her closed in, she found that she no longer had control.

Thornton

Thornton looked ahead to the pillars and was nearly blinded by an explosion of light, followed by a boom that resonated in his chest.

Are we too late?

He pushed his legs into the ground with all his might, hoping that they had made it in time. He had the strangest sensation that he could feel

Gift of the Shaper

his hammer, too. He didn't know how or why, but it was like he knew it was there, the same way he could sometimes feel someone's eyes on him from across a room. It was a strange pull, one that made him uneasy.

Up ahead, Miera was broadening the distance between them, and Thornton swore it looked like she was floating.

No. She is floating, he thought.

Her legs weren't moving; she was being propelled by something. He looked at Yasha, running beside him, who must have noticed too. She looked more puzzled than afraid, but it did not stop her.

The closer they got, the more Miera seemed to change, and if it was not for the fact that he had been face to face with her earlier, Thornton wouldn't have recognized her. She had taken on a cloak of light that made the rest of the world look dim, and she was hurtling toward the point from where the explosion had come.

They had nearly reached their destination when the world shook.

It was an eruption that rattled each of them to the core. Looking up, they could see a blazing point of light floating high up in the air and lording over the one pillar in the center.

Miera spoke, but it sounded nothing like her; the voice was hollow and unearthly, like everything else around them. "It begins!" she said. The words were more like a plea than a declaration.

Thornton looked out and saw, chained to the pillar, a towering black figure thrashing about in agony, with a ball of light hovering in front of it. Whatever the two figures were, there was violent opposition between them as each seemed to vie for dominance. A third ball of light—Miera—went scorching toward them.

Miera

Miera was light. She covered the distance in the blink of an eye.

"D'kane!" she shouted. Her voice was now completely unlike the girl who housed it: forceful and commanding. The Breaker, being drained of his life force, snarled at her as she approached. He was turning from black to gray as the Master Khyth was slowly claiming that which was his. "Stop this! You will unravel the world!"

The sound of laughter blasted like thunder as D'kane threw his head back. He looked Miera in the eye, saying, "You and I both know, even if I wanted to, I cannot stop this now."

Through the pulsing of power that burned his body, she could see the cracks in his skin that were the result of his Breaking. They reminded her that he would stop at nothing to see this through, and he would most likely not have to. All around her, she could feel the fabric of this world pulling apart as D'kane tapped into the very energies that shaped it and held it together.

He never intended to set the Breaker free—he sought to replace Him!

"If you destroy this world, you destroy the power that you wield," she said in a desperate attempt to sway him.

The Master Khyth was not hearing it, though, as he wrested his eyes back to the Breaker. "Then so be it," he shouted.

Thornton

D'kane was the first to strike. He was holding his hand out toward Miera, gripping the Hammer as it continued to drain power from the Breaker below. Then, suddenly, the Khyth shifted in the air, sending forth an explosion of darkness and light that knocked Miera backward as it rippled through the Otherworld.

Thornton and Yasha were there just in time to see her fall.

"Miera!" Thornton yelled. He didn't know how much he would be able to help her, but he tried to cover the distance, nonetheless. She was a falling star, and he was going to try to catch her in his hands.

As he ran, he heard a scream come from Yasha as he dove after Miera. Her light-covered form was rocketing toward the earth like a meteor, and he was afraid that he might not make it in time. Even if he did, what good would it do?

Gift of the Shaper

He was about to find out as he reached out his arms to try to catch her as she fell.

Thornton's arms felt like they would fall off as he caught his friend, dropping to his knees despite the surge of strength he felt. He found his footing, though, and lowered her to the ground. She was bathed in a layer of light that made it hard to look directly at her. Turning his head and squinting, Thornton tried to make sure she was alive. "Miera," he said softly, "are you . . . okay?"

The woman in front of him was somehow different than the Miera he knew. Something inside her had changed, and Thornton hoped it could be contained.

"I am," she said, "for the most part." She coughed and looked up to D'kane, who seemed to be struggling with Yasha. "He must be stopped."

"I know," Thornton said. "But how?"

Miera was silent as her feet found solid ground, and her next words came out softly, like the girl that Thornton had known all along. "I don't know," she said. "And that frightens me."

Thornton had not had time to reflect on the fact that his head was pounding again—until now. He seized his head as it lurched back, groaning in pain as he pressed his fingers into his eyes.

"It's your hammer," Miera said aloud. "It feels you and knows you are here but can do nothing about it."

"Make it stop" was all Thornton was able to say. He ground his knees into the floor in agony, unable to form a coherent thought.

"Thornton, listen to me," Miera said. Her voice had an ethereal quality to it, adding to the weight of the words. "You must use the Hammer of the Worldforge to seal the way to the Otherworld."

The young blacksmith could barely comprehend the words as she spoke. "What . . ." he began to ask, but Miera was not done.

"You will need help from the Binder of Worlds," she said. "She will meet you on the other side."

"And Thornton," she said as she looked back one last time, "I'll take good care of Olson."

"I don't understand," he began, but she was already moving away from him.

Miera, the Shaper of Ages, was moving toward D'kane, the Breaker of the Dawn, in a final heave of desperation, and a dance that had commenced at time's infancy now took the first steps toward its end.

Elyasha

Yasha looked up to her former master, hardly recognizing him. She had known him to be ambitious, but this put any notion of the word to shame. He held the Hammer of the Worldforge in his hands and was slowly draining the Breaker. There was no better example of treachery and pride in all of the stories and legends.

Yasha pushed down the fear that crept into her mind that was telling her she was nowhere near as strong as D'kane. She knew she wasn't, and even in the physical world he was her superior in virtually every way. But fear would avail her nothing, so she cast it aside, opening herself up to the tide of power that had been gently begging entrance into her body since she had crossed the threshold to this place.

It was warm and it was powerful, like the current of a rushing river: strong, uncontrollable, portending death. But she would not resist the power like she had at first. She let it come, and she no longer cared if the waters consumed her.

As if sensing her, D'kane turned his head to try to find her. It was like he knew she was there but was somehow blind to her presence. "Yasha," the Master Khyth growled, "this is simply not your day."

He was pulsing strongly with the Breaker's fresh power and looked to have stripped Him almost completely; the once-mighty mountain of black that hulked over the Otherworld was nothing more than a shriveled gray husk that trembled against His prison. Raising his free hand, D'kane brought it down like he was swatting a fly, and Yasha felt herself being crushed against the ground.

Yasha groaned as she began to push back. "You were always unbearable," she heaved, calling upon all of her inner strength to counteract the power of the Khyth-who-would-be-Breaker. Being only previously capable of commanding the smallest bits of energy of the Otherworld, she suddenly found herself behind a deluge of strength and surprised even herself as she directed it toward the towering point of light that D'kane had become.

Gritting her teeth and letting out a cry of great effort, Yasha pushed again. She could feel a change inside of her as the power rushed through, and she became cognizant of the cracks in her skin that were already starting to form, a byproduct of the effort involved. And, despite not knowing its secrets, Yasha had inadvertently stumbled upon the key to the most sacred of Khyth rituals, the Breaking.

Deep in the recesses of her mind she knew that, without the guidance of a Master Khyth, she could die. But still she let the power consume her, well aware of the dangers both inside of and in front of her, and she chose to give way to the one below in order to contain the one above.

She screamed as the power tore through her. Her eyes flooded with light and her veins carried fire. She had triggered the Breaking on her own, and it was starting to overpower her. Never had she experienced pain like this, and the full force of it brought her to her knees.

D'kane saw what was happening and laughed. "I didn't think you had it in you," he said. He was caught between draining the last of the power from the Breaker and fighting off his relentless apprentice, who was suddenly proving to be more of a challenge than he had anticipated. With a gesture, he redirected some of the power he had siphoned and pushed it Yasha's way, hoping to subdue her.

It worked.

Yasha was bathed in pain and strength as she crumpled to the ground, lungs and body ablaze. *This is how it ends,* she thought. She could barely focus through the excruciating ordeal. The power had overtaken her and had filled her to the point of bursting. Without the help of a master Khyth, she would surely die.

D'kane saw his chance and focused his attention entirely on her. "You never should have come here," he said as he moved both his hands toward her in a pushing motion. The wave of strength that hit her was enough to rattle the consciousness from her body—but still she fought. She clung to life by the thinnest of threads.

"This is not her fight," came a shout from somewhere in the fog. Bolts of light shot toward D'kane as Miera emerged, draped in strength and light. "Leave her out of it."

The last thing Yasha saw before her pain-wracked mind shut down was Miera, hurtling toward Dkane as he drained the Breaker.

Miera

Miera gathered her strength as she looked at Thornton. Through the fog of her mind she knew she recognized him, but her thoughts were scattered and loose, drifting away.

She was bound by compulsion now; nothing inside her would let her stay still. She started to move toward the light that was D'kane, but stopped to look back at her friend.

"Thornton," she said, "you must use the Hammer to seal the way to the Otherworld."

The young blacksmith looked confused. "What . . ." he groaned, but Miera was not done.

"You will need help from the Binder of Worlds," she said. "She will meet you on the other side. And Thornton,"—she looked back one last time—"I'll take good care of Olson."

With those words, she turned and sped after D'kane. She heard, and could almost feel, screams from Elyasha as she felt a sudden surge of power.

"This is not her fight," Miera shouted, with a violent swing at D'kane. "Leave her out of it."

"It's not that easy," said D'kane. He seemed to have nearly finished desiccating the Breaker, who now looked like he would crumble to dust at the slightest touch. "Though you can certainly join her." He ground his teeth together with the effort of redirecting more of the power he was consuming, sending it straight to Miera in hopes of incapacitating her as well. He looked surprised then to see that it had exactly the opposite effect.

The blazing light surrounding Miera suddenly tripled in intensity as she absorbed the influx of strength. The power of the Breaker, though it had taken a different path, had indeed sprung from the same well as hers. It was one and the same, and it filled her with renewed vigor. Pushing herself off the ground, she made for the air, climbing to make herself level with D'kane.

All around them, the Otherworld continued to tremor. It was being pulled apart, Miera knew, and D'kane was not concerned in the least. If he continued and succeeded, it would collapse, and all the energy and power—and everything else it held—would spill out into the physical world.

She had to act, and act fast.

She went for the Hammer.

Flinging herself right at the master Khyth, she lowered her shoulder, and the two of them collided in midair as she did her best to knock the Hammer from his grip, hoping to disrupt the process.

D'kane, in a desperate attempt to finish what he started, tried to keep the Hammer aloft as both of them plummeted to the ground. "It's nearly finished," he said through clenched teeth. The cracks of his burnt body had multiplied and spread, and he looked more like a blackened coal than a creature who once might have been human. The more of the Breaker's power he drained, the more he resembled the ancient being.

"For once," Miera said, "you're right." The two of them collided with the ground with such force that even the towering pillars quaked in response.

Miera looked down at D'kane, seeing that the day had finally come which the Binder had foreseen all those years before, and she knew what had to be done. She only hoped that it would be enough.

With her hands around his throat, she set her body ablaze, and the whole of the Otherworld sang in response as it continued its rapid collapse, shaking and seizing in its death throes.

"No!" D'kane shouted. "I won't let you steal this from me, too!" He knew what she was trying to do and fought back fiercely, trying to wrest away the grip that Miera had on him and on the Otherworld. He twisted onto his side, tossing Miera off of him and struggling to his feet.

Miera crashed to the ground, tucked her chin into her shoulder, then rolled onto her hands, vaulting herself up and onto her feet.

The two of them were standing now, and D'kane had the Hammer in his right hand. He started at Miera and swung, aiming right for her head. Miera, though, had other plans. She reached out to meet the black head of the Hammer in midair, catching it in her hand and staring right at the Khyth who had the audacity to try to usurp the Breaker.

The desperate quaking of the Otherworld had turned cataclysmic as all its power threatened escape.

Miera, still draped in light, locked eyes with D'kane. "You've chosen your fate, just like your master chose His." With unearthly quickness she tore the Hammer from his hand and threw it, never breaking eye contact with the Khyth. "Now learn what solitude means."

The words hung in the air as the world was wrapped in light, bursting forth from a single point and burning all that it touched, swiftly and without mercy, as the Otherworld was consumed.

Chapter 54

Gift of the Shaper

It was not always this way. Not in the beginning.

No.

It was never supposed to be this way.

When they had created the world, each of them pouring a bit of themselves into it, everything had held such promise. Such potential. Such beautiful and unending possibility.

But the Breaker held back. He had secreted away parts of His power that the Shaper and the Binder had both surrendered. He had done it behind their backs—they, who had trusted Him, who had confided in Him. Who had loved Him.

He had betrayed them. And for that betrayal He paid dearly.

"We will seal Him off," She had said to the Binder, "from the creation that He so longed to be a part of. We will seal Him off and make Him forget that we ever existed." Her hand had trembled with rage that day; She knew there was no going back.

The great black eyes of the Binder of Worlds blinked slowly. She knew that the Shaper was right—it was the only thing to be done. He had forced their hand when He made His decision to deceive, and in doing so had sealed His own fate.

"We will use the Hammer of the Worldforge," the Binder had answered. "It will be the instrument of His undoing and the only way that He will atone for what He has done."

The Shaper nodded. She placed the Hammer on the ground, its handle facing the sky. "Then it is settled. Here shall He be bound until one of His own blood returns to take His place."

"So be it," the Binder had answered. The sadness in Her voice had carried across the millennia, reaching out from the moment She had willed the world into existence until the moment Her spirit was snuffed out by the Hammer that She had helped create.

It was never supposed to be this way.

No.

It was never supposed to be this way.

Chapter 55

Kienar

Gift of the Shaper

Tennech

"Back!" shouted Caladan Durakas. "Push them back!" His words scraped across his throat as they crossed the point of shouting and into screaming; his tone reeked of desperation. Ducking as an arrow flew past him, he did his best to keep his footing while he hacked and swung his sword at the advancing Legion.

"It's not working," Duna parried. She was holding her right shoulder as she continued swinging, in an attempt to staunch the bleeding. The broken end of an arrow was jutting out, and the look on her face said that the pain was starting to register.

The two of them had watched the Legion, possessed of some madness, breaking into their ranks without fear or hesitation. Behind them they caught flashes of what looked like a man blasting in and out of existence, cutting down Valurian and Thurian alike, only to disappear as if he were never there.

"Then push harder!" Still mounted on his war horse, Calathet, General Tennech was shouting commands to his armies. He would see this through to the bitter end, he swore, no matter how many bodies they had to stake their victory on. "Abandon the flank!" he yelled. "The front line must hold!"

But he knew that it would not matter in the end. The clashing forces, the bloody confrontation that was misting the forest floor red—none of it mattered, not a bit of it, if D'kane succeeded. They could lose every man that called Gal'dorok home and still come out on top, so long as the Master Khyth came through.

At least that's what he had been repeating to himself as he slashed ferociously at an oncoming Athrani. But when he looked up again to refocus his strategic center, the unyielding mantra that ran through his mind suddenly came to a halt when he saw the spear that caught Sera in the chest, tearing her off her horse and pinning her to the ground. His face went white as the blood drained away, and he found himself riding toward her, oblivious to the needs of his slowly shrinking army.

D.L. Jennings

Duna

"Your own general abandons you! He has given in to death!" Durakas fumed as he watched Tennech charge off, and Duna was certain that the Dagger of Derenar had given up or gone mad.

The thundering of boulders hummed and pounded as the Khyth around them wove their Breaking through the air, taking advantage of the weakened state of their Athrani counterparts. But to see the general storm off like that—certainly not in his character—they began to hesitate. Even Duna was uncertain as she fended off more and more of the Legion. Their number seemed endless, and the arrows from the Kienari above were unrelenting.

Maybe Durakas was right. Maybe Tennech had seen the futility of it all and had chosen the quickest route to death.

With his sudden departure, his army had become like a snake with its head freshly severed, thrashing about madly with no purpose or threat. Even the war-hungry Thurians seemed to be teetering off balance.

But that was not what made up her mind to flee. Not the spears and swords of the Athrani, not the looming and silent threat of the Kienari. Not even the rows of dead that now lined the forest floor.

No, it was when Durakas caught an arrow in the skull, tossing him unceremoniously off his horse and onto the ground below, that Duna finally caught her wits and called for the retreat. The general could rot in the Otherworld for all she cared, and she was not intent on beating him there.

"Fall back!" she commanded. "Fall back to Gal'dorok!" Her cries were echoed by the Captains of the Fist.

The Breaker can wait, she fumed. He would have to. *He's been there this long,* she thought, *and, by the Breaker, he can stand to wait some more.*

Chapter 56

Naknamu

Gift of the Shaper

Thornton

Falling.

Faster, falling. Tumbling. There was no air to breathe, but somehow Thornton knew he was choking.

A woman's voice. He couldn't make out the words.

Miera? Had she made it through?

He sputtered back to life.

Beside him lay the unconscious body of Yasha, who looked to him like the Khyth that he knew, her skin cracked and blistered, charred with power. Behind him, the silver arch that guarded the Otherworld glowed hot. *What had Miera said? What had she done?* His head was cloudy, but he moved through the fog to find her words.

Use the Hammer, she said.

With his head free of the ever-present pounding, he felt relief wash over him like a tide as he traced his fingers back and forth over the smooth grooves of a wooden handle. The grain was familiar to him and gave him a sense of comfort amidst the chaos. It had come back to him, though he had no memory of just how or when.

"Get up," said the voice. Thornton looked up to see the dark eyes of a Kienari staring back at him.

He jumped. "Ynara," he said, startled.

"Once," she replied, "but now I am much more. I am the Binder now, as my mother was before me."

Confused, Thornton closed his eyes tightly to try and understand what she could possibly mean, but before he could come up with an answer, he remembered Miera's words.

"The Hammer," he started. "She said . . ."

"She said we have to seal her in," Ynara answered. "I know. I have always known." Regret seeped from her words like puss. "Yet knowing does not make it any easier." She reached out a hand. "Here. Give it to me."

Thornton did as she asked, standing back as she grasped it just below the night-black head. Taking it in her long fingers, she raised it up as the Hammer, from base to tip, began to glow.

"What are you doing?" Thornton asked.

"What the Shaper wishes," was Ynara's reply. A burst of light streamed forth from the tip, splitting into waves that shot out in separate directions, solidifying, becoming chains. Ynara, the Binder, stood firm as the chains took their place over the portal once again, sealing it shut.

Thornton looked at the portal, lifeless and still, and again to the Kienari. "What did you do?" he asked.

The Binder blinked her huge black eyelids. "I have closed the way to Otherworld. It was the only way to ensure that the Breaker remains trapped."

"But if the Breaker is trapped," Thornton said, digesting the words. "Then Miera is trapped too."

Ynara put a spindly hand on his shoulder. "She chose this fate, young one. It was her decision and the only way to stop him. She knew what would happen if He was set free and chose to leave a world where that never happens."

Thornton's jaw hung open. He was trying to comprehend a world without Miera.

Ynara seemed to sense this and tried to offer him some comfort. "The Shaper had Her reasons for doing what She did," she said. "And though she is gone from this world, she is not dead."

"She might as well be if we can't get to her."

Thornton looked again at the portal, then to his hammer, while his heart sunk in his chest. *There must be a way to get her back,* he said to himself. *And if there is, I will find it.*

The sounds of retreat shook the foundation of Naknamu as the charging Athrani Legion drove off the last of the Khyth invaders.

The voice of Endar rung out in celebration, dwarfing the shouts of his men. "Watch them go, boys," he shouted, "with their tails between their legs. I told you they bleed like us!"

Gift of the Shaper

The Legion cheered in response.

"Come," Ynara said, "help me move her." The two of them picked up the heavy and unconscious body of Yasha, making their way through the maze of roots and soil. "Your part is not yet finished."

"What?" Thornton sputtered. "Where are we going?"

"To Ellenos, where you and your sister will be safe," she answered.

"Sister?" Thornton said. "I don't have a . . ."

Thornton looked at the young Khyth in the darkness that slept below Naknamu, with thousands of questions flying through his head about the girl with the hair like fire. The road back to Ellenos would be long, and he was still trying to wrap his head around how he wound up inside the ancient tree.

But as they walked toward the surface, he realized that their meeting had not been one of chance; it was intentional and it was designed.

And, with everything that had happened in the span of these few short days, he knew one thing for sure: it was just the beginning.

EPILOGUE

Tennech stood above the dunes, looking out over the Wastes.

Beside him, on the back of Calathet, the body of Sera somehow still clung to life. Her breathing was shallow and her pulse weak, but she was alive. The wounds that she had sustained at the battle for the Tree had nearly killed her, and would certainly have killed a human, but she was never one to give up easily. Death rattled in her throat as she breathed, a mixture of blood and saliva that threatened to snuff out the fire inside.

But she was alive.

He still had that much.

He had come far in the days since the battle, traveling by night and avoiding the major roads for fear that he should be discovered. When D'kane had failed to emerge from the Otherworld and, instead, the young blacksmith had come out in his place, he knew they had lost. No amount of pleading with Yetz would spare his life, he knew. He was as good as dead if he ever set foot inside Khala Val'ur again.

As good as dead, that is, unless he had an army to back him up.

He looked back at Hullis and Dhrostain, seated atop their Gwarái, and nodded.

Making his way past the shifting sands of the Wastes of Khulakorum, General Tennech spurred his mount onward, toward the burning dunes of Khadje Kholam and into the very heart of the Wastes, where the Tribes of the Sun dreamed.

APPENDIX

Glossary of Terms

Aidren: A young Athrani half-eye imprisoned in the cell next to Olson and Dailus.

Aldis Tennech: A human general of Khala Val'ur. He commands all the armies of Gal'dorok.

Aldryd: An aged Athrani residing in Annoch, where he holds the title of Keeper. He resides in the Temple of the Shaper.

Annoch: The capital city of Derenar, it is also called The City of the Forge and is home to Athrani and humans alike. Inside its walls lies the Temple of the Shaper. A person from Annoch is called an Annochian.

Athrani: A people who worship the Shaper of Ages and are known for their power to transmute matter, called Shaping. Their distinctive multi-colored eyes allow them to be easily distinguished from humans.

Athrani Legion: A collection of soldiers who march under the banner of Ellenos, comprised of mostly Athrani and half-eyes.

Anvil of the Worldforge: Used by the Shaper of Ages, along with the Hammer of the Worldforge, to create the world. It can be found in the Temple of the Shaper in Annoch.

Binder of Worlds: One of the creators of the world, along with the Shaper of Ages and the Breaker of the Dawn. She is the guardian of the two worlds and helped to imprison the Breaker in His chains.

Breaker of the Dawn: One of the creators of the world, along with the Shaper of Ages and the Binder of Worlds. He was imprisoned by the Shaper ages ago and continues to be a thorn in Her side. His followers, the Hand of the Black Dawn, seek to free Him from his prison in the Otherworld.

Gift of the Shaper

Breaking (power): Gifted by the Breaker and wielded by Khyth. It allows the user to move or reshape matter, but not to change its form. It is able to be learned by anyone and is not limited to those born of Khyth blood. (See also The Breaking).

The Breaking: A ritual undergone by Khyth apprentices that serves to increase their ability to wield the power of the Otherworld. The ritual is often fatal, scarring the Khyth for life and leaving their skin looking burnt and cracked.

Caladan Durakas: Commander of the Fist of Ghal Thurái.

Cavan Hullis: A captain from Ghal Thurái known for his gift for strategy.

Chovathi: A race of sub-surface-dwelling creatures who formerly inhabited Ghal Thurái. They are pale and carnivorous and can only be killed by removing the head.

Dailus: An Athrani half-eye from Ellenos who meets and befriends Olson Woods.

Derenar: A large region encompassing many human and Athrani cities. It is bordered to the east by the region of Gal'dorok and to the south by the Wastes of Khulakorum.

D'kane: An ambitious Master Khyth of the Breaking who resides in Khala Val'ur. He is presumed by all to take the title of High Khyth when his master, Yetz, falls out of power.

Duna Cullain: Second-in-command of the Fist of Ghal Thurái. She is subordinate to Commander Caladan Durakas.

Ellenos: Also called the First City. It is home to the Athrani and is their capital city and seat of their government. A person from Ellenos is called an Ellenian.

Elyasha: Also called "Yasha" by her friends, she is a Khyth apprentice serving under D'kane.

Endar: An Athrani half-eye who ascended to the rank of Commander of the Athrani Legion.

D.L. Jennings

Farryn Dhrostain: A short, fierce captain from Ghal Thurái.

Farstepper: A rare breed of humans possessing the ability to move from one point to another by traveling through the Otherworld. They come from beyond the Wastes of Khulakorum and are known for their skills as warriors and assassins.

Fist of Ghal Thurái: A greatly feared and respected army out of Ghal Thurái, led by Caladan Durakas. Alternatively referred to as the Fist of Ghal Thurái, the Fist of Thurái, or simply the Fist.

Gal'behem: The mountain range that surrounds Khala Val'ur in Gal'dorok. Its name means "the great serpent."

Gal'dorok: A large region encompassing many human and Khyth cities. It is bordered on the east by the Tashkar sea, to the west by the region of Derenar, and to the south by the Wastes of Khulakorum. Its name means "great pinnacle."

Ghaja Rus: A man from G'hen who deals in slave trade.

Ghal Thurái: Also called the Mouth of the Deep, it is a Khyth city built into a mountain. A person from Ghal Thurái is called a Thurian.

G'hen: A city that borders the Wastes of Khulakorum. Its people are known for their dark skin. A person from G'hen is called a G'henni.

Gwarái: An ancient beast created by the Breaker of the Dawn in order to hunt down the Athrani. They feed on the blood of Shapers and can be used to absorb their powers. They were hunted to extinction during the Shaping War.

Half-eye: A derogatory title given to one born to an Athrani father and human mother. One of their eyes appears human, while the other appears Athrani (with a second ring of color behind the first). They are capable of Shaping.

Hammer of the Worldforge: An ancient artifact that the Shaper of Ages used to create the world, along with the Anvil of the Worldforge. Collectively they are referred to as the Pieces of the Worldforge.

Gift of the Shaper

Hand of the Black Dawn: The name of those who serve the Breaker of the Dawn and seek to free Him. They are led by Khyth, but humans are drawn to them as well. They operate primarily out of Khala Val'ur.

Highglade: A village to the east of Lusk, whose claim to fame is Olson Woods, a blacksmith of great renown. A person from Highglade is called a Highglader.

Jinda Yhun: Captain of the Guard of Annoch. He is a Farstepper from beyond the Wastes.

Kethras: a Kienari male, brother to Ynara and son of the Mother.

Keeper: A title given to an Athrani who is charged with the protection of the Temple of the Shaper found in their city. There is one Keeper for every temple, and there is typically one temple in any given city where Athrani are found.

Khala Val'ur: Also called the Sunken City, it is the capital city of the Khyth, as well as the capital city of Gal'dorok.

Khyth (title): One who has undergone the ritual of the Breaking in order to gain access to the power of the Otherworld. Above this title exists Master Khyth and High Khyth.

Khyth (people): A people who worship the Breaker of the Dawn and are known for their power to move and manipulate matter, called Breaking. Their eyes resemble smoke and are inherited by their offspring.

Kienar: A small forest near the Talvin Forest that is home to the Kienari.

Kienari: Creatures of stealth and mystery who are much taller than humans, that call the forest of Kienar home. They are often described as cat-like, with their fine black fur and tails. Their night vision is exceptional and uses heat rather than light to locate their prey. They are master marksmen and feel at home in the trees.

Lash'Kargá: A southeastern city of Gal'Dorok that sits on the edge of the Wastes of Khulakorum. It is nicknamed Death's Edge.

Lusk: A human town on the edge of the Talvin forest that has recently become a hub of trade in Derenar.

Miera Mi'an: A young woman from Highglade who has known Thornton since they were young. She never knew her mother and was raised by her father.

Mordha: A G'henni woman who is part of the city guard of Annoch. She is second-in-command to Jinda Yhun.

the Mother: Often called the First Kienari, she is mother to Kethras and Ynara (see Kienari).

Olson Woods: A highly skilled blacksmith from Highglade and father to Thornton Woods.

The Otherworld: An ethereal place of power that exists parallel to—and beyond—this world. It is where the Breaker of the Dawn is imprisoned and from where the Athrani and Khyth draw their power.

Pieces of the Worldforge: The Hammer of the Worldforge and the Anvil of the Worldforge. Both of these were used by the Shaper of Ages when creating the world.

Seralith Edos: An Athrani woman from Ellenos who left the Athrani city for Khala Val'ur. She serves under General Aldis Tennech.

Shaper of Ages: One of the creators of the world, along with the Breaker of the Dawn and the Binder of Worlds. She gave up Her power to the Athrani so they might defend themselves against the Khyth, who were empowered by the Breaker.

Shaping: Gifted by the Shaper and wielded by the Athrani, it is the ability to transmute matter into any form imaginable. Only those who are of Athrani blood can Shape.

Shaping War: A long-finished but not forgotten war between the Athrani and Khyth, which served to drive a permanent wedge between the two races. It has been a continuing source of hatred for both of them.

Gift of the Shaper

Sh'thanna: The Keeper of the Temple of the Shaper in Ellenos. She is friends with Aldryd.

Thornton Woods: A young blacksmith from Highglade, son of Olson Woods.

Thuma: an Athrani, second-in-command to Endar, of the Athrani Legion.

Wastes of Khulakorum: A desert region far to the south known for producing Farsteppers. Most of the region is referred to by outsiders as beyond the Wastes.

Yasha: See "Elyasha."

Yetz: A mysterious figure who heads the Hand of the Black Dawn. High Khyth of Khala Val'ur.

Ynara: a Kienari female, sister to Kethras and daughter of the Mother.

Made in the USA
Middletown, DE
06 December 2018